agnes
&the
hitman

agnes
&the
hitman

jennifer crusie
&
bob mayer

St. Martin's Press ❧ *New York*

AGNES AND THE HITMAN. Copyright © 2007 by Argh Ink and Robert J. Mayer. All rights reserved. Printed in the United States of America. No part of this book may be used or reproduced in any manner whatsoever without written permission except in the case of brief quotations embodied in critical articles or reviews. For information, address St. Martin's Press, 175 Fifth Avenue, New York, N.Y. 10010.

www.stmartins.com

Library of Congress Cataloging-in-Publication Data

Crusie, Jennifer.
　　Agnes and the hitman / Jennifer Crusie and Bob Mayer. —1st ed.
　　　　p.　cm.
　　ISBN-13: 978-0-312-36304-8
　　ISBN-10: 0-312-36304-4
　1. Murder for hire—Fiction.　2. Weddings—Fiction.
I. Mayer, Bob, 1959–　II. Title.

PS3553.R7858A74　2007
813'.54—dc22　　　　　2007019318

First Edition: August 2007

10　9　8　7　6　5　4　3　2　1

For Meg and Jen,

who never gave up on us

acknowledgments

We would like to thank

Deb Cavanaugh for keeping Bob sane,

Kim "Needles" Cardascia for never breaking a sweat no matter what we came screaming to her for,

the **Cherries** and the **CherryBombs** for taking the trip with us,

our beta readers—**Brooke Chapman, Katy Cooper**, Heidi Cullinan, **Kari Hayes, Robin LaFevers, Corinna Lavitt, Chris Merrill,** and **Valerie Taylor**—for giving great feedback,

Richie Ducharme for getting us the beach house,

John Karle for never losing us on the road,

Russ Parsons, who helped us with the food columnist background and who puts up with Jenny in general (well, he has to because she's family, but she's still grateful),

Doreen Thompson for media training (Crusie-Mayer, He Wrote/She Wrote, romantic adventure, and uh . . .),

Charlie Verral for once again providing us with our NYC home away from home,

Mollie Smith for running our professional lives,

Jennifer Enderlin for being the perfect editor,

and **Meg Ruley** for being the perfect agent.

agnes
&the
hitman

monday

"Pan Hunting"

Do not be seduced by those big-box come-ons, full of "complete sets" of extraneous cookware. A complete set is whatever you need, and maybe all you need is a wok and a hot place to grill your bacon. In a pinch, I can do it all with my good heavy nonstick frying pan. Besides the obvious braising, browning, and frying, I can make sauces and stir-fries in it, toast cheese sandwiches and slivered almonds, use the underside to pound cutlets, and in a pinch probably swing it to defend my honor. If I could find a man that versatile and dependable, I'd marry him.

One fine August evening in South Carolina, Agnes Crandall stirred raspberries and sugar in her heavy nonstick frying pan and defended her fiancé to the only man she'd ever trusted.

It wasn't easy.

"Look, Joey, Taylor's not that bad." Agnes cradled the phone between her chin and her shoulder, turned down her CD player, where the Dixie Chicks were doing a fine rendition of "Am I the Only One," and then frowned over the tops of her fogged-up glasses at the raspberries, which were being annoying and uncooperative, much like Taylor lately. "He's a terrific chef." *Which is why I'm still with him.* "And he's very sweet." *When he has the time.* "And we've got a great future in this house together." *Assuming he ever comes out here again.*

Joey snorted his contempt, the sound exploding through the phone. "He shouldn't leave you out there by yourself."

"Hey, Brenda lived out here alone for years, and she did just fine," Agnes said. "I'm as tough as Brenda. I can do that, too." *Of course, Brenda sold me the house and beat feet for her yacht in the middle of a marina, but—*

"Nah, there's somethin' wrong with a guy who leaves a sweetheart like you alone in a big house like that. You should find somebody else."

"Yeah, like I have the time," Agnes said, and then realized that wasn't the right answer. "Not that I would. Taylor's a great guy. And anyway, I like being alone." *I'm used to it.*

"He's a mutt, Agnes," Joey said.

Agnes took off her glasses and turned up the heat under the raspberries, which she knew was courting disaster, but it was late and she was tired of playing nice with fruit. "Come on, Joey. I don't have time for this. I'm behind on my column, I've got—"

"And there's Rhett," Joey said. "How's Rhett?"

"What?" Agnes said, thrown off stride. She stopped stirring her berries, which began to bubble, and looked down at her dog, draped over her feet like a moth-eaten brown overcoat, slobbering on the floor as he slept. "Rhett's fine. Why? What have you heard?"

"He's a fine healthy-lookin' dog," Joey said hastily. "He looked real good in his picture in the paper today." He paused, his voice straining to be casual. "How come old Rhett was wearing that stupid collar in that picture?"

"Collar?" Agnes frowned at the phone. "It was just some junk jewelry—"

The oven timer buzzed, and she said, "Hold on," put down the phone, and took the now madly bubbling berries off the heat. Rhett picked up his head and bayed, and she turned to see what he was upset about.

A guy with a gun stood in the doorway, the bottom half of his face covered with a red bandanna.

"I come for your dog," he said, pointing the gun at Rhett, and Agnes said, *"No!"* and slung the raspberry pan at the guy, the hot syrup arcing out in front of it like napalm and catching him full in the face.

He screamed as the scalding fruit hit him and then dropped his gun to rip the bandanna away as Agnes stumbled to scoop up the pan and Rhett barreled into him, knocking him down so that he hit the back of his head on the marble counter by the wall and knocked off every cupcake she had cooling there before he collapsed into the doorway.

"God*damn it*," Agnes said breathlessly, standing over him with her pan, her heart pounding.

The guy didn't move, and Rhett began to hoover up cupcakes at the speed of light.

"*Agnes?*" Joey shouted from the phone on the counter. "What the fuck, *Agnes?*"

Agnes kicked the gun into the housekeeper's room and peered at the guy, trying to catch her breath. When he didn't move, she backed up to grab the phone off the counter. "Some guy just showed up here with a gun and tried to take Rhett," she told Joey, breathing hard. "But it's okay, I'm not angry." *Miserable little rat-faced jerk.*

"*Where is he?*"

"On the floor, across the hall doorway. He knocked himself out. I have to—"

"Get the hell *out of there*," Joey said, sounding like he was on the move. "*Take Rhett with you.*"

"I can't get out, the guy's lying across the hall door. If I climb over him, he'll come to and grab me. I have to call—"

"Get out the *back door*—"

"I can't, Doyle's got it blocked with screen and boards. I have to hang up and call nine-one-one."

"*No,*" Joey said, and she heard the screen door to the diner slap shut on his end of the phone. "*No cops. I'm comin' over.*"

"What do you mean, *no cops?* I—"

The dognapper stirred.

"Wait a minute." Agnes put the phone on the counter and held the frying pan at the ready, hands shaking, as she craned her neck to look closer at the dognapper.

Young, just a teenager. Short. Skinny. Limp, dirty dark hair. Stupid, because if he'd had any brains, he'd have grabbed Rhett when he went out for his nightly pee. And now that he was unconscious, pretty harmless looking. She probably outweighed him by thirty pounds.

As she calmed down, she could hear Dr. Garvin's voice in her head.

How are you feeling right now, Agnes?

Well, Dr. Garvin, I am feeling a little angry that this punk broke into the house with a gun and threatened my dog.

And how are you handling that anger, Agnes?

I never touched him, I swear.

The boy opened his eyes.

"Don't move." Agnes held up her pan. "I've called the police," she lied. "They're coming for you. My dog is vicious, and you don't want to cross me, either, especially with a frying pan; you have no *idea* what I can do with a frying pan." She took a deep breath, and the kid glared at her, and she looked closer at his face, and winced at the lurid welts of singed skin where the raspberry had stuck. "That's gotta hurt. Not that I care."

He worked his battered jaw, and she held the frying pan higher as a threat.

"So, tell me, you little creep," Agnes said, *"why were you trying to kill my dog?"*

"I weren't tryin' to kill the dog," the boy said, outraged. "I wouldn't kill no *dog*."

"The gun, Creepoid," Agnes said. "You pointed *a gun* at him."

"I was just gonna *take* him," the boy said. "There weren't no call to get mean. I weren't gonna hurt him. I wouldn't hurt *nobody*." He touched the sauce on his face and winced.

"No, you just broke into this house to terrorize me with a gun," Agnes said. "That's not hurting nobody, that's victimizing *me*. Do I look like a victim to you? Huh? You wouldn't have tried this crap on Brenda, would you?"

He frowned up at her, the raspberry sauce crinkling on his face. "Who's Brenda?"

"Everybody knows who Brenda is," Agnes snapped.

She took a deep shuddering breath and reached for the phone again, and he rolled to his feet and lunged for her. She yelped and smacked him hard on the head with her pan, and he staggered, and then she hit him again, harder this time, just to make sure, and he fell back onto the floor, blood seeping down the side of his face, and lay still. She felt a qualm about that, but not much, because it was self-defense. Brenda would be proud of her, he'd broken into her house and she'd defended it, he'd scared *the hell* out of her and—

Violence is not the answer, Agnes.

That depends on the question, *Dr. Garvin.*

—and she was not out of control, she was not angry, she was calm, she was shaking, but she was perfectly fine, and anyway it was a nonstick pan, not cast iron, so she was fairly certain she hadn't done any permanent damage.

Fingers crossed, anyway.

Beside him, Rhett collapsed, overcome by the number of cupcakes still on the floor.

"I *hate you*," she said to the unconscious boy. Then she picked up her phone and said, "Joey?"

"Don't do anything, Agnes," Joey yelled, the sounds of traffic in the background. *"I'm on Route 17. I'm almost there."*

"That's good," Agnes said, realizing her voice was shaking, too. "He's just a kid, Joey. He said he wasn't trying to hurt anybody—"

The kid lunged to his feet, and Agnes screamed again and dropped the phone to swing the pan again, but this time he was ready for her, ducking under her arm and butting her in the stomach so that she said, "Oof!" and fell backward against the counter. He tried to backhand her, and she swung the pan again and hit him in the head, and then she couldn't stop, she hit him over and over, and he yelled, *"Stop it!"* and grabbed for her while she swung at him, driving him back toward the hall door, screaming, "Get out, get out, get *out of this house, get out of this house!"* as he lurched back, and stepped in Rhett's water dish and fell back against the wall and then *through* it, screaming.

Agnes froze, the frying pan raised over her head as he disappeared, and then the wall was solid again, and she heard a thud, and the screaming stopped, cut off.

She stood there with the pan over her head for a moment,

stunned, and then she lowered it slowly and clutched it to her chest, warm raspberry sauce and all, her heart beating like mad. She stared dumbfounded at the wall, waiting to see if he'd come rushing back through, like a ghost or something. When nothing happened, she went over and pushed cautiously with the pan on the place where the kid had disappeared.

It swung open and shut again, the hideous wallpaper that had covered it now torn along the straight edge of a doorframe.

"Oh," Agnes said, caught between amazement that there'd been a swinging door behind the wallpaper and fear that there was also a crazed moron behind there.

"*Agnes!*" Joey yelled on the phone.

Agnes took a deep breath and stepped back to the counter and picked it up. "What?"

"*What the fuck happened?*"

"There's another door in my kitchen, right next to the hall door." Agnes went back and pushed it open again, avoiding the rusted, broken nails that lined the doorway edge, and peered into the black void. "Huh."

"*Where's the kid with the gun?*"

"Good question." Agnes dropped her skillet on the counter, yanked open the utility drawer by the door, and got out her flashlight. She turned it on, shoved the door open with her shoulder, and pointed it into the darkness.

"*What are you doing?*" Joey yelled.

"I'm trying to see what's behind this door. I didn't even know it was *here*. Brenda never mentioned—"

"*Agnes, you can explore that goddamn house later,*" Joey said. "Take Rhett and get the hell *out of there.*"

"I don't think the kid's a problem anymore." Agnes held the phone with one hand and peered down into the pool of light the flashlight cast on the floor below as Rhett came to join her, pressing close to her leg so he could peer, too. "He fell into a basement. I didn't even know I *had* a basement back here. Brenda never said anything about one.

Did you know—?" She had been playing the light around the floor, and now she stopped as it hit the moron. "Uh-oh."

"*What do you mean, 'uh-oh'?*"

The boy was splayed out on what looked like a concrete floor, and he did not look good.

"I think he's hurt. He's definitely not moving."

"*Good,*" Joey said. "He fall down the stairs?"

"There are no stairs." Agnes squinted down into the darkness as the light hit the boy's face.

His eyes stared up at her, dull and fixed.

Agnes screamed, and Rhett scrambled back, stepping in the raspberry sauce, which he began to lick up.

"*Agnes?*"

"Oh, God," Agnes said as her throat closed in panic. "Joey, his neck's at a funny angle and his eyes are staring up at me. *I think I killed him.*"

"No, you didn't, honey," Joey said around the traffic noise in the background. "He committed suicide when he attacked an insane woman in the stupid house she bought. I'm almost there. You stay there and *don't open that door for anybody.*"

"He's dead, Joey. I have to call the police." *This is bad. This is bad. This is not going to look good.*

"The police can't help you with this one," Joey said. "You stay put. I'm gonna get you somebody until we figure this out."

"Some body. Right." Agnes clicked off the phone and looked back down at the dead body in her basement.

He looked pathetic, lying there all broken and dead-eyed. Agnes swallowed, trying to get a grip on the situation.

How are you feeling right now, Agnes?

Shut the fuck up, Dr. Garvin.

Don't say "fuck," Agnes. Angry language makes us angrier.

Gosh darn, Dr. Garvin, I'm feeling . . .

She put the beam on the boy again.

Still dead.

Oh, God.

Okay, calm down, she told herself. *Think this through.*

She hadn't killed him, the basement floor had.

You hit him many times in the head with the frying pan—try explaining that one.

Okay, okay, but he'd *attacked* her in Brenda's *house.* No, in *her* house. So it was self-defense. Yes, he was young and pathetic and heartbreaking down there, but he'd been a horrible person.

Why do you always hit them with frying pans, Agnes?

Because that's what I always have in my hand, Dr. Garvin. If I were a gardener, it'd be hedge clippers. Think how bad that would be.

She punched in 911 on her phone, trying to concentrate on the good things: Rhett was fine, her column would be finished soon, Maria's wedding was still on track for that weekend, Two Rivers was hers—well, hers and Taylor's—pretty soon she was going to be living her dream, and her cupcakes were burning but she could make more—

There's a dead body in my basement and I lost my temper and I hit him with a frying pan many times, I was not in control—

"Keyes County Emergency Services," the police dispatcher drawled.

"There's a dead body in my basement," Agnes said, and then her knees gave way and she slid down the cabinet to sit hard on the floor as she tried to explain that the kid had been going to hurt *her dog,* while Rhett drooled on her lap.

"A deputy is on the way, ma'am," the dispatcher said, as if dead bodies in basements were an every-evening occurrence.

"Thank you." Agnes hung up and looked at Rhett.

"I have to make cupcakes," she said, and he looked encouraging, so she got up to get the blackened cupcakes out of the oven and clean the floor and get back to work, thinking very hard about her column, and Maria's wedding that weekend, and Brenda's beautiful house that was now hers, and everything except the dead body in her basement and the goddamned frying pan.

Shane sat on a bar stool, in a shady nightclub on the wrong side of the tracks in a bad part of Savannah, Georgia, and tried to estimate how many people he was going to have to kill in the next hour. Optimally it would be one, but he had long ago learned that optimism did not apply to his profession. He felt his cell phone vibrate in his pocket and pulled it out with his free hand, expecting to see the GO or NO GO text message from Wilson. There were only three people who had his number, and they never called to chat. One of them was across the dance floor from him, which left two options. He glanced at the screen and was surprised to see JOEY.

Jesus. First time ever, and he calls in the middle of a job. Shane hesitated for a moment, then thought, *Hell, you gave him the number for emergencies,* and hit the ON button. "Uncle Joe?"

"Shane, you on a job?"

"Yes."

"Where you at?"

"Savannah."

"Good," Joey said. "Close. I need you home."

Shane frowned. *Home? You send me away at ten and* now *you want me home?* "What's the problem?" he said, keeping his voice cold.

"I got a little friend needs some help. She lives just outside Keyes in the old Two Rivers mansion. Remember it?"

Fucking Keyes, SC. Armpit of the South.

"Come home and take care of my little Agnes, Shane."

You adopt another kid, Joe? Gonna take better care of this one? "I'll be there in an hour."

"I appreciate it." Joey hung up.

Shane pushed the OFF button. Joey needing help taking care of something. That was new. Old man must be getting really old. Calling him home. That was—

"I'm a Leo—and you?"

Shane turned to look at her. Long blonde hair. Bright smile plastered on her pretty face. Pink T-shirt stretched tight across her ample chest with the word *Princess* embroidered on it in shiny letters. Effective advertising, bad message.

"What's your sign?" she said, coming closer.

"Taurus with a bad moon rising." The hell with Joey. He had a job to do. He looked at the upstairs landing.

Two men in long black leather coats and wraparound sunglasses appeared on the landing. They took barely visible flanking positions at the top of the metal stairs, just as they had the previous evening at approximately the same time, which meant the target was in-house.

At home, so to speak.

"Do you come here often?" Princess asked, coming still closer, about three inches too close. He scooted back on his stool slightly.

"Never." He looked up again. Too many people had seen *The Matrix*, he decided as he took in the bodyguards' long jackets and shades.

The Matrix probably hadn't even played in Keyes yet.

Princess came in closer, her breasts definitely inside his personal space. "What do you do for a living?"

"I'm a painter."

That's what Joey used to tell people. *I'm a painter.*

Enough with Joey.

Shane glanced across the room. Carpenter was in place, his tall, solid figure near the emergency exit, the flashing lights reflecting off his shaved ebony skull. *I paint them, Carpenter cleans them.* Shane nodded toward the guards ever so slightly. Carpenter nodded back.

"That's cool." Princess began to scan past Shane, probably looking for somebody who'd play with her. She must have found him, because she smiled at Shane blankly and backed off. "Have a good one," she said, and was gone into the crowd.

The phone buzzed once more, and Shane glanced at the screen: GO. He secured the phone in his pocket, nodding once more at Carpenter, who reached into one of his deep pockets. Princess was over by the bar now, dialing on her phone with a blank look on her face as she tossed her head to get the hair out of her eyes. Then she frowned and pulled the phone away, staring at it. Shane knew no one's cell phone within two hundred feet would work now, as long as Carpenter kept the transmitter in his pocket working, jamming all frequencies.

Shane wove his way through the sweaty dancers to the bottom of the staircase and walked up, Carpenter falling in behind him. Both bodyguards stepped out, forming a human wall that he estimated weighed over 480 pounds combined with another ten pounds or so of leather coat thrown in. Which meant they trumped him by over 270.

Fortunately 210 pounds with brains could usually beat 480 pounds of dumb.

"Private office," the one on the right growled.

Shane jabbed his right hand, middle three fingers extended, into the man's voice box, then grabbed the face of the man on the left and applied pressure at just the right places with the fingertips of his left hand, thumb on one side, four fingers on the other. The man froze in the middle of reaching under his jacket, unable to move, while Carpenter caught the man to the right.

"Tell me the truth and live," Shane whispered as he leaned close, ignoring the other guard's desperate wheezing attempts to get air down his damaged windpipe. "Lie and die. Is Casey Dean here?"

"Uggh." There was the slightest twitch of the head in the affirmative.

"Alone?"

"Uggh." A twitch side to side.

Shit. "Left foot," Shane said. "How many are in there? Tap your foot for the number."

The foot hit the ground twice, then halted.

"Good boy." Shane shifted his fingers slightly and pressed. The man dropped unconscious to the floor. Carpenter already had the other man down, sleeping with the leather. At least they'd be warm.

Shane reached inside their coats and retrieved their pistols. He placed one in his waistband in his back and kept the other one out, safety off. He stepped over them as Carpenter reached down and grabbed the back of each man's jacket and dragged them to a small janitor's closet and tumbled them in, then turned and faced the stairway to make sure no one else came up. He wasn't wearing leather.

Shane walked down the hallway to the bright red doorway with a prominent NO TRESPASSING sign hung on it. He kicked right at the lock, the wood splintered, and he stepped in and to one side, eyes taking in the dimly lit scene, pistol up, sweeping the room, gun in concert with his eyes.

Movement. Two people. A man. Seated behind a desk. A redhead standing on the other side, leaning forward, palms down on the desktop, her skimpy halter top hanging loose, exposing her breasts. *Great,* Shane thought. *I had to hit at playtime.*

He strode across the room as the man jumped up and the woman turned, looking surprised. The man was reaching for a jacket when Shane hit him with a cat-paw fist strike to the solar plexus, making him thump back into his chair, gasping in pain and floundering, out of commission for a couple of minutes at least.

The redhead lunged at Shane, who sidestepped her claws, grabbed her from behind, and used her momentum to slam her against the desk, pinning her to it. He got one arm in a half nelson around her neck and pressed the barrel of the gun against the back of her head. He could feel her tight ass pushing back against his groin, and she began to grind as she struggled against him, putting her arms flat out on the desktop and looking over her shoulder angrily. He shoved her shoulders down on the desk and saw a small tattoo of a compass on the small of her back, just above her jeans. *Like somebody needs directions there,* he thought.

She pressed back harder against him.

"Stop it," he said.

"Oh, come on," she whispered. "You like it. We can work this out, you and me. I can—"

Shane pulled the gun back and tapped the barrel against the back of her skull.

The girl rubbed her head. "What the fuck?"

"This is business and you are not part of it. Stay there." Shane backed away, keeping the barrel aimed at her, and when she didn't move, he glanced at the man who was still gasping for air. Not a problem.

Then Shane reached inside his jacket and pulled out an airline ticket. He tossed the plane ticket on the desk in front of the woman. "You've got a problem, here's the solution. A voucher you can use at the airport tonight. Enough for a one-way ticket anywhere in the world."

The redhead stared at him.

"You don't ever want to come back to Savannah again," he told her. "This man hangs with bad men, and they're going to remember you were here and come looking for you."

The girl was nodding, reaching for the ticket at the same time she tried to put her jacket on.

"You can go, but if you say anything to anyone on the way out, you will die."

The girl was still nodding like a bimbo bobblehead doll, one arm in her jacket, the other with the ticket in hand. Shane kept one eye on her struggles as he focused his attention back on the man. When she was ready and holding the ticket in one hand and her purse in the other, Shane pulled out his satellite phone and hit the speed-dial for Carpenter. "You got one civilian coming out. Redhead. Let her go."

There was a telling moment of silence. "A witness."

"A *civilian* coming out," Shane repeated.

"Roger," Carpenter said.

Shane nodded to the redhead, and she scuttled to the door and was gone.

Shane turned his attention back to the man. "Same deal for you, my friend." He slapped another ticket voucher on the desk.

"Who—?" The man coughed and tried again as he managed to sit up straighter. "Who—are—you?"

"Doesn't matter who I am," Shane said. "I'm gonna ask you some questions. Answer honestly, you take this ticket and go. Lie and die."

The man's face was shiny with pain and exertion. "What—do—you—want?"

"You were hired by the mob to kill someone the U.S. government would prefer stay alive."

"You got the wrong—"

Shane hit him, an open-handed slap that was more insult than injury. "You're wasting my time, Casey Dean," he said, and the man flinched when he heard the name. "The people I work for do not make mistakes. Unlike you."

"Really—"

Shane reached out and jabbed his thumb into Dean's shoulder, hitting a nerve junction, and the guy jumped as if struck by an electric shock. "Now here's the deal. You tell me what I want to know and forget about the hit, fly away, and never come back, and it's the same to me as if you were dead."

Dean rubbed his shoulder. "That's it?"

"That's it." Shane slid the ticket voucher across the desk.

"You're really gonna let me go if I tell you what you want and forget about the contract?"

"No. I'm gonna let you go if you forget about the hit *and* give me the names and contact information of whoever hired you *and* the name of the target."

Dean shook his head. "I can't give the contractor up. He'll kill me."

Shane brought the gun level with the point right between the man's eyes. "Which is worse? The possibility he might kill you in the future or the certainty I *will* kill you in the next ten seconds?"

"Shit." Dean slumped, looking suddenly very old. "Listen, I'm just a business manager. I'm—"

Shane pressed the muzzle of the gun hard against the man's skin just above his nose.

Dean's eyes turned inward, mesmerized by the barrel. "I'm telling you, I don't know the contractor's name. I just got a call that services were needed."

"Who's the target?"

"Didn't get it yet. I swear."

Great. Dean was an idiot, but there was a ring of truth in that.

"Listen, I'm cold. Can I get my jacket?" Dean's eyes shifted again, his voice heavy with faked innocence now.

Shane looked at him, almost pitying him in his stupidity. *The dumb fuck has a plan.* He pulled the gun back. "Sure." His assignment was to take out Casey Dean, world-class hitman, but if this guy was a world-class hitman, Shane was Princess's date to prom. Some guys were all PR, no game, and Dean was sure as hell turning out to be one of them.

When Dean had put on his jacket, he looked downright confident, his eyes sly as they went to the desk. "So I really don't know anything, but I'm definitely leaving town, just like you said. Okay if I get my passport from my desk drawer?"

Shane nodded. *You bet. Commit suicide with my gun. That's what I'm here for.*

The man turned his back and opened a desk drawer, and Shane brought his gun up.

Dean swung around, a small gun in his hand, and Shane fired two quick shots, hitting him in the chest. Dean fell back, disappearing behind the desk.

Below, the music pounded, drowning out everything. Shane walked forward, gun at the ready, and rolled the man over, surprised to find there was still a spark of life in his eyes. Not surprised to see his two shots were so tightly grouped they appeared to be one hole, but not happy to see them an inch off target.

Fucking Joey, making him lose focus. Fucking Keyes. Fucking little Agnes, too, whoever she was.

A funny look came over the man's face as Shane aimed the gun at his forehead. His eyes blinked rapidly. "Wait," he gasped. "We can make a deal."

"Oh, come on," Shane said. "You know who and what you are. You lied. You'd have completed the contract because otherwise you'd never get another job."

"No—" Dean said, and Shane fired, the round making a perfect black hole in the center of his forehead. Shane leaned over and checked Dean's pockets, finding a business card with just a phone number on it. He pocketed it.

He pulled out his cell phone and hit number 3 on the speed-dial.

It was answered on the first ring: "Carpenter."

"Painting's done. You'll have to help him on to the next world on your own, Reverend. I won't be at debrief."

There was a brief moment of silence. "Wilson won't like that."

"The target had no information on contractor or his target."

"Roger."

Shane put the phone away and picked up the voucher.

Then he crossed the room to the window, reached under his shirt, retrieved the heavy-duty snap link attached to the rear of his body armor, clipped it to a bolt holding a drainpipe, turned outward and jumped, the carefully coiled bungee cord snapping out until it jerked him to a halt three feet from the street and bounced him back up half the distance. As he went down the second time, Shane pulled the quick release and landed on all fours. Right next to his Defender SUV.

Keyes again.

Fuck.

At eleven thirty, an hour and a half after the kid had gone screaming through her kitchen wall, Agnes pulled another pan of chocolate-raspberry cupcakes out of the oven, stopped rehearsing her story for the next wave of police—*It's a nonstick frying pan, so it's really very light, it couldn't kill anybody*—and wondered what Dr. Garvin would say about all of this. Well, she knew what he'd say. He'd look at her and say, "How are you feeling right now, Agnes?"

And if she said, "Fine, Dr. Garvin," he'd give her that look that said, *My ass, Agnes,* except court-appointed psychiatrists couldn't say that.

She tried to remember the list of terms he'd given her to help her describe how she'd felt when she hit her fiancé with the frying pan: *Mean/Evil. Worthless. Revengeful. Bitchy.* She remembered wondering where *outraged* and *betrayed* and *sickened by the unsanitary assault on a dining surface* had been. "He was actually *doing* her on *my clean kitchen table,*" she'd told him, in what she'd thought was a perfectly calm voice. "I mean, *Jesus Christ, of course I hit him with a frying pan!*"

"Hit who with a frying pan?" Joey said from the doorway.

Agnes looked up from where she'd been talking to the cupcakes. "Am I going to go to jail for hitting the kid with the frying pan?"

"No," Joey said, mystified. "You didn't kill him, he fell through the wall. You all right?"

"Well." Agnes leaned against the counter. "There's some stuff I didn't tell you."

Joey came in and put his arm around her, the weight of muscle going to fat a comfort on her shoulders. "Like what?"

"Remember I told you I was engaged after college and my fiancé cheated on me?"

"Yeah, the bastard."

"Well, when I found out he lied to me, I kind of hit him."

"Good for you."

"In the face. With a frying pan. Nonstick. Broke his nose."

"Oh." Joey nodded, still supportive but wary now. "He file a police report?"

Agnes nodded. "He dropped the charges, though." *Tell me I'm okay, Joey.*

"Well, this is different. It won't—"

"And then three years ago, I got engaged to that crime reporter I told you about?"

"Yeah," Joey said, definitely on guard.

"And two years ago, he cheated on me with my assistant? And I caught him with her on my kitchen table?"

"You didn't tell me that part."

"And I hit him in the back of the head with a cast-iron skillet." *Tell me I'm okay, Joey.*

"Oh, shit, Agnes."

Ouch. "So if the cops look me up . . ."

"Did you kill him?"

"No. They put a plate in his head. He's fine."

"You do any time?"

"Probation with court-ordered therapy and community service." Agnes leaned against Joey, grateful for his bulk beside her. "A soup kitchen. It was nice. Good people worked there." *Tell me I'm okay, Joey.*

"You're good people, too, Agnes." He patted her shoulder. "Don't worry. This was self-defense. You're all right."

Agnes looked up at his dear, ugly mug. "Yeah?"

"Yeah," Joey said, and looked at her straight, the way Joey always did.

"Good." She straightened up to go back to work. Self-defense was legitimate. Brenda would have pounded the kid in self-defense, too. "What were you coming in to tell me?"

He looked uncomfortable. "I called somebody to come help you, and I was waiting for him outside, and then the next bunch of cops pulled down the drive. We got trouble."

Agnes put the cakes on the bread table. "You mean besides the cop in the hallway and the dead body in the basement?"

"The cop in the hallway is a dumb-fuck deputy, he's not trouble," Joey said. "But now we got Detective Simon Xavier comin' across your bridge."

"Who?" Agnes peeled off her oven mitt.

"Xavier," Joey said. "The one cop in Keyes who actually knows what the fuck he's doing."

Agnes felt cold. "Joey?"

There was a crash from the direction of the old housekeeper's room, now her bedroom, and Agnes said, "That's that deputy. He keeps wandering around saying, 'So this is what Two Rivers looks like inside.' Like he's looking for something. I told him to stay in the hall. I even gave him a cupcake."

Joey jerked his head toward the housekeeper's room. "Go get him. I'll talk to Xavier."

Agnes swallowed. "Joey, am I going to jail?"

"No, honey," Joey said. "But don't hit anybody else with a goddamned frying pan."

Agnes went cold. *I'm in trouble if Joey's warning me.* "Right." She forced a smile for him, took a deep breath, and started for the housekeeper's room.

"Aw, wait a minute." Joey caught her arm and handed her the frying pan.

"What's this for?" she said.

"I take it back," he said. "If that deputy tries anything funny, you can use this. They can't get you for self-defense."

"Oh, *funny,*" she said, but she took the pan and tried a smile. "Joey, you're the best."

"Go on," he said, but he blushed just the same. "You okay?"

"Yeah," she told him. "Kind of. This has been a really lousy day, but it's almost over, the cops are going to take the body away, I'm not in any trouble . . . right?" She looked at him, trying not to seem anxious.

"Right," Joey said firmly, but his eyes slid away from hers.

Oh, God. Agnes smiled at him as sanely as she could and headed for her bedroom, not relieved at all.

Once in the housekeeper's room, Agnes clutched her frying pan tighter and felt her way toward the bedside lamp.

"I told you nothing happened in here," she called out, looking around for the cop. "It was all out in the kitchen." *Not that I'm upset with you, sir. Please don't arrest me.*

The wind blew the curtains away from the window by the bed, and she saw that the bedside table was tipped over, and then a hand clamped over her mouth and somebody said, "Shhhh," and she swung the pan up over her head hard and connected with a smack that reverberated into her shoulders.

He wrenched the pan out of her hand. "*Stop it.* Joey sent me."

She yanked away from him, and he let her go so that she tripped, falling against the bed, and then she fumbled on the floor for the light and clicked it on, breathing hard.

He loomed up over her as her heart pounded, a big guy, dressed in black—black pants, black T, black denim jacket—looking like he'd been hacked out of a block of wood: strong, weathered face; black, flat eyes—*shark eyes,* she thought—cropped dark hair going gray at the temples, now a little bloody on the right; tense, hard, squared-off body, all of it alert and concentrated on her. But the thing she noticed most, as she tried to keep from having a heart attack, was that he looked like Joey. Younger than Joey, bigger than Joey, but he looked like Joey.

She swallowed. "Who are you and what the hell are you doing in here?"

"I'm Shane. Joey sent me." He jerked his head toward the kitchen, no wasted movement. "Who's out there?"

Agnes got to her feet, wishing she had her frying pan back. "Shane. Okay, Shane, thank you for scaring the *hell* out of me, but this is my house, so I'll ask the questions." She took a deep breath. "Joey sent you. Why?"

"I'm here to protect some kid. Little Agnes?"

"That's me," Agnes said.

There was a silence long enough to hear crickets in, and Agnes thought, *If he makes some crack about me being not little, I'm gonna hit him again,* and then he spoke.

"I'm here to protect you," he said, sounding resigned. "Unless you hit me again, in which case, whoever I'm supposed to save you from can have your ass."

"Protect me." That wasn't good. She'd been worried about the police finding out about her record, but Joey thought she needed to be protected from something else, something only somebody like this guy could stave off. Which meant something was seriously wrong. Not that the guy who was now a corpse in her basement hadn't been a tip-off, but if Joey thought something was so bad that she needed this guy, it must be really bad, because a guy like this could protect her from . . .

Anything.

Out in the front hall, Brenda's ugly black grandfather clock began to chime the hour in big gongs that sounded like Death's oven timer, and Agnes looked at Shane again.

Big. Broad. Dark. Strong. Handsome if you liked thugs. Looked like Joey. And he was here to keep her safe.

How are you feeling right now, Agnes?

Could be worse.

"Okay, Shane," Agnes said as Brenda's clock gonged midnight. "I got Joey in the kitchen, a cop in the front hall, a dead body in the basement, and you in my bedroom. Where do you want to start?"

tuesday

cranky agnes column #62

"Just Like Mother Used to Fake"

Many of us have a recipe passed down to us by our mothers that pretty much sums up our childhood memories in an ingredient list. In my case, it was "One chilled glass, two parts Tanqueray, wave at the vermouth bottle, stir clockwise if you're north of the equator, and for God's sake, Agnes, don't bruise the gin." Yours was probably a can of cream of mushroom soup poured over a can of green beans. That mother who made baked Alaska from scratch? She also screamed, "No wire hangers!" Those overachievers always have a dark side.

Shane had started in the kitchen, a big warm room with red walls and white counters that smelled of chocolate and raspberry, quiet except for the rumble of voices from the hall.

"That's Detective Xavier and Joey," Agnes said, looking worried.

Everything in Agnes's kitchen was neat and professional, but nothing said big money, ransom kind of money. In fact, the only thing that had caught his eye was the row of gleaming razor-sharp knives stuck to the magnetic bars on the wall, and next to them long-handled forks that looked sharp as spikes, and beyond those more sharpened, shiny tools, every damn one of them lethal as hell.

Agnes worked in the Kitchen of Death.

"You hit him with a frying pan," he said to her. "How come you didn't grab a knife?"

"The frying pan was closer." Her eyes slid away. "It's not like I had time to pick a weapon. It's not like the frying pan is my weapon of *choice*."

He nodded and moved to look at the revolver on the counter, stopping when he saw the dirty white tape around the pistol grip, an old mobster's trick. Any old mobster in Keyes, South Carolina, was going to be somebody Joey knew. Fuck. There went any hope of getting out of there and back to work fast. Wilson was not going to be happy.

Well, that made two of them.

"Where's the body?" he asked her, and she went over to the hall door and pushed on the wall next to it, and a concealed door swung back and forth while she watched. He reached inside his jacket and under his T-shirt and pulled a mini-Maglite out of the pocket sewn onto the outside of his body armor. "Can you stall this Xavier while I go down there and get a look?"

"Sure," Agnes said, not sounding sure.

He moved past her to put one foot through the door onto the two-by-eight on the inside where the stairs had once been attached, and tested to make sure it was solid. Then he swung into the void until both feet were on the board. He bent down, put his fingers on the same piece of wood, and then slid his feet down the wall. Halfway down, he let go and landed lightly in the basement, and then went over to the body and put his mini-Mag on it.

Angry welts on the face. Agnes and her hot raspberry sauce.

Blood underneath the dirty hair. Agnes and her frying pan.

Neck twisted and broken. Agnes and her unknown basement with no stairs.

Joey's Little Agnes didn't need protecting, but he might stay and put up some warning signs for unsuspecting intruders. Something like BEWARE OF THE COOK or AGNES KILLS.

He heard voices and waited to hear the door open wide, but instead he heard Joey say, "Xavier, this here is my little Agnes, Cranky Agnes, from the newspaper. You probably seen her picture over her column."

Shane bent down and began to go through the boy's pockets.

Upstairs he heard a Southern drawl say, "Pleased to meet you, Miss Agnes. Now, you do own this house, ma'am?" and Agnes, so clear she must have been right by the door, say, "Yes. I bought it from Brenda Dupres four months ago. I've been rehabbing it, but I'm still finding things. Mostly dry rot and bad plaster, so the basement was actually a step up. Well, not for the dead guy. Are you sure I can't get you some coffee, Detective? I make a truly delicious cup of coffee."

Good girl, he thought, and played the flashlight around the room. An old pool table in the center, good solid mahogany, the felt now peeling up from the slate. A small bar tucked in one corner, fully stocked, as if somebody had just left it yesterday, the wood now covered with dust and mold. Behind it, a ceiling-high, four-foot-wide wine rack, still filled with bottles, now covered with dust and cobwebs. And a five-foot-high replica of the *Venus de Milo* tucked into the corner, now speckled with mildew. *You'd have thought they'd have taken this stuff out of here before they boarded it up, sold it for good money,* he thought. Well, maybe not the statue.

The door opened above him, and he heard Agnes say, "Cupcakes, then? Fresh out of the oven," and Xavier's voice loud in the doorway saying, *"What the hell?"* and Agnes saying, "Don't shoot him, he's on my side," and Shane looked up to see the muzzle of a truly large gun pointed down at him and behind that a very powerful flashlight, blinding him.

"What *the hell* are you doing down there?" Xavier said.

Shane clicked off his own light. "Just making sure this boy didn't need my help, sir."

The light went off, and Shane heard the clatter of metal as the edge of a ladder appeared in the hole and angled down until the bottom touched the concrete floor. Xavier climbed down, older than Shane expected, probaby Joey's age, his white suit gleaming in the dark, then Joey, then another man, younger, larger, blond, and goofy-looking.

Joey came over to Shane and hugged him, then kissed him on each cheek, but Shane kept his eyes on Xavier and his gun. It was a revolver, which wasn't cutting edge, but it was a .357 Magnum, which was impressive.

Joey let him go and gestured to the guy with the gun. "Shane, this here is Detective Simon Xavier. An old acquaintance of mine. And his partner, Detective Hammond."

Xavier holstered the gun and nodded, and the young blond guy behind him nodded, too, looking friendly. "So, Mr. Shane, you felt you had the right to come down here and bespoil my crime scene because . . ." He raised his eyebrows, waiting for an answer.

"I thought he might need assistance," Shane lied.

"And the untoward angle of his neck did not tell you that he was beyond any earthly assistance you might render?"

"I'm not a doctor, sir," Shane said.

"Neither are you a miracle worker, son," Xavier said. "Should you find any other bodies in my jurisdiction, you *will* refrain from attempting to raise them from the dead."

"Yes, sir," Shane said.

Joey looked down at the body, no recognition in his eyes.

Good, Shane thought.

"Know him?" Joey said to Xavier.

Xavier reached into the dead man's pockets, pulled out a wallet, and flipped it open. He stood up slowly and straightened. "Thought so. Jimmy Thibault."

Joey grew very still.

Not good, Shane thought.

"Aka Two Wheels Thibault," Xavier said genially.

Hammond peered at the corpse. "Yep, that's a Thibault. They breed like rats out there in the swamp. Two Wheels's got more cousins than a dog's got fleas."

Xavier smiled at Joey, showing some teeth. "Oh, Joey knows the Thibaults, don't you, Joey?"

Joey's face closed. "Nah."

Bad lie, Shane thought. "Why would Joey know him? This kid doesn't look like anybody who'd come into the diner."

Joey nodded. "Yeah, this kid never came into the diner. I never saw him before."

Xavier looked at Shane, thoughtful now. "The diner. You wouldn't be that boy who used to work in the diner, now, would you?"

Shane nodded.

Xavier cocked his head, interested. "Now, where you been all these years, son?"

"Here and there," Shane said.

"Who you work for now?"

"Joey. He called me to help his friend Agnes."

"And you came riding into town all dressed in black?"

"Seemed the right thing to do. She's pretty vulnerable out here alone."

Xavier's eyes were flat on Shane. "And you're gonna keep her from being all alone, are you?"

"Yes." *Until I find out what's going on here and get Joey the hell out of it.*

Xavier stared at him for a moment more without comment and then bent back to the body, going through the pockets in silence.

Not much in there, Shane thought. The kid must have been dirt poor.

Agnes called down from the doorway above. "Doc Simmons is here. Okay if I have him look at Rhett while he's waiting for you? Rhett ate a lot of chocolate, and that's not good for dogs."

"Sure, Miz Agnes. Then get him down here," Xavier said.

"Dogs?" Shane said to Joey.

"The coroner is elected here," Joey said to Shane. "Only guy who ran for it was a local veterinarian named Simmons whose business was going under."

Only in Keyes, Shane thought.

"Hammond," Xavier said. "You stay here with the body and wait for the coroner."

Hammond nodded.

"You," Xavier said, looking at Joey, "I'm going to want the pleasure of your company for some conversation later."

You and me both, Shane thought, and followed his uncle and the detective up the ladder, determined to find out what a boarded-up basement, a moth-eaten old bloodhound, and a food writer with a nice ass could have to do with his ex-mobster uncle before his notoriously un-sympathetic boss terminated his career.

By one thirty Tuesday morning, Agnes had answered the same thirty questions at least a thousand times, grateful none of them had been, "Exactly how many men *have* you struck with a frying pan, Miz Agnes?" since the answer now stood at four, if you counted Shane. Hammond had thrown some variety into the mix by asking about Maria's upcoming wedding—"She still as sweet and pretty as ever?"—and Doc Simmons had looked at Rhett and said, "Nothin's gonna kill that ole hound, certainly not your most excellent cake, Miss Agnes," and then, almost as an afterthought, pronounced the Thibault kid dead. Agnes had said, "Thank you, Doc," put some cupcakes in a bag for him, and waved him off into the night, watching as he followed the ambulance crew with the body down the lane and over the rickety bridge to the main road. "Rest in peace, I guess," she said to the tail-lights and went back to the kitchen, but she'd barely gotten there when the door chime went again.

"I'll get it," Joey said, sliding off the counter stool. "You tell Detective Xavier here whatever else he needs to know so he can go home." He patted Agnes's shoulder and kissed her cheek and then ambled out to get the door while Agnes turned to smile at Xavier, radiating innocence.

"You know everything about me already," she said to Xavier, but a minute later, Taylor strode in looking blond, handsome, and concerned, and she had to say, "Except for him. Detective Xavier, this is my fiancé, Taylor Beaufort. Taylor, this is Detective Xavier."

"Detective," Taylor said in his soft drawl as he slid his arm around her. "Sugar, what the devil is goin' on out here? Are you all right?"

"I'm just fine," she said, a little rattled that she'd forgotten he existed. "What are you doing here?"

"I heard somebody broke in," he said, his drawl getting less soft as he scowled in Shane's direction.

Shane looked back with the same expression he'd had since she hit him with the frying pan: none.

"And how was it that you heard about the break-in?" Xavier asked.

"Everybody in town heard, Detective," Taylor said. "Doc Simmons stopped for coffee on his way out here and mentioned it to his waitress who mentioned it to Maisie Shuttle who told my waitress when she stopped by the Inn for dessert." He moved his hand up to Agnes's shoulder. "Agnes, you must have been scared to death."

"I'm fine." He sounded truly worried, and Agnes tried to feel comforted by that.

"A boy broke in and tried to steal your fiancée's dog, Mr. Beaufort," Xavier said. "Would you know anything about that?"

"He tried to steal *Rhett*?" Taylor said, looking at Shane with astonishment.

"Not Shane," Agnes said. "A *boy.* Shane is Joey's nephew. He's here to look out for me. Joey asked him to come."

"I see." Taylor didn't look happy. "Well, no, I don't see. Why would anybody want to steal Rhett? And why would Joey call his nephew? What—?"

"The house is isolated," Shane said. "She shouldn't be out here alone."

Yeah, Agnes thought, and then felt like a wimp. Brenda had been just fine out here alone.

"Keyes is a safe community," Taylor said to Shane. "The former owner lived on her own out here without any problems. I don't see—"

"A kid broke in with a gun and threatened Agnes," Shane pointed out.

"Just a prank," Taylor said stiffly.

"She's not laughing," Shane said. "And he's dead."

"*Dead?*" Taylor looked down at Agnes. "I thought they just *arrested* him. What happened?"

"He fell," Agnes said, skipping the part where she'd swung the frying pan in case Taylor felt moved to blurt out her history with cookware as weaponry.

"He threatened your fiancée with a gun, and she defended herself," Xavier said.

"Yeah," Hammond said. "With a frying pan. Can you believe it?"

"*What?*" Taylor said, alarmed.

Agnes grabbed Taylor's arm and yanked him toward the hall door. "It's late. *Let me walk you to your car.*"

"Wait a minute." Taylor stopped and mouthed the words *frying pan?* at her.

She scowled at him. *You just shut up about that frying pan.*

"She won't be alone," Shane said. "I'm staying with her."

Taylor straightened, forgetting the frying pan entirely, which made Agnes feel absolutely warm toward Shane.

She tugged Taylor toward the door again. "It's *all right,* he's Joey's nephew," she said, trying to move him. "It'll be *okay.*"

"I don't know," Taylor began at the same time Xavier said, "Where is Joey?"

Taylor looked back at the detective. "Oh, he said to tell you it was getting too late for him, so he was going on home."

Xavier swore.

"Come *on.*" Agnes pulled Taylor out the door and into the checkerboard hall, and once they were there, momentum helped her get him through the front door. "Look, really," she said to him once they were outside on the wide front porch, "it's okay. Shane's just here to make sure nobody else breaks in."

"I want to stay," he said, but he drew her down the steps and out across the lawn close to the drive where he'd parked his Cobra, so she knew it was all for show.

When they reached the car, he put his arms around her, and she leaned into his broad chest, trying to recapture the way she'd felt about him in the beginning, when it had felt like he was the perfect man for her. *Was it just because he was such a good chef?* she thought.

There must have been more. Well, the good sex. That was always a selling point. And he'd been sweet. And she'd been so damn *lonely.*

"I don't know about having Maria's wedding here," Taylor said, rubbing her back. "It's causing you so much stress, and this mess with this dead boy will ruin it anyway. You know how Evie Keyes hates gossip. If she finds out somebody died on the premises—"

"Her son isn't getting married in the basement," Agnes said, pulling away. "He's getting married in the gazebo, which is beautiful and corpse-free."

"I'm just saying." Taylor tried to put his arm around her again, and she shrugged it off, feeling like a surly three-year-old. "You've been through a lot. Why don't we just tell Evie to move it to the country club—"

"No!" Agnes stepped back from him, feeling betrayed. "Evie's just looking for an excuse to drag her son's wedding over there, and if she does, we owe Brenda three months' back mortgage payments. That was the deal, remember? We do the wedding in exchange for the first three months' mortgage? Do you have nine thousand dollars? Because I don't."

"Calm down," Taylor said. "Brenda would let us work out a payment plan. I just don't like seeing you stressed like this."

"What's making me stressed is the thought of moving the wedding to the country club." Agnes clamped down on her . . . irritation. Yeah, that was it, irritation. *I'm not angry. I'm annoyed.* "The wedding stays here. The fact that the kid died here has nothing to do with me or the wedding. It's not like I killed him—" She winced at the thought.

"A frying pan, Agnes," Taylor said. "Jesus."

"Go home, Taylor," Agnes said. "You've comforted me enough."

"I'm just trying to help you," Taylor said. "You've been whining at me to get out here, and when I do—"

"Right." She smiled up at him in the moonlight, trying not to bare her teeth. "Hey, you know what? I got the attic bedroom painted last week, and it's the most beautiful pale blue, like water. And the bed's all made up. It's all ready for you to move in—"

"It's hotter than hell up there," Taylor said.

"Not with the windows open and the fan going," Agnes said. "And the low light is beautiful on those wood floors. It's so peaceful and beautiful and—"

"Agnes, I don't have time to move right now," Taylor said.

Agnes crossed her arms over her raspberry-stained T-shirt. "Listen, I've been killing myself trying to get this house and this wedding together and—oh, yeah—write my columns and pay the mortgage to Brenda, and you've been out here, what, maybe three times this last month?"

"Agnes, come on, honey," Taylor said without putting much coaxing into the *honey,* and Agnes thought, *Who am I kidding? This was a mistake from the beginning,* and let her breath out in a huge sigh.

"Okay, I knew this was coming, but I was ignoring it because—" She looked up at his truly handsome face that was going to look great on their cookbook cover and thought, *Because I live for my work and you were good for my career.* "—because I really wanted this to work. But it isn't."

"Agnes, *honey.*" He reached for her.

"No," Agnes said, stepping farther back. "It's not just you. A guy with a gun broke into the house tonight, and you know who I turned to? Joey. I completely forgot about you until you showed up, all I wanted was Joey. That's all I want now." *And Shane,* she thought, and tried to ignore that one. "So it's not just you, it's both of us. I was just lonely and—"

"Agnes, you're upset," Taylor said, taking a step toward her, "but you're forgetting something." He gestured to Two Rivers. "We've got our dream, sugar."

She looked back at the house, the white columns gleaming in the moonlight and the windows shining gold in the darkness. "I know. I've loved this house since Lisa Livia brought me home from school with her that first summer."

Taylor tried to put his arm around her again. "Brenda said it was like having a second daughter when LL brought you home. That's why we belong here, sugar. This is *your family home.*"

That was a complete crock, but Agnes liked the sound of it, just the same. "You know, I sat on the high dock and dreamed about owning a house like this some day, and cooking with butter just like Brenda cooked with butter, and marrying a fine Southern gentleman like Brenda married the Real Estate King." She looked back at Taylor. "And when I saw you here on the lawn saying, 'Agnes, marry me,' I thought I was finally going to be just like Brenda. Or Scarlett O'Hara. With butter."

"Agnes," Taylor said. "You *are* Scarlett O'Hara with butter."

"Taylor," Agnes said. "You have no idea what I'm talking about. It's my dream not yours, you hate this house, that's why you're never out here. So give me some time to find a way to pay you back for your half of the down payment and what you invested rehabbing the barn—"

"Oh, God, Agnes, I'm so sorry!" Taylor swept her into his arms, and Agnes found her nose smushed into Taylor's shirt, which smelled faintly of butter and rosemary, which was probably another reason she'd said yes to him. "I've neglected you, sugar. I'll move out here tomorrow!"

"No," Agnes said into his shirt, but he kept talking.

"I'll make it up to you, you'll see," he said. "It'll be just like we planned it, I swear. We'll be out here, living our dream, writing cookbooks that'll make us even more money than *Mob Food* made you, we'll have it all." He let go of her just enough to get a line on her mouth and then he kissed her passionately, which Agnes went along with because he was a good kisser, but when he broke the kiss, she took a deep breath and stepped back.

"No, Taylor," she said. "I—"

"We'll talk about this next week," he said, opening his car door, "sittin' on our porch with a couple of juleps, talkin' about the books we're gonna write together, just you and me, Scarlett and Rhett at Two Rivers."

"I already have a Rhett," Agnes said, but he was sliding into the Cobra.

"Tomorrow is another day, sugar," he said, and then the Cobra roared to life, and he peeled off toward the bridge, and she watched his taillights fade into the darkness.

Maybe they could keep the business partnership going, and she wouldn't have to pay him back. That would be good, since she had no money. And he was going to look so handsome on that book cover. Joey had looked really good on the cover of *Mob Food*, really authentic, but Taylor was young and handsome and, well, bankable. His picture was going to sell a lot of books.

She could use some bankable. Brenda's house was a real money pit.

Rhett yawned, saying, "Ar ar ar," which was probably a comment on Taylor, too, and then he shambled back toward the house, and she followed him. She could deal with Taylor after the wedding. Tomorrow was another day. Well, not tomorrow, either.

"I am so not Scarlett O'Hara," she said to Rhett, and went back to the kitchen, where Xavier and Hammond were packing up to leave, promising to return later that day, Hammond telling her to please say hi to Maria for him.

When she'd handed them cupcakes, and they'd gone over the bridge into the darkness, Agnes turned to Shane and said, "I suppose you have more questions."

"No," he said, still expressionless. "I got most of it listening to Xavier. You're tired. I'll make a bed down here where I can stay close, and we'll go over everything in the morning."

"Thank you," she said, struck by what a comfort that was, that he knew she was wiped out, that he was going to stay close all night, that he'd be there in the morning. "I'll get you pillows and blankets," she told him, but after she brought them to him, she stood there, not sure what to do or say next, grateful he was there, large and solid and standing between her and the rest of the world, resisting the insane urge to blurt, "Would you like to sleep in the bedroom with me?" because that might be misconstrued, and she might think it was all right if it was misconstrued, that it would be good to have that much strength wrapped around her or at least between her and the window, except she had enough trouble already without sleeping with a stranger who was armed. Plus, there was Taylor, she was technically still engaged, and she held strong views on cheating. Usually backed up with a frying pan. "Thank you very much for watching out for me."

"You're welcome," he said. "Good night."

"Good night," Agnes said, and went into the housekeeper's room, holding the door open for Rhett. The last thing she saw was Shane, leaning against the kitchen counter, looking alert as all hell.

Okay, tomorrow is another day, she thought, and felt positively comforted and definitely not alone.

Shane woke up the next morning when Agnes tripped over him trying to get out her bedroom door. "Good morning," she said, looking half-asleep and completely confused. "You slept on the floor?"

He picked up his air mattress. "If anybody came, I wanted to be close."

Agnes nodded. "Oh. I would have let you sleep with Rhett if I'd known you were that worried."

He thought about telling her that it wasn't Rhett he was protecting, and then wondered if she'd have offered to let him sleep with her, and then wondered if that would have been a good idea. Then he watched her go around the counter and into her dangerous kitchen, wondering if she was naked under the thin red sweats she was wearing, which answered that question. At least for him it did. If it came to it, she'd have to do her own deciding.

Focus on the problem, he told himself. *Then get back to work before Wilson blows a gasket.*

Rhett flopped down beside Shane when he sat down at the counter. The table was right there, but he couldn't watch Agnes from the table.

Agnes put on her red-framed glasses and opened the large double-door refrigerator. She loaded her arms with food, and then she shut the refrigerator door with her hip and came toward Shane to dump the stuff on the counter in front of him and take down a pan from overhead, every move effortless and efficient and distracting, especially with all of Agnes moving softly under her sweats.

"So why would anybody want to kidnap Rhett?" Shane said, mostly to get his mind off Agnes, since he was pretty sure the answer was going to come from Joey. "Was anybody asking about him before this?"

"Kind of." Agnes took a white apron off a hook by the door and put it on—it said CRANKY AGNES'S MOB FOOD on it under a drawing of Agnes in her glasses—and tore open a package of sausages wrapped in butcher's paper and tumbled them into the pan. Then she turned on the heat under it, took down a wicked-looking fork from the magnetic rack, and began to poke the meat with it, not looking at him.

"Kind of." Shane watched her. She didn't look happy.

She turned and bent to look under the counter for something, her sweatpants pulling tight over her round butt. Agnes would never make a supermodel. Agnes was, Shane thought with a great deal of restraint, pattable. "What kind of kind of?"

She put a bowl on the counter and took down a wire whisk. "Right before the kid got here, Joey and I were on the phone and he asked about Rhett. So Joey might know something if you ask him. Coffeemaker's over by the sink if you want some."

"Okay." *Fuck.* Joey again.

Shane went around the end of the counter and found a big white coffeemaker and a coffee canister in the corner just as the meat in the pan began to cook. The smell hit him like a wave: Joey's Italian sausage. Joey's Italian breakfasts from when he was a kid.

Forget that. Shane opened the jar and stared at beans instead of powder. "Uh."

Agnes came over, reached into the cabinet, took out a grinder, placed it on the counter, and then went back to her bowl. She splashed in a little cream and began to whisk the eggs, probably with more force than necessary. "I trust Joey. Joey is the best guy I know.

Joey would never hurt me. Joey called you to come protect me."

"Yeah." *But the old bastard still knows something, and he's gonna tell me about it.* Shane hit the top of the grinder, probably with more force than necessary, and it burst into action, the odor of the ground beans filling the room, competing with the treacherous smell of the sausage while he tried to imagine what his uncle might be up to. When the beans were ground, he had to go past Agnes to fill the pot with water and was careful not to brush against her. Her hair was all tangled curls and she had no makeup on and her skin was rosy with sleep, and that was messing with his concentration, plus there was the damn Italian sausage of Joey's. He'd been in a lot of treacherous places, but Agnes's kitchen was topping them all.

He poured the water in the coffeemaker, closed the top, pressed the button, and leaned against the counter to wait, searching for a safe topic that might tell him more about the mess he was pretty sure she was in. "So who's Taylor?"

Agnes frowned at him. "What do you mean, who's Taylor? You met him last night."

"He have anything to do with the Thibaults and the mob?"

"*Taylor?*" She took another pan down from one of the hooks above her head, set it on a burner, turned the heat low under it, and picked up the butter. "No. God, no. Taylor is a local boy making good. Well, he's forty-four, so the boy part is probably pushing it. He's worked his way up through the kitchens of most of the area restaurants, and now he's chef on the best restaurant on the Island over there on the other side of the Intracoastal." She nodded in the direction of the water. "He's a real self-made man, a hard worker, and a truly good chef. We're just about finished with a cookbook that's going to be a bestseller because his recipes are great, and that's going to set up the catering business he's going to run out of the barn he just renovated here. He has nothing to do with the mob and absolutely no reason to send anybody after Rhett. You choosy about your eggs?"

"I don't want eggs," Shane said. "You don't need to feed me. Would he gain anything if you died?"

"I want to feed everybody." Agnes flipped a chunk of butter into the pan. It slid across the surface and then began to melt slowly, fighting with the coffee and the sausage for Best Morning Smell, Kitchen Division. "If I died, he'd get Two Rivers. We have a partnership agreement for the cookbook and the catering business, so the survivor gets it all. But he needs me to finish the *Two Rivers Cookbook*—his future's riding on that book. It wasn't him." She picked up the red pepper, ran a knife around the stem, twisted it, and popped out the core with one smooth motion.

Shane was impressed. "Did your mother teach you to cook?"

"Oh, please," Agnes said, taking down a knife. "My mother barely *ate*. She had a waistline to maintain. I didn't taste butter until my best friend's mother melted a chunk of it in a pan in front of me right here in this kitchen when I was fourteen. After that, there was no turning back. Any boy with a milk shake and a cheeseburger could have me."

"That explains Taylor," Shane said.

"Humor. Har." Agnes began chopping the pepper with machine gun–like efficiency.

"A catering business. I thought you were a newspaper columnist."

Agnes shot a guilty glance at her laptop, and kept chopping. "I am. But Taylor wanted the catering business and I wanted Two Rivers. So we bought it from Brenda together. I can write anyplace."

"Brenda," Shane said, remembering Joey last night on the phone saying, *"the old Fortunato place."*

"Brenda Dupres," Agnes said, introducing the pepper to the butter. "The Real Estate King's widow and the closest thing to a mother I ever had. Closer than the one I did have, anyway. She's the one who fed me butter. Fabulous cook, throws terrific parties, knows—"

"Brenda Fortunato," Shane said.

"That was before the Real Estate King," Agnes said. "And before I knew her. Mr. Fortunato was sleeping with the fishes by the time Lisa Livia brought me home with her."

Cousin Lisa Livia. Vague memories of an intense dark-haired girl came back. And Aunt Brenda. Good food, he remembered. Fancier than Joey's. But that was before Joey had sent him to military school and everything in his old life had stopped like a slammed door.

Fuck that. He inhaled the melting butter and put his mind back on the problem at hand. "But this wedding will be Fortunato not Dupres. The bride's mother is a Fortunato."

"Lisa Livia? Yes."

"What about her father?"

Agnes hesitated and then said, "He's not around. LL never married him, so Maria's a Fortunato, too."

Great. All Fortunatos, all the time. "What happened to him?"

"Nobody knows," Agnes said, turning away. "He was a bad choice. Twenty-seven-year-old wiseguy meets an eighteen-year-old high school senior. Lisa Livia went bananas for him until she caught him cheating. Then she went off on him and he hit her and that was it for LL."

Shane felt pretty certain he was missing something. "That was it?"

Agnes nodded. "I had a scholarship to a college in Ohio, and we were graduating, so she decided to come with me. Johnny disappeared and we went to Ohio and Maria was born. The two of us raised her together until she was three and LL's boss moved his company west and she went with him. It about broke my heart when they left."

She looked bereft for a moment, and Shane wondered how many times people had left Agnes and how the hell she had the courage to keep inviting them back into her life. Once had been enough for him. "And nobody ever found out what happened to Johnny?"

Agnes turned back to the sink. "Nobody looked too hard. You could say he was a missing person who nobody missed at all."

He was definitely missing something, but since it had happened eighteen years ago, it wasn't something he cared about. "How many people are coming?"

"Not that many. About a hundred."

"That's a lot. And half of them are from Maria's side of the family, right? Fifty Fortunatos? And Maria's father's family?"

"Maria's father is not around. It's just the Fortunatos. But it's not like you think. I know Maria. She's not a mob princess. Lisa Livia raised her away from all that. She's just a nineteen-year-old girl in love with a preppie golf course designer who's got more money than God, and they're going to have a nice wedding on my lawn and then go have babies dressed in Ralph Lauren. Nobody will be kissing the Godfather's ring or whatever the hell that is. He's going to have cake like everybody else and then leave."

Shane went very still. "The Don. Michael Fortunato. He's coming?"

"He's Maria's great-uncle, of course he's coming."

Shane rubbed his head. *Fucking Joey.* "You didn't mention that."

"Shane, I don't think the kid last night wanted to take Rhett because the Don is coming. The Don's never even met Rhett. They don't move in the same circles."

Shane took a deep breath, but then the coffeemaker beeped, and he took a Cranky Agnes mug from a hook under the cabinet and poured out a cup, deciding he'd said enough. "Coffee?"

Agnes looked over at his cup. "That looks like mud."

"I like it strong." He sipped the brew, heartened by the way it reached up into his brain and pressed GO, and then he took his cup back to his seat at the counter, where he had a better view of Agnes, which was the only thing about this mess that was any good at all.

So there was another question for Joey. After *You know anything about that old mob gun at Agnes's, Joey?* and *You acquainted with that Thibault family, Joey?* and *Why did you ask Agnes about Rhett, Joey?* he was definitely going to mention *You think maybe the Don coming has something to do with this, Joey?* Jesus. "Okay, anything else happen this week you want to tell me?"

"Nope." Agnes stirred the red pepper in the butter, and the smell made Shane dizzy, sharp and sweet and pungent. *I want eggs,* he thought, and tried to get his mind back on the job.

"Think harder," he said. "*Anything* this week that was out of the ordinary?"

"Sure. Lots."

Agnes was driving him crazy with the buttery pepper and sausage smells. She frowned down at the pan as she talked, her cheeks flushed from the heat from the pan, her sweats sticking to her with the humidity, and that wasn't helping his concentration, either.

"The baker quit yesterday, so I'm making a wedding cake," she was saying, "*Golf Magazine* did a rave article on Palmer's latest golf course, the Flamingo, calling him a genius of green design, and he's only twenty-eight, so we're all very proud. Doyle told me I was going to have to replace the driveway bridge pretty soon or learn to swim, and I told him I have no money and to shore it up with whatever fell off the house next."

"Doyle?"

"Handyman." Agnes peered over her steamed-up glasses at the pepper. "I moved in and he showed up."

Shane focused. "How long ago?"

Agnes used the back of her hand to push her glasses back up her nose. "About three months. I don't think he's spent them sneaking up on Rhett, if that's what you're getting at." She tipped the eggs into the pepper and butter and then picked up the pan, tilting it so that the egg covered the bottom. Then she looked up. "Listen, nothing out of the ordinary has happened. Well, except for the kid with the gun. And you."

The phone rang and she answered it. "Good morning, Reverend Miller. Yes, I'm sure Maria's a good Christian girl. What?" Agnes scowled, her face twisting behind those big red-rimmed glasses. "Of course she's been baptized—she's a Catholic. Yes, I know for sure, I'm her godmother, I was there." She listened another moment, shaking her head the entire time. "Uh-huh. Uh-huh. Right. You bet. You're welcome. See you Saturday. Good-bye." She hung up and said, "Moron," and turned back to her eggs.

Shane decided to let that conversation pass. "Okay, let's go back to the dog. How many people know Rhett is here?"

"Anybody who read the flyers I put up when I found him on the front porch. Anybody who's been out here in the past four months. Anybody who gets the *County Clarion*." She stuck a spatula under the slowly cooking egg and lifted it so that the uncooked stuff ran underneath it, concentrating on it as if it were the most important thing in the world.

"The County what?" Shane said.

"The *County Clarion*. The local newspaper. One of the papers that prints my column. I did one on cooking for dogs, and instead of my usual column picture they ran a big one of Rhett and me."

Shane sighed. "And you wait until now to mention this."

"What? The paper?" Agnes looked up at him. "Big deal. I'm telling you, everybody around here already knew about Rhett. He rides with me in the truck every time I go into town. There's nobody on the side of the road that hasn't been hit with his flying spit. He is not a secret." She picked up the cheese, took a grater from a hook on the wall, and began to grate cheese over the eggs in long pale strips.

Mozzarella, Shane thought. Memories of Joey's diner sizzled in his brain. "When did this paper come out?"

"Yesterday morning."

Shane closed his eyes. It was a damn good thing she was cute. "And you didn't think this was significant?"

Agnes kept an eye on the cheese and the eggs, and at exactly the right moment, she flipped the omelet over and slid it onto a plate. She took down a knife, halved the omelet with one clean slice, and transferred half onto another plate. Then she piled sausage on both plates, the smell making Shane dizzy with memory and hunger. "No," she said, handing the plate to him. "Salsa?"

"Yes, please," he said, and she went around the counter and put a jar on the table and motioned him over. "So this paper—"

"Toast, English muffins, or bagels?" she asked as he moved to the table.

"Muffin," Shane said, trying not to go headfirst into the omelet. It had looked so simple when she'd made it, but when he cut into it and tasted it, he realized he'd missed some stuff while he'd been making coffee. There were herbs in there or spices or something, and the egg was light—*Fluffy*, he thought—and the pepper still had crunch to it but was buttery, too. "This is good," he said without thinking.

"Thank you." Agnes sat down across from him with her omelet.

Then, having waited to show he was tough, he cut into the sausage and tasted it. "Damn."

"I know, it's amazing, isn't it?" Agnes said. "I don't know where Joey gets it, but it's fabulous."

Shane put his fork down. Fucking Keyes and memories. He picked up his fork again and began to eat. "So the *paper*—"

"Are you suggesting that somebody looked at the picture in the paper and developed a burning desire to own Rhett?" She shook her head. "You didn't see the picture."

"No, but I'd like to." Shane loaded his fork with omelet and sausage together.

"I threw mine out, but Joey will have one."

The muffin halves popped up from the toaster on the counter behind him, and she stood up to get them, the scent of her mixing with the hot yeasty smell of the muffins, and the buttery, peppery smell of the eggs, and the fat, spicy smell of the sausage, and Shane lost track of where he was in the conversation.

"What?"

"The *Clarion*." Agnes put a hot muffin in front of him and passed him the butter. "Joey will have one."

It was real butter. He'd been pretty sure it was from the smell when she'd cooked his eggs in it, but now he bit into the muffin and the taste exploded in his mouth. A man could get used to food like this. "Okay, was there anything in the article—?"

Agnes shook her head, her curls bouncing, and he stopped talking to watch her. "The article was about making your own dog biscuits. There was nothing about Rhett, the house, or anything else that would make anybody want anything here."

He plowed through breakfast in a semi-trance, overwhelmed by the sharpness and the creaminess of it all, which was distractingly like

Agnes, and then his cell phone vibrated and he pulled it out. The letters that scrolled across the screen were unintelligible groupings of
five. Wilson. The real world was calling. So was his breakfast. He put
the cell phone away. He'd decode what the world wanted later.

"More coffee?" Agnes said, and when he nodded, she got the coffeepot and filled both their mugs, leaning closer to him to fill his. She
smelled good, he thought. She smelled—he searched in his mind for
a word. Delicious.

He also liked it that she didn't ask him about the phone or the
message.

A door slammed somewhere in the house, and Shane stood, his
gun out.

Agnes stared at it. "Where did—?"

Shane put a finger on her lips.

She leaned closer and whispered, "It's probably Doyle."

"Why—" Shane began, but then a loud voice with a thick Irish
brogue echoed through the house. "Top of the morning, lass."

Shane put the gun away just as a hulking man limped into the
door from the hall. Probably a boxer in his youth, given the poorly
healed broken nose and the old scars crisscrossing his ruddy forehead
under his shaggy white hair and bushy beard.

"Morning, Doyle," Agnes said. "Want some breakfast?"

"No thank you, lass, although it's mighty tempting." Doyle
looked at Shane with piercing blue eyes. "And who is this fine strap-
ping lad?"

"This is Shane, who is staying with me for a while. Shane, Doyle."

"Pleased to meet—" the old man began, and then he caught sight
of the tear in the wallpaper to his right and stiffened. "And what in
the name of all that's holy happened here?"

"Turns out I have a basement. Look." Agnes went over and pushed
on the wall so that the hidden door swung open. "A kid broke in and
said, 'I come for your dog,' and then he fell into the basement and died."

"Saints be," Doyle said, his joviality gone, and went over to poke
his head into the doorway.

Shane drank the last of his coffee and pushed his chair under the table. "Thank you for breakfast. I'm going into town to see Joey. If you think of anything else, let me know." He looked around and picked up a piece of paper on the counter, turning it over to find a blank space. "Got a pen?"

Agnes reached into a cup on the counter by the back door and retrieved a pen. He took it and wrote down his cell phone number and gave it to her, thinking that now four people had it. A crowd. His life was getting complicated.

"Thank you for the number." She took the paper, tore it in half, scribbled something on it, and held it out to him. "Here's my numbers. Home and cell. What about Rhett? Should I keep him inside?"

Shane took the paper. "No, I'll take him with me just in case anybody else comes after him."

"He likes to hang his head out the window and snort the air," Agnes said. "Sometimes the snot gets intense."

"Great." Shane whistled to the dog.

Rhett looked at him as if he'd said a dirty word.

"Go on, baby," Agnes said to the dog. "Go with your Uncle Shane. He's going to take you for a ride."

Rhett lumbered to his feet, and Agnes bent to pet him, her sweatpants stretching against her butt again.

Uncle Shane turned his eyes away and headed for the hall door, Rhett padding obediently behind him.

He turned back to see Doyle watching him and Agnes standing in the sunlight from the back door, smiling at him surrounded by the scent of coffee and butter and sausage.

"Did you forget something?" she said.

Yeah, he thought. *I forgot this part of Keyes.*

"Be careful today," he said.

"You, too," she said, and he nodded and left.

Shane had toured Two Rivers the night before, checking to see if any-one had been hiding there, and he checked all the rooms again be-fore he left, going through the empty, generously sized living and dining rooms on the first floor; the four comfortable if sparsely fur-nished bedrooms on the second floor, two of them filled with wed-ding presents; and the two rooms at the top of the narrow stair up to the attics, the front attic rough, but the back, riverside room now a finished bedroom with white woodwork and pale blue walls, the low windows in the half walls softly lighting the big, low, blue-satin duvet-covered bed. It would be nice someday, he thought now, as he double-checked the partially finished bathroom that flanked it. Hell, it was nice now, a lot better than the narrow housekeeper's cell Agnes was sleeping in.

Not that he wouldn't move in there in a second if invited. Break-fast had pretty much sealed that deal.

He went outside and walked around to the back of Two Rivers, shaking off the well-organized comfort of Agnes's house. He felt the weight of the phone in his pocket and knew the message from Wilson was waiting and that an attempted dognapping was not his priority, but something was threatening the world that Agnes had created with her hot breakfast and her warm kitchen, and he had to take care of that before he went back to his own world.

Rhett watered the fence around the air-conditioning unit, which gave Shane a chance to see why the house was never cool—a place as big as Two Rivers needed a unit twice that size or at least another same-sized unit—and then the dog snuffled his way to the gazebo, its white wood freshly painted, its red roof neatly patched, one of the few things about the outside of Two Rivers that looked restored. The house was still stately with its double porches and tall columns, but it had been scraped in preparation for painting and it looked like it had a bad case of house mange.

He heard heavy footsteps behind him and turned, hand instinc-tively going for his gun, but he stopped when he saw it was Doyle lumbering toward him.

"Special place, isn't it?"

"It's something," Shane agreed, moving on toward the river.

"Special woman, our Agnes," Doyle said, moving with him.

"She's something," Shane said, moving on faster.

"You be staying long?" Doyle asked, catching up.

"Long as it takes."

"To do what?" Doyle said, and Shane thought of Agnes on that blue bed upstairs and moved on before the old man could read his mind.

He stepped up onto the dock, which creaked ominously, and looked back at Two Rivers, ringed on three sides by tidal marsh and the deep waters of the Intracoastal and the Blood, cut off from the forested land on the farthest side by an inlet, the ancient bridge its only link to the road out. It was beautiful but isolated. *Like Agnes—*

"So how long will you be staying?"

Shane sighed. "Who would break in to steal the dog, Doyle?"

Doyle blinked at him. "That dog? Nobody."

"Somebody did. Who would want to hurt Agnes?"

Doyle scowled. "Nobody. Everybody likes—"

"Somebody did. I'll be staying until I find out what's going on. If you don't like it, take it up with Agnes." He turned and walked along the edge of the property until he could see the bridge ahead to his right. He heard the sound of cars and moved to where he could see the road but be hidden by the foliage, his hand drifting toward the butt of his pistol.

Two cars appeared, a big white Lexus leading the way, followed by a baby blue '80s-era Cadillac. They crept over the wooden bridge and even at this distance, Shane could hear the creak of protests from the bridge supports. Both cars stopped in front of the house, and the driver's door on the Cadillac opened first.

A curvy little platinum blonde wearing a fluttery blue dress got out and surveyed the place like she owned it, her hands on her hips. She turned and looked in his direction, and he recognized her despite the years: Brenda Fortunato. She was still a beauty, passing for early forties in full sunlight even though she had to be in her fifties. She tilted her head as she looked at the house, and she did not look thrilled, possibly because with most of its paint scraped off, Two Rivers looked like hell.

The other car door opened, and the driver of the Lexus stepped out. She was tall where Brenda was tiny, trim where Brenda was curvy, pale where Brenda was tan, tailored in beige where Brenda fluttered in blue, low-heeled where Brenda spiked, and she did not put her hands on her hips or look at Two Rivers as if it were hers; she just tucked her purse under her arm, nodded politely to Brenda, looked at the house and winced, and then began to walk toward the wide central steps. She oozed class and money, and Shane thought, *Evie Keyes.* Mother of the groom and First Lady of Keyes, South Carolina. Which was pretty much like being Queen of the Landfill, as far as he was concerned.

Then Agnes came out the front door and down the steps with a tray of drinks, dark curls bouncing and red-rimmed glasses sliding down her nose again, wearing some kind of red dress with straps that tied on her shoulders and a skirt that whipped around her legs in the breeze, and Shane's thoughts jumped track until she led the other two women around the side of the house to the gazebo.

Agnes had damn good legs. And a great back. One pull on those ties— And she'd smiled at him, standing there in the morning sunlight. Might have been an invitation. Might not have been, too. Probably should make sure before he started untying things.

"You be a watchful sort of fellow," Doyle said from behind him.

"Shouldn't you be painting?"

"Shouldn't you be doing something someplace else?"

Shane considered arguing, but since he was guilty of the thoughts that Doyle suspected him of, he called to the bloodhound and moved away, and Doyle headed back toward the house.

Rhett padded across the inlet on an old log and immediately lost himself in the palmetto on the other side, and Shane followed, so focused on what might be ahead that when the dog stopped suddenly, he tripped over him and hit the ground just as a branch less than six inches from his head exploded in splinters, the sound of the shot echoing through the vegetation.

From the prone, Shane fired twice in the direction of the intruder. Rhett bayed and charged forward, and Shane cursed, realizing the dog was moving into the line of fire. He squeezed off four more rounds as fast as he could pull the trigger, then lunged to his feet and sprinted after the dog, hunched over, not quite believing he was putting his life on the line for a dumb old bloodhound. He continued to fire, dropping the magazine out of the well as he moved, zigzagging, slamming a fresh clip home, firing once more. Then he dived onto Rhett, grabbing the dog's collar as he rolled behind a log, holding the bloodhound to his chest.

Rhett bayed once more, then began licking Shane's face. Shane stared up at the palmetto fronds above, half-expecting to see bullets whipping through them, but they were perfectly still. Since the initial shots, the intruder had not fired, which meant he was either waiting to ambush Shane if he got closer or else had split while the getting was good. Or Shane had hit him and taken him out, which he doubted, given he had fired mainly for cover not effect, having no solid target.

He waited, letting time tick away. He was in no rush and knew waiting put the burden on his opponent, if he was still around. If the guy was a pro, the wait could be long. After fifteen minutes, Shane turned to Rhett, who appeared to be sleeping, and poked him. Rhett opened one eye. Shane poked him again and the dog opened both eyes and took a deep sniff.

No baying. No alert.

Shane got to one knee, pistol still at the ready, and looked around. No sign of the intruder. Between his eyes and Rhett's nose, he felt confident they were alone.

He walked forward, on alert, Rhett trailing him, and stopped when he saw his battered black Defender. He pulled out his remote opener and tapped the small STATUS button and then watched as a small green light flickered green a dozen times, then surprisingly turned red and stayed that way. Shane stared at the Defender. Something or someone had set off the vehicle's motion detector.

He slowly circled the truck, eyes going over every inch. Nothing seemed amiss, but given he had just been shot at, he wasn't willing to bet his life on it. With a resigned sigh, he got down on his knees in the muddy ground, then lay down, sliding forward, feeling the damp soil ooze into his outer clothes as he angled himself so he could see the underside of the high-riding truck. Then he froze.

The shaped charge on one of the plates was easy to spot: it was directly under the passenger seat—whoever had put it there had not taken into account it was a right-hand-drive European vehicle. No wires. It looked like one of Agnes's large mixing bowls painted black and stuck to the plate. A small red LED light glowed, indicating it was armed. Shane doubted it was on a timer since whoever had placed it wouldn't know when he was coming back to the truck.

But no one should even have known he was here. At least no one who had the sophistication to make and plant such a device. The kid in Agnes's basement wasn't anywhere near this level of professionalism. But whoever had just shot at him obviously was.

Shane took a deep breath, then slid to where the bomb was right in front of his face. It couldn't have been armed until it was in place, thus there was an arming mechanism. Which meant there was a disarming mechanism.

He placed both hands on the bowl and slowly twisted it counterclockwise. The bowl moved smoothly and Shane unscrewed it until he felt it give slightly. He carefully lowered the bowl of explosives inside the metal frame to the ground, exposing a small metal canister hung below the plastic top that had been glued to the bottom of the car and into which it had been screwed. He reached up and removed the battery that supplied power to the detonator.

He stuck it in his pocket, then ripped the plastic off the bottom of the truck. He pulled the entire contraption with him as he crawled out from under the Defender. He opened the rear of the truck and placed it all inside, then went around and opened the door.

"Come on," he called to Rhett, who had watched the disarming of the bomb with no interest at all.

The dog jumped, feet scrabbling at the edge of the seat, and then he was in, moving over to the window, where he looked at Shane disapprovingly, a smear of snot on the dark glass.

"It's bullet- and blast-proof glass," Shane said, trying to explain why he wasn't rolling down the window.

Rhett gave Shane a look that said, *I just saved your life, but that's okay.*

Shaking his head, Shane violated standing operating procedures and lowered the passenger window. Rhett stuck his head out, a happy camper.

Shane spared a moment for what Wilson would say if he ever had to explain this—*The dog wanted the window rolled down, and he'd saved me from being shot, so I violated procedure from gratitude*—and then headed for Joey's.

If he wasn't careful, Keyes was going to be the death of him.

Agnes had heard the car doors slam and had said a fast prayer before she smoothed down the skirt of her red cotton sundress in an attempt to look like a lady or at least like Brenda, shoved her glasses up the bridge of her nose, and picked up the tray of lemonade and sweet tea.

Then she'd carried the tray into the hall and out through the beautiful big carved double front doors, propped open now for some cross-ventilation because it was hotter than hell in the house; across the lovely veranda that would be even lovelier if it had some goddamn *paint* on it; down the wide gracious front steps that were a real bitch to negotiate with a tray that heavy not to mention sandals with heels, *thank you;* and over the front lawn to meet the new arrivals: Brenda, looking beautiful as ever in a full-skirted rayon number, and

Evie, looking cool and boring in white-piped beige Chanel and pearls, all but screaming, *I got good taste and you don't.*

"Agnes, you look lovely," Evie said as she glided toward her.

"Evie, I'm sweating like a racehorse," Agnes said. "Let's have the tasting in the gazebo, shall we?"

"Certainly," Evie said, changing course around the house toward the gazebo without missing a step.

"Oh, Agnes, honey," Brenda said, slowing as she saw the front door open. "You shouldn't leave that door open, sugar, it's bad for my grandfather clock."

You shouldn't leave your grandfather clock here, it's bad for my hall, Agnes thought, and then felt guilty because Brenda had given them such a deal on the mortgage, especially the first three months' payments in exchange for holding the wedding there, so she just said, "Well, whenever you're ready to move it out, Brenda, it's right there waiting for you," and steered them around the side of the house.

"The gazebo looks *beautiful,*" Brenda said, gliding along the flagstone walk in her three-inch heels, and Agnes smiled because it really did and because Brenda was pleased with it. Then Brenda added, "That fresh paint just *gleams,* Agnes," and let her eyes slide to the scabby-looking house.

"Doyle's putting the primer on the house today," Agnes said, feeling guilt swamp her. "By Saturday, this place will look like Tara." *With butter.*

"I *do* hate to see you go to so much trouble," Evie said, sweetly, "when the country club is just—"

"No trouble," Agnes said brightly. "Wait till you see the gazebo ceiling. It's going to be perfect for the ceremony. Maria and Palmer will look adorable up there." *Did I just say 'adorable'?* She shook her head and led them across the lawn and up the steps to the table inside. "There now. Isn't this lovely?"

"You know, it *is,*" Evie said, sounding surprised as she looked up at the rafters that Doyle had painted blue and Agnes had added gold-leaf stars to.

Brenda looked up at the ceiling and said, "Oh, Agnes, you do like things bright, bless your heart."

Agnes smiled uncertainly and looked up at the stars again. She'd thought they were beautiful, like an illustration out of an old book. Maybe she should have checked with Brenda first. . . .

"Well, I think they're *very* nice," Evie said firmly. "Neo*class*ical."

Agnes blinked at her in surprise.

"Of course," Brenda said, smiling at Evie. "Neoclassical. Maria's coming with Palmer. They're just so darling together, don't you think?"

"Yes," Evie said, with a noticeable lack of warmth. Her face remained smooth, so it was hard to tell if the coolness was for Brenda for being too familiar with a Keyes or for Maria for having the audacity to marry into the family. Nobody could object to Maria herself, but it might very well be sticking in Evie's craw that this wedding meant she was eventually going to be the grandmother of a child who shared a bloodline with Frankie "Two Hands" Fortunato, now deceased, the whereabouts of his body unknown but presumably shod in paving material.

On the other hand, Evie could rest assured that her grandkid would not be getting beat up on the playground nearly as regularly as his father had.

Brenda said, "Agnes, where is that sweet old bloodhound of yours?"

"Rhett? He went into town—"

The bridge rattled and gravel crunched, and Agnes looked back to see a plain dark sedan pull up and Detective Hammond get out.

Wonderful. "I'll be right back," she said, and crossed the lawn to tell him that he could do anything he wanted in her basement, not adding, *as long as you stay away from the gazebo so they don't hear words like* attack *and* death. *And* frying pan.

She went back to the gazebo, and Brenda and Evie leaned away from each other, as if they'd been conferring about something.

Brenda looked past her and said, "Isn't that Robbie Hammond? Whatever is he doing out here?"

"Checking on some things," Agnes said. "Now, I'll go get the cakes—"

"He was Maria's first boyfriend," Brenda said, sitting back with a fond smile. She turned to Evie. "They were *very* close."

What the hell are you doing? Agnes thought as Evie's eyes narrowed, but before she could say anything, a bright pink Mustang convertible came over bridge. "Mother of God," she said, appalled at what had been done to a classic car.

Evie sighed. "The people at the Flamingo are very pleased with the golf course Palmer designed," she said faintly. "So they sent the car."

"It's *pink*," Agnes said, still staring.

"Flamingo pink," Evie said. "Palmer gave it to Maria."

"He's no dummy," Agnes said without thinking.

"Well, isn't it the cutest thing?" Brenda said, exchanging a glance with Agnes of mutual agreement that it wasn't while Evie grew grimmer.

"I'll just go inside and get the cakes," Agnes said.

When she got back with the cake plate, Maria was in the gazebo, looking incredibly lovely, her long glossy dark hair caught up in a knot at the top of her head, making her big brown eyes and pointed features even more striking. For once, Palmer wasn't staring at her adoringly, his slightly foolish features and slightly receding blond hairline fixed in her direction. Instead he was surveying Agnes's extensive lawn, an unfocused look in his eyes, a dress bag draped over his arm as if he'd forgotten it was there.

"Agnes!" Maria threw her arms around Agnes.

"Hello, honey." Agnes hugged back with one arm while she held the cake plate steady with the other. "How are you?"

Maria smiled at her at little too widely, her eyes a little too bright. "*Fine,* now that I know you're doing the cake." She leaned closer and whispered, "Can you really do this?"

"Yep." Agnes sat the cake plate down to get better traction on the hug. "I have some ideas to cover up the fact that I'm not one of the world's great cake artists, but I will bet you six M&M'S that you will have a beautiful cake anyway, and I swear it will be delicious, much better than Bern the Baker's. His cake tastes like cardboard because he's always concentrating on his sugar paste."

"Six M&M'S. High stakes." Maria grinned the way she had when she'd been little, and Agnes felt her heart tug at the memory. "You're on."

"Such a pity Bern canceled on you," Evie murmured, watching her son from the corner of her eye, as if waiting for a sign that he wanted out of his engagement.

"I was *shocked* when Bern told me he wasn't going to do it after all," Brenda said, her lovely face growing serious. "Some people do not know their places."

"So true," Evie said, looking at Brenda.

Mean, Agnes thought, and moved closer to Brenda.

Off in the swamp, somebody fired a gun several times, and Agnes jerked around, expecting to see a guy in a bandanna come out of the swamp and demand her dog, but nothing happened except that Evie looked displeased. She didn't legally own all of Keyes, but spiritually she did, and she clearly hadn't put in an order for gunfire this morning.

"So we'll all sit down," Agnes said brightly to cover up her nerves and the gunfire that continued. Damn hunters. "And we'll taste cake. Palmer, you sit here, and I'll get another chair—"

"No, no." Palmer turned and smiled, a genuine smile that surprised Agnes with its sweetness. "I tagged along and I don't deserve cake. But I'd like to look at the lawn if you don't mind."

Brenda looked up, puzzled. "Why would you want to look at my lawn—?"

"Not yours," Evie murmured.

"The lawn?" Agnes said. "Of course I don't mind."

Palmer kissed Maria's cheek. "Pick a winner, darling," he said, as if by rote.

Maria patted his shoulder. "I already did, baby," she said, equally without warmth.

That doesn't sound right, Agnes thought, but her real interest was in the woods where the shots had come from. All she needed was a stray bullet picking off a member of the wedding party, and there'd be hell to pay.

Palmer draped the dress bag over the gazebo rail and wandered off, and Maria sat down and said, "So. Cake. Chocolate raspberry?"

"The cupcakes," Agnes said, concentrating on the important stuff, since the gunfire seemed to have stopped. "I know that's your favorite, Maria, but the cake has to be strong enough to support the fondant, and that one's pretty delicate. It'd be wonderful served with raspberry sauce at the rehearsal dinner, though. The raspberry sauce is in the silver bowl. The heart-shaped cakes are Italian cream cake and the round ones are pound cake, which is the only kind I'm positive will hold up the fondant. The square ones are a coconut pound cake that I'm trying out. I think it might work if you're afraid plain pound cake is too boring, but I'm warning you now, I'm not an expert cake decorator, so the stronger the cake you give me to work with, the better chance you have of getting something that makes it through the reception." Agnes picked up a plate.

"I have to confess that I am concerned that the house isn't painted yet," Brenda said as Agnes put cakes on the first plate, and Agnes flinched.

"It will be." Agnes handed the plate to Maria. "Bride first."

Maria handed the plate to Evie. "Absolutely not. Mother of the groom first."

Evie accepted the plate. "Thank you, my dear. You have such lovely manners."

"Because if the house won't be ready—" Brenda began.

"It will be." Agnes plopped cake on a second plate and then shoved that plate at Brenda, wondering what her problem was.

Brenda frowned at the plate. "Now is this the china you'll be using for the wedding, sugar?"

"No," Agnes said, distracted again. "Taylor's got china on order to stock his catering kitchen in the barn, and we'll be using that."

Brenda shook her head. "There's an awful lot that isn't in place—"

"It will all be here," Agnes said firmly. "The china, the house, the cake, the flowers, everything. Which reminds me, I tried calling the florist this morning to double-check on the delivery times, but I couldn't get through. That's not like Maisie. Is she sick?"

"Oh, *Maisie*." Brenda took the plate, shaking her head. "Poor old Maisie, always did have more boobs than brains, bless her heart." She forked up a piece of the Italian cream cake, taking care not to drop any crumbs on her own significant cleavage. "You're not going to believe this. She *canceled*."

Agnes stopped filling the third plate, and Evie and Maria froze, too. "What?"

Brenda bit into the cream cake, hesitated, and shook her head. "Oh, I think that's just a touch too sweet, Agnes, but then it's too soft for your fondant anyway. What? Oh, Maisie. Well, you know how disorganized she is, incompetent really. She just felt overwhelmed by the whole thing and canceled." She tasted the pound cake and pursed her perfect lips, although her forehead did not wrinkle. "I think the pound cake may be too dry. And you know you'll have to cover it with the fondant at least the day before, probably two. So if it's dry now . . ." She shook her head and then met Agnes's eyes. "What? Oh, Maisie? Yes. I'm afraid you'll have to do the flowers, too."

Agnes felt her temper rise, took a deep breath, and put the last cake on the plate. *This isn't like Brenda, Brenda's on my side, I'll just stay calm and find out what happened later, everything will be fine.* She turned to Maria, whose jaw was set, but who did not look surprised. "I'll fix it, you'll have flowers," she said quietly, while beside her Evie looked grim.

Very good, Agnes. You control your anger; your anger does not control you.

The morning's not over yet, Dr. Garvin.

Agnes turned and smiled at the table. "Look at this, I've been so anxious to get you all cake, I didn't serve drinks. What have I been thinking?"

Evie picked up the lemonade pitcher and began to pour. "This coconut pound cake is just delicious, Agnes, you have outdone yourself. Lemonade, anyone? Or sweet tea?"

"You know, the chef at the country club does a nice cake," Brenda said, taking a glass of lemonade.

"This chocolate raspberry cake is really good," Maria said, straightening.

She had two bright spots of color on her cheeks and fire in her eye, and Agnes forgot Brenda's betrayal for a moment because Maria was looking a lot like her mother. Lisa Livia may have grown up in the South, but she was descended from a long line of dons and hitmen and Brenda. And, Agnes thought with a sinking heart, Maria was descended from a long line of dons and hitmen and Brenda and Lisa Livia.

"So, the cake," she said in her best aren't-we-all-glad-to-be-here voice, waving her cake plate in Maria's general direction to distract her from whatever was about to set her off.

"I'm just thinking with everything that's gone wrong, the wedding might be better at the country club," Brenda said, and Evie perked up.

Rot in hell, Brenda, Agnes thought, but before she could say anything, Maria said, "Did you hear about my dress?"

"Your dress?" Evie said, but Maria was smiling at Brenda. Fixedly.

Oh, God, what did Brenda do to the dress? Agnes thought, seeing the entire wedding go south as the bride killed her grandmother in the gazebo with the cake knife. Barbie Clue.

"Oh, yes, the dress." Brenda sipped her lemonade, looking blonde and lovely as ever. "Maria had ordered one from New York, but there was no tradition in that, so I canceled it—"

"*What?*" Evie said, putting down her lemonade.

"—and I'm giving her my wedding dress to wear." Brenda smiled fondly at Maria, who smiled back. Not fondly.

"She's at least a foot taller than you are," Evie said, appalled. "You canceled that dress? She loved that dress. We all loved that dress!"

"It's all right," Maria said, still smiling.

It's not all right, Agnes thought, trying to think of how she was going to get the dress back. And how she was going to get Brenda psychiatric help because she'd clearly gone round the bend. And how she was going to keep Lisa Livia from killing her mother, something that had been imminent all LL's life anyway. "I—"

"In fact, I've been thinking," Brenda said, and a silence fell over the table, even Evie turning to Brenda to see what was coming next. "What with Two Rivers not looking its best—I'm sorry, Agnes—and the florist quitting, and all, well, I have to agree with Evie that the country club is very beautiful, and they have flowers there anyway, so we could probably just use *their* flowers. . . ."

Her voice trailed off as three women looked at her in horror.

"Well, it's too late to get another florist, everybody would understand that, and we can't have it here," she said, the voice of reason. "This place isn't even *painted.*"

You have lost your ever-lovin' mind, Agnes thought.

"We cannot use the country club's flowers," Evie said firmly. "But I do agree that Two Rivers is a little shabby for a wedding of this stature, so I think that moving it to—"

Agnes said, trying to keep the panic from her voice, "Well, *I think*—"

Maria stood up. "You know, I just love my grandpa's big old house. It's just . . . *the South,* don't you think?" She turned to look at it in all its scraped and scabby glory, Tara with leprosy, and turned back hastily. "And I do want a *Southern* wedding, in the fine old Keyes tradition. I do believe in tradition, don't you, Mrs. Keyes?"

Evie nodded, not buying anything yet.

"But I do want a wedding that will make people sit up and take notice," Maria said, looking at Brenda. "I want a wedding that says, Look at us, we have *arrived,* we *belong.* Right, Grandma Brenda?"

Brenda looked up at her, and for a moment she looked hungry, even vulnerable. Agnes thought, *She wants to belong, she feels as alone as I do.*

Maria moved between Brenda and Evie. "That's what I want my wedding to be, tradition and innovation, the best of both worlds, having it all!"

The two older women looked at each other, united in confusion.

Agnes frowned. It was a nice picture, Maria uniting the two fighting houses, but she was Lisa Livia's kid, and her cake, her flowers, and her dress had just been canceled, and now Brenda and Evie were trying to hijack the whole damn thing to the fucking country club.

Language, Agnes.

To the gosh-darned country club.

Agnes pushed her glasses up the bridge of her nose, took a deep breath, and said, "Well, I think that's wonderful, but you can just forget the country—"

"We'll have it all," Maria said, thrillingly. "My wedding in my grandpa's house, which Agnes *will* get painted—"

Agnes started at the steel in Maria's voice and then nodded.

"—and Taylor's brilliant food, and Agnes's wonderful cake, and Maisie Shuttle's gorgeous flowers, which Grandma Brenda *will* get back for us—"

Brenda flinched.

"—and Evie's cousin Wesley's marvelous photographs, and Palmer's fraternity brother's uncle's band, and it's going to be so perfect, so traditional and yet new."

"Well, that's very sweet, Maria," Brenda said, "but—"

Shut up, Brenda, Agnes thought, seeing the red light behind Maria's eyes, so like the light in Lisa Livia's before the carnage began.

"And it will be all of that," Maria said, her voice rising, "because it will all be tied together by our *theme,* the symbol of Palmer's and my future."

"Theme?" Evie said, surprised.

"Theme?" Brenda said, confused.

"Oh, God," Agnes said, bracing herself.

Maria smiled at Palmer, out on the lawn, gazing at the grass.

"Grass?" Agnes said, thinking, *Green, I could fake green by Saturday.*

"Flamingos," Maria said.

"What the hell?" Brenda said, startled.

"You're joking, of course," Evie said.

"Pink," Agnes said, thinking, *Pink, I can fake pink by Saturday.*

Maria opened her bag and took out an eight-inch virulently pink plastic flamingo and slapped it on the table. "Isn't it just hysterical? It's a pen. Dina Delvecchio sent it to me when she found out that Palmer's big successful golf course is called the Flamingo. See, the feet are like the holder, and you pull the pen out—"

"Dina Delvecchio?" Evie said, grasping at straws since the flamingo was probably beyond comprehension.

"Maria's maid of honor," Agnes said, staring at the flamingo pen. "Bless her heart." *Goddammit, Brenda, you had to open your mouth, didn't you?*

"—and we glue the place cards to the beaks," Maria went on. "They're only seventy-five cents each, so they're cheap, too, Grandma. You'll like that."

"That's *seventy-five bucks for place cards*," Brenda said, looking at the pink plastic with horror.

"*And* they double as party favors," Maria said virtuously. "I already ordered them, Agnes. They'll be here Thursday."

"*Maria*," Evie said, staring in horror at the plastic flamingo.

"So, flamingos," Agnes said. It was awful, but it was at Two Rivers, so she was for it. Marginally. "Arriving Thursday."

"And here's the best part." Maria held up the dress bag. "My dress. Or Grandma Brenda's dress."

"Don't call me Grandma," Brenda said.

"The big trend now is in colored wedding dresses," Maria said, unzipping the bag. "So . . ."

She pulled off the bag and revealed an old-fashioned meringue wedding dress with a huge puffy skirt canopied with lace and bows.

All of it dyed flamingo pink.

"*That's my wedding dress!*" Brenda said, standing up and knocking over her chair.

"I know," Maria said, beaming. "I'm going to wear it just like you wanted. Brenda."

Okay, Agnes thought, sitting down in relief. There was no way in hell Maria would wear that horror of a dress anywhere. This was payback. She met Maria's eyes and said, "Fabulous idea. It'll be the talk of the county," and Maria said, "Well, *I* think so."

Fifteen minutes of cool reasoning and heated reproach later, Evie had left for the Keyes mansion in silent shock, and Brenda had gone back to the *Brenda Belle,* the Real Estate King's yacht, in outraged fury.

Agnes grinned. "So, flamingos."

"Of course not." Maria stuffed the dress back in the dress bag. "The dress was the giveaway, wasn't it?"

"I'd pay good money to see you in it," Agnes said. "If I had any good money."

Maria sighed. "Well, I had to do something. Evie's being so snotty about everything that I'd tell her to fuck off if she wasn't going to be my kids' grandma someday. And she's an angel compared to Brenda. Did you *see* that dress? She really expected me to wear it. And she really did cancel my dress, too, but Palmer ordered another one and they're going to express it here Friday if that's okay."

Agnes nodded. "I'll keep it for you."

Maria shook her head. "I swear to God, Palmer told Brenda four months ago that he'd pay for the wedding, but she said no, I was her granddaughter and she was going to take care of it all, and now she's pissed off the baker and the florist and wants to use the leftover flowers at the country club. Why did she offer to pay in the first place if she was going to act like this?"

"I don't know," Agnes said. "This is not like Brenda. I could see her insisting on wearing white to your wedding because it'll look good with her tan, but meddling like this? She's lost her mind."

Maria picked up the dress bag. "Well, it doesn't matter. I've settled her hash."

"So, just checking to make sure here, no flamingos?"

"Oh, the flamingo pens are coming," Maria said. "I don't know how far I have to carry my bluff. But the wedding is just like I planned it, white butterflies and daisies. I'm going to let them both stew for a while and then graciously agree to go back to the original plan, and they'll be so grateful, they'll get out of my way." Maria looked out over the lawn and waved to Palmer, who obediently turned and trotted back toward them.

She watched him with an odd expression on her face, and Agnes felt a chill.

"Are you two okay?"

"Yes," Maria said, and then frowned toward the house. "Is that Robbie Hammond?"

"What?" Agnes said, and turned to see Detective Hammond coming out of the house. "Yep. So Palmer—"

"Robbie and I dated one summer," Maria said, watching him instead of her fiancé, who was now approaching the gazebo.

Oh, great. "He doesn't seem real bright," Agnes said.

Maria scowled at her. "He's a nice guy."

"Not much of a future," Agnes said.

"He serves and protects," Maria said.

"I think he has a girlfriend," Agnes said, having no idea what Hammond had.

"I'm engaged," Maria said coolly.

"Okay, then." Agnes began to clear up the cake plates. "Now I have to get Maisie Shuttle back on the job with the daisies and bake you some cake. What kind do you want?"

"Whatever holds up the icing," Maria said. "The coconut was good."

"Thank you," Agnes said. "I'll give you the chocolate raspberry for the rehearsal dinner."

"Wonderful," Maria said, but her voice was flat as she looked past Agnes to her intended, coming up the steps.

"Everything okay?" Palmer said.

"Yes, dear," Maria said.

They looked at each other in fairly cold silence.

No, no, no, Agnes thought. "Have some cake," she said to Palmer and prayed that whatever it was, they'd get over it by Saturday.

God, I'm shallow, she thought, and headed back to the house to make out her list of cake supplies and to work on her column. That had to be done by Saturday, too. Everything had to be done by Saturday.

Sunday's going to be a good day, she thought.

Assuming she lived that long.

An hour after he left Two Rivers, Shane sat outside Joey's diner in the Defender and worked at the message on his cell phone until he had it all decrypted:

WRONG TARGET HIT

CASEY DEAN STILL ACTIVE

CALL TO SET UP MEET TO DISCUSS

ASAP.

"Fuck." He'd killed the wrong guy. Too many intel screwups like this lately. Somebody needed to go in there and kick some ass. Wilson would have once, but he was getting old.

Rhett was hanging his head out the passenger window, looking miserable. *I know how you feel,* Shane thought. He slammed his head back against the headrest and closed his eyes. First Joey and his little Agnes and his mysteries, and now this screwup.

Shane flipped open the cell phone and punched in number 2 on the speed-dial. It was answered on the second ring.

"Wilson."

"I'm in Keyes."

"Why?"

"Personal business. What happened with the intel?"

Three seconds passed, which was a very long time in Shane's experience dealing with Wilson. The emptiness was filled with clicking noises as the signal was encrypted, bounced between government satellites, and decrypted.

"I'll meet you in Keyes this evening, twenty-two hundred hours," Wilson said. "Location?"

Shane blinked. He always came to Wilson. "There's a floating dock at the junction of the Blood River and the Intracoastal Waterway."

The phone went dead and Shane closed it. He saw Joey lock up his diner and come slowly over, a newspaper in one hand. For the first time, he looked old to Shane.

"What's in the back?" Joey asked, jerking his head toward the large box in the bed of the truck as he got in, shooing Rhett over at the same time.

"Air conditioner unit," Shane said. "The one at Two Rivers isn't enough."

Joey raised his eyebrows. "Agnes come into some money, did she?"

Shane started the truck. "You shutting down for the day for real?"

"There's someone I need to talk to," Joey said.

"Anybody I know?"

Joey hesitated.

Shane figured he'd shown enough patience. "I got some questions, Joey. That's just the first."

Joey nodded. "Charlie 'Four Wheels' Thibault. Grandpa of the kid who died last night."

Shane waited.

"I used to know him. Thinking I better go see him."

Shane nodded. "I'll drive you. Mind the slobber."

"Nice ride," Joey said, thumping the heavy side panel.

Shane pulled into the street and Joey pointed which way to drive. "So how'd you get to know this Four Wheels?"

"He was one of the guys back in the day," Joey said. "How's Agnes doing?"

Not subtle, Shane thought. "She was with Evie Keyes and Brenda when I left."

Joey shook his head. "Poor little thing."

Shane thought of Agnes, round in those thin sweats, attacking that pepper on the chopping block, smacking him with the frying pan. Agnes was a lot of things, but *poor* and *little* weren't two of them. "Why'd you ask Agnes about Rhett last night, Joey?"

Joey looked out the window. "I always ask about Rhett. I worry about them both out there all alone." He turned back to Shane. "I've known her since she was a kid. She used to spend summers down here with Lisa Livia when they was in boarding school. They'd come into the diner and ask questions. Lisa Livia wanted to know how to run the place, she was all about the money." He laughed. "That Lisa Livia, she's no dummy. But Agnes, she wanted to know how to cook. All the time, wanting to know how to make this, why'd you put that in there, Joey?"

Shane kept his eyes on the road. He couldn't get two words about the Thibaults, but about Agnes he was getting a book. *Nice try, Joey.*

"Then they grew up and didn't come back anymore," Joey went on, seeming almost wistful. "I get a Christmas card every year from Agnes, sometimes she'd send me stuff in the mail, stuff she finds she thinks I like, diner stuff. But then about three, four years ago, here Agnes comes again, asking questions 'cause now she has a newspaper column, and she remembered me, she's gonna write about me."

Shane looked over at the old man. He was grinning like it was a joke, but he was proud.

"About me," Joey repeated, shaking his head. "And then this editor in New York read the columns about me and said she wanted a book, and Agnes wrote one. The editor called it *Mob Food*. It came out last month, been selling real good, too, they say. That's where Agnes got some of the money for her half of the down payment on the house." He looked away, out the window. "My picture's on the cover. Leaning on the diner counter." He looked back at Shane. "I told her to forget about it, but Agnes said I had to be on the cover. And you know Agnes."

Shane nodded. "I'm starting to."

"She uses a lot of my stuff in her column, some other people's, too. She got a lot of stuff from Brenda, too, see Brenda's the one who taught her to cook—"

Enough. "So why did you ask Agnes about Rhett right before the kid broke in to take him?"

Joey looked out the window again. "Coincidence."

Shane swerved to the side of the road and slammed on the brakes, putting a hand out to keep Rhett from sliding off the seat. Rhett looked up at Shane, then at Joey, then sighed and put his head back down.

Shane stared at his uncle. "That gun at Agnes's was an old mobster's gun. That kid was the grandson of an old mob guy. There weren't that many old mob guys who retired down here, Joey. Just two, you and Frankie Fortunato, and now I hear about this Thibault guy. And I have to say that you retired down here pretty fucking young. You couldn't have been forty, either one of you. So I'm thinking there's a lot going on here that I need to know. Are you going to tell me this story? Or we gonna sit here all day?"

The seconds ticked away as Joey met his eyes; then he turned and looked out the window at the dark green woods of the swamp. Shane waited. The seconds turned into a minute, then two, and Rhett sighed once more. Then Joey sighed, deeper than Rhett, and looked back at Shane. He had a wan smile and he did look old. "You grown up, haven't you?"

"I grew up a long time ago, Joey. You saw to that."

Joey nodded. "Yeah. That was the idea." He looked out the window, still nodding, and Shane waited. When he turned back, the man Shane remembered was there. Solid. The shark smile. "Okay, Frankie and me was driving down to Miami to do a job for the old Don, Frankie's father. Our engine blew up right outside of Keyes. We got stuck here for a couple of days and we liked it. So we kept coming back every summer and then when we decided to retire, Frankie and I figured we'd come here, do some work for the Don on the side.

"Then Frankie and I got a tip, this would be about twenty-five years ago now, that there was a freight car full of cigs on the rail line, ready to load to go overseas. We made most our money boosting freight cars when the port was still active. We kick up half the take to the Don in Jersey, split the rest twenty/twenty/ten with Charlie 'Four Wheels' Thibault getting the ten percent 'cause all he does is drive. Took Frankie's Caddy 'cause it had the big trunk. Went down to the rail siding, bust in, but no cigs, just a safe, and it has this box on top, got a necklace in it, made of big hearts, junky-looking thing."

Joey shook his head. "I had a weird feeling about it. But the tip come from the Don, so we lift the safe out, and Frankie, he takes the necklace for Brenda because she's on his case all the time, he says, 'cause she thinks he's cheating on her, which he is, but that's Frankie for you. We throw the safe in the trunk of Frankie's Caddy. Beat feet to Frankie's place, where Agnes lives now. Park just over that damn bridge; it was in better shape then. Take the safe down to Frankie's basement, open it up. Inside, no cigs. Five million dollars in nonsequential bills."

Shane raised his eyebrows.

Joey nodded. "Yeah, too much money. Four Wheels, he's scared shitless, he goes home. I go home. Frankie goes upstairs to Brenda. We figure we'll lay low, work something out. Except the next day, Frankie's gone, the safe's gone, the necklace is gone, the five mil is gone. Nobody knows nothin'. Four Wheels moves out to the swamp and shoots anybody who comes close."

"Where'd Frankie go?"

Joey shrugged. "Tahiti. Meet his maker. I dunno. Never seen or heard from again."

"Anybody come after you?"

Joey rubbed the scar over his eye. "A couple of times." He looked away.

There's more, Shane thought. "What's this got to do with Agnes?"

"This weekend, Agnes's column is on cooking for dogs, so her picture is a special one with Rhett." Joey held up the newspaper and gave it to Shane.

Shane spread it open. Inside was a column with a headline that said, CRANKY AGNES and a picture of Agnes, smiling, big glasses and curly dark hair, with her arm around Rhett. *Cute as all hell,* Shane thought. "So?"

"Look at the dog's collar."

Shane peered closer. Rhett had a collar on that looked like it was made out of big junky-looking glass hearts.

Joey tapped the paper. "That's the necklace Frankie showed us that night. No one's seen it since that night, but there it is on Rhett. I think maybe the necklace and the five mil never left the house. And I think Four Wheels saw that picture and that's what he thinks, too. And maybe Four Wheels told somebody that, like one of his dumb-shit grandsons."

"Oh, *fuck,*" Shane said. All of Keyes County could be coming for little Agnes if they thought she was sitting on five million bucks; that was why Joey had called in the heavy artillery. "You couldn't have told me this from the beginning?"

"I haven't told anybody this in twenty-five years," Joey said.

"Great." This, plus he'd killed the wrong guy in Savannah. Not a good week. And it was only Tuesday.

Joey seemed a little more relaxed now that his secret was out. "Xavier was the responding deputy on the case. Hell, the entire police force of Keyes, all four of them, was on the case. Everyone except Xavier kinda gave up when Frankie's Caddy was found abandoned at the Savannah Airport the next day and there was no sign of Frankie. But Xavier, he never gave up on it. It's the one he never solved, and it was his biggest one and he thinks it kept him from becoming sheriff and marryin' Evie Beale, Evie Keyes now. But Frankie wouldn't have blown town without saying nothing to me. We was closer than brothers."

"So who killed him and took the money?"

"No idea." Joey nodded to the road. "This is about Agnes. We go talk to Four Wheels and find out if he sent that little bastard after our girl and what the fuck he knows. Drive."

Shane pulled back out onto the road, trying to find the wedge into Joey's story. Anybody could have killed Frankie for five million, but what that had to do with Agnes now—

"Turn left on that dirt road," Joey ordered.

A large NO TRESPASSING sign was tacked to a tree. It was barely legible given that it had been riddled with buckshot.

As soon as he turned, Shane reached down next to his seat and pulled out his Glock Model 20 and placed it on his lap. He wasn't surprised when Joey pulled out his own pistol from his waistband and did the same. Shane recognized the make: a Colt Python revolver. Powerful and small. And the handle was wrapped with medical tape. Old dogs didn't learn new tricks. Rhett must have sensed the mood change, because he was peering ahead, out the windshield.

The road they were on barely deserved the moniker as it narrowed into a rutted track. The trees overhead linked branches to form a green tunnel.

"I don't like it," Shane said.

"Don't worry," Joey muttered. "Four Wheels ain't got—" He didn't get the rest of the sentence out, as there was a sharp snap and a hairline crack appeared in the windshield. "What the fuck?"

Rhett let out a bark as Shane slammed on the brakes. There was a ping, and Shane threw the truck into reverse as he spotted two teenagers with caps on backward, firing away with rifles from behind a log about fifty yards up the road.

"What the fuck is going on?" Joey demanded.

"Couple of kids shooting at us," Shane said as he gave the engine some gas and swiveled his head so he could negotiate the narrow track. Another ping, which he knew was a round hitting the armored front of the car. "More of the Thibault clan, I assume."

Joey reached for the door handle, but Shane had already overridden both the windows and the locks and the old man fumbled with it for several moments before realizing that.

"Open the fucking door, Shane."

"Nope." Shane saw the end of the track and the main road approaching, and he slowed down. No more shots; he assumed they were out of range and/or sight of the hidden firers.

"You just run away?" A vein was throbbing in Joey's forehead.

"When the odds aren't good, yeah." Shane spun the wheel and they were back on the county road.

"They teach you that in the army?"

"No." Shane looked at his uncle. "You did."

Joey took several deep breaths, then he slowly began to nod, and a resigned smile crept across his face. "Yeah, I did, didn't I? Always play the odds."

"This is the second time today I've been shot at," Shane said.

"*What?*"

"First time was this morning in the woods near Agnes's house." Shane reached down and scratched Rhett's head. He'd thought that the shooting had more to do with him than Agnes, given the message he'd decoded, but he was reevaluating that now. And the bomb was a wild card that he needed to factor in. He was fucking reevaluating *everything.* He loved his uncle, but the old man hadn't put all his cards on the table yet, and that was troublesome. It looked like Agnes had bought more than just a lot of maintenance problems when she invested in that old mansion.

Joey's alarm was obvious. "The shooter. Was he a pro?"

"Hard to tell," Shane said.

Joey was staring out at the landscape whipping by. "I got you out of here when I sent you to school. I should have kept you away."

"Don't worry about it, Uncle Joey," Shane said, thinking about Agnes in her kitchen. "I've been in a lot worse places."

"Maybe you better go," Joey said.

Shane shot him a glance. "Not until this is straightened out."

"Shane, there could be pros out there. The Don's guys. They could be gunning for you now, too."

And there's my last question. "Why would they be doing that?"

Joey looked away. "Figuring you were with me. You know."

Another lie, Shane thought, and began to wonder if there was anybody he could trust.

"Maybe you better just stick close to Agnes," Joey said.

"That's my plan," Shane said.

Agnes sat on the swing on the finished screened-in back porch with a bottle of wine, a splitting headache, her laptop, and a pad of paper, trying to finish her latest To Do List and write her column while the Chicks sang softly in the background. It was hard concentrating with all the distractions, not the least of which had been Robbie Hammond coming back to the house to ask, "Was that Maria Fortunato?" with an expression on his face that said that whatever happened that summer they'd dated had had a major impact on him. "Yes, and she's *getting married Saturday,*" Agnes had said firmly, and he'd gone away, leaving Agnes feeling a little guilty, but not much. Back to work.

The Chicks were singing "The Long Way Around," which seemed appropriate since the To Do List was getting the house painted, getting the bridge reinforced, finding an air conditioner on sale somewhere that also had really lax credit terms, ordering the cake supplies, and hunting Maisie Shuttle down to make her cough up a thousand daisies. The column was about the life-or-death importance of a cake that could hold up pounds of fondant and still taste like heaven when the guests chowed down, and Agnes loathed every boring word of it. She was trying to shoehorn in some insightful facts about the history of wedding cakes, but they were even worse—

"I can't believe you bought this fuckin' dump."

Agnes looked up and saw a vision of petite southern loveliness— Southern Jersey, in this case—standing in the porch doorway: glossy brown ringlets framing big brown eyes, sharp features, and a wide red mouth, over a body built for a tube top and capri pants.

"LL?" Agnes felt tears spring to her eyes. "Oh, God, I've *missed you!*"

She got up from the swing, letting her laptop slide onto the cushions, and threw her arms around her best friend, knocking her glasses sideways in the process. Lisa Livia said, "Oh, honey, *I've missed you, too,*" and hugged Agnes tight for a minute. Then she let go, shoved her own oversized sunglasses farther back on her head like a headband, looked up, and said, "Agnes, you dumbass, you are so screwed."

"Why?" Agnes straightened her glasses. "Did the bridge collapse?"

Lisa Livia threw her huge white patent leather bag on the old metal table and sat down on the swing, shoving the laptop back over to Agnes's side as she turned down the CD player. "No. What the hell is this doing out here?"

"I'm writing my column. Did you know that the Romans used to break the wedding cake over the bride's head?"

"No, but I'm not surprised. Italian men are hell on women. Pay attention here, I've been on that tub, the *Brenda Belle,* going through my mother's stuff."

"She's been living there ever since she sold me Two Rivers." Agnes sat next to her and poured her a glass of wine. "I don't know why she hasn't bought herself a nice condo. *I am so glad to see you.* You missed the meeting with her and *Evie Keyes.*"

"That was my plan." Lisa Livia crossed her killer legs, took the wine and sipped it, nodded, and then drank a good slug of it. "I know why she hasn't bought herself a condo; she thinks she's coming back here, and she's trying to screw up my kid's wedding to do it."

"What?" Agnes said, looking at her over the wine bottle. "That's crazy. Why would she come back here? Why would she hurt Maria's *wedding?* That's her big social coup, that's her in!"

"Because, as I have been telling you for years, she's a fucking nutcase." Lisa Livia settled into the swing. "Ever since Maria's been down here, Brenda's been at her about Palmer, how much he's like his dad, who married pretty little Evie Beale when she was just eighteen and has spent the rest of his life drinking and screwing everything in sight."

Agnes blinked at her. "*Palmer* is like his father? That's ridiculous, Palmer is Evie's baby, Palmer wouldn't say boo to a goose, let alone proposition one. I still don't know how he got Maria into bed." She hesitated for a minute. "Actually, I'm not sure he . . ."

"Yeah, he did," Lisa Livia said. "I asked because I didn't want her marrying him because he was sweet and rich and then getting bored in the first week. She said the sex was great and I should stop making assumptions and she was very happy. Now she's not so sure, because Brenda's planted this idea that he's going to turn out like his father."

"*Why* would she do that?" Agnes said, mystified.

"Because she's trying to stop the wedding. This morning when I got into town, I waited until Brenda left the yacht, and then I went aboard and starting going through her stuff to see what she was up to." Lisa Livia looked at Agnes over her wineglass, her big brown eyes huge. "She's swindling you."

"What?" Agnes frowned. "No. Not Brenda. I mean, I mean she's being difficult, but I think that's just because she's having to deal with these people who have shut her out all these years. You should have seen her face when—"

"She holds your mortgage," Lisa Livia said. "Why didn't you go through a bank, you dumbass?"

"She gave us a better rate." Agnes put her glass down. "Taylor had our lawyer look at the papers. They're standard. I mean, they're *boilerplate*. It's the exact same contract that Evie gave Palmer and Maria for the house they're buying next door to the Keyes place. The only clause Brenda added was that Maria hold her wedding here, and that's not a problem, I *want* Maria's wedding here, plus I get three months' mortgage payments free if I do it. It's a great deal."

"I know it's standard, and I know it's the same one Evie gave Palmer." Lisa Livia rolled her eyes at Agnes's obtuseness. "The difference is, Evie loves Palmer. It's also the kind used by crooked lenders to rip off buyers all the time. You think the Real Estate King became King by playing fair and square? Brenda learned everything she knows about selling houses from him. She's taking you, Ag."

This is ridiculous. Agnes pulled back a little. "LL, the contract just says I have to let Maria get married here, it doesn't say she has to get married. I know you and your mother have your problems—"

"She's a vicious bitch," Lisa Livia said, and finished off her wine.

"—but she's not a crook."

"She killed my father," Lisa Livia said. "Real estate fraud is a step up for her."

Here we go again, Agnes thought. "Look, you're the best friend a woman could possibly have until you get started on your mother—"

"Okay, you think I'm crazy, but just listen to me." Lisa Livia put her glass on the table and leaned forward, her tube top shifting in ways Agnes could not possibly appreciate and yet somehow was glad that Shane was not there to witness. "You know that clause that says that if you're in default of your payments for three months, the lender gets the house back?"

"Yes," Agnes said patiently, "but that's a standard clause, and we're not in default."

"But you will be," Lisa Livia said, just as patiently. "If Maria doesn't have her wedding here, Saturday, by noon, you are in default." She picked up her bag and pulled out a paper and handed it to Agnes. "Remember this?"

Agnes looked at it. "Yes. It's the wedding agreement. We're having the wedding here in exchange for . . . the first three months' mortgage payments."

Lisa Livia nodded. "Those three payments are past due if the wedding doesn't happen *here.*"

Agnes heard Brenda say, *If we held it at the country club . . .*

"What?" Lisa Livia said, watching her face.

Agnes swallowed. "Brenda's trying to move it to the country club. She even had some insane idea about using the flowers there."

"*What?*" Lisa Livia said.

"And Evie wants to have it at the country club, but not use their flowers." *I don't believe this. Brenda would not do this to me.*

"Jesus, I should hope not the country club's flowers." Lisa Livia sat back. "But there you go. Anything that keeps the wedding from happening here by Saturday noon means you lose the house and Brenda gets it back *and* she keeps your down payment. I knew there was no way she'd let this house go. She's been hanging on to it for twenty-five years, but she's broke, she's in debt up to her ears, big debt, Ag, and she's desperate for cash." Lisa Livia shook her head. "I told you, she learned this crap from that shyster she married. Real Estate King, my ass. People used to come to the house and threaten to kill him."

"I don't believe she'd do this," Agnes said, looking at the paper. "It's too far-fetched. I know you and she have your differences, LL, but she was good to me. She taught me to cook, for heaven's sake. She's like a mother to me."

"She is a mother to me," Lisa Livia said. "And I'm telling you, she's doing it."

"Lisa Livia, I have real problems." Agnes poured herself another glass of wine. "A kid died in my basement last night after trying to kidnap my dog at gunpoint, and now I've got this wedding—"

"*Died?* As in *dead?* And you're still *here?*" Lisa Livia's face changed, and she straightened. "Wait a minute. Brenda sent him."

"Oh, for the love of God, LL," Agnes snapped. "Your mother is not responsible for everything."

"She's trying to scare you out so you can't do the wedding so you'll have to forfeit and she'll get the house back. I betcha. Don't you leave this house." She drank more wine.

"I'm not."

"You're not staying here alone, are you? Get that worthless Taylor out here."

Agnes shook her head. "Joey got his nephew to come stay. Shane."

Lisa Livia choked on her wine. "Shane?" she said, wiping her mouth. "Little Shane?"

room window when I was a kid. I got stuck up there a lot when Ma had her parties. You wouldn't believe what I saw." She tilted her head, looking Evie right in the eye. "Like Simon Xavier feeling you up underneath our big oak tree. And that wasn't all. . . ."

Brenda said, *"Lisa Livia!"* Evie stiffened, and Agnes sat down and poured herself another glass of wine.

"I'm trying to remember if you were married then or not," Lisa Livia was saying to Evie, sounding genuinely puzzled. "I'd have to ask around. You know. For *guidance.* To get my dates straight."

"Wine?" Agnes said to Maria, who nodded and sat down next to her, equally resigned, picking up her mother's wineglass.

Evie pressed her lips together so tight, they made a white line in her face.

"It's not the kind of thing I'd ever do," Lisa Livia went on. "I mean, *ever* do, talk like that, I mean, unless somebody, you know, tried to *fuck my daughter over* on something she wanted, because in that case, *if that happened,* I would pour lye over *every single fuckin' inch* of this town. You think Sherman did some damage on his march through here? I'd make him look like fucking *Merry Maids,* what I'd do to you and everybody in this godforsaken hole if you or anybody else *fucks with my kid,* or *her happiness,* so if she says she wants fuckin' flamingos, she gets fuckin' flamingos right here at Two Rivers. The wedding will *not* be at the country club, it *will* be here and it *will* have flamingos and *anything else my kid wants,* do you understand?"

Agnes drank some more wine and so did Maria. She was pretty sure Evie understood. The First Lady of Keyes might not be Caesar's wife, but she was Jefferson Keyes's wife, and Jefferson Keyes's wife did not get felt up under an oak tree by a cop or, God forbid, laid, not even twenty-five years ago.

A quiet fell over the group.

Then Evie stood up. "Very well." She nodded to Maria. "I think this is a terrible mistake, but your mother is correct, it is your wedding. You may have your flamingos here at Two Rivers."

"Now *wait a minute,*" Brenda said, but Evie turned and walked down the steps and around the corner of the house to her Lexus, her dignity unspoiled even if her reputation had a dent in it.

Brenda turned to Lisa Livia. "Well, that was certainly a disgusting display worthy of your father's family."

"*Shut up,* Ma," Lisa Livia said, her hands on her hips. "Like you weren't born in the Bronx, and the Fortunatos weren't a big step up for you. Now you listen to me. You try to move this wedding away from Two Rivers again, I'm gonna clean every skeleton out of every closet you got and make them dance, you hear me? I'll dig up everything you ever buried, including my daddy, and then I'll sink that beat-up rowboat you're living on so you'll be out in the street with nothing. Do not fuck with my kid and do not fuck with my friend, they are all the family I got, and they are off-limits to you. Understand?"

Brenda drew back as if she'd been slapped, and then she glared at LL, and for a moment they were mirror images, two curly-haired mini-furies, one blonde and one dark, little but lethal. Then Brenda said, "I'm not going to listen to that kind of talk from my daughter," and turned to Agnes. "I'd like to speak with you before I go," she said coldly, and went into the house.

"I thought she'd never leave." Lisa Livia turned to Maria, who was sitting on the porch swing beside Agnes, her arms crossed in mirror image of her mother, the third fury in the triumvirate, although she looked more exasperated than enraged. "You got your flamingos, baby," Lisa Livia said, her voice doting.

"I don't *want* flamingos, Ma," Maria said. "I was just trying to make them crazy so they'd give me the wedding I really do want. I'd have talked them back to Two Rivers with the butterflies and the daisies and everything I wanted, but now thanks to you, I got *flamingos.*"

Lisa Livia stared at her daughter for a long moment, and then she said, "I hope someday you have a daughter, and when you do, I hope she breaks your heart the way you just broke mine."

"Yeah, yeah, yeah," Maria said, and went into the kitchen.

Agnes held out the wine bottle to Lisa Livia. "We tried to head you off. Wine?"

"Fuck that," Lisa Livia said. "Get me a bourbon."

"Kitchen," Agnes said, and they both went in.

Brenda was just inside the door, staring openmouthed at the kitchen wall, where the outline of the basement door could be seen easily now since so many people had gone through it.

"Agnes, *what is that?*" she said, as if Agnes had done something vile.

"The door to the basement I didn't know was there," Agnes said. "Your husband's old den is down there. Which you failed to mention when you sold me the house."

"Daddy's rec room?" Lisa Livia said, and went over to it. "Is the Venus still down there?" She pushed open the door and poked her head through. "My God, I'd forgotten all about this." She sounded ready to cry, which was not like Lisa Livia.

"Ma?" Maria said to her, momentarily distracted from her own anger.

Agnes got out the bourbon. "Coming right up, LL."

"If you don't want the Venus, can I have it?" Lisa Livia said to Agnes.

"God, yes," Agnes said. "You can have everything that's down—"

"*Why is this door open?*" Brenda said.

"A boy named Thibault fell through there and broke his neck," Agnes said.

"*Thibault?*" Brenda put her hand on the counter to steady herself.

"He came to dognap Rhett," Agnes said.

Brenda sank down on the counter stool. "Oh, my God."

Agnes took the bourbon to Lisa Livia, who was still peering into the basement, biting her lip now. "You okay?"

"My daddy loved this place," LL said, and took the glass. "Just loved it. My God. And the Venus is still down there?"

The front door slammed, and somebody walked across the hall, and then Shane came into the kitchen, Rhett trailing behind him.

When he saw the four of them standing there, he paused, and Rhett flopped down beside him.

He looked tall and broad and dangerous, all dressed in black. He looked damned good, in fact.

"Joey?" Brenda whispered, dead white now.

"This is Shane, Joey's nephew," Agnes said. "Shane, this is Brenda Dupres. Fortunato—"

"Shane, oh, my God." Brenda put her hand over her heart. "Shane. Of course, what was I thinking? Well. You've grown up since the last time I saw you."

"That's Little Shane?" Lisa Livia whispered to Agnes. "Who knew he was gonna grow up to be that?"

Shane eyed them all warily.

Lisa Livia waved to him. "Hi, Shane. Remember me, Lisa Livia?"

"Hello," Shane said, still cautious, which was something, given the effect Lisa Livia and her tube top usually had on men.

"You think the next time you're in the basement, you could bring up that Venus statue?" Lisa Livia said.

"It's a crime scene, LL," Agnes said, trying not to watch Shane's face. "We'll get it to you, I promise."

"Welcome home, Shane," Brenda said, holding on to the counter now. "Whatever are you doin' back in Keyes? Something for Joey?" Her voice shook a little on *Joey*.

"Looking out for Agnes," Shane said. "We were wondering why nobody cleared out the basement before it was boarded up."

"Cleared out?" Brenda said, her voice a little higher than usual.

"You got a bar full of booze down there, racks full of wine, a good pool table, and that real nice statue of the *Venus de Milo*—"

"*Real* nice," Lisa Livia said, while Maria looked at her in disbelief.

"—but it all got boarded up. Why?"

Brenda blinked at him. "Oh, Frankie. It just all reminded me so much of Frankie, so I just nailed the door shut and papered over it after he disappeared."

"My ass," Lisa Livia said in Agnes's ear. "She killed him. She probably buried him down there, that's why she's so spooked it's open again. She's probably got him buried under the Venus." She sighed. "He'd have liked that."

"Shh," Agnes said, praying that was a joke. "Brenda, what did you want to talk to me about?"

Brenda looked back at her, as if she wasn't quite sure who Agnes was. "What? Oh, Agnes. Well, about the wedding, of course. I was hoping you'd be reasonable about moving it to the country club since you're never going to get the house painted in time but—" She looked back at the wall and then at Shane. "—I think I'm just going back to the *Brenda Belle* now and we'll talk about it tomorrow." She smiled weakly at Shane. "Tomorrow's another day."

"It always is," Agnes said.

"I'll go with you, Grandma," Maria said, and Brenda didn't say a word about the "Grandma."

Shane moved aside, and Brenda glided past him, tottering a little on her heels, still beautiful, but very pale. For the first time, she looked close to her real age.

Maria shot one last baleful look at her mother and followed Brenda out the door.

"What's the *Brenda Belle*?" Shane asked when they were gone.

"Her yacht," Agnes said. "She's been living on it since she sold me this place."

"It's an old tub," Lisa Livia said and looked at Agnes. "Do you believe me now?"

"Maybe," Agnes said.

"Believe what?" Shane said.

"I'll tell you later." Agnes picked up the phone and dialed. "I have to tell Taylor first." Lisa Livia rolled her eyes, but Agnes said, "It's his personal business, LL." She listened to the phone ring once and then Taylor's answering machine clicked on. When she heard the beep, she said, "I need to talk to you tonight. No excuses. Nine o'clock is good." She hung up and turned back to Shane. "So Maria went mental on Evie and Brenda, then Lisa Livia told Evie she saw Xavier feel her up twenty-five years ago, and now it turns out there's a chance I'm going to lose this house, and I'm definitely going to be up to my ass in plastic flamingos by Thursday. How was your day?"

"I talked to Joey, I got shot at twice, and I got you an air conditioner. Why are you going to lose the house?"

"Shot at?" Lisa Livia said.

"This morning while Evie and Brenda were here?" Agnes said. "Because I heard shots then."

"They missed. Why are you going to lose the house?"

Then the other shoe dropped. "You got me an air conditioner?" Agnes swallowed hard. "You got me an *air conditioner*?"

He looked taken aback. "Well, you were having trouble with the central air unit you had—"

"It's too small for the house," Agnes said.

"—so I checked it before I left and you needed another one. It's no big deal, Agnes."

"Oh, my God," Agnes said. "You got shot at and you still got me an air conditioner."

"Agnes, it's an air conditioner, not a kidney," Shane said, and she wanted to say, *It's better than a kidney, after all that, you still remembered me?* but all she said was, "Thank you very much. I'll pay you back."

"No, you won't," Shane said. "Think of it as room and board. What's for dinner?"

"Joey brought me a tenderloin last night and I put it to marinade this morning," Agnes said. "That's easy and then we'll have sandwiches from the leftovers for a while."

"That's worth an air conditioner," Shane said.

"I'll do more," Agnes said.

"You're easy, Agnes," Shane said.

You have no idea. Take me. "An air conditioner. My God."

"So what happened with the house?"

"That's what I have to talk to Taylor about first."

"If you tell me, I'll fix it," he said, and she almost told him, just because he was there, and because he bought her an air conditioner, and because he could do anything, she was pretty sure.

"It's nothing I can't handle," she lied.

"I'll go put the air conditioner in," he said, nodded to Lisa Livia, and went out the back door.

Agnes turned to start dinner and caught sight of Lisa Livia watching her with her arms folded. "What?"

"Finally, something good is happening to you."

"Yes," Agnes said firmly. "I got an air conditioner."

"That's not all you're getting," Lisa Livia said. "And that fathead Taylor is toast. Couldn't happen to a shallower guy, either."

"Don't get all starry-eyed on me," Agnes said, heading for the refrigerator. "Shane is not staying."

"I know, that's the beauty of it. He gives you an air conditioner, evicts that airhead from your life, gives you great sex, and then leaves. My God. The perfect man."

"Are you staying for dinner?" Agnes asked with studied politeness.

"No," Lisa Livia said. "He might decide to take you before dessert. I wouldn't want to be in the way. I'll come back tomorrow for leftovers after I've rummaged around on the *Brenda Belle* to see if Brenda's got anything incriminating packed away. She's about as smart with money in general as you are, so outside of scamming you for this house, I doubt she's much ahead of you on anything."

"I'm smart with money," Agnes said.

"You're an idiot with money," Lisa Livia said. "So is Brenda or she wouldn't be in this cash bind now. You're the genius with words; I'm the genius with money. We should do something together with that. But not tonight. Tonight you're going to be playing footsie with the hotsie."

"You're disgusting," Agnes said, trying not to grin.

"Yeah, but I'm going to save your butt," Lisa Livia said. "I'm not kidding about that Venus. I want it." She took one more look at the basement door and left, and Agnes sighed.

That made two people who were going to save her butt. The place was filling up with people who wanted to save her.

She tried to feel exasperated about that, but she grinned instead.

Then she went to make dinner.

Shane spent the rest of the afternoon wrestling with the new air-conditioning unit and with the idea that his good old uncle Joey was still keeping something from him. Considering what he'd already been told, it had to be something pretty serious, which did not bode well for his getting back to his regular employment, something that didn't bother him as much as it would have the previous night. Doyle came by but didn't offer to help with the AC, saying he needed to focus on the house painting, although Shane figured it would be at least a decade before he got the place painted at the rate he was going. About seven, he went inside and cleaned up, and Agnes fed him tenderloin and fresh corn and new potatoes and ice cream with homemade hot fudge, and he thought about telling her he didn't eat that much and then plowed through all of it. She said, "I think I'm going to make a golf course cake with flamingos for Palmer's groom's cake," and he said, "Okay," because there wasn't much else to say after that, and watched her finish her next day's To Do List. It was long. Then she opened her laptop to work on her column, muttering about wedding cake, and he went out and finished getting the unit hooked up. After that, he sat on the back porch steps and watched the sun set with Rhett and then waited in the moonlight for Wilson to show up, all of which would have been peaceful if Agnes hadn't been so tense and if Wilson hadn't been coming to him. It was unheard of for Wilson to come to him. Plus it was well past nine and that waste of a human being Taylor hadn't turned up yet. Everything was wrong.

At ten minutes to ten, he stood up to walk down to the dock and realized that Rhett wasn't collapsed beside him anymore. He whistled and then, since that never worked anyway, he went around to the front of the house to find the dog and saw that the front door was open.

Fuck.

He took out his Glock and moved silently into the hall and heard Agnes say, her voice tight, "You're *dead,* I saw you *die!*"

"I just need to get the dog, lady," somebody pleaded, and Shane relaxed a little as the voice cracked. A kid.

He edged closer to the door and saw the kid from the back, his jacket shabby, a Confederate Army cap on his head, a gun in his hand. Not good. And his hand was shaking. Even worse. An amateur.

"You are *not* getting my dog," Agnes said. She was behind the counter, unarmed but looking plenty outraged, with Rhett in the open space beside the counter, looking unconcerned. And there were knives and frying pans all within her reach, so it could turn into a major mess fast.

Shane moved up silently behind the kid. Agnes put her hand out to the counter, and Shane saw that it was shaking just as he heard a boat out on the water. Wilson. *Enough,* he thought, and grabbed the kid by the neck and smacked his head into the doorframe.

The kid said, "Urp," and dropped the gun and Shane shoved the swinging door to the basement open, lowered the stunned kid by the back of his shirt into the hole.

Then he pocketed the gun and grabbed the kitchen table and shoved it across the basement doorway just as he heard Taylor's Cobra rumble across the creaking bridge.

"My meeting is here," he said to Agnes, nodding out toward the dock. "And your fiancé finally got here. Keep that table across the door and don't tell anybody the kid is down there. We'll find out from him what's going on after we get done with these guys."

"Okay," Agnes said, looking a little rattled, but determined.

"That's my girl," Shane said, and went out the back door, remembering too late that she wasn't.

He had to get out of Keyes.

Agnes watched through the open back door as Shane walked out to the dock, calm as anything in spite of having just disarmed somebody and dropped him in a basement. They just didn't make guys like him anymore, she thought, and then Taylor came into the kitchen carrying a large box that was heavy from the way he huffed as he put it down on the table Shane had just shoved across the basement door. He didn't seem to notice that the table had been moved. Well, he hadn't been in the house enough to really know where the furniture went.

Keep your temper, Agnes.

"What's he still doing here?" Taylor said, jerking his head toward the dock, and she looked back out to where Shane was silhouetted against the last of the sun.

He looked wonderful out there, although it was a little disconcerting that he held his business meetings on her dock at night. Kind of made her wonder what kind of business he was in.

"I don't like it that he's living here," Taylor said.

I do.

"I mean it, Agnes," Taylor said. "He has to go."

"He brought me an air conditioner. He can stay forever as far as I'm concerned." *Not to mention he just saved me from another damn dognapper.* Agnes turned her back on the window and looked at Taylor in the dim light of the kitchen. He seemed indistinct, fuzzy, and not just because the light was dim. She flipped on the overhead light, and he still seemed not quite there, a little too blond, a little too round at the corners.

Maybe it was because Shane had such sharp edges.

"Well, if you've got him out here, I don't see why you needed me," Taylor said.

"We need to talk," Agnes said, trying to decide whether to break the engagement and then tell him that Brenda was swindling them, or tell him she thought they were being conned and then dump him.

"Not now," Taylor said, opening the flaps on the box. "I'm in a hurry. Look at this." He pulled out a plate.

Agnes pushed her glasses up the bridge of her nose and came around the counter to squint at it. It was a plain white plate, cheap pottery with a thin glaze, nothing to make a snob like Taylor get excited. "So?"

"Aren't they the greatest?"

Agnes looked at him in disbelief. "Taylor, you wouldn't feed Rhett off this plate. Are you telling me this is what you want to use for the catering here?"

"God, no," Taylor said, and then recovered. "I thought you could use this as the china for the wedding. Save some money."

Agnes took it. "It's not china at all; it's pottery." She turned it over. "Incredibly cheap pottery. I can't believe you're not spitting on this."

"I told you, it's for the wedding."

"No." She handed it back. "It's not. Take it back. Listen, we have a problem."

He looked floored. "I can't take it back. Agnes, you'll save a fortune. Look at it again. Look at the bowls." He pushed the box toward her. "They're a nice shape and . . ."

He kept talking, and Agnes tuned him out and looked in the box and saw the receipt stuck down the side. She reached in and pulled it out to see just how cheap this junk was. If it was more than $1.98 for the whole damn box, he'd been ripped off good.

She unfolded the paper and saw scrawled at the bottom of the Visa slip a signature: *Brenda Dupres.*

"Brenda sent you out here with this," she said as her throat closed. "What's going on? Why are you working with Brenda? *What is this?*"

"Uh," Taylor said.

Agnes felt herself flush, heat rising with her temper. There was a plan here, Lisa Livia had been right—Brenda was up to something—except that LL had missed that Taylor was part of it and this horrible thin, ugly pottery with a cheap thin grainy glaze was part of it, she was supposed to use this horrible junk instead of the lush creamy china Maria deserved, and Brenda would have made sure somehow that Evie found out, Brenda had *asked* about the china that morning, and then Brenda would have looked at Evie and said, "The country club has beautiful china. . . ."

Brenda was trying to swindle her out of Two Rivers and Taylor was helping her. Agnes put her hand on the table, furious that he'd *lied to her*—

Steady, Agnes.

—incredulous that he could be that *fucking stupid.*

"Agnes?"

Agnes took a deep breath, controlling her anger with everything she had.

What was he getting out of it? He was going to lose the house, too, the dimwit. What had Brenda promised him?

"Agnes, what's wrong?"

You fucking moronic lying bastard, you sold us both out.

Angry language makes us angrier, Agnes.

Agnes took a deep breath, trying to keep her voice steady. "You sold us out to Brenda."

"I don't know what you're talking about," Taylor said, his eyes shifting left.

"You *lie.*"

Taylor took a step back. "Agnes!"

Physical exercise is often a good way of defusing anger, Agnes. Just walk away now.

Agnes gritted her teeth. "I don't know what promises Brenda made you, you *treacherous idiot,* but if I lose this house, *you lose this house.*"

Taylor drew himself up. "There's no need for insults, Agnes."

Running, Agnes, weight lifting, swimming . . .

"There's *every need,* you *dumbass.* You're screwing *both* of us and you don't seem to *see that!*"

Bowling, assault, battery . . .

"*Agnes!*" He shook his head. "You're really out of line. Last night, trying to break off our engagement, and now accusing me of betraying you . . ."

Defenestration, castration . . .

"I have to tell you, Agnes, *I'm not pleased.*"

"*Shot put,*" Agnes snapped, and shoved the hall door open with her shoulder and picked up the plate and slung it into the hall, where it smashed beautifully on the black-and-white-tiled floor.

Shane placed the pistol next to him on the wooden bench and tried to relax, but the sound of breaking dishes back in the house had him on edge. That, plus he knew he was a conspicuous target sitting in the moonlight on the fixed high dock at the end of the wooden walkway, just above the metal gangplank leading down to the floating dock.

A sniper with a thermal or night-vision scope could nail me without breaking a sweat, Shane thought. He glanced back toward Two Rivers as he heard another crash, but he could see the lights glowing in the kitchen windows and Agnes looking just fine through the back door as she threw things into the hall and yelled at that idiot Taylor, and he realized he'd rather be out here chancing a sniper than in there chancing Cranky Agnes in a rage.

Shane turned back toward the water as the darkened silhouette of a boat painted flat black skirted the near bank of the Blood River, a hulking figure behind the center console, a smaller figure sitting erect to the right rear. Shane stood, sliding his pistol into the holster, and walked down the metal gangplank to the floating dock.

He grabbed the line the driver threw him and quickly tied the jet boat off. It was low to the water and when the engine was cut, the sounds of the low country descended once more.

"Carpenter," Shane acknowledged the driver.

"Shane." The tall black man dressed in a one-piece camouflage flight suit looked around and smiled. "Nice digs."

The sound of more china shattering came floating through the night, and Carpenter's smile disappeared. "Trouble?"

"Not mine."

Wilson, dressed as always in a well-cut gray suit, climbed up on the floating dock, said "Good evening, Mister Shane," walked up the gangplank to the high dock, and took a seat, and Shane followed him.

Wilson had a Boston accent, enriched in some Ivy League school and fostered among the good old boy network of the World War II hotshots from the Office of Strategic Services, of which he was just about the last one standing. Shane knew he was in his early eighties, but the man was as spry as someone twenty years younger, and despite the evening's heat, there wasn't a drop of sweat on the slightly wrinkled skin on his forehead.

"I'm considering retirement," Wilson said.

Shane blinked at the unexpected opening.

"I must consider who my replacement would be. My position has special requirements. An absolute devotion to duty without any personal considerations is one of them."

"That goes without saying," Shane said.

"You made personal considerations a priority last night. This makes me question my inclination to make you my successor."

Shane straightened a little. Running the Organization could do a lot to alleviate the boredom he'd been feeling lately.

"You were not at the debriefing."

"I had a family emergency to attend to. The first in my career."

Wilson's head turned toward the house, as if just noticing the ongoing crashing inside. "It appears the emergency is still in continuance." He turned back toward Shane. "The individual you killed in Savannah was a mid-level mob contact who was to transfer the payment for Dean's hit."

"Then why did the intel indicate Dean was at that club?"

"A mistake from one of our lesser agencies. It's surprising they got that close to Casey Dean."

"It wasn't very close," Shane observed.

"You took out Dean's source of payment. That will upset Dean."

"Who is Dean's target?"

"You have no need to know."

Shane had heard that answer more times than he could count in his time working for Wilson. If he got Wilson's job, he'd know a lot more.

"We believe Dean will still try to fulfill the contract."

"Without being paid?"

"We believe the contractor will still pay."

"Who is the contractor?"

Shane braced himself for another *No Need To Know.* But instead Wilson turned and looked out at the low country. "Don Michael Fortunato. He's coming here for a wedding. We think the Don is doing a preemptive strike, taking out someone who's a threat to him while he's here for the ceremony. It appears the Don fears a rat."

Shane stared out at the swamp. *Fucking Fortunatos.*

"The nuptials should be quite lively," Wilson said.

"*Agnes!*" Taylor had said as Agnes had picked up the next plate and slung it after the first one into the hall, where it smashed onto the tile floor. It had been satisfying, but it had lacked form somehow. "I need a point system," she'd told Taylor, and was working one out—ten points for a dinner plate, maybe eight for a soup bowl, triple that if any of them hit his lying fatheaded skull—when he tried to take the box from her

"*Hey.*" She yanked it back, and started grabbing dishes from it and slinging them out into the hall as fast as she could, one after the other, while he yelled, "Goddammit, Agnes, what the hell are you doing?"

How are you feeling right now, Agnes?

Bite me, Dr. Garvin.

"*I hate a liar, Taylor,*" she said as she sent the last of the teacups after the dinner plates and started on the saucers. *"You've been lying to me, just like you're lying to me about these crap dishes, you've been lying to me about Brenda, and that makes me mad."*

He tried to grab the box from her, but she was in hyperdrive by now, diving to the bottom for soup bowls.

"Because *I don't get it.* I don't get why some people are so *goddamn selfish"*—a bowl went flying—"that they think *it's all right"*—and another—"for them to *lie in their goddamn teeth"*—and another—"so that they can *get what they want."* She stopped for a moment to breathe and looked him in the eye. "Why do you and Brenda get to lie and cheat and *everybody else has to play fair?"*

"Agnes, it's not what it looks like—"

"Hold it," Agnes said, plate in hand, hot anger going cold in an instant. "Do not even *think* about pulling that line on me, you and your *fine Southern gentleman* crap—"

Taylor's face darkened. "Now *wait a minute*—"

"—because you are no *gentleman,* betraying a *commitment*—"

"—I keep my commitments—"

"And you expect me to be your wife?" Agnes shrieked in his face, forgetting she was about to dump him. "Some *fine Southern gentleman,* betraying *his own* wife—"

"I haven't betrayed my wife!" Taylor snapped.

"What?" Agnes said, stopped in her tracks, and then as Taylor's face grew slack with the realization of what he'd just said, she sucked in her breath and said, "You're *married? You're already married to somebody else?"*

"Now, Agnes," he said, and as a red haze flooded the kitchen, she lunged for the counter and grabbed the nearest thing at hand.

"You're my obvious replacement," Wilson said to Shane as he prepared to go. "A seasoned professional, an unblemished record, and, we thought, no personal ties to distract you from your work."

"My uncle is hardly a personal tie," Shane said. "He's called me for help once in twenty-five years."

"Right before you made the only mistake of your career," Wilson said, no expression in his voice at all.

"The mistake was not mine," Shane said.

"You've caught bad intel before," Wilson said. "You should have caught it this time. Can you honestly say you weren't distracted by personal issues?"

Shane met his eyes squarely. "I—"

His cell phone rang.

Since he was staring at one of the four people who had the number, and the second one was in the boat, watching him with nonjudgmental eyes, and the third was in the house, throwing dishes, it had to be Joey.

Wilson waited and Shane knew it was a test.

It rang again.

Shane answered it. "Yeah?"

"Agnes okay?" Joey asked.

"She's in the house throwing dishes at Taylor." *Take a cue from my voice and hang up, Joey.*

"Shit. If that hairball says the wrong thing, she'll kill him."

"You're exaggerating." Shane met Wilson's eyes. He wasn't passing the test.

"She's on probation already," Joey said. "She's bashed two fiancés and had one dead guy in her basement. As long as she's throwing dishes, she's probably okay, but she ends up with another assault charge or, God forbid, another body, and—"

"Hold it," Shane said, and listened.

The house was silent.

"Fuck," he said, and sprinted for the back door.

Agnes stood very still as the kitchen swung around her. There was a faint roaring in her ears, and the floor rocked, and she let the box fall off the counter and onto the tile, where the rest of the dishes in it smashed.

"Agnes?" Taylor said.

"Your wife." She took a step forward and raised her hand, surprised to find a meat fork in it.

She'd been expecting a knife.

"Agnes." Taylor tried to move away, but she put the fork on his Adam's apple and pressed hard and he stepped back against the table, arching his back to get away from her until his shoulders touched the swinging door to the basement.

"Behind you is the door the kid fell through last night," Agnes said calmly. "He died, so I think you should stay very still right now."

"Ag—" He tried to turn his head and sidle away, and she pressed harder, breaking the skin.

"Do you know how sharp this fork is? Of course you do. Stand still and talk fast. How long have you been married to Brenda? You are married to Brenda, right? You didn't bring another woman into this just to mind-fuck me?"

"Agnes, it doesn't mean—"

She pressed a little harder and the blood began to drip down his neck. "Did I ever tell you about my anger problem, Taylor?"

He swallowed, his Adam's apple sliding along the tine of the fork. "Yes."

"How long have you been married to Brenda?"

"Not long."

"You *lie.*" She pressed harder.

Taylor's voice came out strangled, probably because he was afraid to swallow. "May second."

"The day before we signed the house papers." *He knew all along, he's known about the swindle from the beginning, he lied and lied and I believed him, he lied—*

"Agnes, honey, it was a terrible mistake." He swallowed again, sweating now. "I knew it right away, but I couldn't leave her, it was the only way I was sure of keeping the house. For us. *For us.*"

Agnes could hear herself breathing hard, just like in the horror films. Almost like watching herself, listening to herself. *He knew all along, he lied to me, he lied.*

"I did it for *us,* sugar."

You son of a bitch. She clenched her jaw and there was a rushing in her ears as she tried to shove the fork through his goddamn throat, but her hand wouldn't move. She threw her shoulder into it, and it still wouldn't move.

"No," Shane said from behind her.

"Thank God you're here," Taylor said, still pinned to the wall. *"She's nuts. Get her away from me and call the police."*

Shane was holding on to her wrist; that's why her hand wouldn't move. That was annoying. "Let go of me," Agnes said through her teeth.

"No," Shane said to Taylor, still holding Agnes's hand. "You will not call the police."

"The hell I won't," Taylor said, and then realized belatedly that he was still forked. *"Get her off me."*

"I won't kill him," Agnes said to Shane, trying to sound calm and reasonable through the red mist. "You can let go."

"Don't do it," Taylor said. *"She almost killed her last fiancé."*

"He's fine now," Agnes said. "He has a plate in his head. He can't walk under magnets, but how often does that happen? You can let go."

"If the police should ever hear of this," Shane said to Taylor, "she will be the least of your problems."

"All right," Taylor said, keeping his eyes on Shane.

"Let go of the fork," Shane said to Agnes.

"I want him dead," she said.

"Eventually, he will be," Shane said. "Let go of the fork."

"He *lied to me,*" Agnes said, her breath coming hard. "I want him dead *now.*"

"Not your decision. Let go of the fork or I'll take it."

She looked into Taylor's clueless, cheating, lying face, the same dumb, smug, cruel face a million women had probably looked into that day—*it wasn't me, I didn't do it, it's your imagination, I can explain, it's not what it looks like*—and thought, *If we killed them all when they did it, they'd stop doing it,* and tried to lunge, which was when Shane yanked her hand back and almost broke her arm as he dragged her behind him.

Taylor grabbed his throat and turned to run, and Shane hauled him back with his free hand as Agnes clutched her arm and tried to get to Taylor again.

Shane lifted Taylor up off his heels, holding Agnes at arm's length.

"Remember," he said calmly. "No police. If the police come asking anything at all about tonight, Agnes and her fork will look like a pat on the back compared to what I will do to you."

"You don't scare me," Taylor said, looking terrified.

"Then you're dumber than I thought," Shane said, and threw him into the hall.

Taylor scrambled for the front door, slipping on the black-and-white tile floor and cutting himself on the pieces of broken china there, and Agnes thought, *No!* and started after him, but Shane still held the arm with the fork and yanked her back, dragging her into the housekeeper's room and slamming that door behind them while she kicked at him, toppling them both onto the bed.

"Knock it off," he said, pinning her to the mattress while he tried to take the fork from her, but she held on to it with a death grip, so frustrated she wanted to stab it into a wall, and he finally snaked one arm underneath the hand holding the fork and around her neck, applying pressure to get it away from her. He pressed her down on the comforter, her shoulder and neck hurting as he pried at her fingers. "*Let it go*, Agnes," Shane said, and she tried to writhe free and then she heard Taylor's car engine start, rev up, and then fade away, and she thought, *Damn it, damn it, DAMN IT*, as Shane yanked the fork away from her, almost breaking her wrist.

"*Go to hell!*" she said, snarling with rage and frustration and pain, and he said, "Oh, give it up," and eased back. She rolled under him and struck out savagely, so damn mad at men that she wanted to pound him, and he dropped the fork and grabbed her wrists and jerked them over her head, slamming her back down on the bed, on top and in control again.

"Will you give up?" he said, as if she were just an annoyance, and she tried to knock him off, jerking under him, breathing hard, and watched his eyes change, grow darker and hot as she moved.

Oh, right, she thought, *goddamn men,* and then she felt the weight of him on top of her, felt all that rage fuse in her body in a need for hard contact, and all her frustrated fantasies about him hit her, all the lust she'd buried because she'd been *engaged,* damn it, and suddenly she wanted payback, wanted to cheat on Taylor, wanted to pound somebody, wanted to *fuck* somebody, and her anger kicked into something lower and sharper and a lot more focused.

Physical exercise is a good way of defusing anger, Agnes.

Way ahead of you, Dr. Garvin.

Shane let go of her wrists and straightened away from her, and she reached up and grabbed a handful of his T-shirt and yanked him back down, rolling so that he was under her.

He didn't fight her much.

She straddled him, holding wads of his T-shirt in her fists. "I'm *really mad,*" she said, gritting her teeth, her breath coming hard as she smacked his chest on every word. "*Really, really FURIOUS.*"

"Yeah," he said cautiously.

She leaned down on her fists, practically growling at him, her teeth clenched. "My court-appointed psychiatrist says I should vent my anger in *nonviolent physical exercise.*" She smacked him in the chest again, and he winced and caught her wrists.

"You know, Agnes, that's not the hottest thing any woman has ever said to me."

She yanked her wrists free and pounded her fists into his chest again, then let go of his shirt to strip off her dress and throw it on the floor.

He stopped frowning. "Course, it's not the worst thing any woman has ever said to me, either." He ran his hands up her sides to cup her breasts.

"Don't take this personally," she spat. "This is rage, not lust."

"This would be better if you didn't talk."

Agnes rolled off the bed to shove off her underpants.

"Never mind." Shane sat up to strip off his shirt. "Say anything you want."

"No, I'll be quiet," Agnes said, breathing hard as he stood up to take off his jeans. "I mean, *I'm mad as fucking hell*—" She kicked the bed as she thought of that *incredible dickhead* Taylor getting *engaged* to her to *swindle* her, *lying to her*, the *rat bastard*. "—but I realize you're doing me a *favor* here. I can be *accommodating*." She glared at him. "*What do you like?*"

"Women." Shane kicked his jeans away and reached for her.

"I can do that." Agnes shoved him back on the bed. "I was thinking more along the lines of special requests, style, *execution*—" She straddled him again, naked this time, nestling herself against him and watching him shudder at the contact. "—any particular act or *function* you're partial to—" She ran her fingernails down his torso, trying not to rake too deeply and making him wince anyway. "—anything that especially turns you on or makes your eyes roll back in your head—" Thinking of how he'd feel hard in her, wanting to pound on him, wanting him pounding in her, wanting to just pound the hell out of the goddamn world and smacking her fists into him because of it. "—because, and I know you'll think less of me for this, especially since you just watched me spit my ex-fiancé on a toasting fork like the limp bagel he is—" His eyes were closed now, maybe because she was rocking, but she really couldn't help it, he was so damn hard against her. "—but basically all I want is *my brains fucked out.*"

"*Right,*" Shane said, his voice a hoarse whisper. "If you could just wait a minute."

"Condom. Not a problem. Hold on." She leaned over him to reach the bedside table, and he curled up and took her breast in his mouth, and she shuddered at shock of him, feeling the pull in her groin, the suck deep inside her. She gritted her teeth and ran her fingernails through his hair, pressing his head to her harder, rocking harder with the rhythm of his mouth, and his hand shot out and fumbled for the drawer, and she remembered what she'd been doing and let go, yanking the drawer open and finding the condom, while his hand took her other breast. She grabbed onto the headboard and thought, *I should have gotten mad last night,* and then just went with his rhythm, sliding against him, feeling how broad his body was between her legs, how hot his mouth was on her, using the headboard to pull herself up over him until he flipped her over on her back and took the condom from her.

He began to move down her stomach, licking and kissing, and she grabbed his hair and yanked up. *"Later,"* she said, needing full body contact, none of that passive lying around, getting serviced, "fuck me *now,"* and he said, "Right. Now," and put the condom on, shaking his head, but the hell with him, she knew what she needed, she needed to pound somebody, somebody was going to *pay,* goddammit. When he reached for her, she moved over him, straddling him again, and he guided himself into her as she sank down, shivering at the shock of penetration, grabbing on to the headboard and jerking against him because he felt so damn good, thinking *damn it damn it damn it damn it damn it,* banging hard into him with each curse, working off all that frustration and rage while he gripped her hips and held on. She ground into him, not even realizing she'd let go of the headboard and was pounding his shoulders with her fists until he grabbed her wrists and rolled her over, pinning her down while she writhed under him. He rocked inside her and the heat built, but it wasn't enough, she wanted to move, wanted to be the one punishing, and she smacked her head against his shoulder, writhing and biting hard in frustration until he said, *"Damn* it!" and slid out of her. *"No,"* she said, clawing at him, but he flipped her over, and before she could swing on him, he'd pulled her up and slid into her from behind, his hand stroking down her stomach and into her, and she sucked in her breath as he pushed farther up into her, trapping her against him as he rocked. *"Harder,"* she said, pounding on the mattress, and he slammed into her, and she gasped as lust finally wiped out rage, and the full impact of what she was doing with a semi–complete stranger hit her.

Wait a minute, she thought, but the heat was everywhere and so was he, his hands on her, his body wrapped around her, *in* her, her skin itched and crackled and she couldn't stop shuddering, it was too late, and he wasn't stopping, his breathing ragged and out of control behind her, she couldn't even *see* him, massive behind her, surging into her, and the pressure built, and her blood pounded, the tension everywhere, her breath coming in little gasps as she writhed under his hands and his weight, and then he shifted and rocked into the perfect spot, and she screamed, "Oh, *God,*" and came her brains out, rattling the headboard so hard, she woke up Rhett and made him bark right before she collapsed onto the mattress with Shane on top of her.

A moment later, the electricity went out.

In the darkness, all she could hear were the crickets and somebody breathing really hard. That was her. Shane was so still, he was immobile, completely silent, for minutes, hours maybe, while Agnes felt her body spiral back from the good stuff, and then he relaxed, sucking air as hard as she was. He'd been listening, she realized. For what, God knew. Maybe another dognapper.

He pulled out of her and put his hand on her back. "Are you okay?" he said after a minute, still breathless.

Agnes thought about it. "Yes."

She moved away carefully, assessing the damage she'd brought on herself. There was surprisingly little, considering how much banging around she'd been doing. Mostly it was just that every-cell-I-have-has-just-collapsed feeling that a really good orgasm gave her. She breathed for a while, trying to sort things out, and then she said, "How are you?"

"I'm not sure," he said, sounding bemused.

She heard him sit up in the dark and she did the same, cautiously. "Sorry?"

"No. No complaints. What happened to the lights?"

"Sometimes they do this." She tried to catch her breath. It seemed to have gone permanently. "The circuit breaker blows. Or on hot nights sometimes the grid goes." *Well, this is weird. And how was it for you?* She drew another deep breath. "I've got flashlight lanterns stashed all over the place." More breathing. "There's one by the door and a couple more in the kitchen." She could see the paler moonlit blue squares of her bedroom windows now that her eyes were accustomed to the dark. Her body was coming back, too. It was her mind that was leaking out her ears. "Usually when the circuits blow, it's because there's too much power being drawn, but we weren't using any power."

"Oh, there was a surge there at the end."

As pillow talk, it wasn't much. On the other hand, her foreplay had been trying to kill somebody. Definitely time to go back to therapy. "Thank you for taking the fork away from me."

"You're welcome." He got up and put on his jeans, and she could have sworn he'd picked up his jacket and taken out a gun. He put whatever it was in his waistband. "We need to get that kid out of the basement and ask him who sent him, although my money's on Grandpa Thibault. Then tomorrow I'll go take care of whoever it is, and you'll be safe again."

"Oh. Good." Agnes squinted at him, still trying to see what he'd put in his waistband. It wasn't like he needed guns. He was terrifying all by himself. Which reminded her. "Thank you for threatening Taylor."

"My pleasure."

"Listen, did I do anything awful to you? I mean, just now?"

"No, Agnes," Shane said, sounding exhausted. "You had sex with me. I'll take pretty much anything that comes with that."

"Okay." She slid down a little in the bed.

"So we don't have power, which means we don't have air-conditioning," Shane said.

"Right." Agnes realized that sweat was already dripping between her breasts. "Oh, hell. And you got me a new unit, too. Well, it's the thought that counts."

"Doyle got the screens up on the back porch before he left."

"Yes."

He moved and she saw his silhouette against the window as he looked out. Big guy. Well, she knew that. She tried to move and felt the effects of him everywhere. Really big guy.

"After we deal with the kid, let's sleep on the porch."

"We'll have to wake up early," Agnes said.

"I always do," Shane said.

"Okay." Agnes got out of bed and picked up her pillow. "You know, I wouldn't have killed Taylor." *Probably.*

"Hell, Agnes, you almost killed me." Shane picked up his pillow.

"Humor. Har." Agnes gathered up the comforter and opened the door, turning back to get her clothes. "I—"

Shane pointed a gun and fired straight at her twice, the muzzle flash lighting the room, bullets cracking past her ear, then a thud—

Shane went by her, his face expressionless, his hand on her shoulder, pushing her down. "Stay there," he said, and she turned on her knees and saw a guy lying in the moonlight in the kitchen, his arms splayed out at his sides, a gun in one open hand, and Shane, firing twice more into the man's chest as he went past on his way out the back door.

Agnes nodded, even though he was gone.

As near as she could tell, the guy with the bullets in him was big. Older. Not skinny like the kid who'd died in the basement last night. This one outweighed her. He'd have shot her even if she'd thrown raspberry sauce at him.

Not that it was a problem now. He was dead.

She saw her glasses on the floor there, where they'd fallen off when she'd been fighting Shane on the way into the bedroom. She crawled forward gingerly and picked them up, not sure why she was being careful since the guy had four bullets in him. He wasn't getting up again.

She put her glasses on.

Those last two bullets. Just fired right in as he went by. Agnes put her head on her knees and shook.

After a while Shane came back in and said, "He did something to the power. We'll get it back tomorrow." He went over to the body and put the flashlight on the face. "You know him?"

Agnes stood up very carefully and went to look, pushing her glasses up the bridge of her nose. He was older, grizzled hair, broad ugly face, two bullet holes in the center of the forehead, two more in his chest.

Two holes. Like in Taylor's neck.

"No."

He leaned down and picked up the guy's gun.

"Shouldn't you wait for Xavier for that?" Agnes said.

"We're not calling Xavier."

"Oh." Agnes put a hand out to steady herself but there was nothing there. "You sure?"

Shane looked at her. "What do you think Xavier is going to do about another body here after the kid in the basement?"

"Well . . ." Be pretty suspicious about it, but that wasn't why they weren't calling him, Agnes was pretty sure. Still she wasn't going to argue with the guy with the gun, even if she had just had sex with him. She just didn't know him that well.

"What are we going to do with the body?" She had visions of dragging it into the swamp, whispering, "Here, gator, gator," and she made a little sound of distress at the thought.

"I'll take care of it. From now on, I take care of anything like this. No more Xavier."

"What do you mean, 'from now on'? You think there's going to be more of this?"

"It's possible." Shane rolled the dead man over on one hip, found his wallet, and flipped it open. "Wallace Macy." He pulled out five crisp one-hundred-dollar bills and frowned.

Well, he wasn't the only one frowning. He should be having her evening. Jesus wept.

Shane pulled out his fancy phone and punched in a number. "Carpenter," he said into the phone. "I have some woodwork." He listened for a moment, then flipped it shut.

"Who is Carpenter?"

"He's a man of many talents." He looked up at her, and she remembered she was naked. "You might want to get dressed. He'll be here in twenty minutes."

"Is he going to try to kill me?"

"No."

"Already I like him," Agnes said, and went into the bedroom.

She picked up her sundress, patted Rhett, straightened the bed, went into the bathroom, took off her glasses, washed her face, and combed her hair. Then she threw up until it felt as though she'd lost everything she'd ever eaten in her entire life.

When she was done, she splashed cold water on her face again and realized she'd been crying the entire time, ever since Shane had fired those two shots into the dead guy, ever since she'd seen those two holes in his forehead.

"Two holes," she said to her reflection. "I almost killed Taylor. Just like that. Only that didn't seem real. This was real. I could have done this. Oh, *God.*" She put her forehead on the cold mirror and swallowed hard and tried to think what the hell had happened to her life. She'd been writing a successful food column, and engaged to a terrific chef, and living in a great house, and now she was sleeping with a killer, and somebody was trying to take her house, and she'd almost killed her fiancé. . . .

"Ex-fiancé," she told her reflection. "I'm pretty sure that's over."

And then there was the flamingo wedding.

She started to laugh. She couldn't help it, she had to, and then she couldn't stop, even when Shane knocked on the door and said, "Agnes?" she still couldn't stop, and he rattled the door but she'd locked it, so he kicked it in and came in and held her and said, "It's okay," and she held on to him and said, "I know," and cried and then after a while she stopped, and he kissed the top of her head and patted her back, and she said, "That was *bad,*" and he said, "Yeah," and she said, "I won't do it again," and he said, "I thought you meant the shooting," and she said, "That, too," and let go of him and got dressed and put on her glasses.

When she had herself together again, she went out to the kitchen and got Rhett a dog biscuit in case he'd been traumatized. "At least it won't ever get any worse than this," she told him. He seemed comforted by that.

Then as Brenda's goddamned son of a bitch ugly black grandfather clock gonged midnight in the front hall, she went out onto the porch to wait for somebody named Carpenter to come and clean the blood out of her kitchen.

wednesday

cranky agnes column #75
"It's His Fault You're Fat"

Heartache often drives us to consume things we wouldn't otherwise, such as an entire pint of Caramel Pecan Perfection high-fat ice cream, covered in ganache, the crack cocaine of frozen dairy. Twelve hundred calories per pint, six hundred and eighty of which are fat calories, but it only dulls the pain for the moment, there's that carb fog while you're standing at the sink shoving it in your face, and then it's over and you feel . . . used. Like a cheap pickup the Dove people seduced and abandoned in your kitchen, leaving you with sticky hands and an empty cup and a still-broken heart, except now you're mad at Dove, too.

Shane could hear Carpenter whistling inside the house, a good sign. He could also feel Agnes shivering beside him on the porch swing, not a good sign. He still wasn't sure what had happened with Taylor to set her off with the meat fork, but he knew that being shot at by a strange man shortly after having angry sex, shortly after having tried to kill your fiancé, shortly after having a dognapper point a gun at you was a bad night for anybody, even a woman as tough as Agnes. Although she'd certainly been up for the sex. Energetic woman, Agnes. He hadn't been surprised when she'd come unglued there at the end of it all, but he had been surprised that she'd managed to get it all over with in about ten minutes. Energetic *and* efficient. One in a million.

She shivered and he put his arm around her.

"So you and Carpenter," Agnes said. "You're like, partners?" She shifted on the swing so she could look up at him through those ridiculous red-rimmed glasses. Her lips were very close, and her curls brushed his neck, and she was warm against his arm, and she was braless in that strappy dress, squished against him. . . .

"Okay, then," Agnes said when he didn't answer her. "Who do you work for?"

"We work for a very special organization," Shane said, trying to sound noble.

"That sounds so . . . UNICEF-ish." She looked back toward the kitchen. "It's not UNICEF, is it?"

Carpenter came through the screen door, a body bag over his shoulder, and Agnes's big eyes got wider. "I've got the package ready for removal and the scene cleaned. I'm sure you checked the wallet and saw the half a dime. Not a professional. Four shots—overkill, don't you think?"

"I was annoyed," Shane said. *The shithead fucked up my afterglow.*

Agnes looked from one to the other. "I was just going in," she said. "Very nice to meet you, Mr. Carpenter, thank you for cleaning up my kitchen." Then she got up and left, taking her warmth with her.

Shane stood, too.

Carpenter said, "What does she know?"

"Now, nothing," Shane said. "Shortly, probably too much. She's in the middle."

"Wilson won't like it."

Shane stood, silent.

"You would make a good department head," Carpenter said. "I would enjoy working for you."

"With," Shane said.

"This job could end it."

"This job could make it. Wilson told me Casey Dean's hit will be here."

Carpenter considered that. "Casey Dean is a professional. He'd never have anything to do with this—" He shook the body bag ever so slightly.

"True," Shane agreed. "So something else is going on."

Carpenter looked back inside to Agnes, who now appeared to be talking to the wall over the table. "What about her?"

"Someone appears to want her dead."

"Why?"

"I'm not sure."

"You sure she was the target for this guy?"

"Not positive."

"Is it our business if she is?"

"It's my business."

Carpenter nodded back toward Agnes. "There's a kid in the basement. Connected to this?" He jerked the body bag on his shoulder as if it were full of feathers and not dead meat.

"I don't think so. This guy was coming to shoot. The kid was like another one who came last night, after something."

Carpenter looked thoughtful, as if he were calculating something, and Shane was taken aback when he said, "I understand she cooks."

"Yes."

"I am often hungry in the morning."

Shane paid attention. "She makes an excellent breakfast."

"Perhaps I should come for breakfast."

"That would be . . . new."

Carpenter nodded. "A good partnership is flexible."

"Wilson might not like it."

"Wilson is retiring," Carpenter said. "You are in a complex situation. And I am often hungry in the morning." He touched a finger to his forehead in a salute and readjusted the body bag over his shoulder. "Be centered."

Then he was gone and Shane went inside to see what Agnes was saying to the wall.

Agnes had gone inside and watched as Carpenter talked to Shane with the body bag over his shoulder as casually as Palmer had talked to Maria with her dress bag over his shoulder. She looked at the basement door and then back to Shane and Carpenter and then back to the basement door, and then she went to the wall, leaned over the table blocking the door, and pushed open the door a crack.

"Hello?" she whispered.

"H'lo?" came a cautious whisper back.

"So who are you?" Agnes whispered.

"I heard shootin'," the boy said, his voice a soft drawl.

"Yes."

"Damn." There was a moment of silence, then, "Listen, I got my rights."

"No, you don't," Agnes said, annoyed at his lack of groveling. "You attacked me in my house. I hit the last kid who attacked me with a frying pan." *And then there was the meat fork,* she thought, shuddering at the memory of the blood running down Taylor's neck. "Now who the hell are you?"

The boy sighed. "I'm Three Wheels Thibault."

"The kid who died here last night was named Two Wheels Thibault. Relative of yours?"

"Cousin," Three Wheels said.

"Well, I'm sorry for your loss," Agnes said, and added hastily, "I didn't kill him."

"He were a dickhead. Always callin' names. Actin' like a big shot. Pokin' fun. Made me *mad,* you know."

"No," Agnes said. "I wouldn't know about that." She looked over her shoulder at Carpenter and Shane, who were still talking. That wouldn't last long. "Can you climb up out of there?"

"No, ma'am, I tried." The boy summoned up some outrage. "I think I hurt my ankle. I'm gonna sue that guy who dropped me in here."

Agnes looked back again at Shane and Carpenter. Shane looked roughly the size of a grain elevator. Carpenter was bigger. "Three Wheels, these are not men who get sued."

"Think they're better'n everybody else," Three Wheels groused.

"No, it's because anybody who might sue them stops breathing," Agnes said, acknowledging what she'd been trying to ignore about Shane's career choice.

"Oh," Three Wheels said, all grouse gone. "That was the shootin' thing?"

"Yes."

"They with the mob? My grandpa used to work for the mob."

"Who's your grandpa?"

"Four Wheels Thibault."

"Four Wheels?" Agnes said, and had an out-of-body Two Wheels–Three Wheels–Four Wheels–I-Just-Had-Sex-with-a-Professional-Killer-and-Almost-Died-Three-Times epiphany. "Jesus Christ. Never mind. Who sent you to kill me?"

"Grandpa. 'Cept I weren't supposed to kill you, just supposed to get the dog with the collar on't. He said it'd be easy. You was supposed to be *alone*."

"Yeah, well, bad luck for you," Agnes said, and then Shane turned back to the house, and she said, "You be *quiet*," and shut the door and stepped away from the wall, realizing as she did that, while she didn't know the kid she had imprisoned in her basement well enough to trust him, she didn't know the man she'd just had sex with at all.

Shane came through the door braced for whatever Agnes was up to now. She said, "Is Carpenter gone?" a little more loudly than necessary, leaning much too casually across the basement door, and he thought, *Wonderful. She's bonded with the kid in the basement.*

"Yep." Shane closed the back door. "And so is Macy."

"That was an interesting conversation," Agnes said. "'The package.' 'Not a professional'? 'Half a dime'?"

"The body. Not a professional killer. Five hundred dollars." Shane jerked his head toward the porch, changing the subject. "So you want to move out there for the night? Carpenter said he'll have the electricity back by morning. Until then, it'll be cooler out there."

"Sure." Agnes took a deep breath. "Okay, so the kid in the basement. He's just a kid. I don't think he was trying to hurt anybody."

"He had a gun, Agnes."

"He says he was only after Rhett. I'm sure he didn't mean any real harm. I think we should just let him stew down there for the night, talk to him in the morning, you scare him, make him see the light. That'll be plenty enough." She turned and went past him toward the housekeeper's room, and then stopped and turned back when he didn't follow. "So you coming to help carry stuff?" She looked nervously toward the basement door.

Shane sighed. "Agnes, I'm not going to hurt him."

"He just came to get Rhett," Agnes said, pleading with him from behind her glasses.

She wasn't wearing a bra under her dress; in fact, he was pretty sure she wasn't wearing anything under her dress. He was tired, but not that tired. "What else did he tell you?" he said, trying not to give away that she could probably get pretty much whatever she wanted from him.

Agnes sighed. "His name is Three Wheels Thibault, and his grandpa, Four Wheels, who used to work for the mob, sent him to get the dog. The kid last night, Two Wheels, was his cousin who always picked on him. He says he hurt his ankle when you dropped him in the basement and he was going to sue you but I talked him out of it. I think he's bluffing."

"What's his favorite color?" Shane said.

"Blue," Agnes said.

He shook his head. "You sure you're okay?"

"No. People keep trying to kill me."

"And I keep stopping them," Shane said.

"And don't think I'm not grateful," Agnes said. "You're getting a really nice breakfast tomorrow."

"Make enough for Carpenter," he said.

Agnes blinked. "Really?"

"That a problem?"

"No," Agnes said, her brow furrowing as she thought about it. "No. He seems like a good guy. I mean, his skill set is upsetting, but so is yours, and I'm for you. People are trying to kill me and you're saving me, so I'm definitely for you."

Shane nodded. "All right, then."

"So come help me get the pillows," Agnes said. "Do not shoot Three Wheels. Save yourself for Grandpa Four Wheels, who sent both boys."

"I'm not going to shoot Three Wheels," Shane said, exasperated. "What do you think I am?"

"A hitman," Agnes said.

Shane nodded. "Good call."

Agnes wrapped her arms around herself. "You could have lied to me, you know."

"I'm guessing that's when you pick up the meat fork," Shane said, and pointed her toward the bedroom.

"I'm giving up meat forks," Agnes said, and she sounded as though she meant every word of it.

"We'll see," Shane said.

Half an hour later, Agnes lay curled into an insomniac fetal position on her back porch under a sheet, trying to take stock. The man she'd planned on marrying was not only married to another woman, he was trying to cheat her out of her house with the other woman, and she'd almost killed him in retaliation. The Southern–Italian wedding of the season that she'd planned with meticulous care was now going to be a flamingo-themed pink-fest. Two different men had shown up with guns and pointed them at her tonight, for reasons that appeared to involve her dog, and one of them had definitely intended to kill her. A man the size of a truck had just removed a body from her kitchen. An underage kid named after a tricycle was trapped in her basement, because the hitman she'd just had angry sex with wanted to talk to him in the morning. And her column still wasn't done.

She was definitely turning over a new leaf. Her next fiancé was going to be a nice, steady, nice, regular nice guy, a non-lethal, non-lying nice guy. A good guy.

Agnes shifted on Shane's air mattress. She was definitely not sleeping with the hitman again. That was just insane. The whole concept of "messy breakup" alone could—

"You sure you're okay?" Shane said, half asleep beside her now.

"Yes," Agnes said.

Which wasn't a lie. She was exhausted, but she wasn't angry or frightened or insane anymore. If she'd been this calm when they'd had sex, she might have noticed some of the details. It was a shame she'd missed that.

She shifted again.

"Something wrong?"

"No." *But it would be really nice if you wrapped your arms around me. And then did some stuff. To keep my mind off some other stuff. And make me so tired, I pass out.* And then tomorrow, *I'll be sane and never sleep with you again.*

"You scared?"

"No," Agnes said. "You're here."

"What then? I'm trying to get to sleep, and you're tense as a board."

"Yeah," Agnes said. "About that."

"Whatever it is you need, I'll take care of it in the morning." He stretched over and kissed her forehead, and she lifted her chin to catch his mouth, putting her hand on his cheek and kissing him back, and after a minute, he pulled back. "Agnes?"

"Well," she said in a reasonable voice. "It's morning *somewhere.*"

He rolled over on his back and stared at the porch ceiling. "You're an odd woman, Agnes." He sighed. "You have any special requests? Anything you like?"

"Men," Agnes said. "Men who save my life and then make me come on my back porch."

"I can do that," Shane said, and put his arms around her, and Agnes sighed and began to concentrate on the details.

They were very comforting.

Shane woke feeling naked and exposed. And content. He cracked an eye at the mop of dark curly hair lying across his chest, which he knew was a mistake, because he should be checking the perimeter first to see what had wakened him. He was making a lot of mistakes lately.

He looked over at Rhett and noted that the bloodhound had his head up, which he took to be a sign of high alert for the dog. Probably the apocalypse coming, and the Four Horsemen were pounding toward the bridge over the inlet right now. With luck, it would collapse under them. Shane slid out from underneath Agnes and realized he was very exposed. A sniper could take him out easily.

Shane grabbed the rumpled sheet and went to drape it over Agnes, but paused, taking in her soft, round naked body for a few seconds, then carefully placed it over her. He reached down and grabbed his pants and put them on, fastening the holster for his Glock in place. He slid his feet into his boots.

A figure wearing a straw hat walked down the dock, a tackle box in hand, casting a long shadow over the water to one side. Shane opened the screen door, and Rhett shambled down the path to greet the invader.

They met near the gazebo.

"Detective Xavier."

"Mister Shane Smith."

"How do you know that?"

"Saw the scrapbook your uncle keeps in the diner under the counter. Saw that picture of you in the hospital bed, getting the Silver Star when you were in the Rangers. Your uncle talked some about you."

"My uncle has a big mouth." *Joey has a scrapbook on me?*

"Not big enough. So you were a war hero and got wounded?"

"I was in the wrong place at the wrong time," Shane said.

"Don't want to have that happen again," Xavier said.

Rhett peed.

Shane said, "So where is Detective Hammond this fine morning?"

"He volunteered to get some background on the wedding," Xavier said. "See if that might explain the unfortunate break-in. I believe he knows the bride."

Rhett continued to pee.

Shane noted the tackle box. "Going fishing? Water's back where you came from." He nodded to the small boat tied off at the floating dock.

"What I'm fishing for is in the house." Xavier tried to get around Shane.

Shane moved to block his way. "And that is?"

Xavier halted. "I don't like that basement."

"It is dank and dark."

"I don't like that crime scene." He made to get by once more.

Shane folded his arms. "You said it was an accident."

"It was."

"Then?"

"I want to poke around." Xavier tried to step around once more, and Shane edged into his way.

"Poking around can be dangerous."

Xavier looked up at him, exasperated. "What are you trying to say, son?"

"Already said it."

Rhett finished peeing and came over and sniffed Xavier's shoes, seemed satisfied, and ambled toward the house. *Great guard dog,* Shane thought.

Xavier looked at Shane's outfit of pants, pistol, and no shirt, and then glanced up at the porch. "You sleep outside?"

Shane turned and looked through the screen door. There was no sign of Agnes or the sheets that had been tumbled there. A woman who could wake up fast and then remove evidence silently. His kind of girl.

"Yep. I like fresh air."

Xavier nodded, his exasperation evaporating into amusement. "Right. Miss Agnes up yet?"

"I wouldn't know."

"Right." Xavier gave a lazy grin and walked around Shane. "Quite a woman, that Miss Agnes."

"Yep," Shane said, following him up the walk.

"Bit sharp-tempered, though."

"I'd call her fiery."

Xavier turned his head toward Shane and nodded amiably. "Fiery. That's good."

They walked up the path, Rhett ambling with them. Xavier trooped up the steps to the porch and spared a glance at the air mattress and Shane's T-shirt, crumpled in a ball. "Restless night, son?"

"Slept like a baby."

"I bet you did," Xavier said, and went into the kitchen.

Agnes had awoken slowly to voices out by the gazebo and then quickly to the realization that she was naked on her back porch with a teenage boy imprisoned in her basement and a cop walking up to her back door.

Shit. She grabbed for her sundress and slipped it on, trying to stay below the screens while gathering up as much of the bedding as she could carry, then did a low dash into the house to get Three Wheels out before Xavier saw him. She shoved the table away from the basement door, pushed the door open, whispered, *"Wake up down there,"* and dropped one of the kitchen chairs into the opening. *"Climb on that and boost yourself up here."*

She stood back as Three Wheels clutched and clambered out of the hole, skinny and dirty, seemingly made entirely of elbows and knees with a shock of reddish-blond hair sticking out from under his old Confederate army cap. When he was on his feet, she grabbed his shirt.

"Listen to me," she said. "In about half a minute, Detective Xavier is gonna come through that door and ask who the hell you are. You agree with everything I say, and you won't go to jail for threatening me with a deadly weapon, you understand?"

Three Wheels looked tired, scared, and mad, but when he heard Xavier's voice, his eyes widened and he nodded.

Agnes shoved him into the nearest seat and said, "I'm making you breakfast. You'll eat it."

"Yes'm," Three Wheels said.

Agnes started to put coffee on and then shifted course to the fridge and poured Three Wheels a glass of milk instead. She put that in front of him, stuck bread in the toaster to get him started—if his mouth was full of food and drink, all the better—poured coffee beans into the grinder, turned the gas on under the griddle, fired up her CD player, and then got out her bowl to make pancake batter. The toaster heated up, so Carpenter must have fixed the electricity. That was—

Three Wheels was staring at her.

"What?" she snapped.

"Nothin'," he said, looking away, blushing.

She looked down and remembered: no bra. "Oh, for the love of . . ." She reached over and grabbed her Cranky Agnes apron and put it on to cut down on the shifting problem under her dress. Then the toast popped and she loaded four slices up with butter and jam and put it all in front of Three Wheels. "Chew, don't talk."

"Yes, ma'am," Three Wheels said, and began to eat as if he'd never seen food before.

She almost felt sorry for him, but he'd broken into her kitchen, pointed a gun at her, and tried to take her dog, so the hell with him.

She started the coffee brewing and melted butter in the microwave, then dumped flour, sugar, baking powder, baking soda, and salt in a bowl just as Shane and Xavier came through the back door from the porch, followed by Rhett, who immediately flopped down in a patch of sunshine and fell asleep. Well, it was a long walk up from the yard. She smiled at Xavier—*see how friendly and unworried I am?*—and said, "Detective Xavier, what brings you out here so early in the morning?"

"The smell of that wonderful coffee brewing in your kitchen, Miss Agnes."

"It reached all the way into Keyes, did it?" Agnes smiled wider at him, trying to make the words warm instead of sarcastic. "Well, then I'll pour you a cup as soon as it's ready."

"I'd appreciate that." Xavier nodded to Three Wheels, who

crammed the rest of his piece of toast in his mouth. "And who might this be?"

"This is—" Agnes began, and then Doyle came in from the front of the house, calling "Top of the morning!" Agnes crossed her fingers mentally and then said to Xavier, loud enough that Doyle could hear, "This is Doyle's assistant. He's helping with the painting, trying to get the house finished for the wedding." She turned to Doyle. "Pancakes coming right up, Doyle."

Doyle's bushy white eyebrows had shot up, but she met his eyes and he nodded. "All right, darlin'. I could use . . . some pancakes."

Thank you, Doyle, she thought, and turned back to Xavier. "Did you come for breakfast, Detective?" *Please God, say no. Three Wheels will never be able to fake it through a whole breakfast.*

"No, Miss Agnes, I came for your basement," Xavier said. "I'll just be going down there now."

Agnes looked at Shane.

"I'll just be going with him," Shane said.

Agnes nodded. It was a real shame she wasn't going to be sleeping with him anymore. A man that fast on the uptake was a treasure. Of course, given his line of work, a man slow on the uptake was dead.

Xavier looked into the hole. "Why is there a chair in here?"

"I put it in there so people could get in and out," Agnes said. When Shane and Xavier both looked at her as if she were insane, she added, "It seemed like a good idea."

"I'll go get the ladder," Doyle said, and left.

Xavier set the tackle box on the kitchen counter, and Agnes went back to her pancakes. Anything was better than just standing there, looking Xavier in the eye.

She went to the fridge and got buttermilk, sour cream, eggs, and ham while Xavier gestured to the box and said, "This is my crime scene investigation kit." He held up a can. "Luminol." He looked at Agnes. "It detects blood even if someone's cleaned it up so you can't see it with the naked eye."

Agnes cracked an egg too hard and got shell in the bowl. "Blood?"

She picked the shell out and thought of how she'd spilled Taylor's blood right about where Xavier was standing. She glopped in the sour cream and began to whisk. Whisking was very good for nervous energy, especially with "Tortured, Tangled Hearts" twanging as back-up music.

Doyle came back with the ladder.

"You know," Xavier said as the ladder clattered into place, "it is kind of strange that those stairs are missing. Seems like someone was trying to hide that room for some reason."

Agnes kept whisking. "Brenda said she boarded it up because it made her think of her poor departed Frankie and she wanted to forget."

"Poor old widow woman," Doyle said, his voice full of Irish.

Xavier shrugged. "It was mighty convenient that old Two Wheels—"

Three Wheels choked on his milk.

"—hit right here where he would fall through and—"

"You said Agnes was clear," Shane interrupted.

"I said I believed her story about the events of the other evening," Xavier said. "Other stories I am not so certain of. Your uncle Joey, for instance . . ."

Three Wheels crammed in more toast.

Agnes tried to tune Xavier out, whisking the cooled butter and buttermilk into her eggs and then pouring her wet ingredients into her dry. She folded them together with a spatula and then poured pancakes onto the griddle, sprinkling them with pecans as she thought about hooks for her column—*the rise of the two-thousand-dollar wedding cake: a sign of the apocalyse?*—but it was all too clear that Xavier was loaded for bear and he'd decided the bear's name was Joey. *Damn it, Joey, what have you been up to?* She grated cinnamon on top of the pancakes and was watching them carefully for bubbles, worried for Joey, angry with everybody else, trying to figure out what the *hell* had happened to her life, when she felt a gentle tug on her sleeve over the counter.

"Ah have to go to the bathroom," Three Wheels whispered.

"Out in the hall, under the stairs," she said, talking low. "But you come back, we're not done with you. You hear?"

"Ah will," he said, looking down, and she realized he was looking hungrily at the pancakes.

She flipped them, and they landed perfectly golden, the pecans studding them like garnets.

He sighed.

"Okay, then," she said, and let him go.

She looked over to see Shane at the basement door, holding the dinette chair she'd dropped into the basement, rolling his eyes because she was letting Three Wheels leave the room.

I got Three Wheels covered, she thought. *You take care of Xavier.*

He pushed the chair under the table and disappeared into the hole, and she put the pancakes on a plate and poured the next batch as Doyle said, "So you be having the law in the basement, I be having an assistant in the bathroom, and somewhere we be having a grieving widow who sealed everything off from devotion?"

"That's about it." Agnes looked around her kitchen, saw that everything was under control, and picked up her cell phone.

"You're a very trusting lass, Agnes," Doyle said.

"Not so much anymore," Agnes said, and punched in Lisa Livia's number.

Shane held the ladder steady as Xavier climbed down, tackle box in one hand, but when he got to the bottom, he ignored the center of the room to detour over to the ancient bar, nodding to the mildew-speckled Venus as he passed her.

Shane pointed at the concrete floor. "The boy hit there."

Xavier nodded. "Thank you, son. My concern today, though, is what happened twenty-five years ago in here."

Fucking Joey, Shane thought as he watched Xavier open up the tackle box. "Twenty-five years ago?"

"Long ago in the mists of time, son, your uncle ran arm in arm with the man who owned this house, one Frankie Fortunato." Xavier took out the can of luminol and began walking slowly around the room, spraying. "Who subsequently disappeared. As mobsters are sometimes wont to do. You do know your uncle Joey was once with the mob?"

"Yep. But he left that behind a long time ago. He's an honest man, my uncle." *Maybe.*

Xavier laughed with genuine amusement as he sprayed. "Joey the Gent? He's got more stories than the library. And most of them are indeed fiction, but I'm interested in the nonfiction ones." He put the luminol can down on the old bar and reached into the kit and pulled out a bulky light, which Shane recognized as infrared. "Care to turn off the overhead?"

Shane flicked off the light as Xavier flipped on his own.

"Well, I'll be damned," Xavier said.

No, you won't, Shane thought, looking at the dragged blood trail that led straight into the wall. *But Joey might well be.*

Agnes listened to Lisa Livia's cell phone ring as she put the pancake platter on the table, the phone crammed between her ear and her shoulder.

Doyle said, "This lad who is now my assistant?"

"I know," she told Doyle. "I'm grateful. And I don't think you'll really have to—"

"H'lo?" Lisa Livia said, her voice slurred with sleep.

"I know, I know," Agnes said to her. "I know it's way too early, but I thought you should know, you were right, and I was wrong, wrong, wrong." She took down a frying pan, unwrapped the ham, and dropped the slices into it to fry, then turned back to pour more batter on the griddle, lowering her voice. "Brenda is swindling me on the house."

"Well, duh," Lisa Livia said around a yawn. "You couldn't wait until noon to tell me that?"

"There's more," Agnes said, and then Three Wheels came back in. "Hold on." She looked at Three Wheels. "Did you wash your hands?"

"Yes, ma'am."

"Pancakes are on the table," Agnes said. "Maple syrup's in the pitcher. Butter's in the dish. Ham's coming right up. Are you allergic to nuts?"

"No, ma'am."

"Because there are pecans in the cakes and I don't want you swelling up and turning blue on me."

"No, ma'am."

"Do you swear on the Bible you washed your hands?"

"Yes, ma'am."

"Eat."

"Thank you, ma'am."

Agnes turned back to the phone and began to slice more ham. "So there's more."

Lisa Livia said, "Tell me that wasn't Shane you were talking to."

"That wasn't Shane."

"Are those your sour cream buttermilk pancakes?"

"Yes."

Lisa Livia stopped yawning. "I'm coming over."

"Fine, but about Taylor. He's in on the swindle."

"You're kidding me. He signed the papers, too. How dumb is he?"

"Not that dumb. He—"

"So what's your name, me lad?" Doyle said to Three Wheels as they both helped themselves to pancakes.

"Three Wheels."

"No, it is not," Agnes said to him, and then into the phone she said, "Hang on a minute." She turned back to Three Wheels. "Do not say that around Detective Xavier, because he will make the connection that you're related to Two Wheels, understand?"

Three Wheels nodded.

"That's not the name on your birth certificate, right?" Agnes said, not sure. The Thibault clan didn't seem to be wound real tight; it was entirely possible Three Wheels had a cousin legally christened Steel-Belted Radial.

"Nah, that's what Two Wheels called me when I fell off'n my tricycle when I were little," Three Wheels said, semi-morosely. "He were always makin' fun."

"Well, those days are over," Agnes said. "What's your given name?" When Three Wheels looked confused, she added, "Your real name, the one on the birth certificate?"

"Garth."

Agnes nodded. "Garth."

"They kept tellin' my momma she was shameless, and that was Garth's big hit that year plus she just really liked his music so—"

"Garth it is," Agnes said. "How are those pancakes?"

"Grade A, Miss Agnes."

"Excellent," Agnes said, and went back to Lisa Livia and the cakes on the griddle, flipping them as she cradled the phone, and then moving on to turn the ham. "You still there?"

"Getting dressed," Lisa Livia said, her voice muffled. "I'm trying not to miss any of this. Who the hell is Garth?"

"The kid who pointed a gun at me and tried to steal my dog last night."

"What?" Doyle said, looking sharply at Garth.

"I'm *real* sorry about that," Garth said, forking up another pancake.

Agnes double-checked the cakes on the griddle, took the empty platter, and filled it again, then filled another with the ham.

More batter, she thought, and began a second bowl. Garth must not have eaten in a week. Or he was a teenage boy.

"He tried to steal Rhett, so you're feeding him sour cream pecan pancakes this morning," Lisa Livia was saying. "Makes perfect sense to me. I've missed you."

"Wait'll I tell you the next part," Agnes said. "Taylor—"

Somebody knocked on the back door, and she stepped back to see who it was.

"Morning, Miss Agnes," Carpenter said.

"Good morning, Mr. Carpenter," Agnes said, surprised. "Thank you for my electricity. Would you like breakfast?"

"Yes, ma'am," he said, and came inside, pretty much filling the kitchen.

"Have a seat," she said. "Shane's in the basement with Detective Xavier, but I imagine he'll be up shortly."

"Everything in its time." He took a glass from her open shelf, sat down, and poured himself some milk.

"Help yourself to the cakes and ham, too," Agnes said, and put some speed on whisking the wet ingredients for the second batch of cakes as she spoke into the phone again. "Lisa Livia?"

"Who's this Mr. Carpenter? Did he steal your dog last night, too?"

"You really have to come out here for the unabridged version," Agnes said. "The big news is you have—"

"How's my little Agnes!" Joey said, breezing in from the front hall.

"Joey!" Agnes cast a cautious glance at the rest of the crowd. "Xavier's down in the basement!" *And he thinks you did something horrible twenty-five years ago. What the hell's going on?*

"Where's Shane?"

"He be in the basement with Detective Xavier," Doyle said, sitting back with a cup of coffee, surveying the crowd with amusement now. "It be like a museum down there. Our Agnes should open it for the public. Get one of them fancy velvet ropes, put me in a uniform, let me decide who goes in and out." He gestured to the door. "Step right this way, ladies and gents! See the historic basement!"

Joey faltered for a moment, and Agnes couldn't tell if it was Doyle's basement humor or the sight of Carpenter and Garth eating pancakes and ham, but then he kept on going toward the basement door.

"Pancakes?" Agnes said, trying to delay him as she mixed the wet ingredients into the dry with a lot less care than with the first batch. Speed, that was the ticket.

"Later," Joey said, and slid a huge package wrapped in butcher paper across the counter to her. "Ribs."

"Thank you," Agnes said, hoping there were enough for everybody, since the thought of Carpenter and Garth in a smackdown over a rack of country ribs was not a pretty one. Carpenter had the edge over Garth on size and training, but Garth had youth and Thibault viciousness on his side. She shook her head and went back to the phone, turning her back on the rest of them. "Lisa Livia?"

"What's going on over there?"

Agnes dropped her voice. "Breakfast. Now here's the news: Your mama's married. Taylor's your stepfather."

"*What?*"

"I'll see you real soon," Agnes said, and hung up to finish the next batch of pancakes, cut more ham, start the marinade for the ribs, and then begin today's To Do List before moving on to write her damn column.

"You be real careful down there in that museum, Joey," Doyle called, and Joey gave him a funny look before he climbed down the ladder.

"Excellent pancakes," Carpenter said. "The ham is particularly fine."

"Is there more?" Garth said, holding out the empty platter, and Agnes took it back and filled it again while she thought about just what the hell was in Joey's museum in the basement and when she should start the next batch of pancakes.

"Joey the Gent," Xavier said when Joey reached the basement floor. "Just the man I want to talk to."

The last half hour in the basement, Shane had kept his mouth shut as he watched Xavier use more equipment from his tackle box. Sophisticated the old detective wasn't, but efficient he was. Shane had a feeling Xavier and Carpenter would get along quite well. Old school and new school, same brain.

Xavier pointed to an aged stool between the bar and Venus. "Have a seat, old friend. I found something quite interesting here in Frankie Fortunato's rec room."

"One of Frankie's fine wines?" Joey asked, glancing at the wine rack, but he went to the stool and sat down.

"Not wine," Xavier said. "I found blood."

"Yeah, that bum kid—" Joey began, but Xavier cut him off.

"Not from the Thibault kid. That you can clearly see. This was old blood that someone had tried to clean up. Only showed up with the luminol and the infrared light. It's a blood trail. Leading from there, where the bottom of the stairs had been, around this bar, right up to that wine rack and ending at that wall behind the rack. Blood from a long time ago."

Joey's eyes had that dead look, and he was staring at the detective. Shane had a feeling he was witnessing two old warriors picking up their swords once more.

"I'm willing to bet," Xavier said, "that blood is twenty-five years old. I'm willing to bet that it's Frankie Fortunato's blood type. And I'm willing to bet that when we knock down that wall right behind you, we find Frankie's body."

"How much you got to bet?" Joey asked. "You want me to put some action on this? Give you some kind of odds? You know Keyes, Xavier. Lots of secrets, lots of strange things going on all the time. Lots of skeletons in closets. Sure you want to go poking around?"

As denials went, Shane thought, it was pretty bad.

"In your closet, Joey? Sure."

"This ain't my house or my closet. How long is it going to take you to get that blood test done? I know about your little tackle box, Simon. *CSI: Las Vegas* you ain't."

"The blood test won't take long at all, and I'm good enough at what I do to get a warrant to find out what's behind that wall."

Joey snorted. "You think so? Agnes's got a wedding to put on here.

And Jefferson and Evie Keyes aren't going to like you fucking around with their only son's wedding. Maybe Jefferson calls the sheriff and they put the brakes on your little one-man show. You're right, you're gonna need a warrant to get behind that wall. Which means you're gonna need the judge to sign off on it. You know, the judge who golfs with Jefferson every week. Whose wife is best friends with Evie."

"And how are the Keyes going to know about this?" Xavier asked.

Joey gave his shark smile. "It's a small town, Simon."

Xavier shook his head. "I'll find out what's behind that wall. One way or another." He climbed up the ladder.

"Now *I* want some answers," Shane said.

"Everybody wants answers. I want breakfast," Joey said, and went up the ladder right behind Xavier.

Like that's gonna work, Shane thought, and followed him up.

When Agnes put the third platter of pancakes and the second plate of ham on the table, the atmosphere lightened considerably. There was something about being full enough to relax yet still hungry enough to enjoy food with plenty of it still on the table, that just mellowed the hell out of people.

And there were a lot of people at her table, she thought happily.

"So, Garth," Carpenter said genially.

"Is here to paint the house with Doyle," Agnes said brightly.

Carpenter smiled at her gently. "I was here last night, Agnes."

"Right," Agnes said.

"Who sent you, Garth?" Carpenter said. His voice was soft, but there was no denying it.

"My grandpa. He found that newspaper picture on his window-shield, you know, the one with the dog in it? And he wanted me to get the necklace it had on it in the picture, except the dog don't *have* no necklace on it."

Carpenter looked at Agnes, and she said, "I have no idea where the necklace went."

Doyle put up a hand. "That was my foolish doing. I found that piece of junk when I was clearing up around here, and I put it on Rhett as a joke."

"A joke," Carpenter said. "And where is this joke necklace now?"

"I pawned it," Doyle said. "I asked Agnes if she wanted it, and she told me I could have anything I found cleaning up, so I took it to Atlanta and pawned it. Sorry."

"You pawned it?" Agnes said. "I thought it was junk."

"It was," Doyle said. "I got five dollars for it. You want the five dollars? If I overstepped, I'm real sorry, lass."

He didn't look sorry, and when Agnes thought about it, she couldn't exactly remember telling him he could have anything he found, either. He probably could—she wasn't interested in most of the stuff he turned up—she just couldn't remember *telling* him that.

Which was just like the old reprobate.

"No, I don't want the five bucks," she said. "I don't care about the necklace."

"Why Atlanta?" Carpenter said. "Savannah's closer."

"I was *in* Atlanta," Doyle said. "Now, would you be suspecting me of something, Mr. Carpenter?"

"I have an unfortunately suspicious soul, Mr. Doyle," Carpenter said. "I would also like to know who arranged for Mr. Four Wheels to find the newspaper picture in his car."

"Don't know that," Garth said, and shoveled in more food.

"And what is it that you do for a living, Mr. Carpenter?" Doyle asked.

"I am, among other things, a man of the cloth, Mr. Doyle," Carpenter said, and Agnes almost dropped her spatula.

"And what denomination would that cloth be of?" Doyle asked.

"I am a Spiritual Humanist," Carpenter said. "We believe in helping others improve their conditions. In living, for example, Mr. Doyle, a life free of deceit."

"So, how about those pancakes?" Agnes said. "I've still got Shane and Xavier to feed and then there's Lisa Livia coming over, and you wouldn't believe how she can put them away, so I'm thinking at least another batch. And then there are ribs for lunch. Are you staying for lunch, Mr. Carpenter?"

Carpenter kept his eyes on Doyle. "Why, thank you, Miss Agnes, I would be delighted to stay for lunch."

"Well, then I'll get these ribs marinating and perhaps you can man the grill—"

The phone rang and Agnes answered it.

"Miss Crandall?" Reverend Miller said, pitching his voice deep for effect as usual, thereby sounding, as Lisa Livia had once said, like God making an obscene phone call.

"Good morning, Reverend Miller," Agnes said, wondering what excuse the minister had come up with this time for barring Maria from wedded bliss with a Keyes under his watch.

"I was just wondering if Miss Fortunato is what you'd call a regular churchgoer?" Reverend Miller asked.

"Hell, yes," Agnes said, having no idea. "Every Sunday. She wouldn't miss. I'd love to chat about that, but I've got a kitchen full of people to feed, so if that was all you wanted . . ."

"You're sure about that," Reverend Miller said. "Because I feel strongly—"

"I do, too," Agnes said. "You have a good day." Then she hung up.

Xavier came out of the basement, followed by Joey and then Shane. Xavier looked at Carpenter and said, "Who is this?"

"My business partner," Shane said as he cleared the doorway.

"And what business is that?" Xavier said.

"Housework," Carpenter said.

Shane introduced Joey to Carpenter, and Agnes grabbed Garth's sleeve and pulled him close.

"When breakfast is done," she whispered, "I'll distract them and you get out of here. I'll tell them I told you to go. It'll be all right."

Garth's pale bony face looked stricken, his freckles standing out against the white. "But what about the ribs?"

"What?" Agnes said.

"And the paintin'?" Garth said. "I gotta help Mr. Doyle paint the house, right? And then have ribs. And this house needs a lotta work. You need help." He was nodding at her, serious.

Agnes put her hand on her forehead. "Uh, Garth—"

"I'll work for room and board."

"*Garth*—"

"Don't send me back to the swamp, Miss Agnes," Garth said, his voice pathetic. "I hate it there. I'll sleep in the basement, honest."

"You can't sleep in the basement," Agnes said, appalled.

"You got a barn or somethin'?" Garth said.

"Well, yeah," Agnes said. "Taylor turned it into a catering hall. It even has a loft apartment with a bathroom. But—"

"It's got a *bathroom*?" Garth said.

"Oh, hell," Agnes said, and then her baser self took over and reminded her that she really did the need the house painted and God knew what else was going to turn up before the weekend. And with a Thibault on the premises, maybe the rest of the clan wouldn't show up to shoot her. And he liked her cooking.

Well, he probably liked anybody's cooking, but it was a real pleasure to see that boy eat.

"Yeah, sure, you can stay a couple of days," she said, knowing she was going to hell for exploiting the bathroom-less and then thought about the rest of her day.

To Do List, she thought. *Feed cast of thousands, several of whom are killers and one of whom is an underage dognapper now living illegally in my barn. Plan flamingo wedding. Remember not to screw hitman's brains out again even though he's really hot. Find nice normal guy without gun permit.*

The back door opened and Lisa Livia came in, looking gorgeous in pink capris and a black T-shirt that said EXPENSIVE in rhinestones. "So," she said to Agnes, seemingly oblivious to the fact that conversation had just stopped and six pairs of male eyes were now riveted to her rhinestones. "What's the plan?"

Take revenge on the sleazy bitch who's trying to swindle me out of my dream house.

It was going to be a very busy day.

Shane escorted Xavier outside without giving Agnes a chance to invite him to breakfast, and made sure the detective actually got in the boat and cast off, puttering away down the Blood River, before he returned to the kitchen, where he found his uncle at the table with the rest of the people Agnes had collected. He thought about dragging Joey out onto the porch, and then decided to sit back and watch.

He learned a lot by watching.

There was Lisa Livia, looking damn good, and there was Carpenter, surveying the kitchen population as if they were part of the mission, and Doyle, looking at Three Wheels without much enthusiasm and at Lisa Livia with a wistfulness that was almost sad, remembering lost days maybe. Three Wheels, eating ham and pancakes at the speed of light and watching Agnes with no intent to kill, although, some other kind of intent maybe—*try anything and die, kid*—and Rhett, asleep under the table once again, like a particularly lumpy brown rug. And Joey . . .

Joey met his eyes and then looked back down at his cakes and ham.

Agnes put a plate full of pancakes and ham in front of Shane. "Eat." She poured coffee and put that in front of him, too.

He began to eat, only half-distracted by Agnes's food this time— the ham crisp and sweet, the cakes thick and light, studded with pecans, the syrup falling in ropes to mix with the melting butter—but getting in the way was Joey, who was up to something that was probably going to get them all jailed or worse.

Doyle looked from Shane to Joey and back again and then said, "Garth, my boy, it is time we began our work day," and removed a reluctant Three Wheels from the warmth of Agnes's stove, Three Wheels slapping a slice of ham between two pancakes as he went. Agnes and Lisa Livia took their coffee out onto the porch, and Carpenter sat back, relieved from the distraction of the rhinestones, and watched Joey and Shane finish off their breakfasts.

Joey evaded Shane's eyes in the ensuing silence until he couldn't stand it anymore. "There's really an old blood trail down there?"

"What the fuck?" Shane exploded. "You think I'd just stand there and let him bullshit you if there wasn't? I was down there for half an hour watching him sniff around. I'm surprised he didn't take an ax to that wall, but he's a smart cop. He's playing this straight and legal. You telling me you don't know anything about that blood trail or what's behind that wall?"

"Oh, come on, Shane," Joey pleaded.

"Don't fuck with me, Joey. You been lying to me since you called me. Is Frankie Fortunato behind that wall?"

Carpenter raised his eyebrows and sipped his coffee.

"Damned if I know," Joey said. "I told you what happened that night."

Shane glared at his uncle. "Is someone else behind that wall, then? You guys whack someone way back when and put the body there?"

"You think we were that stupid?" Joey asked. "Put a body where somebody's gonna find it someday?"

That Shane believed. "All right." He pointed a finger at Joey. "You swear to me right now, on your beloved Angelina's soul, that you don't know what happened to Frankie Fortunato."

Joey closed his eyes for a moment, and then nodded. "I swear on my dear wife's soul. I don't know what happened to Frankie Fortunato after I left him alive and well with that safe that night."

Shane sighed. There was still a seed of doubt in the back of his mind, and he tried to take apart the way Joey had phrased it to see if his uncle had built in wiggle room with the oath. "Okay, you didn't put anybody behind the wall."

"Well, thank you for that," Joey said, all injured dignity.

Shane fixed him with a stare. "What *is* behind that wall?"

Joey sat very still.

Carpenter grinned behind his coffee cup.

Joey shifted in his chair, clearly thinking *Oh, fuck.* He sighed deeply. "Frankie's bomb shelter."

Shane straightened. "What?"

"Frankie's fucking bomb shelter. But you can forget about getting in, 'cause Frankie had the only key."

Shane pushed his plate away and tried to will some patience. "What 'fucking bomb shelter,' Joey?"

"Frankie put a damn fallout shelter in the backyard." Joey jerked his thumb toward the river. "Had it brought over on a barge and lifted by crane at high tide at night into the yard; then he covered it up and built the gazebo on top. Even if Xavier knocked the wall down, he ain't gonna find a body. He's gonna find a fifty-foot tunnel 'cause Frankie used a tunnel to go from the rec room to the shelter. Only people who knew about it were Brenda and me and Four Wheels."

"A bomb shelter?" Shane was still trying to wrap his mind around this development.

"Government surplus," Joey said. "Survive-a-nuclear-blast type of thing. Foot-thick, steel-reinforced concrete walls. Fucking indestructible. Loaded with food and all sorts of survival stuff. Frankie was a little bit paranoid."

"You think?" Shane leaned forward in the chair. "And Frankie had the only key to the shelter?"

"Yeah. Big damn thing almost six inches long. He kept it next to his gun."

No stairs. The entrance covered. The blood trail. The bomb shelter with only one key. Shane thought about strangling Joey with his bare hands. "Four Wheels is coming for the necklace because he thinks Agnes opened the bomb shelter and found the five million bucks from the robbery. That's why you called me in. You knew it wasn't a dognapper and you knew it wasn't just anybody thinking maybe the five million was here. You knew *exactly* what it was."

"Maybe," Joey said.

"Maybe we need to open the bomb shelter," Carpenter said, and they both looked at him in surprise, Joey probably because he was talking, but Shane because opening a bomb shelter was not in the mission statement.

"Wilson," Shane said to him.

"I am a curious man," Carpenter said.

"You can't do it without the key," Joey said. "That door is *thick*. And the lock—"

"Eat your breakfast," Shane said, knowing Carpenter could open anything he damn well wanted to. "We need to go look for a tunnel."

Agnes and Lisa Livia had taken their coffee out onto the back porch and sat down on the swing.

"So how about this," Agnes said. "Traditional wedding cakes had white icing because refined sugar was the most expensive, so white cakes were the most expensive. Now the most expensive ones are the elaborate ones that come in all different colors. Irony. Great column hook, huh?"

"Taylor's my fucking stepfather?"

"Yep." Agnes gave up on her column, put her coffee on the table, and turned to face Lisa Livia, prepared to be supportive in the fury to come. "He married Brenda the day before we signed the house papers."

"That makes sense," Lisa Livia said.

Agnes looked at her in disbelief. "That makes *sense*?"

"Well, yeah." Lisa Livia gave the swing a shove and they began to move back and forth, creaking in the summer breeze. "If you accept the insanity that my mother sold the two of you this house with the intention of swindling you out of it and he was in on it, he'd have to marry her. That way when he lost the house to her, he'd get it back because he was her husband. It's the only way he profits from the deal."

"Jesus wept," Agnes said, feeling her rage rise again.

Angry language, Agnes.

It's a Bible verse, Dr. Garvin.

"So of course he's married to my mother," Lisa Livia said grimly. "But he's gonna pay in ways he can't even begin to dream of. She'll probably kill him, too, just like she killed my daddy. So if you're thinking revenge, just wait. It's coming right up on its own."

"You *really* think she killed your dad," Agnes said, more willing to believe it today than she'd ever been before.

"He'd never have left me," Lisa Livia said. "He *loved* me."

"Well, you were right about the swindle, so I'm inclined to believe you about this one." Agnes picked up her coffee and blew on it and then sipped it. "Poor Taylor. I almost killed him last night and now Brenda's going to off him anyway."

"You almost killed him?" Lisa Livia's eyes widened. "When he told you about Brenda?"

"Went for him with a meat fork." Agnes shook her head at her own insanity. "Shane took it away from me. Thank God."

"You owe Shane big," Lisa Livia said. "You realize that if you'd killed Taylor, Brenda would have inherited half of this place back?"

Agnes sat up. "Oh, *God.*" Then she stopped. "No, she wouldn't have. I would have. We have a survivorship agreement. If one of us dies, the other gets everything. We have to survive the other one by twenty-four hours and then we inherit, so if Brenda had managed to off me, she'd have gotten the whole place but—"

"You wouldn't have inherited." Lisa Livia shook her head over her coffee. "You'd have killed him and you can't profit from your own crime. So she'd have gotten it."

"Oh," Agnes said, deflated. "Oh, crap. There really wouldn't have been an upside to forking him, would there?"

"Aside from the simple pleasure of the act itself, no." Lisa Livia gave the swing another push. "We have to figure this out. This is bad. We need a plan."

"A plan." Agnes nodded, trying to relax with the swing as she thought. "A plan is good. Something that puts the house in my name, not in Taylor's."

"Yep."

"And that makes it mine permanently, so Brenda can't ever have it."

"Yep."

"What would do that?"

"Taylor and Brenda dead."

Agnes stopped the swing. "LL, get your mind out of the mob. We're not killing anybody."

Lisa Livia looked at her, her big brown eyes wide with innocence. "It's efficient. We'd have to pin it on somebody else so you could keep the house, but there are a lot of people I'm annoyed with we could stick with the blame. Palmer's best man and his damn practical jokes are bugging the hell out of me. Some jail time would do him a world of good. What's his name? Downer. Downer is an idiot. Let's send him to the slammer."

Agnes started the swing again, fairly sure Lisa Livia was kidding. "Okay, put it down as a backup plan."

"Yeah, we have to wait until the cops are out of here anyway, you can't throw a rock without hitting one. That Hammond kid even came out to the boat to ask Maria about the wedding, although I think that was just an excuse."

"Oh, hell," Agnes said, "he's not going to confuse Maria and make her cancel the wedding, is he?"

Lisa Livia shook her head. "My kid is not that dumb."

"Okay." Agnes went back to stopping Brenda. "What else is there?"

"Blackmail."

"I like that. They're scum, they're bound to have done something horrible." Agnes slowed the swing again. "You really think your mom killed your dad?"

"I know she did. That night he disappeared? I saw her drive his Caddy away. She was the only one in it. They said he ran away because they found his car at the airport, but she was the one who drove it away."

Agnes sat very still. "You were thirteen, LL. How can you—?"

"Yeah, but I was a thirteen-year-old Fortunato," Lisa Livia said.

Agnes nodded, trying to be open-minded. "What if we found proof? We could blackmail her with that. Unless you wanted to turn her in to the cops now." It did seem odd, talking like this about Lisa Livia's mother, until you remembered that Lisa Livia's mother was Brenda Fortunato. Rasputin's kid probably had the same conversations.

Lisa Livia was shaking her head. "I couldn't turn her in. They'd prosecute her, and it would be in the papers."

"So?"

"My uncle Michael would find out," Lisa Livia said with obvious patience. "You know, my uncle Michael, the Don?"

"Yeah," Agnes said. "So?"

Lisa Livia looked at her as if she were insane. "My daddy was the Don's brother. That means my mother whacked the Don's brother. You know how long she'd live once he knew she killed him? Maybe ten seconds. I don't like my mother, but I don't really want her dead." Lisa Livia looked out through the screens to the Blood River. "I just want to know for sure."

"Okay," Agnes said, suddenly feeling better about her own parents. They'd been neglectful and deceitful and they'd deserted her at ten, but they hadn't murdered anybody. Point in their favor. "So where do we look for evidence that your mother, uh, whacked your father?"

"The boxes on the *Brenda Belle*," Lisa Livia said. "Everything she owns is on that damn boat."

"You think she'd keep evidence? That sounds dumb. Brenda is a lot of things, but dumb isn't one of them."

"I think she wouldn't know." Lisa Livia put her coffee cup down. "She has all her papers packed into boxes and I think she doesn't even know what's there. She'll leave the boat sometime today, she's going stir crazy on there, pacing back and forth, making phone calls and then slamming down the phone, cat on a hot tin boat. The only thing that's keeping her together is the knowledge that she'll be evicting you on Sunday and moving back here. She can't *wait* to get back here. As soon as she leaves again today, I'll go through as much of it as I can."

"I owe you," Agnes said.

Lisa Livia shook her head, a little sadly. "No, I shoulda done this a long time ago. Besides, you're putting on my kid's wedding. I owe you. I—" She stopped as they heard two sets of car doors slam, and she got up and craned her neck to see who was coming around the corner of the house through the porch screen. "Oh, God, it's Evie and Maria," she said after a moment, dread in her voice. "I gotta eat crow here and get my kid her white wedding back."

"No, wait." Agnes shoved her glasses up the bridge of her nose and stood up, too. "I think I can do it. Let me do the talking this time. My trade for you getting me the stuff to blackmail your mother."

"That's fair," Lisa Livia said, and then she put on a smile as the screen door opened and Maria came in, followed by Evie with a dress bag over her arm.

Dress bags, the new hot accessory, Agnes thought, and plastered a smile on her face as she thought fast about how to get rid of the flamingo theme.

Maria said, "Evie called me to meet her here. She has a surprise to show us."

Evie looked like six kinds of hell. "I've come to apologize. Palmer scolded me last night for being overbearing and rude, and he was right. If Maria wants a flamingo wedding, then she should have a flamingo wedding." She reached for the dress bag and unzipped it.

"Well, actually," Maria said, looking jolted.

"I think we can talk about that," Agnes said, stepping forward. "I'm sure we can compromise—"

"I shouldn't have opened my big mouth," Lisa Livia said.

"So I went to my dressmaker last night, and we worked on the dress," Evie said as if they hadn't spoken, pulling a lot of pink fabric out of the bag again. "Maria, would you please try Brenda's wedding dress on for us?"

Maria took a deep breath and took the dress, which looked a lot lighter, and went inside, detouring into the housekeeper's room.

"Really, Evie," Lisa Livia began.

Evie turned to her. "I did not appreciate what you said to me, Lisa Livia, but if someone had spoken to my son the way I spoke to your daughter, I would have felt the same way. I apologize, I sincerely do."

"Oh, *don't*," Lisa Livia said miserably. "*I* apologize. I was completely out of line."

"We've been talking," Agnes said. "And we're really both sure Maria will be *fine* with a white wedding. We think you were right to insist on something classic, like daisies and butterflies, Maria has always loved those, maybe with tiny flamingo accents and then a flamingo groom's cake—"

"No, no," Evie said. "A girl should have the wedding she wants. I made a mistake. I was glad to spend last night fixing it. My dressmaker is a genius. You'll see."

"Oh," Lisa Livia said.

Agnes looked at Lisa Livia and knew she was thinking the same thing: How do you tell a woman who has stayed up all night and spent a small fortune in dressmaker overtime fees that the flamingo thing was a joke her future daughter-in-law played to teach her a lesson about meddling?

Agnes and Lisa Livia looked away from each other and shut up.

"So have you talked to Maisie Shuttle?" Evie said to Agnes, after they'd discussed the weather and hoped it would hold for the weekend, and how the weatherman was predicting that it would, and how the gazebo was certainly looking lovely.

"Who's Maisie Shuttle?" Lisa Livia said.

"Florist," Agnes said. "Not yet, I'm still getting her machine. Don't worry. Maria will have her flowers, which I'm thinking will still be white, with maybe tiny pink accents—"

The screen door slapped open, and Maria came out in Brenda's dress, but it was Brenda's dress reborn, the hoop skirt and lace overlay gone along with the meringue sleeves and poufy overskirt and all the other froufrou. It was still flamingo pink, but lighter—Evie must have soaked it forever to rinse out part of the dye—and now the cut was streamlined and strapless, with just an edge of netting along the top of the bodice, the skirt still full but with a crinoline not a hoop. Maria looked lovely. Pink as all hell, but lovely.

"That really did take you all night," Agnes said, looking at all the work that must have gone into just *removing* fabric.

"I wanted to apologize *today*," Evie said. "I didn't want Maria to think I wasn't . . . I didn't want her to feel . . . I . . ." She looked at Maria. "I'm so sorry. I don't know what got into me. After Brenda and I went to lunch yesterday and talked, I—"

"*Brenda,*" Agnes snarled, imagining what that lunch had been like, Brenda dripping poison into Evie's ear.

Maria took a deep breath. "Thank you, Evie, this is a beautiful dress and I'll think of you when I walk down the aisle."

Oh, hell, Agnes thought as she heard somebody walk through her kitchen. "You know what would make this dress perfect? *An all-white backdrop with just tiny pink accents—*"

Maria turned to her eagerly, and then the screen door from the kitchen slapped and Brenda stepped onto the porch, invading from the house. "Well, here I am, Evie," she said, looking like she hadn't slept well. "What was so important?" She caught sight of Agnes and smiled, looking predatory. "Agnes, sugar, you had the front door open again, and you know that's bad for my clock, so I just closed it for you. And you've got a big ol' truck coming across the bridge, too. Is that a good idea?"

"It's about time you got that clock out of my hall," Agnes said, and watched Brenda's face sharpen, and then a beat later, she thought, *A truck? The bridge can't support a truck.* "No," she said, and started for the door, only to be blocked by Brenda, staring at Maria's dress.

"Where did you get that?" Brenda said to Maria.

"It's your wedding dress, Grandma," Maria said, smiling bravely. "I'm wearing it for my wedding."

"My wedding dress?" Brenda said, her pretty face darkening.

"Where's my Italian lace? Where's my bouffant sleeves? Where's my *goddamn hoop skirt?*"

The same place as your goddamned morals, you worthless tramp. "It's been modernized, Brenda," Agnes said. "When you pass something on to someone else, you have to expect changes. *You don't get it back.*"

Brenda glared at Agnes. "I can expect my wedding dress to stay my goddamn wedding dress."

"Ma, it's beautiful," Lisa Livia said. "Evie and her dressmaker worked on it all night. We're really grateful. *All of us.*"

Brenda turned on her, glaring. "Well, I'm not grate—"

The air was split with the sound of honking, frantic honking, as if a giant duck were being turned inside out, and Agnes said, "What the hell?" and shoved Brenda out of the way to see what was going on.

There was a deliveryman on her back lawn setting loose a large pink bird.

"What is that?" Agnes went out through the screen door and down toward the bird as it broke free of its crate and bolted for the river. It was at least five feet tall, and while she actually did know what it was, she was having trouble accepting the fact.

"Delivery for Maria Fortunato and Palmer Keyes," the deliveryman said, giving up on catching the bird. "They here?"

"Maria!" Agnes yelled, but Maria was right behind her. "Did you order a flamingo?"

"No," Maria said, staring at the bird as it loped, honking, toward the water, but she signed for it when the uniformed chinless wonder with the blond crew cut jabbed the clipboard at her. Then he handed her an envelope and drove off, leaving the crate and the bird behind as he made Agnes's bridge groan again in his getaway.

"That's a flamingo," Lisa Livia said, coming up behind them as Maria opened the envelope, and Agnes said, "Yes, it is," staring in equal disbelief.

"It's a wedding gift from Downer," Maria said, reading the papers from the envelope, and her inflection on "Downer" told them all they needed to know about how she felt about Palmer's best man. "Its name is Cerise."

"What in God's name?" Doyle said, and Agnes turned to see him and Garth crossing the lawn, gaping at the bird, which was still honking frantically, now knee deep in the Blood River.

"Flamingo," she told him. "How's that house painting coming?"

"We need sprayers," Garth said. "That's a flamingo. Hot damn."

"They eat shrimp," Maria said, still reading the papers. "What are we going to do with a flamingo?" Her voice quivered on *flamingo,* and Agnes realized that after the dress and her grandmother, the big pink bird was probably the last straw.

"Jimbo can get us all the shrimp we want," Garth said, and Agnes took the papers out of Maria's hands and gave them to him.

"You are now chief flamingo wrangler," she told him. "Take care of Cerise until we figure out where she belongs so we can send her back. Feed her lots of shrimp. Maybe that will shut her up."

"Cool," Garth said.

"And paint the house," Agnes added.

"On it," Garth said, and was gone.

Agnes turned to Maria. "You really do look beautiful in that dress, honest to God, and the flamingo will be gone by your wedding, I swear."

Maria nodded, trying to smile, and then Agnes turned to the rest of the group, raising her voice to be heard above the honking.

"So, who's for a mint julep?" It wasn't quite ten yet, but it was definitely turning into a drink-your-brunch day. If Cerise didn't shut up soon, she was going to get a julep, too. With a syringe if necessary.

Evie shook her head, trying to look away from the flamingo and failing. "Thank you, Agnes, but I'm going home to bed." She finally tore her eyes away, kissed Maria on the cheek, halfway between a real kiss and an air kiss, smiled weakly at Lisa Livia and Brenda, and tottered off to her Lexus.

"She's startin' to show her age, bless her heart," Brenda said with satisfaction.

"She was up all night working on your dress for your grand-daughter," Lisa Livia snapped.

"She was up all night *ruining* my wedding dress," Brenda shot back.

"Bless her heart," Agnes said.

Brenda jerked back to glare at Agnes.

"I'll have Shane and Joey put that clock in the truck and bring it out to your boat," Agnes said.

"That clock is the only heirloom from my family," Brenda said. "You just leave it where it is."

"It's in *my house*," Agnes said.

Brenda took a deep breath and then stopped, the blood rising in her face.

"I think I'm going up to the gift bedrooms to change," Maria said, her voice cracking. "It's quiet up there. And I can look at my china. I'll like that."

When she was gone, Lisa Livia said, "Come on, Ma, let's go back to the boat and leave Agnes to work on the wedding in peace." She shot a glance at Cerise, still honking her head off. "Sort of."

"*Yacht,* not boat," Brenda snapped. And then she smiled, which was almost worse. "You go on, honey. I've got some things to do in town. But I could use a glass of water before I go. You don't mind if I get it myself, do you, Agnes? I feel as though I still own the place, you know." She turned on her heel and walked across the lawn and into the house.

"My mother," Lisa Livia said. "A complete waste of oxygen. Bless her heart."

"She's insane," Agnes said. "Normally, I'd just go berserk and scream at her, but I'm trying to be an adult and use the Dr. Garvin approach."

"I am no fan of Dr. Garvin, but in this case, yes. Play nice until we find something that we can nail her to the wall with." Lisa Livia went toward the house, pulling Agnes with her. "Does she even know that you know? About Taylor and the swindle, I mean?"

"Depends on whether Taylor's had time to talk to her. He is a great avoider of conflict, so maybe not. Go get me something good from those boxes."

"You know, another place to look is here at Two Rivers," Lisa Livia said, opening the screen door. "She might have left something behind somewhere."

"Left it? Like where?" Agnes said, and then stopped in the kitchen doorway, where Brenda was staring at the open doorway to the basement.

"What do you mean, *they're down there looking for the tunnel?*" she was saying to Joey, sheet white.

Lisa Livia looked at Agnes. "Like in the basement," she said.

Shane looked around the rec room, trying not to linger on the Venus de Mildew and thought, *The Fortunato taste in decorating. Probably causes genetic damage. Which would explain a lot about the family.*

"This is a great house," Carpenter said as he flipped open the clasps on his large plastic case.

"You think?"

"Can't you feel it?" Carpenter asked as he brought out a foot-long infrared wand. "Cut the light."

Shane turned off the light, and Xavier's blood trail glowed. Carpenter looked like a ghoul holding the wand. He nodded. "Lot of blood. Someone cleaned it up, you can see the smears, probably with bleach." Carpenter walked the trail from where the stairs had ended, across the floor, around the edge of the bar, to the wine rack. "Turn the light back on."

Shane flipped the switch. "Why do you think this is a great house?"

"The vibe." Carpenter ran his large hands lightly over the old wooden rack.

Shane thought about Agnes, maybe in that cool blue bedroom at the top of the house. "Might be a good house to come home to."

Carpenter stared at him for a few seconds, then nodded. "It might be. You tired, my friend?"

Shane wiped a hand across his forehead. "I didn't get much sleep last night—"

"Not that kind of tired." Carpenter shrugged his broad shoulders. "I'm tired. And you do the real dirty work. I'm willing to bet you're real tired, deep inside."

Shane stared at Carpenter, surprised, and then thought about what Wilson had said out on the high dock. Taking Wilson's job would mean he'd be out of the field. He'd be giving the orders rather than having to execute them—literally. Sending somebody else out to do what he did.

Carpenter lifted the huge wine rack out of the way and put it to the side. Then he placed his hands on the wood-paneled wall. "There's something that looks like a stethoscope in my case. Except bigger. And it has headphones."

Shane looked in the case and retrieved the device. He brought it to Carpenter, who placed the headphones on and then put the cone at the other end against the wall. He turned a knob on the control and began slowly sliding it along the wall in short swaths, working from the floor up to the ceiling.

Shane waited, wondering what mischief Agnes and Lisa Livia were up to upstairs. And why all of a sudden he and Carpenter were having conversations instead of short exchanges about packages and cleanups.

"There is indeed a void behind here," Carpenter said, removing the headphones.

"You can hear a void?" Shane asked.

Carpenter handed him the equipment. "It sends a pulse out, like sonar." He was staring at the paneling as if it were going to speak to him.

"What—" Shane began, but Carpenter held up a hand indicating silence. Shane figured he was waiting for the vibe to speak to him again. Or maybe the void.

Carpenter looked left, then right, at the ghastly imitation of the *Venus de Milo*. He reached out and began to run his hand over the statue.

"Carpenter?" Shane said when his friend put his hands over her breasts. Maybe the rhinestones had gotten to him. "I think Lisa Livia wants that."

Carpenter pressed both breasts and at the same time took the toe of his boot and jammed it under the floorboard of the paneling in front of him. There was a slight noise, and Shane moved forward and knelt, putting his fingers next to Carpenter's boot. He hooked them under the floorboard and lifted. A section of the paneling slowly began to lift, protesting against the inertia of the years it had been stuck in place.

"I am curious." Carpenter went over to his case and pulled out two headbands with flashlights attached to the front of them and tossed one to Shane. "Frankie was the older son, but not the Don. Stuck down here with his Venus de Milo Bomb Shelter. And your uncle, he's worried, but he's not saying anything. Doesn't strike me as the type to scare easy, your uncle." He turned on his light and faced toward the void.

Shane did the same, feeling very troubled. Joey didn't scare easy, but something had kept him quiet and stuck in Keyes for a long time.

The tunnel was about four feet wide going up to a rounded roof slightly over six feet high. It was lined with brick, very old brick, and it was deep, black as hell beyond the light cast by Carpenter's beam.

"Let's see what lies ahead." Carpenter started in, and Shane followed. He couldn't see past Carpenter's bulk as they moved down the long tunnel, and he almost bumped into him when he came to an abrupt halt after fifty feet. The cleaner moved aside so Shane could see that the passage abruptly ended in a steel wall. No, a steel door, Shane realized as he saw the metal wheel in the center and the outline of a hatch.

Carpenter knelt and examined a keyhole to the left of the hatch, probing it with a long flexible rod he pulled out of one of the many pockets on his coveralls.

"Not pickable," Carpenter decided. "Plus, the moisture down here has rusted whatever mechanism is in there solid anyway."

"Blast it?" Shane suggested.

Carpenter rolled his eyes. "Always using the hammer when finesse will work. Wait here." He edged past Shane and went back down the tunnel.

Shane looked at the steel hatch and rapped on it with his knuckles. Solid. Blasting it would probably bring the house down on top of them. That would piss Agnes off. *Don't want Agnes pissed off,* Shane thought. Fiery, okay. Pissed off, no. At least not at him. If Taylor came by and infuriated her again, he was willing to lend a hand. Or whatever she needed. He began to wonder if Agnes was alone upstairs—

Carpenter was coming back.

"You know," Shane speculated, "if someone whacked Frankie Fortunato and didn't have Joey's skills as a cleaner, this would be a good place to stash the body. And if Frankie had put the safe with the money in here already and that person had shut the door with the key on Frankie's body and then found out the five mil was in there, that person might have been getting pretty steamed over the past twenty-five years."

"Why kill Frankie if not for the money?" Carpenter carefully placed a wooden box on the floor and opened it, revealing several glass vials. He also laid out a long green nylon case. He peeled open the Velcro holding it shut, revealing steel rods.

"Maybe the killer thought the money was elsewhere," Shane said. "Maybe in the trunk of Frankie's Caddy. And when the killer found out that five million was in here, he was screwed because he couldn't get in without getting noticed and that would bring attention to the body, so . . ."

"You say *he*," Carpenter said as he began setting up what looked like an IV drip holder. "You have your suspicions." He angled a glass tube into the keyhole.

"There are suspects. If Frankie is in there."

"Do you suspect your uncle?" Carpenter put a glass tube with a stop-cock on the bottom onto the IV drop holder.

"No. Joey has his faults"—*a lot of them*—"and he'll lie to you without blinking, but his oath is good. Hell, the mob calls him Joey the Gent." But Joey was lying about something else. And that meant he must have a damn good reason for lying.

Carpenter very carefully turned the stop-cock until a single drop of the liquid dripped into the long tube and slid down it, disappearing into the keyhole. There was a hissing sound, and a small puff of smoke appeared.

"Don't breathe the fumes," Carpenter advised. "Poisonous."

Shane stepped back.

Carpenter looked at his watch. Several minutes passed. A second drop of acid dripped down with the same result. Carpenter nodded. "All right. I'll have to adjust the tube a few times, but I estimate this will burn through the locking mechanism by around noon tomorrow, give or take an hour. Then we'll know if Frankie's in there."

"Noon tomorrow," Shane said. "Helluva lot can happen before then."

"Like finding Casey Dean?" Carpenter said.

Right. The mission. "That was my next move," Shane lied, and headed back down the tunnel, focusing once more.

When Lisa Livia had followed a shaken Brenda over the bridge, Agnes went down to the river to see what she could do about calming a hysterical five-foot-tall pink bird with a honk like an amplified mutant duck. When she got there, Cerise looked her in the eye and honked louder, flapping her wings and going nowhere, splashing in the Blood, agitated and miserable, and Agnes began to feel for her.

"I'm sorry," she said. "Whatever it is, I'm really sorry, and I will get you back home as soon as I can, *I swear,* and I will have that idiot Downer roasted slowly over hot coals while I'm at it, but *please* stop honking—"

"She's lonely," Garth said from behind her, and Agnes turned to see him standing there, as gawky as before in the same dirty denim, but now frowning with purpose, holding a bunch of papers. "I looked it up, like you said, on the Internet."

"What?" Agnes said, dumbfounded, Garth and the Internet not compatible in her mind.

"They taught us in school," Garth said, indignant. "Computers. I graduated elementary school and junior high."

"Of course you did," Agnes said, feeling awful for feeling surprised. Bad grammar did not mean bad brains, she knew that. "Uh, congratulations."

Garth nodded. "I'd go back next year, but Grandpa says there's no use for it."

"Hey," Agnes said. "There's use for it. You go back."

"You could talk to Grandpa about it," Garth said, looking away. "That would be right nice of you. Like in the movies."

"Uh," Agnes said, wondering what the hell movies Garth had been watching. Probably something where the nice lady got shot. "Yeah. Let's cross that bridge later. Flamingos first."

Garth went back to his Internet printouts. "I went and Googled *flamingos*. And flamingos, they ain't ever alone, they's always in big bunches, lots of them. It ain't right that there's just one."

He looked at the still-vocal Cerise with real sympathy, miserable for her, and when Agnes looked back at Cerise and saw the wildness in her eyes, her heart clutched, too.

"Fucking idiot Downer," she said as her throat closed, and then she pulled her cell phone out and punched in Maria's number, listening to Cerise, who wasn't honking anymore, not to Agnes's ears— now Cerise was moaning, "Alone, alone, alone, I'm so alone, alone, alone. . . ."

"Oh, *God*," Agnes said, and thought about all those damn nights in that little housekeeper's room, waiting for that rat bastard Taylor to come out so they could move up to that lovely cool pale blue room in the attic because moving up there would mean they were starting their new life, and if she didn't wait, if she moved up there alone, it would mean she'd be alone forever—

Alone, alone, alone, alone . . .

And before that, those lonely nights after her engagements had broken off when she'd wondered what was *wrong* with her that men always lied to her and left her alone, and before that those miserable days after Lisa Livia had taken baby Maria and followed her job west with her lying boss, who'd promised never to move his business, and before that those godawful holidays alone in boarding school before Lisa Livia had come along, brassy and defiant to anybody who'd tried to make her miserable and who'd brought her home to beautiful Two Rivers and Brenda for every summer and holiday after that so that for a while Agnes hadn't been—

"Hello?" Maria said, answering the phone.

"Get that shithead Downer to send this poor bird back where it belongs," Agnes said, close to tears. "They're *never* supposed to be alone. Her heart is *breaking. She's not supposed to be alone."*

"Oh, *no,"* Maria said. "I'll *kill him.* I'll get Palmer on it *right now."*

"Thank you," Agnes said, and clicked off the phone.

"I called Jimbo for some shrimp," Garth said over Cerise's moaning. "He should be bringing it right up to the dock any minute now. Maybe food will make her feel better."

"Not even three pints of Dove's Caramel Pecan Perfection," Agnes said from experience, staring miserably at Cerise, who stared miserably back.

Alone, alone, alone . . .

Lying bastards.

When Shane climbed up into the kitchen, he found a new long To Do List on the counter that was headed "Paint sprayers." He put it in his pocket and went out to the side of the house, where he heard hysterical honking. From the front of Carpenter's van, he could see down onto the riverbank, where Agnes and Garth seemed to be trying to feed something to a giant agitated pink bird.

Carpenter came out to join him, Rhett at his heels.

"That's a flamingo, right?" Shane said as he watched Agnes start toward the house, her red sundress flipping around her legs in the breeze again.

"Yeah," Carpenter said, looking as bemused by the whole thing as Rhett did.

"Thought so." He watched her move up the path, the ties of the sundress jaunty on her shoulders, and he wondered why she'd bothered with ties since she didn't have to untie anything to get it off, the whole thing just slipped off over her head. Probably so he'd think about untying it. Which he was doing right now—

His phone vibrated and he checked it and saw a text message from two hours ago. He pulled out his sat phone and punched in speed-dial 1 and Wilson answered on the first ring.

"Where have you been? I transmitted the intelligence to Carpenter's van two hours ago."

Eating pancakes. Checking out a bomb shelter. Thinking about ways to get Agnes alone. "Checking out what I can here." *What intelligence?*

There was a long silence, which indicated what Wilson thought of that.

"Check the intelligence ASAP." The phone went dead.

Shane closed the phone. "Wilson sent some intel, probably on Casey Dean. Can you check and prep it for me?"

"Roger that," Carpenter said, and nodded to the drive. "Isn't that Agnes's fiancé?"

Taylor's Cobra was coming down the road followed by a van with the county logo stenciled on the side. They bumped over the bridge and parked at the side of the house, and Rhett ambled down the path to investigate.

"Yep, that's him."

The county van meant some kind of inspector. That was going to annoy Agnes. Maybe even make her furious.

Carpenter looked at him with interest. "You don't seem to mind him being here."

"Nope." Shane watched Taylor get out and confer with the self-important little man who'd gotten out of the van. Agnes was going to hate him, too. Anger, coming right up. "I'm feeling pretty cheerful right now."

Carpenter shot him an odd glance, then shrugged. "So about the intel?"

Shane looked at his watch. "I can give you half an hour. Then I'm going to have to save this idiot's ass again."

He went over to the van and climbed inside with Carpenter who got the air-conditioning going full blast. One wall of the van was lined with computers, communication equipment, and other machines Shane didn't know the purpose of. The other side was lined with lockers holding the various tools of their trade.

Shane sat in one of the swivel chairs bolted to the floor while Carpenter took his in front of the large computer screen and brought up the intel that Wilson had sent.

"The FBI intercepted a call to Don Fortunato," he said, looking at the screen. "Traced back to a pay phone in Savannah directing the Don to go to a pay phone away from his house and await a call in fifteen minutes, which would have been untraceable, but Wilson had a tail on the Don with a directional mike. The tail followed him to the pay phone and picked up most of the Don's end of the conversation."

Shane read the screen over his shoulder:

DF: Yeah?
　　(six-second pause)
DF: How the fuck do I know?
　　(eight-second pause)
DF: No shit.
　　(four-second pause)
DF: Hell yeah, I still want the job done.
　　(four-second pause)
DF: Fuck you. We agreed on a price.
　　(seven-second pause)

DF: All right. All right. Fuck it. We got a contract. You make sure you do your part. The rest can come on the back end. My consigliere only got the cash we agreed on with him for the front end.

(three-second pause)

DF: Yeah, that's the target. How'd you know?

(eight-second pause)

DF: No shit? But you do nothing until I get there. I wanna be there. I wanna see it. I'm giving you an extra hundred large for that. Which you get when it happens, but not before the wedding. Got to be after. Got to show some respect.

(eight-second pause)

DF: Today? Fuck. Yeah, he's in Keyes. My consigliere. And he's got the down payment in cash. But—

(nine-second pause)

DF: The what fucking bridge? Talmud?

(two-second pause)

DF: Okay, Talmadge. Two P.M. local. Breakdown lane, southbound, center of span.

(five-second pause)

DF: Yeah, yeah. The money's packed like you said.

(two-second pause)

DF: You better be fucking worth it.

End of conversation.

Shane was already checking his watch. The payoff was taking place in an hour. "Where's the Talmadge?"

"Did you cross a large suspension bridge coming out of Savannah heading into South Carolina when you came up here?"

"Yeah."

"That's it."

"How far away?"

Carpenter got out of his seat and slid open the door leading to the driver's compartment. "I'll make it in fifty minutes unless we get caught in traffic."

"That's cutting it close."

"Perhaps we should have been monitoring instead of in that tunnel." Carpenter got in the driver's seat and started the van.

"That's not helpful now." Shane opened up the weapons locker.

"What about Agnes?" Carpenter said, but he was already heading down the drive.

Shit. "Maybe she won't kill him."

"What if she does?"

"What's one more body among friends?" Shane said.

Agnes had come in from consoling Cerise with shrimp and called the florist, powering through some rabbit of an employee on sheer leftover rage from the flamingo-napper who'd taken Cerise from the loving wings of her flock.

"Hello?" Maisie said.

"This is Agnes Crandall," Agnes snarled. "You can't cancel the Keyeses' wedding flowers if you ever expect to sell flowers in Keyes again. Are you *insane?*"

"*Oh,*" Maisie said, her baby-doll voice even higher than usual. "Oh, I'm so sorry, but I can't, I just can't, they'll *kill* me."

"Who?" Agnes said. "And don't you dare hang up on me or *I'll* kill you. And don't think I won't, Maisie."

"The *Fortunatos,*" Maisie whispered into the phone.

"Why would the Fortunatos kill you for doing the flowers for one of their weddings? They're a lot more likely to kill you for *canceling* on them."

"You don't *know them,*" Maisie said.

"Yeah, *I do.* A hell of a lot better than you do, evidently."

"Not better than *Brenda,*" Maisie said.

"Maisie, Brenda is trying to stop the wedding. She doesn't care that she's putting you in harm's way. The *Don* is coming for this wedding, he's giving Maria away. Don Fortunato. The Silicon Don. That's much tougher than Teflon. If he gets here and there are no flowers, you think he's going to be happy?" Agnes dredged up memories of any mob movies she'd seen. "He's going to ask who disrespected his grandniece. And you know what everybody is going to tell him?"

"What?" Maisie said, her voice a little moan.

"Maisie Shuttle."

"Oh, dear."

"Get those daisies out here by Saturday morning and you won't be sleeping with the fishes, Maisie. He'll never know the hell you put us through. But if you don't, I will tell him everything. I'll tell him where you live, Maisie. I'll tell him about the Scottie dog on your mailbox, so help me God, I will."

"Oh, no, all right, all right." The words were almost inaudible.

"Do *not* fail me, Maisie," Agnes said, putting steel in her voice. "Or the first thing the Don will put a bullet hole through will be the Scottie on your mailbox and the second thing will be *you*."

"No, no, *no*."

"The flowers, Maisie, the daisies will be out here Saturday morning, *won't they?*"

"Yes, Agnes."

"Thank you, Maisie. You won't be sorry. And the Keyeses will be *very, very grateful*. Oh, and Maisie? Put in some little flamingo pink touches, will you? *Little* touches."

Agnes hung up, trying to feel guilty for having beat up on a helpless Southern florist, but basically, Maisie should never have canceled on a wedding; any good florist should have known better. She looked for her To Do List to mark Maisie off so she could go take a shower and put on something that had less of a history of sex and violence attached to it—*I may never wear this dress again*—only to hear cars rumbling over the bridge just as the phone rang again. She waited until the rumbling stopped without an ensuing crash of timber and then picked up the phone.

"Agnes Crandall," she said. "Our bridge doesn't collapse."

"Pardon," the man on the other end said nervously.

"Humor," Agnes said. "Har. What can I do for you?"

"This is Wesley Hedges, your photographer for the wedding this weekend." His voice was so tight, it broke on *weekend*.

"Don't even think about canceling, Wesley," Agnes said, her voice level.

"I'm *not*," he said. "I *wouldn't*. But I can't make it."

"Let's review," Agnes said, her temper rising.

"But I'm sending my assistant," Wesley said quickly. "She's as good as I am. Some people say better. But they're all men. She's very attractive. I'm actually better, but . . ." Wesley sounded calmer now that he was being bitchy.

"Wesley, if you're trying to make me happy about your assistant coming—"

"No, she's really good," Wesley said, nervous again. "I mean, she's new, but I've seen her portfolio. I wouldn't send anybody bad. I have my pride. Even if they put a gun to my head, I would protect the sanctity of Wesley's Wonderful Wedding Memories."

Agnes was distracted by the alliteration. "Shouldn't that be 'Wesley's Wonderful Wedding Wemories'?"

"I don't feel bad at all for canceling on you," Wesley said. "Kristy will be out tomorrow to talk to you and get a feel for the place."

"Thank you, but—," Agnes said, but Wesley had already hung up.

"Photographer cancel, too?" Taylor said from behind her, and when she turned, he was standing in the kitchen doorway, smiling like he owned the place, instead of just half of it. He was wearing a suit jacket and an ascot, and he looked ridiculous, but she shouldn't really criticize since the ascot was probably to cover up the fork holes.

"You look ridiculous," she said. The dumbass had lied to her and left her all alone out here. And he'd never fed her shrimp, either.

Beside him was a tubby little man who looked around with the air of an inquisitive basset hound, alert but patient.

Rhett ambled in from the front hall to collapse in front of the counter. He didn't seem too perturbed with either of them.

"This is Mr. Harrison," Taylor said, still smiling. "Mr. Harrison is our health inspector in Keyes. I told him you had some health violations out here, and he's concerned about you serving food to a hundred vulnerable people on Saturday at the wedding."

"Yes, I am," Mr. Harrison said, smiling, too, the smile of a man who has been well paid to find health violations. "Concerned, that is."

"Taylor, you're the one catering that wedding," Agnes said. "That's your big break, catering the most important wedding of the season for this godforsaken county. Will you never learn not to shoot yourself in the foot?"

"I'll be catering it at the country club, too," Taylor said. "My foot is just fine."

"It won't be when Shane gets finished shoving it up—" Agnes began, and then Dr. Garvin said, *Agnes.*

Where the hell have you been?

You haven't been listening. Don't threaten people in front of witnesses, Agnes.

But it's okay to threaten them otherwise? What are you, Dr. Garvin's evil twin?

"What were you saying, Agnes?" Taylor said, his smile widening.

"I was saying you're an evil moron whom fate and karma are going to take care of," Agnes said. "Now your line is 'Who's Fate and Karma, and what did I ever do to them?'"

"That's not funny," Taylor said.

Agnes looked at Mr. Harrison. "I thought it was a little funny, didn't you?"

"A little," he said, smiling. Taylor glared at him and he shrugged. "So what am I supposed to look at?"

Taylor pointed to Rhett, now asleep on the floor of the kitchen. "That dog is unsanitary."

Harrison looked back at him. "You want me to shut down this place because there's a dog on the premises? We have to make this plausible, Mr. Beaufort." He looked around. "This is a clean kitchen. I can go through it, but you're going to have to do better than that."

Taylor glared at him. "There's a basement that hasn't been cleaned in twenty-five years."

Harrison sighed. "I'll poke around under the sink." He bent down and patted Rhett and then opened the cupboard doors under the sink. Everything was packed in plastic tubs with airtight lids, clearly marked as to the contents. He looked up at Agnes.

"I'm a Virgo," she said. "We do that."

He closed the doors and stood up. "This could take a while. Let's see the basement."

Agnes pushed on the door in the wall. "There's a ladder."

Harrison looked taken aback and then poked his head through the door. "This doesn't look like you, Miss Crandall."

"We just found it two days ago," Agnes said. "And I can't put stairs in and clean it up because it's a crime scene."

"That must be hard for you," Harrison said with real sympathy, and then he turned to Taylor. "This is probably where we'll get her."

"Told you," Taylor said.

"Hold on a second." Agnes grabbed her cell phone and punched in Joey's number on the speed-dial. When it rang, she got his message. "Joey, this is Agnes. Taylor is here with a very nice man named Mr. Harrison from the health department. Taylor's bribed him to shut me down for the wedding, and they're going down to the basement now to find something so he can do it. Is there somebody higher up you can confer with to take care of this? Thanks. Love you." She clicked off.

"Mr. Harrison is *head* of the health department, Agnes," Taylor said.

"Then he's about to meet Joey," Agnes said, but her heart sank.

"So," Harrison said, looking down into the hole, "a ladder."

Five minutes later, they were at the end of the tunnel looking at the acid dripping through the glass tube, and Harrison was legitimately upset.

"That's dangerous," he said, covering his nose. "Those fumes are *dangerous.*"

"And if I was serving dinner down here, that would be a problem," Agnes said, thinking, *What the fuck is that thing?*

Language, Agnes.

"You never know where fumes will go, young lady," Harrison said sternly. Then he retreated down the tunnel at a good clip, and Taylor followed him, all but chuckling.

When they were back in the kitchen, Harrison wrote up his prelim report and handed the pink copy to Agnes. "You can't cater that wedding here," he told her, as if he'd been rehearsed. "You'll have to move it to the country club."

She handed the pink slip back to him. "The wedding's going to be here. You know damn well that whatever that is down there will not affect a dinner in my barn on Saturday. And if you try to stop it, I will not only sue your ass for damaging my career," she turned on Taylor, "I'll have you arrested for bribing a public employee, and you," she turned back to Harrison, "arrested for taking that bribe."

Harrison shook his head. "That's not how it works here in Keyes, Miss Crandall."

Agnes sighed. "I see. Then it'll have to be Plan B."

Harrison blinked. "Plan B?"

"He didn't tell you about the bride's family, did he?"

Harrison looked at Taylor. "The bride's family? Well, the Fortunatos, yes, but Mrs. Dupres, the bride's grandmother, wants the wedding at the country club—"

"The bride's mother doesn't," Agnes said. "And the bride's uncle, who runs the local diner? Joey Torcelli? I just called him. He—"

"Give up, Agnes," Taylor said. "Mr. Harrison doesn't scare that easy."

Agnes looked at Harrison. He didn't look happy. He had to know who Joey was. Probably had tried to inspect the diner once.

"I wouldn't file that report just yet," she said to him. "I'd give yourself some room to maneuver. Just in case the bride's family would rather the wedding was at the bride's old family home. Did Taylor tell you this is Frankie Fortunato's old place?"

Mr. Harrison shot Taylor a look of loathing and walked out of the kitchen.

"I've got you, Agnes," Taylor said, not fazed in the slightest.

"You had me, Taylor," Agnes said. "Now you've got Brenda, you poor, doomed sap. And Joey 'The Gent' and Shane after your ass. You better go now. Your flunky is out in his van, and his feet are turning to ice while you wait. At any minute now, he's going to tear up that report and go somewhere far away until the wedding is over."

"Nah, he—"

"And Shane's coming home any minute."

Taylor looked over his shoulder.

"Yeah, well . . ." He looked back at Agnes. "You give me back the ring and I'll go."

"What?"

"The engagement ring." He nodded at Agnes's hand. "Give me my ring back and I'll go."

Agnes looked down at the ring he'd given her. She'd actually forgotten about it. Five thousand dollars he'd said it'd cost him. That could buy some stuff for the house. Like landscaping maybe. *Wonder if Garth can landscape?*

"No," she said. "Go away."

"I want the—"

"You broke the engagement, I get the ring."

"You stabbed me with a fork!"

"You married another woman first," Agnes said. "Go away. I have things to do."

"You won't get away with this," Taylor said.

"That's the best you've got?" Agnes said. "Beat it or I'll have Doyle take a hammer to the Cobra."

"Hey!" Taylor said, and then evidently realizing his ride was vulnerable, he left.

Agnes looked at the ring and then at the basement door.

"Why can't anything this week be *simple?*" she said, and went to call her lawyer.

"We're about five minutes from the bridge," Carpenter said. "I can see the towers."

Shane checked his watch. Ten minutes till the payoff. He poked his head in the opening to the front of the van and saw two suspension towers straight ahead on the horizon. Left and right was swamp as far as the eye could see.

"Ideas?" Shane asked.

"I would think a direct approach is needed here, which is your specialty. It's not like we're going to be able to sneak up on the drop site."

"Pull off before you hit the on-ramp for the bridge. I want to see if I can get an over-watch position with a clear shot with the long rifle."

"Roger that," Carpenter said, "but it's going to be a tough angle up to that midspan."

Shane saw what he meant as they came around a slight curve, and the road rose precipitously toward the nearest tower. "Pull over here," Shane said before they got so close that he wouldn't be able to see the midspan.

Carpenter waited until they crossed a concrete bridge over a creek, then pulled over to the side of the road.

"Open the sunroof," Shane ordered as he placed his M21 sniper rifle in the passenger seat, muzzle up.

Carpenter did so, and Shane stood between the seats, putting a small spotting scope on the roof of the van.

"Not inconspicuous," Carpenter noted.

"Feel free to contribute Plan B," Shane said.

"We grab the consigliere and the money *before* the exchange. Maybe Casey Dean will work a deal with us or break off the contract."

"Wilson wants Dean terminated."

"Did he say so?"

"He doesn't send me out to talk to people." Shane leaned forward and looked through the spotting scope, adjusting the focus.

"He's testing you."

Yeah, and I fail if I don't shoot Casey Dean.

Shane saw a black Lincoln Town Car pulled over in the break-down lane, right side of the bridge, center span. These goombahs were nothing but predictable, he thought. He checked his watch. Three minutes before two. Casey Dean was a professional, which meant the drop would be made right on time. Shane slid back down in the van, crouching between Carpenter in the driver's seat and the sniper rifle in the passenger seat, taking the spotting scope with him.

"The consigliere is there." He held the scope as he peered through the windshield. The view wasn't quite as good, but he could clearly see the black Town Car.

"Two minutes," Carpenter said. "And we've got flashing lights coming down the road behind us."

"Cops?" Shane could hear the sirens now.

"Looks like, followed by an ambulance." Carpenter reached forward and turned on the special radio, tuning it to the local emergency band, the volume turned low while Shane kept his focus on the bridge.

"There's a report of an accident on the bridge," Carpenter relayed from his position, leaning close to the radio speaker.

"Bullshit. There's no accident up there. Dean called this in as a distraction." Shane was shifting, trying to find where Dean was.

"One minute," Carpenter announced.

The door on the Town Car opened, and a tall, thin man with gray hair stepped out, holding a shiny metal briefcase. He was looking about, obviously unsure which direction Dean was coming from.

The sirens were getting closer as Shane reached out with his free hand and grabbed the rifle.

"You're not going to shoot with cops around?" Carpenter asked.

Shane could hear the sirens go by and saw the flashing lights reflected in the windshield. But his focus was on the bridge. The consigliere suddenly reached into his jacket pocket and pulled out his phone and answered.

"Dean's making contact," Shane said.

"One state patrol car and an ambulance, reaching the ramp for the bridge," Carpenter reported. "And I've got another police car in the side mirror coming this way."

This was definitely cramping his style. He couldn't pop out the sunroof and blow Casey Dean away with one shot while the police were driving by. He squinted as the consigliere walked over to the side of the bridge and looked over the edge.

"Oh, shit. Dean's underneath." Shane slid into the passenger seat and put the rifle across his lap. "Drive!"

Carpenter threw the van into gear and pulled onto the road just as a sheriff's car blew past. "Which way?"

"Ahead and then—" Shane thought fast. They couldn't go onto the bridge with all the cops around. He still had the scope to his eye and he saw the consigliere drop the case over the side of the bridge and get back in his car. There was one exit before they hit the on-ramp.

"Take that exit," Shane ordered.

Carpenter turned hard right. The road curved around and then under the ramp, but there was dense, impenetrable vegetation between the road and the Savannah River.

"We've got to see the water," Shane said, powering down the passenger window.

"Hold on." Carpenter jerked the wheel hard and they skidded onto a dirt trail. The van's specially built suspension grappled with the ruts and rocks as Carpenter accelerated down the narrow track.

"Whoa!" Shane yelled as the Savannah River suddenly appeared ahead of them, a rusting chain-link fence indicating the end of the trail.

Carpenter had hit the brakes even as Shane gave the warning, and the van skidded to a halt, the front bumper less than two feet from the fence. Shane was moving as it stopped, throwing open the door and jumping out, the rifle in his hands.

He brought it up to his shoulder in the ready position, the muzzle resting on top of the fence, but he kept the eye closest to the scope closed, while he scanned with the free eye. There were three boats visible. An old tug chugging upriver, and two personal craft heading downriver. Shane put his gun eye to the scope and checked the farthest boat, a cabin cruiser about a half mile away. An old man and woman were visible in the flying bridge.

Not Casey Dean.

He shifted to the second boat, a smaller, faster craft that was kicking up quite a wake and expanding the distance between it and Shane's gun at a rapid pace. A figure dressed in black, hood pulled up over the head, was at the center console.

Shane aimed at the figure and his finger caressed the trigger. He could feel his heart beating and begin to slow down as he got in the rhythm for the shot.

"You sure that's Casey Dean?" Carpenter asked.

"No," Shane said.

"Give me your phone and the card," Carpenter said.

Shane kept the rifle in place, one eye on the boat, which was fast getting out of range and approaching a bend in the river, where it would be out of sight. He knew exactly what Carpenter wanted to do and preempted his partner by using his off-hand to pull out the phone and card and then dialing the cell phone number as fast as he could. He kept his firing hand on the rifle.

Shane was slightly surprised when there was a ring. Then another and another. The figure on the boat didn't move. After four rings, a mechanical voice informed him he could leave a message.

"Casey Dean," Shane said. "I've got you in my sight."

The figure still didn't move.

The boat reached the bend in the river and was just about out of sight when the figure at the console put his right hand into the air and Shane could see the middle finger extended just as the boat gathered speed and disappeared.

"Look on the positive side," Carpenter said. "You know what

Casey Dean looks like from behind, dressed in dark sweats with a hood over his head. That's something to report to Wilson."

"*Fuck,*" Shane said, and got back in the van.

"What do you mean, I can't dissolve the partnership?" Agnes said into the phone ten minutes later. "He's trying to *sabotage it,* Barry."

"Which is a damn good reason to dissolve it, Agnes," her lawyer said. "But it's a partnership. The two of you have to dissolve it together. And Taylor doesn't want it dissolved. He already called."

"Barry, he's trying to get the health department to shut down a wedding we're catering," Agnes said. "Isn't that some kind of breach of contract?"

"I'd sue him," Barry said. "But then, I'm a lawyer."

Agnes heard the front door slam and turned to see Lisa Livia come into the kitchen with a shopping bag that said BETSIE'S BON TON.

Rhett hadn't even bothered to lift his head.

"You got a truck coming across your bridge," Lisa Livia said, and Agnes hung up on Barry and went to the front door to look, almost tripping over five pieces of Lisa Livia's pink leather luggage in the hall on the way.

"Brenda caught me going through her stuff and threw me off the boat," Lisa Livia said. "She kept screaming about betrayal. Can I have my old room back?"

"Sure," Agnes said, heading out the front door. "What truck—?"

It was already crossing the bridge, which groaned its displeasure, and then it was sweeping down the drive and over the lawn—"Will you *stop that?*" Agnes yelled at the driver—and then it stopped and the driver got out and opened the back and wheeled out a crate that looked familiar.

"What the—," Lisa Livia began, and then the chinless wonder of a driver who also looked familiar opened the crate and another flamingo staggered out, honking like mad, and Cerise went crazy.

The driver came toward Agnes with his clipboard.

"No," she said. *"You take them both back."*

"I'm just the delivery guy, lady," he said, his rabbity face twitching. The patch on his uniform said, BUTCH, but he so wasn't.

"I'm not signing that," Agnes said. *"Take them back. They need to be in a flock."*

"Can't do it," he said. "Just sign this."

"No." She pushed her glasses up the bridge of her nose and looked at him closer. "You're not from any delivery service. And you delivered Cerise. Downer paid you to do this. *Who are you?*"

He met her eyes for a moment, and then bolted for the truck.

"Come back here, you bastard!" Agnes started after him, but fear made him fast: He dived for the front seat and had the truck in gear and moving before the door was closed.

She walked back to Lisa Livia, who was still carrying her Bon Ton bag, but who'd now picked up the clipboard he'd dropped.

"This one's name is Hot Pink," LL said.

Agnes looked down to the river. Hot Pink and Cerise were deep in honking conversation of mutual outrage, but Cerise didn't seem to be as manic as before. "Is there a return address?"

"No," Lisa Livia said. "This is like an information sheet. Like a zoo might give out."

"A zoo." Agnes closed her eyes. "Call that moron Downer and ask if he had these guys stolen from a zoo." *What "if"? Of course that idiot had them stolen from a zoo. Who sells flamingos?* "Call Downer and tell him we know he hired Butch to steal Cerise and Hot Pink and if he has them taken back right now, we won't have him arrested and shot."

"Right," Lisa Livia said, taking out her cell phone. "Then we should talk. Brenda threw me out, but I'd already put some of her stuff in the car, so I brought it with me. Like all of her real estate stuff, including her house book."

"Her house book?" Agnes said.

"Her scrapbook of everything she wanted to do to the house but never had the money for after the Real Estate King died." Lisa Livia handed Agnes the clipboard. "It's her dream house book. I know we only have two days, but all we have to do is the outside of the house. She wanted black shutters. And black carriage lights. And pink hydrangeas and white lilacs. It would really fry her to show up on Saturday and see her dream house finished and know you had it and she didn't. And then I stopped by Betsie's Bon Ton and got us our mother-of-the-bride dresses."

"Us?" Agnes said.

"Yeah, you raised Maria with me for the first three years, you're her mother, too. Wait'll you see them. I got one for Evie, too. Betsie was having a sale."

"Them?" Agnes said. "LL, they're not all alike?"

"We'll be cute as buttons," Lisa Livia said. "Hot, too." She opened the bag almost dropping her cell phone in the process. "And they had both a four *and* a twelve!"

"What were the chances?" Agnes said, and Lisa Livia said, "Pretty good, they had them in all sizes."

She pulled the smaller one out and held it up against her. It was a hot pink halter dress with a ruffled sweetheart neckline and peplum bodice, also ruffled, ending in a pencil skirt, the whole thing covered in lighter pink hearts. "What do you think?"

"It's so . . . me," Agnes said, stunned. She was going to look like a flamingo in that thing. A hooker flamingo.

"Well, it should be you," Lisa Livia said. "You can't wear a Cranky Agnes apron to the wedding." She held the dress out so she could see the front, and Agnes got a good look at the back. There wasn't any.

"I don't really have the body for this, LL," Agnes said.

"Are you kidding?" Lisa Livia said. "Your ass will look fabulous in this. I have no control over Evie Keyes, but you're gonna wear this dress. Well, you're gonna wear the twelve."

"How did you know what size to get Evie?"

Lisa Livia shot her a look of contempt. "Like every dress shop in Keyes doesn't know what size Evie Keyes wears. Besides, it was marked down to fourteen ninety-five. I could afford to make a mistake." She held hers out again. "We need hats. And pink fuck-me shoes."

"Oh, yeah," Agnes said. "That's what we need. Give me the house book and call Maria to call Downer."

Lisa Livia shoved the dress back in the bag, handed the book over to Agnes, punched in Maria's number on her speed-dial, waited a moment, and then raised her voice. "Maria? That dipshit Downer sent another flamingo."

Agnes took the book and headed for the house, thinking, *I bet Garth can landscape,* as she tried to ignore the flamingos honking at each other behind her. *Hot flamingos,* she thought. *I got hot flamingos and a $14.95 Whore Mother of the Bride dress from Betsie's Bon Ton. That can't be good. Maybe.* Shane would probably like it. Not that it mattered since that was over with. Only guys who hadn't killed from now on—that was her motto.

There was some progress: She'd broken up with a lying, swindling pig of an adulterer and stopped sleeping with the secretive but adept hitman who put acid in her basement.

"Who says I never learn?" she told Rhett when she was back in the kitchen, and went to take her shower.

Later that evening, after Shane had come back, monosyllabic and surly again, and Agnes had gone through the house book and made notes—Brenda really did have excellent taste—she finished the cake designs; made her To Do List for Thursday; packed up her engagement ring for resale; and fed ribs to Lisa Livia, Carpenter, Garth, Joey, and Shane (which was good, like feeding a large, demented, but sort-of-functional family). Then she and Lisa Livia cleaned the kitchen and socked away the leftovers while the men went down to the basement to bring up the Venus, making a lot more noise than just lifting a statue should have entailed, after which she left Carpenter and Lisa Livia on the screened porch discussing Greek art and automatic weapons with a bottle of bourbon; sent Garth out to the barn after telling him he should ask a girl to the wedding—"Me?" he said; "It's the hottest ticket in town," she told him, "and you've got a backstage pass."—and took bourbon and coffee out to where Shane was sitting on the high dock.

She sat down beside him. "So, how was your day?"

"I've had better." Shane took one of the mugs and the coffeepot from her.

She opened the bourbon and held out her mug, and he poured coffee into it and into his mug, and then she topped off his mug with the bourbon and did the same for hers.

"Listen," she said. "About last night. You and me. I'm not really ready for . . . I mean, this thing with Taylor and all . . . I think I need . . ."

"Okay," he said.

That was easy, she thought, not sure how relieved she should be about that.

They sat back and watched the rest of the sun leave the sky and she could feel some of the tension leave his body in the peace of the evening.

"What did Taylor want?" he said finally.

"He brought the health inspector out to shut down the wedding."

"Did you kill him?"

"No. He wants his engagement ring back, can you believe it?"

"Yeah. No class at all. Want to tell me about the health inspector?"

"Joey's on it. But what exactly did you put in my basement?"

"Acid," he said. "It's to open the bomb shelter down there."

"A bomb shelter wasn't on the inspection checklist when I bought the house. Why do you want to open it?"

She was surprised that Shane actually looked a bit sheepish. "There's a chance Frankie Fortunato's body might be in there. And the five million dollars he stole twenty-five years ago."

"Five million dollars," Agnes nodded. "And you were going to tell me this when?"

"I didn't know until Joey told me yesterday."

"Did it ever occur to anybody to tell *me* that the reason people kept showing up in *my kitchen* with *guns* pointed at *me* was that there was *five million dollars* in *my basement?*"

"We didn't want to worry you," Shane said and told her the story Joey had told him, part of which Lisa Livia had told her years ago anyway, except for the bomb shelter part.

"Lisa Livia is not going to be happy about this," Agnes said, but a part of her mind slid to the fact she could have five million dollars in her basement.

"We'll know tomorrow," Shane said.

Agnes took a deep breath. "All right. So how was your day? You kill anybody?" She stopped, realizing with horror that he might have. "That was supposed to be a joke. You know, like you asked me if I killed Taylor. I don't really want to know—"

"I didn't kill anybody."

"I'm sorry, I'm sorry."

"Agnes—"

"I'm still sort of . . ." She searched for a word that wasn't insulting. ". . . freaked . . . by your . . . job."

"Good," he said.

She jerked her head up. "Good?"

He shrugged. "Some women get turned on by it. Not that I'm against that, but it's not—"

"Turned on?" Agnes looked out over the water. "Huh. Well, it wasn't unappealing when you killed the guy who was trying to kill me. I mean, after I stopped throwing up, I was definitely on your side." *And if you find five million dollars in my basement . . .*

"Agnes—"

"And I'm sure that anybody you've killed had done something to deserve it—"

"Agnes—"

"Like John Cusack in *Grosse Pointe Blank*—"

"Agnes, it's okay."

"Did you ever kill the president of Paraguay with a fork?"

"The fork is your weapon." He took her hand. "If it helps, every target has known exactly why I was there."

Agnes swallowed as his palm touched hers, warm and safe, and then she nodded. "This very special organization you work for. Is it the mob?"

Shane looked at her as if she were nuts. "No. Jesus, Agnes. I work for the U.S. government."

"You what?" She drew her hand away from him, stunned. "The government *kills people?*"

"Yes, Agnes," Shane said. "It sends them to war and it sends them to the electric chair, and sometimes, when it wants to be more efficient and merciful, it sends me. I'm much more precise and efficient than a bomb dropped from ten thousand feet."

"Isn't there due process or something?" Agnes said. "They can't just *kill* people." He looked at her steadily, and she thought, *Of course they can.* "Never mind."

The ensuing silence was filled with flamingo honking. It had been going on all along, but it was easier to tune out now that there were two and the under-note of panicked loneliness was gone. The honking was now a duet of "Can you believe we're stuck with these morons in this godforsaken backwater?" which was much better than Cerise's earlier solo of "My God, I'm alone, I'm alone, I'm alone, I'm alone, I'm alone. . . ."

"I'm glad you work for the government instead of the mob," she said. "I mean, that's a great retirement plan, right? Health benefits?"

Shane put his arm around her.

His arm was nice, a warm weight on her shoulder without really weighing her down. She let it stay there. It was a friendly arm, she decided, not a sexual arm. She wasn't going back on her decision to not have sex with him by not moving away from him now. They were pals. That was it. That was a pal arm.

She looked up at him. "Is it okay if I pretend you're an insurance salesman for a while?"

"Sure," Shane said.

"How was your day, dear?"

"I almost sold a policy, but the client gave me the finger."

"Well, don't give up. You'll get Salesman of the Year yet."

"Yeah, I want that gold watch."

They sat again in companionable silence—theirs, not the flamingos'—until the mosquitoes got too bad, and then Agnes reluctantly moved away from his warmth and stood up. "Time to go in."

She looked back toward the house, where Lisa Livia's bedroom on the second floor was lit up. "It's nice to see the second-floor lights on. Makes the house look happier."

He looked back at the house, too. "That Lisa Livia's room?"

"Yep."

"Why didn't you take a bedroom up there instead of that dark little housekeeper's room?"

Agnes thought about her big, cool, blue bedroom in the attic. "I was making a master suite on the attic floor, for when Taylor moved out here with me. It was going to be a symbol of our commitment, moving into that bedroom together. But he kept putting off coming out here, and I kept getting sidetracked by other things, and I think . . . if I moved up there without him, it meant I knew I was going to be alone, that he wasn't coming out." She smiled at him. "You should take the other bedroom on the second floor. Two of the bedrooms are full of wedding gifts, but the one next to Lisa Livia's is made up for guests."

He shook his head. "Too far away from you. I can sleep on the air mattress across the doorway." He stood up.

Agnes nodded, feeling guilty as all hell. "Okay. Seems awfully uncomfortable."

"I've had a lot worse," Shane said.

He walked her down the dock, stopping with her when she slowed at the path for the barn.

"Could you check on Garth for me?" she said, squinting down the path. "He's all alone out there in the barn, and I feel funny going down there at night. A guy should be checking on him."

"I don't want you alone in the house."

Agnes shook her head. "I'm not alone. Lisa Livia is in there. And you're right here. Somebody would have to be suicidal to try anything now. Besides, bad things come in threes. I've been attacked in there three times already. I'm safe."

"Yeah, that works," Shane said.

"The whole town knows you're here now," she said. "The place is getting to be like Grand Central Station. I'm not alone anymore. I'm safe."

He shook his head, but he let her go up to the house alone as he turned toward the path for the barn, and she felt warmed by his concern.

Okay, she thought as she went up the steps, *he's a killer.* But he killed for the government, so that was . . . well, disturbing.

But the thing was, of all the people she knew, the people she trusted most were Joey, Shane, and Lisa Livia, and she trusted Carpenter, too, and he was Shane's partner. Meanwhile people like chefs and county inspectors were venal and vile and treacherous. So . . .

Confusing.

She went through the screened porch and into the kitchen and screamed, "OH!" when she saw somebody standing by the basement door, realizing a second later that it was the Venus.

"It's okay, she's unarmed," she told Rhett, who'd jerked awake. He growled and she said, "Humor. Har," and bent to pat him, and then a movement in the hall doorway caught her eye and she saw a guy with a gun pointed at her and screamed again. Rhett launched himself toward the man, baying, and knocked her to one side as the guy fired, and then the man cursed as Rhett clamped his teeth on his leg, and Agnes flung herself at him, too, trying to keep him from shooting her dog, and he backhanded her, her glasses flying off as she hit the wall, and he shook Rhett off and turned the gun on her. She braced herself for the shots, but when they came, the guy jerked backward as bullets hit him, slamming him through the doorway as he shot wildly at the ceiling, into the hall, and out of sight, glass shattering and the clock gonging, and Shane walking through the kitchen, firing impassively until there was a click, and even then he kept walking toward the hall, smoothly sliding the empty magazine out of the pistol and slamming another one home.

"You all right?" he said from the doorway to the hall when the noise stopped.

"No," she said, crawling onto her knees and then getting shakily to her feet to follow him into the hall and stand behind him.

The man was splayed out on the checkerboard tile, his chest splattered with blood, his eyes staring up vacantly. There was a lot of blood and glass and splintered black wood from Brenda's grandfather clock, which was dead, too.

"I think you got him," she said, trying for cool and offhand.

"He hit you," Shane said, and his voice sounded strange.

"Well, he won't do that again." Her jaw began to hurt where the guy had slugged her. She put her hand on it. Ice, maybe.

Shane knelt, went through the man's pockets, pulled out a wallet, opened it, and extracted fifteen brand-new one-hundred-dollar bills.

"Did my price go up?" Agnes asked, still trying for cool. "Is that what I'm worth now?"

"No. The price didn't go up. You're worth a lot more than that. This is a food chain."

"What?"

Shane stood, staring down at the man, his face like it was the first time she'd seen him, completely stonelike, but then he relaxed, and when he spoke again, his voice was almost normal. "Somebody put out a hit on you and hired a shooter, who looked at the target—a woman alone in an old house in the middle of nowhere—and figured anybody could do it. So he kept most of the money and hired this guy to do it for two thousand. And this guy hired Macy for five hundred. So when Macy failed last night, he had to do it."

"So the guy who hired this guy is going to be showing up tomorrow? It's going to happen *again*?" She could hear her voice going up at the end, almost a shriek, and she stepped on it, trying to keep calm.

Shane turned to her. "No. I'm taking this out of the house. Tomorrow, I'll find the next person in the food chain, and from him, I'll find out who let the contract, and I will end this."

He looked huge in the hallway and very certain.

Agnes swallowed. "You can do that."

"Yes."

"I'm over any problem I had with your career choice."

"Good," he said. "How's your jaw where he hit you?"

"It hurts."

"Let's put some ice on it."

She looked at the body and the blood thickening on her nice hall tile. "And then we call Carpenter?"

"And then we call Carpenter."

She nodded, desperately thinking of the good things in her life like Carpenter, who was new, and Garth. . . .

"This was the third time."

"What?"

"Garth," she said. "Garth wasn't a bad thing. This was the third bad thing."

He took a deep breath. "Let's get some ice, Agnes."

"Okay," Agnes said, and went to get the ice.

Shane had watched Agnes to see if she'd come unglued again at the shock of the shooting and the blood, but she'd held it together this time, except for that crazy little blip about the third bad thing, and then another moment when she looked at the Venus in the kitchen and said, with real relief, "She didn't get hit." Lisa Livia had come cautiously downstairs to find out what the hell the shooting had been about and had taken the blood in the hall pretty well, but then she was a Fortunato. Carpenter had shown up within fifteen minutes and removed the body from the house within the same amount of time, earning Lisa Livia's admiration and Agnes's gratitude, and his gentleness with them both was a lesson in itself, but when the hall was clean and he was gone and Lisa Livia had returned to her bedroom, Shane stopped Agnes from going back to the housekeeper's room. "No," he said. "Upstairs. It's too damn easy to get you in there."

Agnes went still for a moment and then called to Rhett and headed for the stairs.

The bedroom on the second floor next door to Lisa Livia's was larger than the housekeeper's room, with a door to the back veranda and a good view of the Blood River, a door that also made it more vulnerable to attack from the outside, but anything was better than downstairs. Agnes needed to sleep someplace she'd never been shot at, and Shane figured that ruled out the first floor at Two Rivers completely.

"The bathroom's here," Agnes said, opening a door off the bedroom. "The other door's off the hall, but we can lock it and then it's like a private bath—"

"Right," Shane said, watching her carefully. "Why don't you just relax?"

"Sure," she said.

"You'll be safe in here. I'll make sure of it."

Agnes nodded, but it wasn't a very certain nod. Shane went over and ran his hand up her neck and entwined his fingers in her hair, pulling her to his chest. "It will all work out."

"You sure?" she murmured into his shirt as her arms went around him.

"I promise." The words were out before Shane realized he said them, and once they were out there, he felt the weight of them. He couldn't remember the last time he had promised anyone anything. It had always been a job. Shane took a deep breath and Agnes pulled her head back and looked up at him.

"You all right?"

Shane nodded, afraid to speak. Who knew what would come out of his mouth next?

Agnes pulled away and walked over to the door to the veranda and opened it. Shane followed her outside. The only sound was the lap of water on the beach and the creak of the floating dock bobbing in the water. Even the flamingos were quiet.

"I was always safe here," she said, her voice tight. "I mean, I was alone, but it was Keyes. Everybody knew there was nothing to steal. Everybody knew I was Joey's friend. There was no reason for anybody to hurt me and a lot of reasons for people not to, so I was safe. I was alone but I was . . ."

She stopped, and he knew she was trying not to cry. He shifted his hands, wrapping his arms around her body, pulling her in tight.

"You're not alone," he said, and kissed her on the neck. She shivered, but not from fear, he thought. He hoped. "Come to bed," he whispered into her ear and she nodded and then turned in his arms, and he knew what she was going to say. "I'll sleep out here. You'll be fine inside."

"No," she said. "I won't be fine inside unless you're in there, too. I know it's just for tonight, but please stay with me."

What if it's for more than tonight? he thought, but he wasn't sure about that, either, so he followed her back through the French doors and watched while she undressed, not ripping off her clothes in a rage this time but letting them drop as if she were too tired to do anything but let gravity take them, her round body lush in the moonlight, and he reminded himself that she needed comfort and sleep, not sex, even as he thought about taking her in every way possible as she climbed into the big guest bed by the glass doors. Then she patted the bed beside her, not bothering to cover her breasts as she leaned forward to him, and he stripped and joined her, the weight of his body in the bed tipping her to him so that he caught all her softness against him, trying to remember to be thoughtful and understanding instead of rolling her on her back. But she whispered, "Make me forget tonight for a while," and he moved his hands down her curves, tasted her again as she moved hot beneath him in the quiet dark. He felt needed above all else, and knew it was more than just lust or even fear as he fell into her warmth and wetness, her body's slide against him. And then even that thought faded as he lost himself in his need for her.

And when they'd both shuddered and come, he held her as she

slipped into sleep, quiet next to him, no nightmares, and he watched the clouds in the night sky scuttle by and thought, *This is a better room,* and then he spooned himself against her and fell asleep, too.

thursday

cranky agnes column #92

"Eating for Your Beating Heart"

There are very few recipes that couldn't be improved by the addition of three-quarters of a pound of butter and a cup of heavy cream, but this is cold comfort when you're laid out like a slab of beef in intensive care, listening to the blood pound in your ears as you seriously consider going toward the light. Think before you eat, people: Food should be the life of you, not the death of you.

at eight thirty the next morning, Shane cradled a cup of Agnes's good coffee in Carpenter's van as his partner looked at the mug shot on the computer screen and then at the real mug on the body on the floor of his van lying in the unzipped body bag and said, "He looks better dead."

They were parked away from the house. Carpenter had come back to eat the omelets Agnes had made for them, complimenting her on the food to the point where Shane thought he'd have to add to the body count. Agnes had smiled through all of it in spite of the bruise on her jaw. That was another thing he loved about her: Sex made her cheerful as all hell.

The bruise on her jaw made him want to kill the guy all over again, though. He'd have to settle for making the moron who'd sent the guy sorry he'd ever been born.

He heard another vehicle pull up, and he glanced out the small one-way bulletproof window and saw Joey's pickup. He opened the back door and gestured, and the old man came over and hopped in, pausing when he saw the body wrapped in thick black plastic on the middle of the floor. Shane slammed the door shut.

"Who the fuck is that?" Joey demanded.

"The guy who came to whack Agnes last night," Shane said. "The second one. The first was night before last, some guy named Macy."

"What the fuck?" Joey exploded.

"Good question," Shane said. "What we got here, Joey, is a food chain of hitmen, and I need to know who got the original contract and who let it. And I need to know it fast, before some pro shows up here instead of these amateurs. So you got any idea who would try to have Agnes hit?"

Carpenter was typing on his computer, but Shane knew he was listening to everything.

"Hold on," Joey said. "You're saying someone's trying to whack Agnes?"

"Yes."

"Why?"

"No idea."

"Shit." Joey sat down and passed his hand over his face. "Is she okay? Is she in there *alone*?"

"She's never alone now," Shane said. "Lisa Livia's in there, Garth's in there, Doyle's working on the bridge. Now answer my question."

"Right." Joey nodded. "Jesus. Well, Four Wheels probably ain't too happy about Two Wheels moving on to the afterlife and Three Wheels disappearing."

"I don't see Four Wheels sending Garth and Macy on the same night," Shane said.

"Or somebody might not like you guys trying to open up that shelter and might figure whacking Agnes will stop that."

"Nobody knows we're opening that shelter," Shane said.

Joey stared at him like he was stupid. "Lots of people know about the basement being opened. Stanley Harrison, the health inspector, was down there yesterday. He's been telling everybody about some acid thing you're doing down there. There ain't many secrets here in Keyes."

You're keeping some, Shane thought, but he shook his head. "I still don't see how killing Agnes is going to stop us from opening up that damn shelter."

"Excuse me," Carpenter said. "But as I understand it, if Agnes dies, Taylor inherits the house as part of the partnership agreement because of a survivorship clause."

"What?" Shane said, taken aback. "How the hell did you find that out?"

"Lisa Livia told me last night," Carpenter said. "What I'm saying is, maybe the hit isn't about stopping us from entering, maybe it's about allowing someone else to enter if they think there's five million dollars in that bomb shelter."

"That fuckin' hairball is tryin' to hurt my little Agnes? I'll kill the bum." Joey pulled his gun out. "Let's go whack him."

"No," Shane said, though it was tempting. "We have to stop the immediate threat. Agnes can take care of Taylor with a toothpick, she doesn't need us for that." He turned to Carpenter. "What do you have on the stiff?"

Carpenter read from the screen. "One Vincent Marinelli, aka Vinnie 'Can of Tomatoes' Marinelli."

"Oh, fuck," Joey muttered.

"I thought you didn't know him," Shane said.

"I never met him," Joey corrected. "But I heard of the mutt. Small-time muscle man out of Savannah. Works for the Torrentino brothers sometimes. They're the closest thing to the mob down in the low country since Frankie disappeared. They kick up, when they remember, to the boss in Atlanta, and the boss in Atlanta collects when he remembers those guys exist in Savannah. Small-time stuff."

Carpenter's fingers had been working the keyboard while Joey was talking. "The Torrentino brothers. Your uncle is right. Small time, but somewhat connected."

"So somebody put out a hit on Agnes, and whoever got it subcontracted it to this Marinelli guy, who subcontracted it to Macy," Shane said.

Carpenter looked over from his computer. "The package that I disposed of Monday night in Savannah was also affiliated with the Atlanta mob. I'll print you out the information."

"What the fuck is he talking about?" Joey asked. "What package?"

"Put the gun away, Joey," Shane said absently. A plan. He needed a plan. He turned to his uncle. "You gotta level with me, Joey. It's important. Are you planning to rat out the Don when he comes here? Or whack him?"

"Hell no. Why would I do that?"

Shane rubbed his forehead, trying to forestall the headache that was growing. He was starting to sympathize with Wilson. "There's a rumor someone is planning on ratting out the Don when he comes here for the wedding, and that the Don has hired somebody to hit that person in return. I want to know who that person is. And I want to know if any of that can be connected with these amateurs who are showing up here to hit Agnes."

"How?" Joey asked.

"Are you going to answer any of my questions with anything other than a question?" Shane asked.

Joey sighed. "Rat the Don out about what?" He held up a hand. "Sorry. The Don's been doing bad stuff for decades, and he's never gotten caught."

"There's no statute of limitation on murder," Shane said. "If the Don had Frankie killed and someone here has evidence on that, the Don would want that person silenced."

Joey rubbed his hand across his chin. "Agnes wasn't here then."

"You were," Shane said.

Carpenter leaned forward. "If there's evidence in the vault pointing to the Don, he might be trying to keep us from getting in there."

Shane looked at his uncle. "I was in Savannah to take out a professional painter named Casey Dean that the Don had brought in to take out this rat. A preemptive strike. The job got screwed up, and Casey Dean is still out there."

Joey pointed at the body on the floor. "This mutt ain't a professional and Macy sure wasn't. And a professional wouldn't subcontract. Especially on a job ordered by the Don."

Shane was trying to fit the pieces. *Think like Wilson.* "That means we're dealing with *two* contracts. One from the Don, put out on the rat. The other from somebody put out on Agnes. Plus we got Four Wheels sending the little Wheels out here looking for the necklace and the five million."

"What a fucking mess," Joey muttered.

"No shit," Shane said. "Carpenter, stay here with Joey and watch Agnes. I'm going down to Savannah and talk to the Torrentino brothers and explain to them that either Amateur Night gets canceled or they do. I'll be back in time to see what's in the bomb shelter when the acid burns through the lock."

"Any instructions?" Carpenter said.

"Yeah," Shane said. "Shoot anybody who looks at Agnes funny. And anybody else you don't like. I'm getting tired of this shit."

"Somebody needs a hug," Carpenter said.

"Humor," Shane said. "Har."

Then he left the van and headed for Savannah.

The Dixie Chicks were singing "Goodbye, Earl" on the stereo, Rhett was asleep under the kitchen table, and the Venus was standing unscathed by the basement door as Agnes made her sixth omelet, this one for Lisa Livia, and tried to write her column in her head.

"The hall is really clean," LL said, taking her toast out of the toaster. "I'm sure some luminol would beg to differ, but the man is good."

"Carpenter? Very good." Agnes flipped the omelet closed. *Okay, wedding cake, there must be something original to say about wedding cake.* Maybe if she led with the Romans bashing the bride with it—

"Probably because he's a man of the cloth."

"You know, I find that so hard to believe." Agnes slid the omelet onto a plate.

"I don't see why." Lisa Livia buttered her toast. "He's a Spiritual Humanist. I think he's very spiritual. He's ordained and everything."

"Uh-huh." Agnes thought about saying, *Do you know what the man does for a living?* and then remembered that she was talking to Lisa Livia Fortunato. Of course she knew what he did for a living.

She handed LL her omelet as the phone rang and then answered it.

"Agnes," God intoned.

"Good morning, Reverend Miller."

Lisa Livia stopped with her fork poised above her omelet.

"I've been wondering," Reverend Miller said. "Does Maria intend to have children?"

You putz. "Yes, Maria definitely plans to have children. Palmer wants enough for a foursome at least. Although what business that is of yours, I have no idea. Good-bye." Agnes hung up and said to Lisa Livia, "Don't even start, I know he's an idiot."

"Jesus Christ," Lisa Livia said. "Carpenter's ordained. Let's keep him on as backup for the wedding." She cut into her omelet.

"Yeah, I'm sure Evie Keyes will go for a Spiritual Whatsis performing her son's wedding ceremony." Agnes began to break eggs into her blue bowl for her omelet. "You haven't seen my To Do List, have you? It has my cake order on it, and I don't think I'm going to make it into Savannah today, so I'm going to have to call it in and then rush in tomorrow and pick it up—"

"Why don't we both go later today?" Lisa Livia said. "I need to get some stuff to clean the mildew off the Venus anyway. And we can sell Taylor's ring then, too. Pay for some landscaping if Garth can't steal what we need."

Agnes frowned at her as she began to whisk. "Garth is not stealing anything. We are not contributing to the delinquency of a minor. I've got to go talk to his grandpa to see if he can stay in school. And I've got to get him some better clothes. He went home last night and snuck some out of his trailer, but they're worse than the ones he was wearing."

"Considering the minor in question, I doubt we'd be contributing much." Lisa Livia forked up more omelet. "I think he's fully funded his juvie trust. This omelet is really good."

The phone rang and Agnes answered it and then heard silence.

"Hello?" she said, and then Brenda said, "Agnes. I was just calling to see if Lisa Livia was all right. We had a disagreement and—"

"She's right here," Agnes said, thinking *you treacherous bitch.*

"That's all right, then," Brenda said. "As long as she's safe. Everything okay out there?"

"Yep," Agnes said. "Wedding's on schedule. Everything's fine. Here's LL." She held out the phone to Lisa Livia. "Your mother."

LL rolled her eyes and took the phone. "Hello, Ma. Yes, I'm fine. Agnes gave me my old bedroom back. Just like old times. What? Yes, I know it isn't like old times unless you're here, but Agnes is making me breakfast, so it's damn near. Okay." She frowned at the phone and then handed it back to Agnes. "I have no idea what that was about, but she cut me off and hung up on me when she heard you were making me breakfast. Jealous much?"

"I really don't care." Agnes dropped butter into the omelet pan for her own breakfast and watched it melt. "Listen, Garth is not a juvenile delinquent. He's really smart. I know he's not educated," she said when Lisa Livia looked like she was about to sneer, "but he's a fast learner, he's picked up everything that Doyle has thrown at him so far, and he was amazing with the flamingos. I bet his mama was smart. That whole naming him Garth because of the 'Shameless' song makes her sound like our kind of people, you know? And when it comes to cunning, you can't put anything past a Thibault. I'm thinking Garth could really be something if he gets a chance. And good clothes are a start, give him some pride."

"Oh, God." Lisa Livia sighed. "You're going to save Garth."

"I am not." Agnes poured her eggs into the melted butter. "But it's not exactly saving a kid to make sure he gets to go to high school. Come on, LL. And if he wants to live here in the barn as a caretaker where there's heat and plumbing and a computer for his homework, and his grandfather says it's okay, then I don't see the problem."

"He's a teenaged boy," Lisa Livia said. "Try sex, drugs, and rock and roll."

Agnes shook her head. "Like he wasn't going to get those in the swamp. At least here he'll go to hell with the Internet and hot water."

"Okay," Lisa Livia said. "I'll put Palmer on the clothes. It'll give him something to do. Grooms are useless before a wedding anyway. But you're not fooling me—you just like feeding him. You like having a lot of people milling around that you can cook for. If you could get Cerise and Hot Pink up here, life would be perfect."

Agnes grinned at her, feeling all sunny and warm inside around the dark hollow parts she was trying not to look at. "You know as hellish as this week has been, and even considering I have to wait until last to get my omelet, this has been the happiest I've ever been. I mean people are trying to kill me, but this house is full of the best people and they're all eating my food and watching out for me and . . . I'm happy. Is that crazy?"

"Maybe," Lisa Livia said. "But I'm loving the omelet, so I'm not arguing."

"I like having you here," Agnes said, throwing grated cheese onto her eggs. "I like it that Joey shows up every day and that Carpenter wanders through and that Garth is putting in hydrangeas right now even though he has no receipts."

"And?" Lisa Livia said.

"And what?" Agnes said, keeping her eyes on her eggs.

"Shane," Lisa Livia said. "God, are you transparent."

"Shane." Agnes nodded. "He's a good friend, but that has to be it. I mean, he's a hitman, and I'm giving up violence, and he's never going to be stable, and my next guy is going to be permanent, a nice regular guy, you know? But Shane's a good guy, a good friend." She caught Lisa Livia looking at her with contempt. "What?"

"You're insane, that's what."

"I don't see why that's insane. I think that's a good plan. Dr. Garvin would approve."

"No, you're insane." Lisa Livia cut into her omelet again. "There's nobody I'd go to faster in a crisis, but you are nuts. And not in a cute way. You have been since I met you."

Agnes looked at her, stunned. "I was fourteen when I met you."

Lisa Livia nodded, chewing omelet. "And everybody in that damn boarding school was scared of you. You know what the first thing they told me was? Don't make Agnes mad. *Seniors* told me that."

Agnes looked down at her omelet and began to lift the edges automatically. "They said that? I thought they thought I was an untouchable because my dad and mom never came back."

"They never got that far. Evidently something happened the first week you were there and they saw the red light in your eyes and you became legend. Anyway, by the end of the first week I was there, I knew exactly who you were. My kind of people. And I asked to be your roommate and here we are."

Agnes swallowed. "They were afraid of me?"

"Agnes, it was a good thing," Lisa Livia said. "Because otherwise, they'd have made your life hell because you had no parents and wore cheap clothes. Thank God they thought you were Carrie."

"Oh, God." Agnes turned off the heat under the omelet pan because she'd lost all concentration.

"Look, I'm sorry, I'm not trying to ruin your day—"

"Somebody tried to kill me last night, Lisa Livia," Agnes snapped. "Ancient boarding school news is not likely to ruin my day today."

"—I'm just trying to explain why finding a nice guy is not in the cards for you," Lisa Livia finished. "What the hell are you going to do with a nice guy?"

"*I can be nice,*" Agnes said.

"Why would you want to be?" Lisa Livia said.

Agnes stopped, dumbfounded.

"Agnes, you're furious and fascinating and wonderful. You should probably not stab anybody with a meat fork again, but why be nice when you can be Cranky Agnes?" Lisa Livia pointed her fork at the red glasses logo on Agnes's apron. "You think you're syndicated in a hundred newspapers because you're *nice*? You think you'd be in *any* newspaper if you wrote a column called 'Nice Agnes'?"

"I'm talking about my personal life—"

Lisa Livia slapped her hand on the table. "I'm talkin' about *you.*
Stop pretending you're normal. You're insane. Make that work for
you. That Dr. Garvin shit where you step on yourself all the time,
that's not good. Forking people isn't good, either, but jeez, Agnes, you
talk about finding some normal guy—hell, that's how you ended up
with Taylor, remember? You talked about nice he was, how normal he
was, how easygoing he was. You went out and found the most white-
bread guy in America, and he turned out to be a jackal. *Maybe that's
not a good plan for you, Agnes.*"

"Well, hell, Lisa Livia," Agnes said mildly. "Maybe a hitman isn't
a good plan, either."

Lisa Livia picked up her fork again. "Well, he sure put a smile on
your face this morning."

"That's just sex," Agnes said, and thought, *That's a lie,* and then
Rhett woke up and barked, and Agnes realized somebody was standing
on her back porch looking at her through the screen door. "Hello?"

"I knocked," the woman said, her drawl more of a chirp. "I truly
did, but you all didn't hear. I'm Kristy. From Wesley's Wonderful
Wedding Memories."

Lisa Livia rolled her eyes.

"Come on in, Kristy," Agnes said. "This is Lisa Livia, the mother
of the bride, and I'm Agnes."

Kristy opened the screen door and came in, cute as a bug with her
pixie face, short dark hair, and tight little body strung with cameras
and bags and a lot of other stuff that looked professional but could
have been garbage for all Agnes knew. Rhett looked at her and barked
again, and Agnes shushed him, so he sighed and went back to sleep as
Kristy smiled at Lisa Livia.

"You can't possibly be the mother of the bride," Kristy said to her.
"You must be her sister."

"Right," Lisa Livia said, and kept eating omelet.

"Have you had breakfast?" Agnes said to Kristy, looking at her
cheese omelet with longing, but ready to give it up for hospitality's
sake.

"No, ma'am, but thank you for the offer," Kristy said, and Agnes liked her better.

"Well, feel free to look around," Agnes said. "The wedding is going to be in the gazebo and the reception is in the barn, which you'll find if you follow the flagstone path off to the right of the porch there. Anything you need to know?"

"I'll just wander around taking some trial shots," Kristy said, batting her big blue eyes. "Any of the wedding party present besides Mrs. Fortunato?" She nodded to Lisa Livia.

"Miss. Never married." Lisa Livia picked up her toast.

Kristy nodded again, having evidently given up on bonding.

"Nope," Agnes said. "Unless you count the flamingos."

Kristy nodded, smiled, and escaped through the back door.

"I'm just saying," Lisa Livia said when she was gone, "you have a lot more in common with Shane than with some normal guy. Taylor freaked when you attacked him with a meat fork. Shane took it away from you and made you come your brains out. I think that's significant."

"He kills people," Agnes said.

"Lucky for you," Lisa Livia said.

Agnes picked up her omelet and took it to the table and sat down across from Lisa Livia. "I'm definitely not going to have sex with him again."

Lisa Livia nodded. "I'm definitely going to sleep with Carpenter."

Agnes sighed.

"Agnes, stop fighting your nature. You're a killer. Accept that and you'll be a lot happier."

"I've never killed anybody," Agnes protested, and then stopped, realizing that might have sounded holier than thou, considering the people she was hanging out with.

"And with the grace of God you never will," Lisa Livia said. "The important thing is, we know we can if we have to." She finished her omelet and pushed her plate away. "So what are we doing today?"

"I have to bake the wedding cakes," Agnes said, "and call in that cake supply order to the bakery in Savannah. And write my column. Clean up the Venus with you. And sometime in there, I'd like to go through your mother's boxes and find something that will completely destroy her life so that she'll never again feel the warmth of the sun on her face or know a happy moment."

"There you go," Lisa Livia said, and got up to take her plate to the sink.

"And then I have to make lunch," Agnes said, and began to eat her omelet.

Shane pulled up to the old warehouse on the edge of the swamp on the east side of Savannah. He'd already decided subtlety was not the desired course of action. He just didn't feel like it. He kept his sunglasses on and got out of the Defender into the humid heat just as a stocky man with the rippling muscles of a steroid-injecting weight lifter and the sloping forehead of Cro-Magnon man stepped out of a personnel door set in the larger sliding doors in the front of the steel building. He wore flip-flops, swim trunks, and a black muscle shirt, which showed off not only the aforementioned muscles, but also a dazzling array of tattoos from his wrists to his shoulders.

"Whaddya want?" the man asked.

"You speaking to me?"

"Yeah, I'm speaking to you."

Shane shook his head. "You're supposed to say: 'I don't see nobody else standing there.'"

"What?"

Shane sighed. No one watched the classics anymore. "The Torrentino brothers in?"

The man's head jerked in what Shane assumed was a negative. "No, and you ain't going in there."

"Wrong," Shane said, and hit the weightlifter in the throat with a quick strike of his fist, avoiding all the layers of muscles elsewhere on the body. Weightlifter's hands flew up his neck as he gasped in pain.

Shane snap-kicked into his groin, eliciting a squeal of pain, and the weightlifter went to his knees, curling over, his hands going from neck to balls. Shane did an elbow strike to the back of the man's head and he was out, prostrate on the ground.

Shane checked the unconscious body for weapons and found none, but he did find a money clip, with "Rocko" picked out in rhinestones, holding twenty-eight crisp hundred-dollar bills. He flex-cuffed Rocko's bulky arms behind his back just in case he came to before the business inside was done, and then went inside the warehouse, but the weightlifter had been telling the truth, the place was empty. He did a quick search and found evidence that the Torrentinos had been there, including two La-Z-Boys and a large-screen TV with an impressive collection of porn videos stacked to one side.

The Torrentinos as the masterminds behind the hits began to seem less likely than ever. But Rocko with those hundred-dollar bills . . .

Shane heard cursing and abandoned the warehouse. Rocko was sitting up, moaning, for which Shane was grateful, doubtful he could toss that much unconscious weight into the Defender. It also meant Rocko had a very thick skull, which wasn't surprising.

"On your feet," Shane said, giving Rocko a quick poke in the back with the muzzle of the Glock.

Rocko muttered something, but staggered to his feet. Shane guided him over to the Defender and shoved him into the passenger seat, his hands still awkwardly secured behind him with the plastic flex-cuff. Shane got in the driver's seat. He threw the truck in gear and drove out of the parking lot. Then he remembered something. He dug in his pocket and pulled out Agnes's To Do List.

Shane reached down and turned on the navigation system and punched in the address for the bakery in downtown Savannah. He was glad for the tinted windows as he drove into the city. Rocko was becoming more agitated as consciousness seeped into his brain, so after Shane double-parked in front of the bakery, he whacked him on the head again.

Then he walked into the bakery.

"Can I help you?" the woman behind the counter said.

Shane checked the list. "I need fifteen pounds of fondue and—"

The woman said, "Excuse me?"

"It's for a wedding cake."

"You mean fondant."

"Whatever. And . . ." He handed Agnes's To Do List over to her.

She squinted at it. "Is this the Agnes Crandall order?"

"Yeah."

She handed it back. "She called it in. I thought she was going to pick it up later. Doesn't matter. It's ready."

Ten minutes later, two bags of miscellaneous cake stuff and three five-pound tubs of icing heavier, the Defender was heading north.

He glanced over. Rocko was blinking the blood out of his eyes from the second whack. He had an incredibly thick skull.

"Try not to get blood on that cake stuff."

"Fuck you," Rocko said, shaking the blood off his face and onto one of the tubs of fondant.

Shane sighed. "You set up the Two Rivers hit. Who hired you and who was the target?"

Rocko turned his beady little eyeballs toward him. "Who are you?"

Shane sighed. "My name is Shane."

Rocko spit on him. "Fuck you, Shane."

"Rocko, we can do this hard or we can do this easy. You got paid five thousand for a contract. You subcontracted Vinnie 'Can of Tomatoes' Marinelli two thousand to do the actual job. He subcontracted it to a dumbshit named Macy for five hundred. Both Vinnie and Macy are dead. I killed them. The job isn't done. So whoever paid you isn't gonna be happy. Who paid you?"

"Fuck you."

Shane crossed an old turn-bridge over the Savannah River. He saw a sign for the Savannah National Wildlife Refuge and turned off, drove down a one-lane dirt road, then onto what could barely be called a track until he was pretty sure they were deep into the swamp. Then he stopped the Defender, got out, went around to the passenger side and opened the door, quickly stepping back, Glock at the ready.

"Get out."

"You going to kill me?" Rocko demanded.

"Not if you tell me what I want to know." Shane reached into his pocket and pulled out an airline voucher. "Then you take this to the Savannah Airport, get on a plane, and no one around here ever sees you again. Got it?" He slapped the voucher down on the hood of the Defender.

Rocko's eyes shifted from the voucher to Shane. "Bullshit."

"Who gave you the contract and who was the contract on?"

A very large alligator basking in the sun about fifty feet away was eyeing them, perhaps sizing them up for a snack. Shane squinted. The gator had a scar where one of its eyes should have been. It was a hard life everywhere, even in the swamp. The one-eyed reptile slid into the water with a splash and began to lazily move toward them.

Rocko heard the splash and glanced over his shoulder. "I took an oath. I ain't violating it."

"What are you talking about?"

Rocko frowned. "To make my bones with the mob, I gotta stick with the oath, right? I can't violate the contract. It's like, ya know, that doctor–patient thing. Or when a lawyer talks to a client."

Spare me from idiots, Shane thought. "That's movie bullshit." A mosquito landed on his neck and took a bite. Halfway from its resting spot, the gator had paused, sizing up the situation with one eye. Shane figured it had more brains than Rocko.

Rocko's head moved back and forth on his bull neck. "Can't squeal. Mob oath."

"Mob oath. You telling me Don Fortunato hired you?" Shane asked.

Rocko's eyes widened. "You from the Don?"

"If I was from the Don, would I be asking you if the Don hired you?"

The furrow appeared in Rocko's forehead as he tried to figure that out. "I'd like to work for the Don."

Scratch the Don, Shane thought. He saw the muscles in Rocko's shoulders begin to bulge and he knew what he was doing and he also knew that the plastic flex-cuff probably wasn't going to hold. The tattoos on Rocko's arms were rippling now from the effort. A naked woman on the right bicep was swaying seductively.

"Rocko," Shane said with a deep sigh. "I really don't want to kill you. But I will if you come at me. Think, damn it. There's no mob oath if you're not working for the mob. So you can tell me."

The flex-cuff went with an audible pop and Shane shot Rocko in the left thigh as he started to charge at him. Cursing, the weightlifter grabbed the leg and hopped about.

"I told you not to do that," Shane said.

The gator was moving forward again, smelling blood.

Shane moved toward the truck. "Rocko, we need to get out of here."

"Fuck you," Rocko said, hopping away from the Defender. "I can't believe you fucking shot me."

"I'll shoot you again if you don't tell me who the contract was on. Agnes Crandall?"

Rocko was in too much pain to hide the look of recognition that flickered across his face at the name.

"Okay, got that. Now tell me the guy who hired you and I'll get you back to the truck before the gator gets you," Shane said, and when Rocko looked even more stubborn, he added. "I'm telling you, you dumb fuck, *there is no mob oath.*"

"Hey, she made me take it, right there on the phone. I *took* the mob oath—"

"She?" Shane said.

Rocko glared at him. "Fuck you, I ain't tellin' you nothin' and I ain't breakin' the oath, neither." He turned and began a limping run along the edge of the swamp.

"Damn it, Rocko!" Shane yelled, but it was already over, the gator came out of the water, an explosion of green scales and big teeth, and closed the ground between them in seconds, its jaws snapping shut on Rocko's leg. Rocko screamed, and Shane fired a couple of rounds into the gator, feeling bad for it, but the bullets seemed to have no effect as it rolled with Rocko into the dark water, dragging him into the depths.

The surface of the water boiled for a few seconds, then became still.

Shane waited to see if Rocko would reappear, but after a couple of minutes he knew Rocko was sleeping with the gator.

He got back into the Defender, pulled onto the dirt trail, and accelerated, heading for the refuge exit. *They don't make 'em like Rocko anymore,* Shane thought as he drove back toward Keyes. Darwin had pretty much explained why. He'd have felt bad except that Rocko's next stop would have been heading to Two Rivers to drill Agnes in exchange for five large after having sent two assholes to terrify her two nights running. For that, the dumbfuck deserved the gator.

And now nobody else would be showing up to shoot Agnes.

One more stop at a jeweler Joey knew to cash in Agnes's engagement ring for top dollar and then he could go home and see what was in the bomb shelter. First guess, Frankie's body. Second guess, five million dollars. Third guess, a bunch of bad survival food and a dozen *Playboy* magazines from 1982. The third one was the most likely—

Shane's sat phone rang, the tone designating the cut out number he had used to call Casey Dean. Shane looked at the text message:

SORRY I MISSED YOUR CALL.
ENJOY THE WEDDING.
SEE YOU THERE. CD.

"Humor," Shane said to the phone. "Har."

He punched the jeweler's address into the GPS and wondered what Agnes was making for lunch.

"I know a little more than I did before I left," Shane said as he drank the tall glass of lemonade Carpenter had brought out onto the porch after lunch. "I know the Marinelli/Macy contract was let on Agnes. I don't know who let the contract, except that a woman made the call, and Rocko thought it was mob related. Whatever that means."

"Well, that's a help," Joey muttered.

Shane turned on his uncle. "Don't start with me, Joey. You called me into this mess and you're still holding something back from me. I think the contract is defunct, given that I've taken out the food chain, but I still want to know who hired Rocko in case whoever it is decides to try again. Plus we've still got your old pal Four Wheels out in the swamp sending his descendants in here." He looked at Carpenter, who was leaning back with his lemonade, smiling as he listened to Agnes and Lisa Livia talk in the kitchen. "And then I got this." Shane handed his cell phone to Carpenter, letting him read the text message from Dean.

"Interesting," Carpenter said.

"What's the status of the hatch?" Shane asked him.

"The lock's burned through," Carpenter said. "I rigged a hydraulic jack to pull it open when you got back, so whenever you're ready."

"Who's in there?" Shane asked, nodding toward the house.

"Agnes, Lisa Livia, and some woman named Kristy," Joey answered. "Wedding photographer. A box came full of flamingo pens with pink feathers on their heads, and they're lookin' at 'em." He seemed bemused by that.

"Why—" Shane stopped when he spotted Xavier pull up to the bridge and park just short of it and Doyle come crawling out from underneath the bridge like some kind of troll. "What the hell is Xavier doing here?"

"Damned if I know," Joey said.

Xavier got out of his car and came over the bridge, where Doyle met him, but the detective's focus was on the house as he crossed the lawn, Doyle following, yammering at him.

"Let's just invite the whole damn town." Shane looked at his uncle. "You know, Joey, if we find Frankie in there, and anything at all points to you having killed him, there isn't much I can do to keep Xavier off your ass."

"I ain't worried," Joey said. "I didn't kill him. I just want to know what happened that night."

Xavier came up the porch steps, Doyle stomping up next to him.

"What can we do for you, Detective?" Shane asked.

"I understand there's been some excavation work in the basement," Xavier said. "I even heard a rumor there's some sort of bomb shelter out there in the backyard and a tunnel that leads to it. And I heard that you fellows have opened up that tunnel and are getting ready to open the hatch to that bomb shelter."

"You sure heard a lot," Joey muttered.

"And where is Detective Hammond?" Shane asked, not wanting that doofus wandering around unsupervised.

"Detective Hammond appears to have taken a long lunch break," Xavier said. "I believe at the marina. Missing all the excitement, that boy is. Sort of like when they opened Capone's vault on TV."

"There was nothing in Capone's vault," Shane noted.

"I'm hoping for better results here," Xavier said.

"Some could say you was trespassing," Joey said.

"Some say you might have some trouble if that bomb shelter gets opened," Xavier said.

"Like who?" Joey demanded.

"Oh, there's been a lot of talk." Xavier pulled a piece of paper out of the pocket of his white coat. "For example. This here is Miz Agnes's criminal record. I was quite surprised to note the contents. Turns out she's wielded a frying pan before with violent effect."

Shane looked at Joey and noted that shut the old man up for the moment.

"I also heard your Miz Agnes is pretty handy with a cooking fork to the neck."

Fucking Taylor, Shane thought. There was going to be one fewer chef in the world shortly.

"Somebody swear out a complaint?" Joey said, still cool.

"No," Xavier admitted, and Shane thought, *Not Taylor then, somebody Taylor told.* The detective scowled toward the river. "What the hell is that noise?"

"Flamingos," Joey said. "So all you got is some gossip and some old paper, I don't—"

Agnes came out onto the porch with Lisa Livia and a trim brunette draped in cameras. Opening the shelter was not going to be the clandestine affair Shane had had in mind. He had indeed forgotten what Keyes was like. He looked toward the bridge, expecting to see the local high school marching band come across with cheerleaders and the rest of the town population.

"I brought a flashlight." Xavier cheerfully held up a heavy-duty light.

"I rigged lights," Carpenter said. "You won't need it."

"Can we get this over with?" Lisa Livia said, and Shane could feel the edge coming off her, nothing like her usual voluptuous vibe. He glanced at Agnes and she nodded curtly, but her tension was for LL, standing at her elbow, and he remembered that for Lisa Livia, Frankie wasn't some dead mobster, he was her father, and they might be about to open his tomb.

"You sure you want to—"

"Yes," Lisa Livia snapped, and Shane led the way into the house, past the kitchen table that held a box full of lurid pink pens with feather tops, and down the ladder, holding it in place as everybody else climbed down.

They all waited in the rec room while he and Carpenter went down the fifty-foot tunnel and manned the hydraulic jack. It was a complicated arrangement of cables and blocks of wood that Shane didn't even attempt to figure out. He had enough of a headache trying to figure out who was trying to kill who and why.

"Grab that," Carpenter said.

Shane grabbed the lever indicated.

"Ready?" Carpenter asked.

Shane nodded.

"Let's do it."

In concert, they began to apply pressure. At first there was no obvious result except a tightening of the steel cables. Then an ominous creaking of the wood blocks, the cables ran over. "Don't worry," Carpenter said. "I've done this kind of thing before."

"Opened twenty-five-year-old bomb shelters?"

"I opened a bank vault once that had been shut for sixty years."

"What happened?" Shane said as he leaned into the level.

"Wall cracked a little," Carpenter said, and Shane looked up at the arched ceiling above him.

"How much is a little?"

"I got it open. It'll pop, just like—"

The hatch popped open with a whoosh and a creak of rusty hinges that echoed down the tunnel and through the house.

Voices rose from the other end of the basement, a babble of questions and some contention.

"It's all right," Shane called back.

"No, it isn't," Agnes yelled back to him. "*Brenda's* here."

Brenda's voice floated down the tunnel. "Is the shelter open?"

"No," Shane called back, but she came tapping down the long tunnel in her heels, and the rest of them followed her. He sighed and turned toward the open hatch and stepped over the lower edge.

The first thing he saw was a safe, its door wide open.

Inside the safe was a frying pan, its rim crusted with very old blood.

Inside the frying pan and piled around it in the safe were empty money wrappers. Lots and lots of them. Enough, Shane thought, to go around five million dollars.

"Oh, *my God!*" Brenda said, her voice full of drama.

"That's *not* my frying pan," Agnes said from behind him, and he turned and saw them, crowding the door, Brenda with her head turned away, Xavier and Agnes behind her, and next to Agnes, Lisa Livia looking pale and the thin brunette holding up her camera.

"I told you," Brenda said to Xavier, her voice rich with distress. "I told you. Joey and Four Wheels killed him. I can't bear to look."

"Look at what, Miz Dupres?" Xavier said.

"At . . ." Brenda turned to look into the shelter, at first with dread and then with disbelief. "What . . . *Where's Frankie?*"

"He's not in there," Lisa Livia said, her voice as stunned as Brenda's, and Agnes put her arm around her friend.

Lisa Livia turned and walked back down the tunnel.

"She wanted her dad dead?" Shane asked, and Agnes shook her head, giving him a look that said she'd tell him later.

"Joey came in and moved the body," Brenda was saying to Xavier, grabbing his sleeve. "Him and Four Wheels. They moved it!"

"How?" Xavier asked, but Carpenter had already moved past the safe and was looking up.

"Hmm," Carpenter said, and began to climb up an old metal ladder welded to the side of the shelter.

Shane went to see what his partner had seen and realized that there was a door at the top, and when Carpenter pushed on the door and flipped it open, sunlight poured in, and above that, a ceiling, blue with gold stars.

"That's my gazebo," Agnes said from beside Shane.

Shane turned back to where Xavier was looking at the frying pan.

"Well, someone got whacked a good one," Xavier said, and looked at Agnes.

"That is *not* mine," Agnes said again.

"This is now a crime scene—" Xavier began and then the earth began to shake. "What the hell?"

"Did you order some trucks?" Carpenter said to Agnes from the top of the ladder.

"Trucks?" Agnes said.

"Five of them. Dump trucks. Heading for your bridge."

"*No,*" Agnes said, running for the tunnel.

Shane went to follow her and caught a glimpse of Brenda.

She looked like the news about the trucks was making her feel much better.

Agnes ran through the kitchen, past the Venus and Lisa Livia, who said, "What now?" as if she didn't care, then out through the hall and across the lawn, waving her hands and yelling, "Stop, no, *go back,*" but the dump trucks kept rolling across the bridge; first one, bumping over the fragile supports, onto the drive, across the lawn and down to the riverbank, where Cerise and Hot Pink honked their rage; then another, the bridge groaning before the truck went to the river; then a third, the supports screaming this time before the truck went on; and then, inevitably, the fourth hitting the bridge, the supports splintering with a crash, that truck sinking into the cut, leaving the fifth and last truck marooned on the other side.

"What are you *doing?*" Agnes screamed as she got to the bridge, but the driver was just as furious, waving his paperwork at her, asking what the hell business she had ordering five trucks of sand to cross a substandard bridge. "I'm suing you people," he yelled.

"I didn't order this," Agnes yelled back. "What the hell is it?"

The driver pulled out an invoice. "Eighty cubic yards of pink sand, for a wedding at Two Rivers mansion."

"*Pink sand?*" Agnes said, dumbfounded.

"Who ordered it?" Shane asked, and she jerked back, surprised to find him beside her.

The driver squinted at the invoice. "A Brenda Dupres."

Agnes turned and yelled, "*Brenda,*" but Brenda was already tapping down the steps in her spike heels, looking enraged, a tiny blond D-cup tigress.

"*What did you do to my clock?*" she said, stamping across the grass, pulling her spike heels out of the earth with vicious energy.

"Some shithead showed up last night to kill me," Agnes said to her, "and he shot up your damn clock instead. *Now what the hell is all this pink sand?*"

"Maria wanted a flamingo-themed wedding," Brenda said, reining in her temper as she drew herself up. "I thought pink sand would fit right in with everything else here. I know how nasty the shore can look when the tide is out. But I never *dreamed* it would break the bridge." She looked down to the river, where the first three trucks were dumping their sand on the shore, Kristy dutifully snapping pictures of it all. "One, two, three . . ." She blinked her eyes at the truck stuck in the cut. "Four. There should be another truck—oh, yes, there it is." She waved at the driver on the road to the bridge. "Five."

"There ain't nothing more coming out here, lady," the driver from the wrecked truck said, "except a tow truck."

"Oh," Brenda said, sadly. "Looks like it's the country club for the wedding then." She smiled at Agnes. "Fiddle-dee-dee."

Agnes turned on her. *"No, it is not the country club."*

Anger is not your friend, Agnes.

Neither is Brenda Fortunato, Dr. Garvin.

Brenda smiled. "Agnes. Honey. The baker canceled. The florist canceled." She took a step closer. "The photographer sent an assistant who doesn't have a clue what she's doing. The health inspector won't let you serve dinner. You tried to kill the caterer." She took another step closer. "The house is only half-painted. The bridge is out. Your kitchen is a crime scene. And you owe me for a very expensive antique grandfather clock." She was almost nose to nose with Agnes now. "You simply can't do it, Agnes. You're finished." Her eyes narrowed. *"Give up."*

Agnes felt her breath go, felt the old dizziness take hold as the red washed over her again, and then she heard Lisa Livia in her head again, saying, *Face it, Agnes, you're a killer,* thought of Shane, putting those two bullets in the guy in the laundry room, walking through the kitchen firing at the guy in the hall until his gun was empty, never losing his temper, no expression on his face at all. Another part of her brain knew that Shane had his arm around her waist, ready to haul her off if she went for Brenda's throat, but the part of her brain where the red mist lived was changing course, looking at Brenda now, knowing that professional killers did not get mad.

They just ended things.

"You listen to me," she said to Brenda, her voice like ice. "On Saturday at noon, the cake will be beautiful, the flowers will be magnificent, the photographer who is taking pictures of the sand right now will be taking pictures of the bride, the catering will be amazing and legal, and the bridge will not only be back, it will be so strong that twenty trucks could cross it. And the house will be the house you have always dreamed of having, and, as God is my witness, *will never have* because I will defeat you utterly and completely, I will grind your face in the dust, I will make you nothing before the world, Brenda Dupres, and my kitchen will not be a crime scene because I will have proved that you picked up that goddamned frying pan in that goddamned bomb shelter and whacked your goddamned husband with it twenty-five years ago, and you will spend the rest of your life in an orange jumpsuit in prison where there is no moisturizer and your face will look like old luggage and the only man you'll be able to seduce is a guard named Bubba with no teeth, so go back to your boat and pray, Brenda, get down on your knees and pray to whatever obscene and vicious god that made you that you do not cross me again *because I will destroy you.*"

Brenda had stopped, her mouth open, gaping, and Shane had loosened his hold on her, and a silence had fallen over the landscape in general.

"Agnes Crandall," Brenda said finally, her voice tremulous, "I do declare, you're insane."

"And don't you forget it," Agnes said, and walked back toward her house.

When Agnes was gone, and a shaken Brenda had picked her way across what was left of the bridge supports to her Caddy parked on the far side, Shane found Carpenter. "Stay here. Check out that shelter. See if you can figure out anything about who came and went via that hatch in the gazebo. And keep an eye on Agnes."

"Roger that," Carpenter said, but he didn't sound happy. "Where are you going?"

"The swamp. I stopped Rocko, now I'm going to stop Four Wheels from sending any more kin to upset Agnes." He looked back at the house. "I think she's really upset. She was . . . different."

"What about Casey Dean?" Carpenter looked as close to exasperated as Shane had ever seen him.

"Dean isn't going to make his move until after the wedding," Shane said, ignoring Carpenter's real question, *What about the mission?*

"How do you know that?" Carpenter said. "Because he sent you a text message and you believe it?"

"Because the Don told him not to do anything until then."

Carpenter's face was as impassive as ever, but his eyes said, *Uh-huh.*

"Fine," Shane said. "You observe the situation and develop a theory that will get me a line on Dean, I'll go after him."

"All right," Carpenter said. "I'll work on that. Does that mean you don't want me with you going after Four Wheels?"

Shane nodded toward the house, where one of Thibault clan was spraying paint with abandon as he finished finishing the house at last. "I'm taking Garth. He knows the terrain."

Carpenter looked even more doubtful. "I don't think he's going to be much help if you run into trouble."

"I think I can handle one old man in the swamp, even if he is surrounded by his family."

Carpenter shook his head. "So far we haven't handled much of anything."

Shane bristled. "I'm doing all right."

"You're not focused. You haven't been since your uncle called you in Savannah. Have you tried to figure out the big picture in this mission? Because there's something about this that I don't like—"

"Wilson's given us an op to run," Shane said, ignoring the instincts that were telling him the same thing. "Take out Casey Dean. I know I screwed up—"

"Twice."

"I know I screwed up twice," Shane said, his voice tight, "but I will take out Casey Dean. I'm going after Four Wheels to close out the problems that have been distracting me."

Carpenter glanced over the house. "You think Four Wheels Thibault is your distraction here? If you don't get focused, you're going to end up in a body bag. Casey Dean has also screwed up by not taking us out. There's something wrong with this whole mission, and it's going to come down to whichever side stops making mistakes and does the job right. Soon. Don't forget that."

"I'm not," Shane said, not looking back at the house. "I'm closing out one loose end, finishing the job here. Then we take down Casey Dean and move on."

Assuming we can convince the general population that there's no five mil at Two Rivers, Joey didn't kill Frankie, and I can leave Agnes.

Better not to share that with Carpenter.

He went to get Garth.

Lisa Livia was sitting on the counter stool, her feet on Rhett and her forehead on the counter, when Agnes got back to the kitchen.

"I was so sure she'd killed him," she said into the counter as Agnes went around her to get the bourbon bottle out. "I was *positive.* I'd seen her driving the damn Caddy away that night. I *knew* she'd done it. *That's her damn frying pan down there.*"

"Well, don't give up." Agnes grabbed a glass and poured Lisa Livia two fingers of bourbon and slid it across to her. "You haven't thought this through. Just because the body wasn't there today doesn't mean it wasn't there last week."

"You think she could have gotten a twenty-five-year-dead body up that ladder and out through the gazebo?" Lisa Livia said, skepticism thick in her voice.

"I think she's capable of chopping a twenty-five-year-dead body into paperweights, carting them out in a basket, and selling them to the Daughters of the Confederacy as memento mori." Agnes poured herself a glass. "We're talking Brenda here. Do not give up hope. It is still entirely possible that your mother bashed your father with that frying pan twenty-five years ago, and that he's still deader than a doornail today."

Lisa Livia's lips quirked as she straightened and picked up her glass. "Yeah. No point in hoping that my mother's innocent and my father's alive."

"Exactly." Agnes lifted her glass. "Why look for a silver lining when there might be a cloud? If South Carolina has the death penalty, there could be an orphanage in your future yet." She clinked her glass with LL's and drank, and Lisa Livia laughed shortly and drank, too.

"Okay," she said when she'd drained her glass. "There's still hope."

Agnes looked at LL's empty glass. "I don't suppose you'd want to pace yourself."

"I don't suppose," Lisa Livia said, putting her glass on the counter. "Hit me, I'm having a bad day." She looked over at the Venus. "Hit her, too."

"She has enough problems." Agnes looked for something to distract LL from more bourbon, went over to the CD player, and punched up the song she'd been playing that morning before breakfast. "Remember this song? You had this on when you bailed me out after I cracked Rich with the frying pan. You made me sing it with you in the car on the way home, remember?"

Lisa Livia bit her lip and looked away.

"There is no good reason," Agnes sang as she leaned over the counter to LL, "*we* should be so *all alone*."

LL took Agnes's bottle of bourbon and poured herself another glass and then joined in, and they belted out the Chicks paean to self-pity. "God, I love the Chicks," Agnes said when the song was done and she'd moved the bourbon out of LL's reach. "And God do I need them this week."

"They've gotten us through some real bad times," Lisa Livia said, pushing her empty glass across the counter as "Hello Mr. Heartache" began. "Hit me. Again."

"If you could slow down a little," Agnes said, "I could use some help destroying your mother."

"Right, the house." Lisa Livia nodded. "How's that goin'?"

"I've decided to take your advice and embrace the killer within, and I'm trying to be a colder, more effective murderous bitch. No emotion. Run silent, run deep. The female Shane."

"Oh," Lisa Livia said. "Well. Glad I could help."

They looked at each other and Agnes poured them each another drink while they tried to work out a plan. All of Lisa Livia's ended up with "and sink her damn boat," so Agnes eventually called a halt to both the planning and the liquid refreshment.

"I can't get drunk," she said as she sipped her last one, knowing she was well on her way. "I have to write a column and make wedding cakes and write a column today. And you have to prepare to be a mother of a bride. All of this mess is making us forget the wedding. Our little Maria is getting married to a rich kid who loves her. To Maria!" She lifted her glass to Lisa Livia.

"I can get drunk," Lisa Livia said, and then added, "To Maria!" and knocked the rest of her drink back.

"Okay, then." Agnes put her drink aside and got out her mixing bowl, trying to keep her mind from sliding back to the chaos of real life, because she was going to stay cool and calm. She thought of Shane, walking through the kitchen the night before, firing that gun with no expression on his face. Yeah, that was gonna be her from now on.

"Speaking of Maria . . ." Lisa Livia slid her now-empty glass across the counter and picked up Agnes's full one. "Are you ready for this? Brenda's been sabotaging Palmer, too. Remember I told you she's been telling Maria that Palmer is just like his daddy, the drunken whoremonger?"

"Right." Agnes went to the refrigerator for butter, sour cream, milk, and eggs.

"Well, she's been telling Palmer that Maria's marrying him for his money."

Agnes stopped and turned around, her arms full. "And he believes this garbage?"

"She's subtle. She just tells him how excited Maria is about living in a big house and having great cars and lots of clothes and big diamonds. He asked me about it, trying to be discreet, poor dork, and I told him Maria doesn't give a rat's ass about any of that, but Brenda's been working on him for a while. He really believes it, and it's giving him cold feet. And having that moron Hammond hanging around isn't making him feel any better."

"Crap," Agnes said, transferring ingredients to the counter. "Okay, so I'll fix that, and then we'll have the wedding, and Brenda will lose the house and die screaming, 'I'm melting, I'm melting.'" It sounded like a plan to her, but Lisa Livia looked skeptical.

"I don't think my mother's going to be that easy to defeat. Not without holy water and a stake."

"Reverend Miller will call again tomorrow morning to ask if Maria's ever been a whore," Agnes said. "I'll ask him to bring some holy water to the wedding to sprinkle on Brenda. He's met her. He'll understand."

Agnes went to the sink to fill her measuring cup with water, glanced out the window at the sun sparkling on the water, and froze.

There was an old paint-peeling yacht easing up to the shore, bobbing up and down in concert with the floating dock, taunting her. It banged clumsily against the rubber bumpers and then the engine cut, and Brenda climbed over the side onto the dock to secure the mooring lines.

"*Fucking bitch,*" Agnes said, and dropped her measuring cup.

"What now?"

"*Your mother has her goddamned yacht moored off my dock!*"

"What?" Lisa Livia came around the counter to look out the window. "I'll be damned." She shook her head in reluctant admiration. "She's getting ready to move back."

"*Bitch,*" Agnes said again, staring at the boat. "We're *sinking* that damn thing."

"Now?" Lisa Livia said, sounding sedated but ready.

"No, I have to make cake now." Agnes went into the pantry and then began taking ingredients off the shelves—cake flour, sugar, baking powder, coconut, plus the supplies that Shane had brought back from Savannah—and then brought them out and dumped them all on the counter.

Lisa Livia caught one of the tubs of icing as it almost rolled off.

"Ick," she said. "What's on this? It's sort of sticky." She looked closer. "This is blood."

"Well, Shane picked it up for me." Agnes got a paper towel and wiped off the tub.

"Thoughtful of him." Lisa Livia went to wash her hands several times and then poured herself another shot of bourbon. "So, you serious about him?"

"No," Agnes said. "I'm not even going to sleep with him anymore."

"Right." Lisa Livia tossed back her drink, tried to sit down on the stool, and fell on the floor.

"So how we doin' here?" Agnes went around the counter and helped her up.

"My mother is a liar and a cheat and a murderer," Lisa Livia said when she was back on the stool. "And she's had her face lifted. Twice."

"Well, now I've lost all respect for her," Agnes said.

Lisa Livia regarded her seriously. "You really have changed."

"I've matured," Agnes said, looking out the kitchen window at Brenda's yacht. *I have a lot on my plate right now and I'm holding on by my fingernails. But as soon as I get a grip here, which is going to be shortly, I swear, Brenda and her boat are going down.*

That's a felony, Agnes. You'll need a really good plan.

Dr. Garvin?

"Agnes?"

"We're going to be all right, LL," Agnes said, and took the glass away from her.

"This ain't such a good idea," Garth said, peering around the Defender at the swamp.

Another critic, Shane thought as he opened the back of the truck. "I just want to talk to your grandfather."

"He ain't the talking type."

Shane looked down the thin trail, too narrow to drive down, squinting to see where it disappeared into the gloomy green. Slightly higher forested ground competed with lower areas covered with black water full of reeds, trees struggling to stay alive, and who knew what kind of nefarious wildlife. Besides the Thibault clan.

He opened the locker in the back of the truck and lifted out a plastic case. Flipping it open, he pulled out a gun that resembled a submachine gun, except it had a large plastic hopper on the top.

"You going to use a paintball gun?" Garth asked in disbelief as Shane screwed a CO_2 canister on below the barrel and poured small round balls into the hopper. "My cousins ain't gonna think that's funny. They use *real* guns."

Shane cocked the weapon. "This isn't loaded with paintballs." He picked up one of the small round balls and held it out for Garth to see. "These are pepper balls. They hold hot pepper and break on impact. Stings to get hit by the projectile in the first place; then the hot pepper is an irritant that causes coughing and a burning on the skin in the eyes and mouth. Pretty much incapacitates anyone it hits. You don't want me killing all your relatives, do you?"

Garth seemed to take the question seriously for a few moments. "Nah." He was still looking at the gun. "You got one for me?"

Shane surveyed Garth. He appeared lost in the coveralls Carpenter had given him, the cuffs rolled up around his ankles, his bony arms sticking out. Reluctantly, Shane pulled out a paintball pistol and loaded it. "You've got ten rounds," he told Garth as he handed it to him. "So don't waste your shots. And use it only if someone's threatening you. And don't shoot unless I do."

"I've shot a gun before," Garth said indignantly as he brought the gun up and aimed into the swamp. *"Pow, pow, pow."*

"Let's go." Shane moved forward toward the trail. He had the stock of the gun tight against his shoulder, scanning, the muzzle following his eyes, finger on the trigger.

"I've got to tell you something," Garth said in a harsh whisper.

"What's that?" Shane was sliding his left foot forward when he sensed something. He looked down and noted a thin piece of fishing wire across the trail. "There are booby traps," Shane said without looking over his shoulder. "That what you wanted to tell me?"

"Yeah."

"And you were waiting to tell me because?" Shane didn't expect an answer. He knelt and traced the fishing line with his eyes. On the right side it disappeared into a bush at the base of a tree. "What's it hooked to?"

"Branch with spikes, most likely."

"No alarm? Can tied to a string, that sort of thing?" Shane looked up and saw that someone had pulled back a branch, tying it off with more line. Several sharp sticks were tied off to the branch. Cheap, rudimentary, but it would hurt like hell if it hit you.

"Nah. Grandpa don't kill people, he just don't want no strangers sneaking up on him without them getting hurt. He figures the screams when they get stuck'd be enough warning. Jimmie, he got stuck once, and boy did he scream. I told you this weren't no good idea."

"Step back." Shane triggered the line with the tip of gun. The branch whooshed across the trail just in front of him and then came to a halt. "Any more traps you know about ahead?"

"My cousin Fred sets 'em," Garth said. "He ain't much good for much else, but he's a good trapper. Caught a gator once."

"I take that as, you don't know whether there are more and where they are."

"That's what I said. Fred knows. But Fred don't like me none. Once he—"

"Silence." Shane moved forward, eyes moving, body light as he walked on the balls of his feet. He was sliding his feet along, not lifting them, alert for the slightest abnormality.

He safely sprang two more traps in the next quarter mile as they went farther into what Shane wouldn't exactly call the heart of darkness—more like the bowels.

"There's Fred's place," Garth said after Shane had disarmed the third one.

A battered trailer sat forlornly underneath a large oak tree. There was no sign of life.

"Fred usually sleeps during the day," Garth said. "The rest of the family is spread out from here to Grandpa's place. There shouldn't be no more traps."

"All right," Shane said. "You lead the way to your grandpa's place."

Garth held the paintball pistol out in front of him, dramatically sweeping it back and forth in front of him, half the time the gun pointing one way while his eyes were looking another. *Too many cop movies,* Shane thought. More broken and battered trailers appeared, spread out in the thick green vegetation like alien pods. A poor alien race that loved cheap beer and booze, based on the number of empty cans and bottles scattered about.

Shane caught movement out of the corner of his right eye and smoothly turned. A skinny young man with a shotgun in his hands was bringing the weapon up to his shoulder when Shane pulled the trigger, firing a burst of five, the projectiles hitting the guy in the chest and exploding in puffs of hot pepper.

The youngster cursed, dropping the shotgun as his hands went to his chest, where he'd have ugly welts developing soon. Of more immediate concern was the gas that clung to him. He doubled over and began hacking and coughing.

"Let's go," Shane ordered, shoving Garth forward.

"That's Jimmie," Garth said. "He ain't gonna be happy."

"*I'm* not happy," Shane muttered. "Worry about me."

Someone stepped out of a trailer to their right, and Shane fired another quick burst, hitting the man, causing him to disappear back inside as fast as he'd appeared.

A half-burned trailer was on their left, and Garth skidded to a halt as he saw a scrawny, middle-aged woman appear like a wraith in the burned-out portion. "Mary-Louise!" Garth hissed. "What're you doing in my house?"

The woman blinked, rubbed bleary eyes, saw Garth and Shane, and then screamed at the top of her lungs. Shane cursed, then fired, hitting her in the stomach with three rounds. The screaming was abruptly cut off and she staggered backward into the darkness of the intact part of the trailer.

"Leave for just a couple days and they grab your home," Garth was saying. "No respect."

Shane could see why Garth wanted to stay at Two Rivers. He had no time to reflect on this as he saw four people moving toward them among the foliage, weapons in hand. Shane fired, squeezing off three rounds bursts, ignoring a bullet from one of the shooters that cracked by. He hit all four, incapacitating them as Garth blindly blasted away with the pistol, one of the pepper balls exploding on a tree less than five feet in front of him.

Shane heard a car engine start to his right front. Ignoring Garth, who was still pulling the trigger of the empty paintball gun and coughing from the near round hit, Shane ran forward around a trailer and hurtled over one of the gasping shooters.

A battered replica of the General Lee was pulling away from a double-wide trailer. Shane was about to drop the paintball gun in exchange for his Glock when he caught movement to his left and the sound of a shot being fired in that direction. He turned, firing, and then released the trigger when his uncle Joey cursed as a pepper ball hit him in the chest and exploded.

"Damn it!" Joey swatted at the mess on his T-shirt and then began coughing.

The General Lee disappeared in a cloud of dust and dirt.

"What the hell are you doing here?" Shane demanded.

"Same thing you," Joey coughed. "Trying to get Four Wheels. And you just fucked it all up." He hacked and then spit. "Fucking Brenda told Xavier that Four Wheels and I whacked Frankie."

Nothing has gone right since I hit Keyes, Shane thought. He amended that thought—there was Agnes. He shook his head. Mind on mission.

"Dumb shit is probably heading for Agnes now that we got him riled up," Joey said.

Fuck. "Let's go." He grabbed Joey, who was reaching up to rub his eyes. "Don't do that." He looked around to see a blinded Garth walk into a tree and almost knock himself out.

"Great." Shane grabbed Garth with the other hand. "My team." A Spiritual Humanist cleaner, an old mobster, an addled swamp rat, and an angry food columnist.

"We'll get 'em next time," Garth said between coughs.

"Wasn't all your fault," Joey said, trying to get his shirttail up to his eyes.

Go team, Shane thought, and pointed them in the direction of the Defender.

The tow truck had arrived and pulled the wrecked sand truck out of the crumpled bridge, and as a bonus had taken Brenda away, too; she'd hitched a ride to get her Caddy from town now that she'd moored the *Brenda Belle* at Two Rivers. Kristy had toured the grounds to "like, take some background shots and get the hang of the place," and then she'd come back in time to help Agnes get LL's bourbon-sedated body upstairs into bed to sleep it off, abetted by a curious Rhett, who had followed them up the stairs to see what they were going to do with her. *He's seen way too many bodies moved lately,* Agnes thought, and then her cell phone rang and she answered it.

"Hey." Joey said hoarsely. "Somebody might be coming to the house who might be dangerous."

"Really?" Agnes said. "Because that almost never happens here. With advance notice. Should I get my frying pan?"

"No joking, Agnes, it's Four Wheels."

"This would be Grandpa, right? The guy who drove for your robbery and then went out to the swamp to breed the rest of the Wheels?"

"That's him."

"Great." Agnes crossed the second-floor hall from Lisa Livia's room into one of the front bedrooms, now full of Maria's wedding gifts and the dress form with Maria's newly arrived white wedding dress, and looked down the lane. Nothing. Rhett peered out the window, too, unperturbed. "It looks peaceful out there now. Should I call the police?"

"Shane says Carpenter can handle it, and we're on our way."

A bolt of red came shooting down the lane in a cloud of dust, swerving to make the turn, and Rhett barked.

"Whoops."

"What?" Joey called out from the phone.

"Spoke too soon. I think Four Wheels is here," Agnes said as the car spun out, a decrepit, rusted-out, engine-misfiring red rattletrap, the Stars and Bars painted on the hood.

"Stay inside and lock the doors," Joey ordered. "Let Carpenter handle him."

"Carpenter's in the basement, and Doyle's out there all alone."

Doyle walked out onto the front lawn, holding his paint sprayer on his hip like a six-shooter.

The driver's door flew open as the car rocked to a halt in front of the ruined bridge, and an old man spilled out onto the gravel, face-first, struggling to get to his feet, a bottle rolling away from him.

"This might not be the trouble you're afraid it is," Agnes said into the phone. "He's drunk. Standing up seems to be beyond him at the moment."

"Is he armed?" Joey asked.

"I don't see a gun."

Doyle shouted something and stomped across the lawn toward the bridge, waving the paint sprayer.

"Oh, hell," Agnes said. "Doyle's going after him. Hurry up, Joey." She turned off the cell phone, told Kristy to stay inside with LL and keep Rhett with her, and ran down the stairs to save her handyman, yelling for Carpenter as she went.

"I ain't tellin' you again," Doyle was yelling as she came out the front door. "Get off me lass's land or I'll pummel you."

The old man had managed to pull himself up to one knee. He was bleary eyed and blinking, trying to focus.

Another car turned down the lane: Brenda Dupres coming back to Two Rivers in her baby blue Caddy.

"Fabulous," Agnes said, and then yelled, "Doyle, get back here!" as the handyman walked across the remaining support beam of the bridge.

"Where the hell is—" Four Wheels bellowed. "Where the— Where is—" He kept stalling out, his brain refusing to get in gear. Agnes saw him look up into Doyle's face and blink. "Who?"

Doyle grabbed the old man's overalls in one meaty fist and hauled him upright, pointing the sprayer at him. "Where's what, boyo?"

Four Wheels seemed to gain some degree of sobriety as he lost the flow of oxygen to his brain, and he grabbed a shotgun from inside the door and swung it into Doyle's groin. The Irishman grunted and dropped the old crook and the sprayer, and Four Wheels shoved him hard, toppling him past the smashed bridge and into the inlet. Agnes yelled, *"Doyle,"* and ran for the cut just as Brenda turned her big car in a wide loop and pointed it at them.

Four Wheels spun about, shotgun in hand, screaming, "Who the fuck is Agnes?"

Agnes reached the muddy inlet and looked down to see Doyle trying to climb up the side, still gasping from the blow to the groin.

"Stay there, Doyle," Agnes said. "He's got a gun."

Four Wheels shifted the large double muzzle so it was pointing down at Doyle. "Try it, you dumb mick. I'll blow your ugly mug right off."

Doyle stopped, breathing hard, his nostrils flaring in anger, but he smartly took several steps back down into the cut. Agnes saw Brenda's car creep a little closer and then stop again, about forty feet away, Brenda invisible behind her tinted glass, probably praying that Four Wheels would pick off Agnes.

Oh, hell, Agnes thought, realizing for the first time that this could be her plan. She might even have sent the old drunk to Two Rivers, and if she had, she was going *to be sorry,* the dumb bitch—

Oh, shut up and be smart, Agnes. You've wasted enough time swaggering around stupid.

Dr. Garvin?

Four Wheels straightened and looked at her and then slowly brought the shotgun up and pointed it at her.

Calm and smart, Agnes. Think.

"Hi," Agnes said to Four Wheels. "I'm Lisa Livia Fortunato."

The sound of wheels on the dirt road made them both look around, and she saw Shane's truck coming down the lane. She heard footfalls behind her and looked over her shoulder and saw Carpenter running across the lawn toward her.

Okay, better odds.

The relief was gone as the shotgun swung back toward her. "You ain't Lisa Livia. You're that Agnes. I seen your picture in the paper."

"Uh . . ."

"You killed my grandson."

"*No,* I didn't. He fell." Agnes took a step closer. "It was an accident, I swear. I'm really sorry for your loss." Out of the corner of her eye, she saw Doyle start to climb up the bank toward Four Wheels.

"Bullshit." Four Wheels twisted his head as he heard Shane's truck stop.

Shane opened the driver's door and got out, gun pointed at Four Wheels. Joey got out of the passenger side, gun pointed at Four Wheels. Carpenter was at Agnes's side, gun pointed at Four Wheels.

Agnes looked at Four Wheels and wondered if he was in any condition to gauge odds.

Carpenter put his hand on her shoulder and pulled her back.

"What the hell are you doing here, Joey?" Four Wheels called out.

"You leave my little Agnes alone," Joey yelled. He was moving to Four Wheels's right while Shane was moving to the left and toward them. And Doyle was taking another shuffling step up the embankment.

Four Wheels staggered slightly, the muzzle of the shotgun wavering. He got a tighter grip on his cane as his head swiveled, back and forth, trying to keep track of everyone. "Everyone just fucking stay still!"

"Ain't gonna happen," Joey said. "You got two shots, and I bet it's just buckshot anyway. Then you're done."

"And you'll never get the first one off." Shane had his pistol up at eye level, aimed right at Four Wheels. The muzzle of his gun wasn't wavering at all.

The old man was perspiring now, booze and sweat, his eyes wide. "I just want some answers. Where's Three Wheels? What'd you do with him?"

"He's fine," Shane said, still heading her way. "Put the shotgun down and tell us why you sent him here with a gun."

"I don't have to tell you anything. Where's my boy?" the old man yelled, and Agnes thought, *Wait a minute, he's got a right to know that.*

"It's all right," she said, and took a step forward.

"Agnes," Carpenter said, but she pushed his hand back and said, "Stay there, you're scaring him," and walked carefully across the remaining bridge support to Four Wheels.

"I swear Garth's all right, Mr. Four Wheels," she said when she was next to him, standing beside the shotgun instead of in front of it. "I think he's probably in the truck. He's helping Doyle paint the house and do odd jobs for me. He can leave whenever he wants to." She leaned a little closer, in spite of the alcohol fumes, seeing Shane moving closer out of the corner of her eye. "I think he likes the food."

The old man's eyes were bleary. "Food?"

She turned in the direction of the Defender. "Garth? You in there?"

Garth's head came up slowly from the backseat, and he waved cautiously.

"Your grandpa's worried about you," Agnes called. "You want to come tell him you're all right?" *But don't tell him about the food because I don't want him to stay.*

Garth nodded and opened the door of the truck, and Four Wheels began to put the shotgun down.

And Brenda gunned the Caddy and drove straight for them.

Agnes froze, but Shane yanked her toward the bridge, where they both fell into the cut, landing hard in the mud, Shane cushioning the fall for her as the Caddy hit Four Wheels square on, the old man screaming as the car smashed into the inlet, crushing him into the mud on the other side of the bridge.

"Don't look," Shane said, pulling her head to his chest, but Agnes said, *"Doyle,"* and she heard the handyman say from under the bridge, *"Fucking bitch!"* which sounded about damn right. Shane held her tight while she shook, and she said, *"She killed that old man,* Brenda *killed that old man, why* did she do that?" and he said, "She wasn't aiming for him, Agnes," and held her tighter while the truth sank in.

Then Brenda opened the door of her wrecked Caddy that was nose down in the cut, hanging suspended in the seat by her safety belt, and Agnes turned in time to see her say, "My God, that man almost killed our Agnes!" her blue eyes wide with innocence.

Doyle picked himself up out of the mud under the bridge and looked at Brenda with so much loathing that it was a miracle she didn't melt from the corrosion. "Burn in hell, you miserable hag of witch," he said, and began to climb out of the cut.

Agnes met Brenda's eyes and saw them narrow.

"She tried to kill me?" she said to Shane, her voice a whisper. "With her *car?*"

"Can you make it out?" Carpenter said from above them, and Shane nodded and sat up, bringing Agnes with him.

Agnes stood up slowly, holding on to Shane as he stood, too. "She tried to kill me with her *car?*"

"Climb out of the ditch, babe," Shane said, his voice telegraphing *steady, steady.*

"She killed that old man!" Agnes looked up the embankment, and saw Garth standing beside Carpenter, looking sheet white. "Oh, God, Garth, did you see—"

"Weren't no call to do that," Garth said soberly. "He was puttin' the gun down."

"I *know*," Agnes said, and held out her hand to him.

Garth took it and pulled her up the embankment. "Is she goin' to jail?"

"If she doesn't," Agnes said, looking soberly into his eyes, "we'll make her pay. I swear to you, we will."

Garth nodded. "All right, then."

"Shane?" Brenda called. "Could you give me a hand, please?"

"No," Shane said without looking at her, and followed Agnes up the embankment. He put his hand on Garth's shoulder. "I'm sorry."

Garth nodded. "Miss Agnes is gonna make her pay if the law don't."

"I beg your pardon!" Brenda said from her car. *"But I am injured."*

"Shut your ugly mouth, you bitch-faced yap, you tried to kill our Agnes," Doyle yelled at her as he reached the top of the bank.

"We'll all make her pay," Shane said to Garth.

"The team," Garth said. "Like you said in the swamp."

Agnes looked at Shane, who winced and then said, "Yeah. The team."

"You are neglecting a wounded woman," Brenda shrieked from her car, practically strangling herself on her seat belt. *"God knows, there's not one gentleman among you!"*

"Call on the devil to save you, you limb of Satan," Doyle yelled down at her. *"God couldn't see you if he tried, you black-hearted whore."*

"The team thing works for me," Agnes said, holding her bruised ribs, and went to call the cops while Doyle stomped back to his house painting, Carpenter took Garth aside to talk to him soberly and give comfort, Shane took a shaken Joey to get the weapons out of sight, Brenda continued to shriek from the cut, and Four Wheels moldered beneath her ruined Caddy.

Shane leaned against the front rail of the Two Rivers porch, watching a couple of deputies try to make a crime scene of the remains of the old bridge under Hammond's direction. Hammond did pretty well, once he stopped asking if Maria was around. An ambulance was parked nearby where an EMT had just finished wrapping Agnes's ribs and was now trying to check out old Doyle, who was resisting removing his shirt with all the vigor of a maiden aunt, while Xavier focused on Agnes, which made Shane tense.

"Go arrest Brenda," Agnes told Xavier. "She just murdered that old man."

"I talked to her," Xavier said. "Now I'm talking to you." His eyes slid around to look at Shane, and Shane stared back, biting back the urge to drag him away from Agnes. Any fool could see that Agnes wasn't the one the law should be talking to, and Xavier was no fool. And yet . . .

He looked over at Brenda, who seemed unconcerned that she'd just killed a man. She was sitting on the swing twenty feet away, drinking deeply from something a lot stronger than lemonade, her shapely legs kicking back and forth, and smiling tensely at a clueless young deputy whom Shane had a feeling Xavier was going to smack upside his crew cut head as soon as he got him out of sight.

"Mrs. Dupres says Thibault was threatening you with a shotgun, Miz Agnes," Xavier went on. "She seems to think you were in imminent danger."

Shane spoke up at that. "We had it under control."

Xavier looked up at Shane. "You did now, son?"

"There was no need for Mrs. Dupres to kill the old man," Shane said.

"She says it was an accident," Xavier said.

"What?" Agnes almost fell off the porch.

Xavier continued. "She was so horrified because that old man was going to shoot you that her foot slipped off the brake, and when she went to stomp the brake back on to keep the car from rolling into you, she hit the gas instead."

"Fuckin' bitch," Joey said.

"She lies," Agnes said.

"She wouldn't be the first person on this porch to do that," Xavier said, looking at her with intent.

Shane moved closer. "You throw a lot of accusations around, Detective. You accused my uncle of killing his best friend. Now you're going after Agnes. I think it's time to drop the good ole boy bullshit and do some real police work."

Xavier stiffened as if he'd been punched. "You think you know how to do my job?"

Shane could see Carpenter looking at him, eyebrows raised in question. Yeah, Wilson wouldn't be happy about him getting involved with the local law. But it was Agnes and Joey on the line here—

There was a stir at the end of the porch as Brenda stood up, taking in everyone on the porch. "Can I go now?" she asked. "I have had a terrible day, a terrible accident, trapped in my car for hours, left unaided by callous, uncaring—"

"*Go to hell, you fucking bitch,*" Doyle called from around the corner, where he was painting the house.

"—inhuman people, and I really am simply unable to continue."

"Yes, Mrs. Dupres, you can go, but don't leave town," Xavier warned her.

Brenda blinked at him. "How could I, Detective Xavier? My little Maria is getting married Saturday. Although how the wedding can take place here, after this gruesome accident, I simply do not know."

She met Agnes's eyes for a long moment, and then she added, "Of course, with the bridge out, it's impossible to have the wedding here anyway." Then she went down the steps and around the side of the house away from Doyle, heading for the path to the dock.

"Where's she going?" Xavier said.

"She's docked her boat out back," Agnes said with blood in her voice.

The honking in the background got louder.

"Flamingos?" Xavier said to Agnes.

"Yes. They hate her, too."

Xavier turned to go. "The boys will be here awhile, getting things in order, but I think I have everything I need to do some *real* police work."

Agnes looked at him steadily. "You're not going to arrest Brenda, are you?"

"Do you have proof she did it on purpose?"

"No," Agnes said.

"Neither do I, Miss Agnes," Xavier said, putting on his hat. "Neither do I. I will be forwarding my notes from the investigation to the DA, however. He should be interested."

He tipped his hat to her and then walked toward the porch steps and stopped when he was opposite Shane.

"You think you know how to do my job, son? You think you know the politics involved when you have to *follow the law* to get your results? When you have to care about something besides just getting those results?"

Shane glared at him. "You think I don't care about anything but results?"

Xavier grinned slyly up at him. "I think you do now," he said, and walked down the steps.

When the police had gone with Four Wheels's body, Garth had turned to them and said, "The paintin's done. What's next?" and somehow, offering him a couple of days off to mourn hadn't seemed like a good idea. So Agnes had said, "Uh, we need shutters," and shown them the pictures from Brenda's house book, and then gone on to explain the idea of the house book, how Brenda had wanted the house to look like this and how this was the best revenge Lisa Livia had been able to think of, that Brenda would see the house she'd always wanted and know she'd never have it, and suddenly four men were determined to get black shutters on the house before dinner.

When Lisa Livia came tottering down the stairs two hours later, two hitmen, a handyman, and a kid from the swamp had shutters unloaded and ladders at the ready, along with new carriage lights for the porches and stone planters for the bridge, exactly like Brenda had planned.

"What the hell?" she said as Carpenter and Shane went up the ladders on each side of her bedroom window. "This racket woke me up, which is saying something, considering Cerise and Hot Pink."

"We've almost got Butch tracked down," Agnes said, watching Shane wrestle his shutter into place on the brackets. "Once we find him, we'll get the birds back where they belong."

Shane looked really good lifting heavy things, she thought. And the shutters, those were really nice, too. She was willing to think about damn near anything to take her mind off the mess to her right, where her bridge used to be. She could tell Lisa Livia that her mother had murdered an old man with her car later. It wasn't like Lisa Livia would be surprised.

Lisa Livia frowned. "So you have Shane and Carpenter hanging Brenda's black shutters."

"It's like the HGTV Hit Squad," Agnes said.

"*Designed to Kill,*" Lisa Livia said.

Shane turned around and yelled, "Is this where you want it?"

Agnes gave him two thumbs up.

Lisa Livia shook her head. "I hope he's getting a lot of sex for this."

"Not anymore," Agnes said. "But he had some good times before. And you'll like this part: He paid for everything with the money he took from the two guys who came out here to kill me. So whoever hired them just redid the outside of my house. It even paid for the paint."

"Do we know who that is?" Lisa Livia asked.

"Some woman, Shane said."

"Brenda." Lisa Livia looked up at the windows. "Damn fine shutters."

"Wait till you see the carriage lights," Agnes said.

Carpenter smiled down at them and waved with his free hand, the other one supporting about twenty pounds of shutter.

Lisa Livia smiled and waved back, trying not to wince from her hangover. "They used to be grim killers who moved silently through the night, answering to no one. Now they're checking with you for proper shutter placement."

"I like to think of it as, 'Do a window treatment, save a life,'" Agnes said, and went closer to tell them how great the shutters looked.

Three hours later, after the shutters were up, and after a dinner of peppermint tea and whole-wheat toast for Lisa Livia and chicken marsala and new peas for everybody else (the chicken cutlets pounded flat with the back of her frying pan, making Shane roll his eyes but stay out of her way), Agnes started toward the dock with bourbon and coffee only to see the *Brenda Belle* sitting there like a big wart on the landscape. Shane wasn't on the high dock, which just confirmed his good sense. She went back through the house where Carpenter was talking softly to Lisa Livia, and then out onto the front porch, where Shane was sitting on the wicker love seat, his hands behind his head, staring down the road, Rhett at his feet, also staring down the road.

"Waiting for something?" she said, setting the coffee and booze down in front of him.

"Yep."

"Want some coffee while you wait?"

"Yep."

"Talkative devil." Agnes poured two cups of coffee and then offered him the bourbon bottle, but he kept his eyes on the road, so she poured that, too. "Got plans for after you're finished road watching?"

"Yep."

Agnes nodded. "Anything I should know about?"

"Sex with you."

Agnes nodded again. "Okay, I know I said this yesterday and then, you know, changed my mind, but I really think since we don't have a future together, that us sleeping together . . ."

He didn't seem to be paying attention, still listening for something, so she gave up and sipped her coffee, staring out at the ruined bridge, and after a minute he said, "You okay?"

She shook her head. "She killed him, Shane."

"I know."

"She's going to get away with it."

"No."

"How are you going to stop her?"

He turned to look at her, his eyes flat, and she remembered what he did for a living.

"You can't kill her," Agnes said.

"No."

Agnes nodded, relieved. "Then what?"

He turned back to the road. "Something will come up."

"Just like that."

"She'll make it happen."

"Why?"

"Her type always does." He went still, the way Rhett went still when he heard something she couldn't hear, the way Rhett was going still now, and Agnes listened, but there wasn't anything.

She sighed. "Okay, listen, what I was trying to tell you is, as much as I have enjoyed getting naked with you, I really need something permanent and solid in my life. And no offense and please don't kill me for saying this, but somebody who shoots people for a living probably isn't going to blink about cheating on his girlfriend. I'd rather be alone than lied to again." That sounded pathetic, so she shut up, but it was true.

"Agnes, I eliminate only the targets I'm assigned," Shane said.

"Yes, but compared to that, cheating doesn't seem that bad, right? I mean, you shoot somebody in the morning, a little nookie on the side must seem like jaywalking. I need to be with somebody who understands that love is serious business, that I am serious business, someone who will stay forever, someone who won't betray me and then come around with a 'Hey, I'm sorry, I won't do it again' the next day and think that makes everything just dandy. I've got a hole in my heart here. I'm not taking any more chances."

His eyes were still on the road, and she stumbled on, trying to make him understand.

"Look, I just cannot afford that kind of pain again, okay? I can't do it. I have to find some good, kind, boring guy who would rather slit his throat than hurt me because I can't take another shot to the heart. It'll kill me and I'm not kidding. I can't do it again. I have to choose really carefully this time. And a hitman, well, that kind of doubles my chances for the shot-to-the-heart thing."

Something rumbled down the road, and Rhett barked as Agnes turned to look. A big-ass truck came into view carrying what looked like a big-ass tank except there was no turret on top, just a scissors-shaped thing, all of it painted army green.

Agnes looked at Shane, not concerned, because he was there, but definitely puzzled. "Are we being invaded?"

"No," Shane said. "You're being invaded. Later. By me." He stood up as the truck stopped and then backed up in line with the ruined bridge.

"What is that?" Agnes said, postponing for the moment her exasperation because he wasn't listening to her.

"It's an AVLB," Shane said, as the tank rumbled off the flatbed it had been on.

"Of course it is."

"An armored vehicle launched bridge. The army uses them to put in bridges during an attack. Watch and learn."

"A bridge?" Agnes lost her breath. "That's a bridge? Why is the army giving you a bridge?"

"The army isn't giving it to me. It's more of a loaner. To get us through the wedding. Then we'll work on something more permanent."

Us. We. "We will?" Agnes said faintly.

The tank moved up to the edge of the cut, making more racket than Cerise and Hot Pink multiplied by twelve. Black smoke puffed out into the darkening evening sky as Rhett howled and the flamingos honked, and Agnes cringed at the way the tracks tore up the gravel roadway but it wasn't the time to point that out. She was getting a bridge. She squinted, trying to understand *how* she was getting a bridge as the folded-over sections on top of the tank body slowly began to extend upward into the air.

Carpenter and Lisa Livia came out onto the porch.

"I was going to complain about the noise," Lisa Livia said, still looking fragile but much better than she had before, "but now I'm just impressed. Leave it to the army to mechanize an erection."

"Laugh now, funny girl," Shane said. "That's gonna be a bridge in about a minute."

"And that bridge can hold over sixty tons," Carpenter said.

"So it's a strong erection," Lisa Livia said, looking at Carpenter.

"Oh, yes," Carpenter said, standing more erect himself.

"Do you mind?" Agnes said, watching the miracle of her bridge literally unfold. "I'm having a moment here."

The road sections reached their apex and began to go down, the hydraulic arm in the center scissoring them apart. Within a couple of minutes, the near end touched down and the far end was in place; then the tank driver disconnected the bridge from the body of the tank and drove back onto the transporter, and the transporter drove off into the gathering darkness.

Rhett settled down, secure in the knowledge that he'd driven off the invaders.

"Wow," Agnes said, looking at her bridge.

"Was it good for you?" Lisa Livia said. "It was good for me."

"That bridge was built for tanks," Shane told Agnes proudly. "It'll take your wedding traffic and then some. It's even better than what you had."

"Thank you," Agnes said to him, trying not to sound hero-worship-y.

"But it's temporary," Lisa Livia said, warning in her voice.

"It's a bridge," Agnes said. "It's right here. And it's even better than what I had."

"Good point," Lisa Livia said, leaning on Carpenter a little.

Carpenter put his arm around her.

"And I'm thinking the price is right," Agnes said, and sipped her coffee as Shane settled his arm around her.

"And my mother is going to have a stroke," Lisa Livia said.

"It's a *beautiful* bridge," Agnes said, and tried to forget all the hell swirling around her and the need to be practical and not get hurt.

She could be smart tomorrow. Tonight she had a bridge and she was holding on to him.

Three hours later, Agnes heard laughter from Lisa Livia's room next door, rolled over, put her chin on Shane's chest, and said, "It really is a beautiful bridge."

"Uh-huh," he said, in postcoital stupor.

"It's nice about Lisa Livia and Carpenter, too. I mean, it's a little bit Bobbsey Twins—you and me, her and Carpenter—but then neither one of you is sticking around after the wedding anyway, so it's not as tidy as it seems, right?"

"Mmmhm."

"I mean, basically, Lisa Livia and I are just extended one-night stands, it's not like we're anything special. I've known that from the beginning, that's why I kept making those pathetic attempts to end this before you ended it and left me. Which I'm giving up, by the way. You got me a bridge, you got me. My God."

Shane lifted his head, waking up more, and frowned at her. "What?"

Agnes gave up. "Thank you for my bridge."

"Yeah. Before that."

She sighed. "Nothing."

Shane put his hand on the back of her head, pulled her to him,

and kissed her, fighting his way to full consciousness. "You're welcome. Can we talk about whatever that was in the morning?"

"No," Agnes said. "Forget it, it was dumb. Four Wheels didn't
send those guys to kill me, did he?"

"No," Shane said, letting his head fall back on the pillow.

Agnes moved back to her own pillow. "Then it's Brenda."

Shane yawned. "Or somebody else who thinks you're sitting on
five million and killing you is the way to get it, but since everybody
knows we opened the shelter and there was no five mil, yeah, I think
it's Brenda."

"I'm going to sink her yacht."

"She can probably swim."

"I don't care. She's gone crazy. It was selfish and horrible to try to
swindle me out of the house, but what she did today to Four Wheels,
that was just insane. So I believe she's trying to have me killed. And
I'm glad you're here to stop her. And I'm going to sink her yacht."

"You're not a one-night stand."

Agnes caught her breath. "Just ignore that I said that."

"I don't know what you are, but you are not a one-night stand."

His voice was so insistent that she went still, as if everything
would go wrong if she moved.

"I don't know what the hell's going on," Shane said, sounding
tired. "Four days ago, I knew exactly who I was and what I was doing.
Tonight, all I know is that I want you."

"You've got me." The words were out without her thinking, and
she wouldn't have taken them back if she could.

"Not just tonight."

"I know," Agnes said. "You've got me. I know you're going to
leave. Just come back when you can. Make Two Rivers home base.
Don't get killed. Come back to me." She heard the need in her voice
and felt ashamed for a minute. "If you can't, just say so, don't lie
about it, but—"

"I wouldn't lie," he said.

"Of course you would," Agnes said, annoyed. "You work for the

government. You'd have to lie. Just tell me you can't tell me or something. Don't lie—"

He rolled over on his side and slid his arm around her waist, and
the weight of him there felt good, secure, pulling her in. "Agnes, I
don't know who lied to you in the past—"

"Taylor, my two fiancés before Taylor—"

"—but it wasn't me."

"—and my father," Agnes finished.

"Your father," Shane said. "That one's new. Tell me you didn't hit
him with a frying pan."

"I was ten," Agnes said. "He told me he and my mom were going
to work for the Peace Corps for a couple of weeks, and then he
dropped me off at boarding school."

"The Peace Corps for a couple of weeks?"

"I was *ten,*" Agnes said. "He was my dad. I believed him. Sue me."

"And then he didn't come back for a year?" Shane said.

"He never came back. Fortunately, I had a court-appointed psychiatrist to explain the significance of that to me later." She refused to
meet his eyes. "Do not feel sorry for me. My dad loved me. He called
me his baby girl. And then he took me to boarding school and that
was the last time I trusted a man. Until Paul. Paul asked me to marry
him in college. I was crazy in love with him. Lisa Livia didn't like him,
Maria cried whenever he came over to the apartment, but I was sure
he was the one. Then I stopped by his apartment and caught him doing some other woman against the kitchen wall. So I picked up the
frying pan on the stove and hit him with it. Broke his nose. You'd
have thought that would have cured me, but no, I met Rick. Rick was
terrific, smart as hell, an investigative reporter at the paper where I
was doing lifestyles. He's the one who talked the editor into giving
me a column, and when some guy wrote in and said, 'I like that
cranky Agnes woman,' he's the one who told the editor to call the column 'Cranky Agnes.' He's also the one who found out that my dad
went to prison for securities fraud and died of a heart attack six
months later. Well, he'd always been a fool for high-fat food, and the

prison cooking wasn't healthy, plus the stress, you know. It was inevitable."

Shane put his hand on her waist and she talked faster. "That was a bad day, the day Rick told me that. Then I came home a week later and found him doing my student intern on my kitchen table. So I picked up my cast-iron skillet and hit him on the back of the head. I don't think I hit him because of my dad; I'm pretty sure it was for the bimbo intern." She looked at Shane finally. "It's like I'm standing to one side watching myself. The world goes red and there's this screaming and I have to kill them. You wouldn't know about that. You're always calm when you kill them."

She rolled over away from him, feeling stupid. They'd had perfectly great bridge sex and then she'd gotten weird about the one-night-stand thing and now there Dr. Garvin was, in bed with them, along with her entire life's history. *Nice going, Agnes.*

She looked back. "I'm fine, really. But I should probably live alone."

Shane pulled her back, close against him.

"What happened to your mother?" he said in her ear.

"Oh, she kept writing me." Agnes sighed and let herself relax against his warmth. "Telling me how wonderful the Peace Corps was and signing my dad's name. Then six years later she showed up at school, telling me my dad had been killed by the native tribes, offering to take me home to mix her martinis for her. But by then, I was sixteen and I liked school and I was spending summers here with LL and Brenda, and I just wasn't interested. And neither was she, really. She married again, to somebody with money. She's where she should be; I'm where I should be." *Here, with you.*

Shane was quiet behind her, so quiet that she thought he'd gone back to sleep, and then he said, "I won't lie. I won't leave you. I don't know what's happening in the future. There's a chance my job will change some, that I'll have more of a desk job. Maybe more of a life."

A desk job. Agnes swallowed and rolled back over so she could look at him. "I could move."

"What?"

"I could move. To wherever you have the desk job. I could—"

"You'd leave Two Rivers?"

"It's just a house," Agnes said. "I love it, it's great, but it's not Tara, for God's sake, it's just a house." *Home is with you.* It was a terrible thought, the final betrayal, betraying herself.

"No," he said, and she flinched and thought, *You moron, why did you leave yourself open like that?*

"Right, sorry," she said. "That was—"

"I'll come here," he said. "I'll come back."

The whole world went still, and then she realized she wasn't breathing and took a deep breath, tears stinging behind her eyes—*Do not cry*—and she said, "Oh," and tried not to clutch at him. "That would be good. This would be a good place to come back to. A place to come home to. Whenever you could." The tears were coming and she couldn't stop them, so she tried not to breathe so he wouldn't hear her crying in the dark.

He nodded. "Can we have pancakes for breakfast tomorrow?"

"Yes," she said on a sob, and then she did wrap her arms around him and held on to him, tighter than she'd ever held on to anybody as he pulled the blanket up over them and smoothed back her hair and rocked her as she cried, and she thought, *He's coming back to me, he's coming back,* and gave up being smart and just loved him.

friday

cranky agnes column #12

"Coke Would Like to Teach the World to Cook"

Some people are critical of Coke, pointing out that when you drop a nail into a Coke, and leave it there for four days, the nail dissolves completely; imagine, they say, what that same Coke does to your stomach. Those who are fans of Coke Ham point out that when you pour Coke over a ham and bake it in a 300-degree oven for two and a half hours, the ham tastes delicious. But anybody who has put a nail in a can of Coke and waited four days knows that it doesn't dissolve at all. Why do people believe everything they hear? On the other hand, Coke Ham really is good. Better than that, it's criminally easy.

the next morning felt eerily calm to Shane, sitting at Agnes's kitchen table in the sunshine with Rhett underneath it draped over his feet and Garth across from him, resplendent in a brand-new shirt and jeans, which he was endeavoring not to get maple syrup on. Shane's life was crumbling at the edges, but in the middle was Agnes, making love and breakfast, wanting him to come home to her, and a big old dog, keeping his toes warm. *Screw the edges,* he thought, and poured himself a mug of coffee brewed from fresh ground beans as Agnes put his plate of pecan pancakes in front of him. Still he knew that it wouldn't work in the long run. Casey Dean was out there, determined to kill somebody after the wedding, and somebody else was out there, determined to kill Agnes. Agnes's coffee and pancakes were good, but they could only hold off reality for so long.

"I have to go to work today," he said, trying to prolong the illusion that it was a normal breakfast between two normal people who had just made love until they'd both collapsed and were now smiling at each other in a sunlit kitchen, giddy with mutual approval.

Garth nodded, his mouth full of pancake.

"Selling insurance," Agnes said, going back to the grill for the bacon she had crisping there.

The pancakes were golden, the butter he slathered on slid off the tops in fragrant melting rivers, and then Agnes reached across the counter and handed him the syrup pitcher Garth had left up there, and he absentmindedly watched her breasts move under her T-shirt as he took it.

"Right, insurance," Shane said, and poured the syrup, its scent reaching deep into his brain.

Garth gave them both the fish eye and shoveled the last of his pancakes in.

"To get that gold watch," Agnes said.

"Yep." Shane cut into the pancakes and forked up a bite: light, tender, nutty, sweet, and buttery, just like Agnes. Home cooking.

The phone rang and Agnes answered it. "Good morning, Reverend Miller. What is it this time?" She listened for a moment and then said, "*What?* No, she's not pregnant. Jesus wept, man, are you insane? Do you know what Evie Keyes would do to you if she knew you were calling people and insinuating that her son is going around knocking up girls?" She listened again and then said, "Yes, that is exactly what you just implied, and I am shocked, just shocked that you'd spread gossip like that about a Keyes. And you a man of the cloth. What the world is coming to, I do not know. God must be listening to you right now and reaching for the bottle, that's all I can say." She hung up and said, "That man needs medication."

"They should just put it in the water here, medicate the whole damn town." Shane said, but he said it without venom—Keyes was what it was and a lot of it was good, the breakfasts, for example—and took another forkful of pancake.

Agnes filled a plate with bacon and came around the counter with it, as Garth got up to go. "I'm gonna go pick up that ground cover for the bare spots around the gazebo," he said.

"Let me give you money," Agnes said, but Garth said, "Nah," and went out the back door as she called after him, "You look really nice in that shirt," and got a grin through the screen door in return. "Please don't steal plants from people," she yelled as he went down the path and he waved without turning around.

"I wouldn't ask any questions about the landscaping," Shane said when Garth was out of earshot.

Agnes nodded. "I'll deal with that later. Listen, I know this has probably been screwing up your job, babysitting me and the wedding—"

"No," Shane said. "It's part of my job. The wedding is my job." He watched the warmth fade from her face and the wariness creep back in. "I didn't know that when I came here. The Don set up a hit here, at the wedding. I'm here to take the hitman, named Casey Dean, out, to stop it."

Agnes drew a deep breath. "At the wedding."

The phone rang and she went to answer it. "Yes, Butch, you bastard," she said, her eyes on Shane, "that was me who left you the message. I know who you are and I know the zoo where you work. If you don't get Cerise and Hot Pink back there today, I am going to turn you in. I don't care about your three children or your grandmother with the operation." She listened for a minute and then she said, "No, two is not enough for a flock as you well know. You take them back today, Butch, or your ass is grass and I am a John Deere super-classic riding lawn mower with a V6 engine and a double cutting blade, do I make myself clear? Good." She hung up and went back to the griddle and flipped the second batch of pancakes, perfect golden pancakes, while the coffeemaker brewed its second fresh-ground pot.

"Is it a coincidence that all of this is happening at once?" she said. "That Brenda is using the wedding to take the house back, and that your hitman is using the wedding for his hit, and that somebody was in the vault for the first time in twenty-five years just this week?"

Shane put his fork down. "I don't know. I don't like coincidences. But I don't see how they connect, do you?"

She frowned, thinking hard, and he just looked at her for a minute. Agnes. On his side. In her kitchen full of life.

"Who does the Don want dead?" she asked.

"Don't know."

She smiled at him weakly. "I don't suppose there's a hope in hell that it's Brenda?"

He smiled back. "I wouldn't count on it."

The phone rang again and she answered it. "Kristy. Hi. I wondered what happened to you yesterday. Yeah, probably a smart thing to do, leave when Brenda starts killing people. No, she swears it was an accident. Right, tonight. Rehearsal dinner's at six, bachelor and bachelorette parties right after that. Pictures at the beginning only, please. Right. Mother and father of the groom, mother and grandmother of the bride. No father of the bride. Yep. See you then." She hung up and looked at Shane. "So. Life goes on. Unless you're Four Wheels."

Carpenter came in from the hall. "Good morning, all. Pancakes?"

"Just in time," Agnes said, and loaded a plate for him, adding enough bacon to feed a family of four.

Shane nodded to him. "Any ideas on who could have broken into the shelter and put that frying pan and the money wrappers there?"

Carpenter sat down and frowned at him over the plate Agnes put in front of him. "Good morning to you, too." He picked up the warm maple syrup. "Have some respect for fine cooking." He took the syrup and poured it over the cakes and breathed in the sweet maple perfume.

Agnes got him a mug of coffee, looking worried, and Shane felt like hell for having unloaded the hit and the Don on her, but she had to know. Keeping her in the dark wasn't fair, either. Although lately the dark was the place they were both happiest, so maybe that wasn't such a bad plan after all.

Carpenter cut into the pancakes and tasted them. "Marry me."

Hey, Shane thought, and it must have shown on his face because Carpenter grinned.

Lisa Livia yawned in the doorway and said, "So this is what happens when I sleep late."

"Damn fine pancakes," Carpenter said, and kept eating as she came into the kitchen, patting his back as she sat down.

"You up for pancakes?" Agnes said, and Lisa Livia nodded and Shane watched Agnes serve up more food, round and warm and flushed, happy again, looking very pattable.

Too many people in this kitchen.

He was wondering what the chances were of luring her back upstairs, when his phone buzzed and he pulled it out. He glanced at the identifier, which indicated that it was a message from Wilson. He was surprised to see it was in plain text, not encrypted:

DOCK. FIVE MINUTES. BRING CARPENTER.

He looked up at his partner, who was wolfing down breakfast. "We have to meet the boss."

Carpenter nodded and spoke around pancake. "When and where?"

"Five minutes on the dock." He watched Agnes, wondering how she felt about her dock being used for his business meetings. Probably not as upset as her wedding being used for his hit.

Carpenter's eyebrows were up a notch. "Let's get moving, then." He scooped up another forkful of pancake and got to his feet. "That was an elegant breakfast, Miss Agnes," he said. "Simply wonderful," he added, smiling at Lisa Livia.

"Thank you," Agnes said, and smiled back, but she watched Shane, worry in her eyes.

Shane got to his feet, too, displacing Rhett, who snorted and then slept on. "That was my line," he said to Carpenter. "The breakfast one. Except in the movie it was dinner." He paused, realizing both Agnes and Lisa Livia were looking at him blankly now. Apparently they didn't watch the classics, either. "Okay. Yeah. Great breakfast." He tried a smile for Agnes, which didn't really work. "Sorry."

"No," Agnes said, catching his meaning, another good thing about her. "It's good to know." She drew a deep breath. "I sure am looking forward to Sunday."

"What happens Sunday?" Lisa Livia said.

"With any luck, not a damn thing," Agnes said, and when Lisa Livia still looked blank, she said, "The wedding will be over, the house will still be mine, we'll all be alive, and Shane and Carpenter will have sold that life insurance policy."

"Life insurance policy?" Carpenter said.

"To Casey Dean," Shane said. "Who will have cashed it in."

"Ah," Carpenter said, looking surprised at the security breach.

"It was on a need-to-know basis," Shane told him. "She needed to know."

"I guess she did," Carpenter said, and Agnes smiled at him, a damn good smile this time.

"I miss a lot when I sleep late," Lisa Livia said, looking from one of them to the other.

"Yeah," Shane said, wishing for the first time in his life he could take the day off. He nodded to Carpenter. "Let's go meet the boss."

He wasn't supposed to tell me that, Agnes thought, watching Shane and Carpenter walk down the path to the dock. *He broke rules to tell me that.* That made it better, that she was special enough that he'd break rules for her. And he was coming back to her, too. *Maybe this time,* she thought. *Maybe—*

"So today we sink my mother's boat," Lisa Livia said.

"I really don't have time." Agnes put more cakes on the griddle for her. "I have to decorate a wedding cake and a groom's cake because your rattlesnake of a mother did something to the baker, remember? There's a wedding tomorrow."

"Oh, right." Lisa Livia sat down in Carpenter's chair. "Maria's bridesmaids come in today, don't they?"

"Bachelorette party is upstairs on the second floor, which is also where they're staying tonight. Bachelor party in the barn." Agnes watched the pancakes bubble. "Taylor talked Palmer into it so he could get the money for renting it twice. Rehearsal dinner first. Joey's taken over the catering, so that's something, and Kristy just called and said she'll be here tonight to take the pictures, and Butch swears he'll get Cerise and Hot Pink out of here as soon as he gets his work done at the zoo and can sneak a truck out. This afternoon, I have to get the bows on the gazebo, but Garth is a fast learner so he can help, and most of the real prep will be early tomorrow morning. The rental stuff's all here, so that's not a worry. Really, as long as Maisie gets her daisies here and I get the cakes done and Joey gets the catering done . . ." She felt her stomach cramp as she thought about all the ifs between now and the wedding. ". . . we'll be fine. Plus, you know, my column." *My career. Mother of God, I have to get my priorities straight. Once I figure them out.*

"I believe you." Lisa Livia picked up Carpenter's fork and began to finish off his breakfast. "My plan for today is just to get the mildew off Venus, so I have time to help with whatever you need. When do you plan to switch out the flamingo theme for the daisies-and-butterflies theme?"

"I don't know." Agnes flipped the cakes. "I'm trying to take my cue from Maria because she doesn't want to upset Evie after all the good flamingo work she's done, but—"

Lisa Livia's cell phone rang, and she pulled it out and answered it. Her face went rigid while she listened. "What? I can't be—" She listened again. "Give me your number." She held out her hand and Agnes grabbed a pencil and her To Do List off the counter and handed it to her and she wrote a phone number down. "I'll call you back." She hung up, sheet white, and said, "Where's your laptop?"

Agnes pointed to the end of the counter and LL went and got it. "Internet?"

"Wireless," Agnes said. "Through the phone lines. What—"

Lisa Livia shook her head, her breath coming faster, and began to hit the keyboard, typing fast. She stopped and looked at the screen and said, "No," and then typed again and looked at the screen and said, *"No,"* and typed again, and Agnes came around to see what she was doing.

Bank accounts. One after another until it looked like there were ten open windows on the screen. "Jesus fucking Christ," Lisa Livia said under her breath.

"LL?"

"She took it all," Lisa Livia said, her breathing short and shallow.
"All what?"

Lisa Livia shook her head and Agnes looked at her and said, "Put
your head between your legs. *Now*," and forced her head down, just
as LL started to slide.

"Brenda took your money," Agnes said, her hand on LL's neck,
keeping her head down until she got some blood back in her brain.

"Not just mine." LL's voice was muffled. "Let me up."

Agnes stepped back and Lisa Livia straightened, some color in her
face.

"She must have gone onto my laptop," Lisa Livia said. "When I
was staying on that fucking boat, while I was asleep or out here, she
used my laptop and somehow she figured out my password. She
didn't just take everything I own, she looted the accounts I manage
for my clients. She did it because I was working with you, fighting her
on this house. Because I said you were family, not her. She cried all
over me that night about that. I told her she should have thought
ahead before she killed my daddy." She nodded at the laptop. "This is
her payback."

"Oh, God," Agnes said, and sat down hard. "How much?"

Lisa Livia swallowed hard. "I'll have to . . ." She drew a deep
breath. "In a minute when I can do this without passing out, I'll add it
up. But somewhere around eight or nine hundred thousand."

"*Dollars?*" Agnes swallowed hard, too. "We'll get it back. We'll go
out to that damn boat and—"

Lisa Livia closed her eyes. "She'll have it in the Caymans by now. I
can't even kill her to get it, that bastard Taylor will inherit."

"Jesus," Agnes said. "Can't we go ransack the boat and find the
numbers or something?"

"She'll have them hidden in one of the millions of places the Real
Estate King had built into that damn thing. I wouldn't even know
how to look for them." She shook her head, keeping her jaw set, fighting tears. "Pretty ironic. I spend my whole life working, neglect my

kid to build up this safety net for us, and then because I want to be there for her at her wedding, I lose everything, including my future. And then I screw up her wedding by sticking her with flamingos."

"Lisa Livia, it's not—"

"I am such a fuckup."

"No, you are not." Agnes put her arm around her. "You don't even believe that. I have no idea how to fix this, but we will. We'll get your money back. We'll do your daughter's wedding, then we'll sink your mother's boat, and then we will get your money, Shane and Carpenter and I, we'll help you get it back. *I swear to you, we will.*"

Lisa Livia looked at her. "You don't even know how to sink a boat."

"I am learning many new skills this week," Agnes said. "Eat your pancakes."

To Do List, she thought. *Throw Maria's wedding. Return stolen flamingos. Clean up the Venus. Get Lisa Livia's money back. Kill somebody named Casey Dean.* She looked out the window to the dock where Shane and Carpenter were conferring with their boss. *Sink Brenda's boat. Write my goddamn column. Believe in Shane when he tells me what I'm dying to hear.*

She went to the pantry to get the wedding cakes.

"I didn't explain things to Agnes very well," Shane said when they'd started down the path to the dock.

"You have to speak from the heart," Carpenter said.

"The heart."

"Yes. You have to open up to the world and learn optimism, and the words will come to you, and you'll tell Agnes how you feel."

Shane stopped. "What?"

Carpenter looked at him, serene. "Contentment with the past, happiness with the present, and hope for the future. Learned optimism."

"Oh." Shane frowned. "I told her I wanted to come back here. She seemed pretty happy."

Carpenter nodded. "That's a start. Once you open yourself to the world, my friend, good things will come to you."

"I don't think going to meet Wilson is the best time for me to get optimistic and, uh, open my heart."

"Indeed not. In some ways, your heart opening up is causing a lot of trouble and, I believe, precipitating this meeting."

He nodded down the dock to where Wilson was already sitting on one of the benches, dressed impeccably in his suit. Shane felt like he was walking the gangplank as they made their way down the long dock to him. Brenda's yacht bobbed on the water, but there was a sleeker, much newer and larger boat just off the low dock: Wilson's mode of transportation. A dark figure was on the bridge of the boat running the engines, keeping it in place against the tide. The jet boat Carpenter had driven the last time Shane met Wilson was tied down on the front deck next to a small crane.

"I'm disappointed," Wilson said as they arrived at the high dock.

Cerise and Hot Pink chorused their disapproval, too.

Without being asked, Shane sat down across from his boss while Carpenter took a seat beside him.

Wilson looked at Shane, his eyes as sharp as ever. "You've had two opportunities to take out Casey Dean, and not only have you failed in both, you have allowed Don Fortunato's consigliere to complete down payment for the contract."

Shane didn't say anything, because he knew there was nothing he could say.

"There has been another death here at the house, and the local police were involved once more. This is not the performance I would expect of the man who would replace me. One thing we have always prided ourselves on in the Organization is our discretion."

"I think you know much more than you're telling me," Shane said.

Wilson looked at him without reaction. "Of course I know much more than I tell you. That is the nature of my job. To know, to give orders, and to take responsibility."

"I take responsibility—" Shane began, but Wilson cut him off.

"You are answerable to me. I am answerable to many others and you are my responsibility. This is something you need to understand about my job.

"The FBI is not pleased we took their information regarding Casey Dean and squandered it," Wilson continued. "I *do not like* having to explain myself to the FBI. I am tempted to pull you from this operation. Casey Dean has been a thorn in our side for years, we gave you the two best opportunities we've ever had, and you fumbled both of them."

Carpenter leaned forward. "Third time is the charm."

"Unfortunately," Wilson said, "I don't—"

"We've got a line on Casey Dean," Carpenter said.

Wilson stared at Carpenter in silence for several seconds then turned to Shane, who had used all the self-control he had to refrain from also staring at Carpenter. "And that is?"

"Carpenter developed it," Shane said, "so it would be best if he explained it."

Wilson folded his arms. "I'm waiting."

"We've got Casey Dean's cell phone number," Carpenter said. "And Casey Dean has called a blind number on Shane's phone that he set up. Dean seems to enjoy taunting us. We can turn that against him. He's using a bounce signal with his cell phone, so we can't use towers to track his exact location. But I can set up three receivers in the area and triangulate his location."

"If he answers his phone," Wilson said.

"He'll answer," Shane said.

"Why do you think that?" Wilson asked.

"Because we've suckered him into being overconfident."

"Good plan," Wilson said with a bland look on his face. Cerise and Hot Pink picked up some volume in their vocals, and Wilson's eyes went past Shane. "We have company."

Shane looked over his shoulder and saw Joey ambling down the dock, dressed in his usual black slacks and red shirt.

"How you guys doing?" Joey asked as he arrived.

"Mr. Wilson, this is my uncle Joey," Shane said, getting to his feet to do the introductions. "We're having a meeting, Joey," he added pointedly.

Joey nodded at Wilson and sat down on the bench. "You're Shane's boss."

"Yes. And you're Joey Torcelli who used to work with Frankie Fortunato."

"That was long ago."

"The past catches up to us."

"Something catching up to you?" Joey asked.

"Time," Wilson said, "catches up to everyone."

Shane glanced down at Carpenter, who raised his eyebrows. *At any minute,* Shane thought, *one of them is gonna say, "The crow flies at midnight," and then I'm gonna shoot them both.*

"Sometimes things come full circle," Joey said.

"Sometimes," Wilson said.

"What the hell are you guys talking about?" Shane asked.

"And sometimes things change for the better," Joey said. "People get a second chance."

"People don't change," Wilson said.

Shane tensed as Joey leaned toward Wilson. "I think they do."

"Gentlemen," Carpenter said. "My friend Shane and I have a job to do."

Joey stood. "I'm going with you."

"I don't think—" Shane began, but Wilson nodded.

"Some experience might be helpful."

What the hell? Shane thought.

"We need the jet boat," Carpenter said.

"All yours." Wilson stood. "A pleasure to meet you, Mr. Torcelli."

"I bet," Joey said.

Wilson moved off to his boat, Carpenter with him to claim the jet boat, and Shane watched Joey's eyes follow them. "What the hell was that?" he asked the old man.

"Nothin' good," Joey said, looking away.

Shane stepped closer. "You're fucking with my life here, Joey. If you know something about this, anything about this, you tell me now. This is life and death, not some old mob game."

"It was always life and death, Shane," Joey said as Carpenter pulled up in the jet boat. "Guys like Wilson, they ain't no different than the Don."

"Damn it, Joey—"

"We'll talk in the boat," Joey said, remnants of authority in his voice that told Shane something of what he'd used to be.

"You're damn right we will," Shane said, but he followed Joey onto the jet boat.

Carpenter stayed at the wheel in the center console of the jet boat. Shane locked down an M60 machine gun on the front pole mount and loaded a band of ammunition into it. Along one side of the jet boat, Joey was securing an orange coast guard logo. He'd already put one on the other side of the boat as they pulled away from Wilson's cabin cruiser. Carpenter pushed the throttle forward and they picked up speed until the boat planed out and they were cruising out of the Blood River onto the Intracoastal.

"Why am I doin' this?" Joey said.

"It explains the machine gun mounted in the prow of the boat to anyone stupid enough to ask questions of a boat with a machine gun mounted in the prow," Shane said, and then called to Carpenter. "Where are we putting the first receiver?"

Carpenter pointed at the GPS screen on the console in front of him. "On the eastern tip of Barataria Island. Second one, here on Middle Marsh Island, southern tip. Third one to the south, on Bull Island. That will give us good coverage."

"Why are we looking on the water?" Joey asked, finished with his task.

"Casey Dean was on a boat the last time we saw him," Carpenter said. "I think it makes sense he's probably living on a boat. Makes him mobile in this area, and he can hide among the thousands of barrier islands and waterways."

"This Wilson guy," Joey said. "You like working for him?"

"I might not be working for him much longer," Shane said.

Joey smiled. "You going to stay here?"

"No, I'm in line to get his job."

The smile disappeared. "You want that?"

"It's a step up," Shane said.

"To where?" Joey asked.

Shane glared at his uncle. "You're the one who sent me away twenty-five years ago to military school. This is the path you put me on. Why are you asking me questions about it?"

"I sent you away to protect you," Joey said.

"From who?"

Shane was surprised as his uncle seemed to grow smaller in the swivel seat. "Shane, what's going on now, it's all part of stuff that was never taken care of twenty-five years ago. There's been a truce all those years. But this Wilson guy, that ain't where you should be. You don't want to be like him."

"A truce between who?" Shane asked.

Joey hesitated. "The Don and me."

"And now the truce is over?"

"I don't know. But it wasn't no coincidence you was in Savannah when I needed you."

Considering he'd been working overseas 90 percent of the time in the previous five years, Shane didn't think it was a coincidence, either. "Why would Wilson want me in the area? I'm getting a little tired of you old men playing me. Why is the truce breaking down now? What's at stake?"

"You're at stake," Joey said.

"First transmitter goes in here," Carpenter announced as he slowed the boat to slide the prow of the boat onto the tip of an island.

Shane didn't move. "What do you mean, Joey?"

Joey sighed and ran a hand across his coarse beard. "Your father . . ." He stopped and shook his head. "This ain't good. You don't need this now."

"My father." Shane stood over his uncle, looking down at him. "You never told me a damn thing about my father. You've always acted like he never existed. That he was some fly-by-night guy who got my mother pregnant. Big family secret."

"Nah," Joey said. "Your father was a stand-up guy. He treated my sister right. I promised them both when you were born, if anything ever happened, I'd take care of you."

"And then you sent me away," Shane said, anger pulsing in his veins.

"I sent you away to save you." Joey stopped and shook his head.

Shane grabbed his uncle's T-shirt, pulling him close. *"Enough."* He could feel the blood pounding in his head, a rushing in his ears, Carpenter coming close to him, but his focus was on Joey. "Enough with the *fucking games,* Joey."

"You're a Fortunato," Joey said, talking faster. "Your father was Roberto, the oldest brother, the one who was supposed to be the Don. You're the Fortunato heir, Shane."

"Oh, *fuck,*" Shane said, and let Joey go.

Agnes was rolling out grass green fondant and swearing at it, when Rhett growled at the hall doorway, and she looked up, ready to pulverize anybody with a gun.

Instead it was Taylor, equally pulverizable, looking like hell.

"Your murdering slut of a thieving wife is out on her boat," Agnes said, jerking her head toward the dock. "Next time, don't come through the house."

"I'm sorry," Taylor said, and his voice was low, not the coaxing, flirting tease she'd come to loathe. "I truly am sorry, Agnes. I've screwed up everything."

"True. Get out." Agnes rolled the resisting fondant over the pin and moved it to the first layer of Palmer's groom's cake, smoothing the top and then beginning on the sides, where things quickly went wrong. *You can do this,* she told herself. *Goddamn fondant.*

"I mean it," Taylor said, coming into the kitchen and making Rhett growl louder. "She just said all the right things, Agnes."

"She's good at that. Leave." Agnes frowned as she smoothed the fondant. It looked so easy when they did it on TV—

"She killed that old man, didn't she?" Taylor said, and Agnes looked up. "I heard about it. They were talking about it in town, that she drove right into him. Almost into you. She was aiming for you, wasn't she?"

"Yeah," Agnes said, watching his face. He did look truly miserable. "And she stripped Lisa Livia of everything she had, and now she's trying to destroy her granddaughter's marriage. She's a real fucking prize, your wife."

"She stole from Lisa Livia?"

"Taylor, she was going to steal this house from me, why is it so hard to believe she'd rip off Lisa Livia?"

"Geez." He paused. "Well, I won't lie to you, Agnes—"

"Sure you will," Agnes said, and went back to her rapidly hardening lurid green icing.

"I was going to help her cheat you out of this house." Taylor shook his head. "I figured you were going to do another book, you'd have plenty of money, what the hell."

"Fuck you," Agnes said, bent over the edge of the cake.

Angry language, Agnes.

Fuck you, too, Dr. Garvin.

You're an idiot, Agnes. Anybody can say "Fuck you." Do something smart for a change.

Agnes straightened and stared at her fondant.

Did you just call me an idiot, Dr. Garvin?

Dr. Garvin?

"But I'd never have helped her kill you," Taylor was saying. "Jesus, Agnes, you're worth twenty of her."

"Twenty thousand." Agnes looked at Taylor, perplexed, trying to figure out what it was about him that she was missing, that Dr. Garvin thought she should be paying attention to.

Tall, blond, gorgeous, desperate. Nope, he was the same complete waste of humanity she thought he was.

She went back to the cake. Maybe she could put the flamingos over the lumps. Maybe the lumps would make the flamingos look three-dimensional. Always a silver lining.

"You're right," Taylor was saying. "You're twenty thousand times better than her. Agnes, if you'll take me back, I think we can make it work."

Agnes jerked her head up. *"What?"*

"You and me, honey. We can make it work." He came closer, his face eager. "I was so damn dumb, I didn't see that I already had it all with you. Two Rivers, the *Two Rivers Cookbook,* that cool blue bedroom upstairs . . ." He cocked his head at her and smiled the smile that had curled her toes a week ago. "Come on, sugar, we were great together."

"I've had better," Agnes said, and went back to her fondant.

"Since when?" Taylor said, outraged, and Rhett barked at him, a little snarl in there for garnish.

Taylor took a step back.

"Since this week." Agnes patted a fondant lump gently to smooth it out. No dice, it was going to have to be a flamingo.

"That Shane guy? Jesus, Agnes, did you even wait a minute after you stabbed me with that fork before you went to bed with him?"

Agnes stopped patting fondant to think about it. "Couldn't have been much more than ten minutes. Fifteen, tops."

"Agnes!"

Agnes straightened. "Taylor, you are in no position to become indignant. You got engaged to me to swindle me out of my life savings, and now you've discovered you married a murdering whore, and you're trying to dump her and latch on to me to save yourself. It's not going to work. Even if I were stupid enough to take you back, you think

Shane's going to come home, find you in his bed, and just say, 'Oh, okay, no problem'? Do you know what the man does for a living?"

"No," Taylor said. "But I think if you explained that we'd reconciled—"

"Yeah, well, we haven't." Agnes picked up the cake round and turned to take it to the pantry and saw Brenda staring at them through the screened door. *Oh, sweet Jesus,* she thought, almost dropping the cake. "If you've come to borrow a cup of sugar, the answer is no," she called to her. *Although I'll trade you a cup for those account numbers in the Caymans.*

"I came to see what Taylor was doing in here," Brenda said, coming into the kitchen and fixing him with a basilisk stare.

Rhett growled again, but this time he crawled under the table.

Smart dog, Agnes thought.

"Hello, Brenda," Taylor said weakly.

"We were just talking about the catering," Agnes said, taking the fondant-covered tier to the counter by the window. As she got closer to Brenda, she could hear her breathing. She was almost hyperventilating. *Anger,* she thought. *Been there, done that.*

"I thought Taylor had decided he couldn't do the catering," Brenda said through clenched teeth, staring at her husband.

"He was just reiterating that," Agnes said. *The stupid son of a bitch.*

"Yes, I was," Taylor said, trying to sound stern.

"And I was telling him that I understood that." Agnes picked up the next cake tier and brought it down the counter. "So now you can both vacate my premises so I can finish this cake for Palmer."

"Green?" Brenda said, contempt all but curling from her mouth.

"Golf course." Agnes unwrapped her next ball of grass green fondant. "With flamingos. He's going to love it."

"Well, nobody ever accused you of having *taste,*" Brenda said. "Bless your heart."

"Taylor," Agnes said. "You can go now. You and the whore you rode in on. Bless her heart."

Brenda exhaled through her teeth.

Taylor looked helplessly from Agnes to Brenda while Agnes began to roll fondant, the heat of her anger making her strong and the fondant smooth.

"We can go into town now if you want, Brenda," he said.

Brenda lifted her chin. "I suppose. I do hate picking my way across that dangerous splintered old bridge, though. I surely don't see how anybody's going to get to the wedding now. So I'll call Evie—"

"Oh, the bridge is fine," Taylor said. "Sturdy as all get-out. Much better than the old one. I drove right up to the house, so you just have to walk along the path."

Brenda's lips parted, but no sound came out.

Agnes smiled as she rolled fondant like a maniac. "That Shane. He sure is a miracle worker. Got that bridge in last night. It's a beauty. And after that he hung the prettiest black shutters you've ever seen on every single window in Two Rivers. If you didn't notice them, you make sure you look, Brenda, because they certainly are gorgeous. Check out the carriage lamps, too." She beamed at Brenda. *"Now get the hell out of my house."*

Taylor went over to Brenda and ushered her out the back door, turning as she went out to give Agnes one last look.

"No," Agnes said, and he nodded and went out, a lost soul, which was what he deserved.

She rolled the fondant onto the rolling pin, lifted it over the cake, and flipped it on. "Don't give me any crap," she told the icing and smoothed it swiftly down over the sides.

Perfect.

"No flamingos for you," she said, and went to get the next layer, wondering exactly how much Brenda had heard and exactly how much trouble Taylor was in.

And why her subconscious thought she was an idiot.

Shane knew Carpenter was behind him, perfectly still. He could almost sense his friend's calmness in the face of his own surging anger.

Fortunato. Fuck.

"What happened to my father?" Shane asked finally. "And my mother. You told me she died in a boating accident."

"She did," Joey said. "The same accident your father died in. I couldn't tell you who he was, because that would have made you a threat to the Don, as the son of the eldest brother. He's got no kids, he ain't gonna have any, so you're the heir, that's no good. So I made a deal with him. I'd raise you, tell you nothing of your father, and he'd leave you in peace, he'd—"

Shane was on his feet before he even realized it. He punched Joey square on the mouth, knocking the old man to the floor of the jet boat, and then Carpenter was there, wrapping his powerful arms around Shane, pulling him away.

"Easy, my friend, easy," Carpenter said.

Shane allowed Carpenter to push him back to one of the chairs and shove him into it. All the rage he'd suddenly felt was just as quickly gone. He couldn't believe he'd lost control like that. He never lost control. And he could see it now, what his uncle had done. "You did it to protect me."

Joey nodded as he dabbed off the trickle of blood on the side of his mouth with a handkerchief he'd pulled out of a pocket. "I did. It was okay as long as Frankie was here. He was protecting you, too. Protecting all of us. Him staying down here was part of the deal, too. Let Michael become Don even though he was youngest. Frankie didn't want it anyway, though it sure pissed Brenda off. Then Frankie disappeared the night of the robbery, and I knew I had to get you out of here. That's when I shipped you off to military school."

"You could have told me," Shane said.

Carpenter let go of him and went back to the wheel, reversing them off the beach and turning south down the Intracoastal.

"What good would it have done?" Joey said. "The name would have been a weight around your neck. And my deal with the Don was that you didn't know. I kept my part and he kept his. He didn't go after you, even though you being alive has always been a threat."

"Why are you telling me this now?" Shane asked as Carpenter pointed the boat toward another island.

"Because the Don's coming here for the wedding. And he knows you're here and who you are. And all this crap is coming up about Frankie and the robbery. I don't know what's going to happen, but it's best you be prepared."

The bow of the boat scraped onto a beach, and Carpenter grabbed the second receiver and jumped overboard. He slammed it into the beach above the high-tide mark.

"Tell me the truth, Joey," Shane said. "Are you planning to whack the Don?"

"No."

"Because he's got a professional hitman in the area who is supposed to take out someone who is a threat to—" Shane froze. "He's here to hit me."

Carpenter was climbing back on board and caught the last part. "One theory. And all the more reason to take out Casey Dean first." He came over and slapped Shane on the shoulder. "Let's focus on the present. And get the son of a bitch."

Carpenter revved the engine and they pulled off the sand, back into deeper water. He turned and steered the boat between two islands. Shane took a deep breath and tried to reorient on his environment and get his head back in the mission, because he knew Carpenter was right. Casey Dean was the priority—even more so now.

They were surrounded by low-lying barrier islands, some small, some stretching out for over a mile in length. Many had thick clumps of trees, others were just covered in water grass. Small inlets and openings cut off to either side, disappearing into the trees. It was beautiful, the perfect place to hide a boat.

"Here." Carpenter turned the wheel and brought them to shore on the edge of one of the larger islands.

"I've got it." Shane grabbed the third receiver, jumped into the warm knee-deep water, and waded ashore. He shoved the receiver into the sand and flipped the switch on top. He waded back out and climbed on board. He saw that Joey had his Colt Python in his hand, ready for action. Shane opened a case and pulled out another MP5 submachine gun. He held it out to his uncle.

"Here. More firepower."

"Thanks." Joey tucked the Python back into his waistband and hefted the submachine gun.

"We're on line," Carpenter announced, looking down at the GPS unit.

"Now we've got to get Casey Dean on the phone." Shane pulled out his phone and dialed in Casey Dean's number. It rang four times; then the answering service came on.

"Casey Dean, this is Shane Fortunato. Seems like we might have some things to talk about. I don't think you're going to be able to complete your contract." Shane cut the connection. *Shane Fortunato. Fuck.*

"Now what?" Joey asked.

"We wait," Shane said as Carpenter drove them over to a small inlet and brought the boat to a halt in the shade of overhanging trees.

"What if the mutt don't call?" Joey asked.

"You got something better to do?" Shane asked. "If I'd have known the truth—"

Joey cut him off. "If you'd have known the truth, you'd have never achieved what you have. You'd have been looking over your shoulder all the time and asking too many damn questions."

"So you know what's best for me?"

"I believed I knew," Joey said. "Now you got to make your own decisions."

"Thanks for—" Shane began, but his cell phone buzzed. He checked the screen as words appeared. Carpenter was at work with his equipment near the GPS.

SHANE FORTUNATO. PLEASURE TO HAVE MET YOU.
PERHAPS WE'LL MEET AGAIN SOON.
THE CONTRACT WILL BE FULFILLED.
CASEY DEAN.

The letters stopped coming. Shane looked up at Carpenter in question. Carpenter smiled as he grabbed the controls and put the boat in reverse, pulling them out of the inlet and into the waterway. Shane moved past the center console and manned the M6o machine gun.

"About three miles from here," Carpenter called to him, checking his small screen.

Shane looked back at his uncle Joey, who was hanging on to the boat with one hand, the other holding the submachine gun. "Let us deal with this," Shane called to him.

"I can still pull a trigger," Joey said.

"Two miles, ahead and to the right," Carpenter announced.

Shane looked ahead. They were in a quarter-mile-wide waterway between an island covered in sea grass on the left and thickly forested mainland on the right.

"One mile," Carpenter said as he pulled back on the throttle, slowing them. He turned the bow of the boat toward an opening in the trees. It was about two hundred yards wide and curved out of sight less than a quarter mile inland as it narrowed. "I'd say Casey Dean's boat is up this waterway."

The jet boat picked up speed. The sides began to close in as they curved left, giving them less than a quarter mile of width.

"Not far now," Carpenter said. "Around the next bend."

Shane had his hand wrapped around the pistol grip of the M6o machine gun and the stock of the weapon pulled in tight to his shoulder. The jet boat banked and they skidded around a tree-covered point of land, revealing the same cruiser from the previous day sitting in the middle of the waterway less than two hundred yards in front of them. Shane began to squeeze the trigger and then paused in surprise. A beautiful redhead was lying on her stomach on the bow of the boat, just below the cabin. She wore a thong and skimpy top.

"What the fuck?" Joey said.

She lifted her head and waved at them, making no effort to cover her slender well-tanned body. Shane scanned the rest of the boat, but there was no sign of anyone else. Carpenter was throttling back, slowing them further. They were less than a hundred yards from the cruiser when the woman got to one knee, reached down, and brought up a long green object.

There was a flash of explosion, and a rocket-propelled grenade roared forth from the RPG launcher she held, straight at the jet boat. Shane pulled the trigger on the machine gun just as Carpenter slammed the throttle forward and pulled the wheel hard left, causing Shane's rounds to go high and left.

"Geez!" Joey yelled as the RPG round whooshed by less than two feet from Carpenter's position and slammed into the trees behind them, exploding. Shane was scrambling to bring the machine gun to bear, but Carpenter was doing a full circle and the cruiser was suddenly behind them, and he couldn't fire down the length of his own boat. He abandoned the gun and ran aft, joining Joey.

There was no sign of the woman now, just a dark figure in the bridge, and the cruiser coming straight toward them. There was a flicker of red just below the bridge, and Shane yelled "Get down," just as the sound of a machine gun firing echoed across the water and the first rounds cracked overhead.

Shane slammed Joey to the floor of the jet boat, protected by the Kevlar plates on the rear. He looked over his shoulder. Carpenter was crouched down as far as he could be and still have a hand on the wheel and see where they were going.

More rounds cracked by overhead, and Shane popped his head up to risk a glance back. The cruiser was picking up speed.

"Faster!" Shane yelled to Carpenter.

His partner slammed the throttle full forward and they raced back down the waterway. Shane slid the tip of his submachine gun over the rear fantail and blindly fired off an entire magazine. He popped his head up once more. The cruiser was still coming and still firing. The only good thing was that the fixed machine gun wasn't accurate, firing high.

Carpenter drove them through the twists and turns. Shane fired off another magazine, this time aiming, seeing the rounds hit the dark glass at the front of the cruiser's bridge with no effect.

"That was some dame, huh?" Joey said with a lopsided grin.

"Yeah," Shane agreed. "I especially liked the rocket launcher accessory."

"We're clear," Carpenter called out as they came out of the narrow waterway into the river. He turned right. Shane got to his feet. "Spin us and I'll fire as it clears," he ordered as he ran past Carpenter back to the front of the boat.

He grabbed the M60 and aimed back where the waterway met the river, finger on the trigger. The bow of the cruiser appeared and Shane fired. The first rounds hit low, right in the water in front of the bow. Shane walked them up into the hull and then up higher as the rest of the boat appeared, focusing the string of bullets on the bridge. The 7.62 mm rounds slammed into the bulletproof glass and Shane knew it would only hold for a little while longer against the onslaught.

"Watch it!" Joey screamed as the woman popped up through a hatch in the bow, RPG on her shoulder. She fired and disappeared. Shane cringed as the rocket-propelled grenade streaked toward them. It hit the Kevlar armor on the front of the jet boat and exploded.

Shane felt a powerful hand slam into his chest and lift him into the air. Time seemed to move in slow motion as he flew upward over Carpenter, over Joey, over the entire boat and tumbled into the water behind the boat. He went under, the weight of the gear he was wearing taking him down. He couldn't breathe, the force of the explosion having knocked the air out of his lungs.

Shane unbuckled his combat vest and tore it off. He felt pain radiating through his chest and could only wonder at what wounds he'd sustained. They wouldn't matter if he couldn't get back to the surface and air.

He blinked, trying to figure which way the surface was. He forced himself to remain still for a moment and looked about. He kicked toward the light.

Shane popped to the surface right behind the jet boat. Carpenter and Joey were leaning over the rear, Carpenter stripping off his gear, getting ready to jump in.

"I'm all right," Shane managed, but he couldn't hear his own voice, just a loud ringing.

A brief smile crossed Carpenter's face and his mouth moved, but Shane could only hear the ringing. Then the smile was gone and Carpenter was looking over his shoulder, shouting something. He shoved Joey over the side, diving off himself. Just as the bow of the cruiser sliced over and into the jet boat, crushing it and forcing it under. Shane blew the air out of his lungs and went back under, seeking the safety of the deeper water.

He was buffeted as the cabin cruiser churned by overhead, propellers ripping what remained of the jet boat to shreds, slicing by scant feet above his head. He forced himself to remain underwater as he watched the propellers move away. He stayed under until his lungs were screaming for air; then he went for the surface, using a piece of the wreckage to cover breaking the surface.

He sucked in air as he watched the cruiser continue to plow away. When the cruiser disappeared around a bend of the river, he looked around for the others. Carpenter was hidden by an overhanging branch, holding on to a piece of wreckage with one arm, the other around Joey, who had a cut on his forehead, blood seeping down his face.

"That didn't go as planned," Carpenter said.

"Lousy work," Shane gasped, his ears still ringing. "We'd have stayed to clean up."

"Well, thank you, Mr. Dean, for being a sloppy-ass killer," Carpenter said.

"We should deliver that in person," Shane said.

"We should do that later," Carpenter said, nudging a dazed Joey toward the bank.

"Yeah," Shane said, looking back in Casey Dean's direction. "But we're definitely gonna do it."

When Joey hadn't shown up by five, Agnes began to panic. The rehearsal dinner was at seven, and while Garth could set up the tables and even put out the plates and silver, she had to be down there dressing the place with flowers and favors. Beyond that, catering was not within her grasp. Family cooking she could do; catering a rehearsal dinner for the first family of Keyes? No.

She wiped her hands on her Cranky Agnes apron and stepped over Rhett to open the fridge and looked at the turkey Joey had put in there. Taylor had promised that he'd make Palmer's favorite meal, turkey and dressing, and Joey had sworn he could handle it. But now it was too late to make the turkey, and Palmer had wanted some special kind of gravy with bourbon in it, and . . . She looked at the turkey and thought, *I'm screwed.*

Rhett bayed, and she heard Taylor say, "Agnes?"

Agnes turned around to see him standing in the doorway again. "Not now." She turned back to the fridge. There were new potatoes in there. That could be simple. Maybe butter sauce—

"I want to work this out."

Rhett growled.

Agnes closed her eyes. "Well, that's just great. No. Now get your ass out of here. I'm busy."

Pay attention, Agnes.

"Where's Joey?"

"I don't know," Agnes said. "Beat it."

Don't be stupid, Agnes.

She heard him come closer, and Rhett growled again.

"He's not here?" Taylor said.

"No."

"Do you want me to cook?"

She turned around. "You quit, you lying, cheating bastard—"

Agnes, you dumbass, you need *him.*

"I know," Taylor said. "That was wrong."

Agnes . . .

Dr. Garvin, I hate *him.*

Okay, first of all, this isn't Dr. Garvin, this is you, talking to yourself, obviously, so pull yourself together.

Second, you need help and he owes you big.

Third, you can use this to your advantage, if you'd get your head out of your butt and stop doing the easiest thing, which is anger, but no, you have to wallow in your emotions and hide behind your rage, so go ahead and screw up your life again. Go ahead. Feel free.

I want Dr. Garvin back.

"What's Joey got in there?" Taylor reached around her and opened the fridge, and Rhett growled again, and Agnes hesitated and then bent to pat the dog.

"It's okay, Rhett," she whispered, and the dog looked at her as if to say, *Sucker,* and then padded back to his place under the table and collapsed into semi-slumber.

"Huh," Taylor said. "Okay. Sure." He began to take things out of the fridge. "Get me a tray or a box or something so I can get this stuff down to the kitchen in the barn. Did you do the dessert?"

"Raspberry–chocolate heart-shaped cakes," Agnes said. "I covered them with ganache and plated them, and I'm going to use raspberry sauce as . . . Look, Taylor—"

He closed the fridge door and opened the cupboard next to it. "I screwed up. I know this won't make up for it, but it's something. And besides . . ." He grinned down at her. "I want to show the Keyeses I can cook."

You gonna be smart or you gonna be dumb, Agnes?

Agnes drew a deep breath. "You want back in. You've looked around and realized you backed the wrong woman and that the Keyeses aren't going to side with Brenda, especially since she's losing her grip and killing people now, and your future is going down the tubes, and you want to switch sides."

"Yes." He looked embarrassed but determined.

"So you want to come back so you can be part of the wedding and have the catering business and the *Two Rivers Cookbook* and everything we were going to do."

"Yes." He was eager now, and she began to see how easy it had been for Brenda to lay things out for him. Almost like leaving a trail of bread crumbs for him to follow.

"Okay," Agnes said, starting her own trail. "You can cater the dinner tonight and the wedding tomorrow, on two conditions. The first is that you work your ass off on this wedding and *make sure it happens.* You are on my side now, and you do everything in your power to make sure this wedding happens and that I keep the house."

"Yes," Taylor said.

"The second is that you sign your share of the house over to me."

Taylor's face went blank.

"I'll finish the cookbook with you, and I'll let you cater out of the barn, but you sign your share of this place over to me. You tried to swindle me out of it, you sign it over to me. The house belongs to me entirely. I get it *all.*"

"Agnes," Taylor said, trying to smile. "Agnes, honey, with the down payment and everything I put into the barn, that's over a hundred and fifty thousand—"

"The high price of being a bastard," Agnes said. "You sign your half of the house over to me, and I'll finish the cookbook with you and let you cater from the barn. Otherwise you lose *everything.*"

Taylor tried one more charming smile, which slid right off Agnes, and then he nodded. "All right. But maybe when you've had time to think about us again—"

"I never think about us," Agnes said. "Us is deader than a doornail. I have a new Us, and I'm keeping it. The only thing I want you for is this rehearsal dinner and the wedding tomorrow. Cook. And show Garth how to do everything, because you need an assistant and he needs skills, and for God's sake, try to remember whose side you're on this time."

Taylor nodded and emptied her cupboards while she went to get a tray for him, not even trying to understand why he'd do anything like what he'd done to her, just crossing her fingers he'd stay on her side until the wedding was over or until Brenda found out what he was doing and came after him with whatever she was driving next.

She was really going to miss Dr. Garvin.

"We're much obliged, Mister Jimbo," Carpenter said as the shrimp boat edged up to the floating dock at Two Rivers three hours later.

"Just Jimbo," the burly man at the wheel of ancient boat said.

Shane watched in the furious silence he'd maintained since they'd hauled Joey ashore on the closest island and then used Carpenter's sat phone in its waterproof case—of course Carpenter had his phone in a waterproof case—to let Joey call for help.

It had taken Jimbo a while to reach them, and Joey had done a guilt-stricken play by play over letting Agnes down on catering the rehearsal dinner, saying now they'd be sitting down to the dinner, now it was dessert, now they'd be breaking up for the bachelor and bachelorette parties, until Shane thought about holding his uncle's head under water just to shut him up. It should have been a great relief to be on board the shrimp boat, watching Jimbo expertly reducing the throttle while turning the large wheel at the same time, but it was just one more thing that was pissing Shane off. He was supposed to be an expert, too, but if you judged by his performance the past couple of days, he was a fucking beginner, they'd have kicked him out of Hitman Prep, hell, they'd have kicked sand in his face at the Hitman Preschool—

The boat touched the floats on the edge of Agnes's dock with the slightest of bumps. Shane's chest throbbed with pain, but it didn't appear that anything had been broken, so at least his body hadn't betrayed him—

"I owe you one," Joey said to Jimbo, touching the white bandage on his forehead.

"Call me any time you need help, Joey," Jimbo said.

Shane could see lights on in every window in the main house and hear loud music thumping away in the barn, pretty much in time to the vein pulsing in his forehead—

"Sounds like we made it back in time for the bachelor party, but not the dinner," Carpenter said. "I sure would have liked to have had some of that turkey—"

Shane ignored him, and Carpenter fell silent as they trooped off the boat onto the dock.

Shane led the way up the metal plank to the high dock and then down the long walkway to land.

"You know," Joey said, "it wasn't your fault—"

Shane shot him a look, and Joey shut up.

At the top of the dock Carpenter said, "My friend, you are taking this too much to heart," and Shane faced him. "That's three times— four if I count the time I ran into Casey Dean in the woods—that he's beaten me. It's obvious he uses women to front for him and protect him. That redhead in the room in Savannah with Marinelli was one of Casey Dean's people, the same one with the RPG on the boat while he drove. And I let her go."

"You might be missing something," Carpenter said.

"That's what I'm saying. I've been missing a lot of things," Shane said with a glare at Joey. "But that's done with."

He turned and went on and then stopped short of the house, hearing the sound of girls giggling and catching the silhouette of a skimpily clad woman in one of the upstairs windows. "Great," he muttered.

"Bachelorette party," Carpenter said. "Lisa Livia told me that—"

"I don't care," Shane snapped. He cocked his head, listening to the music coming from the barn.

"Bachelor party," Carpenter said. "You know, Casey Dean's target, given that it's not your uncle here—"

"Hey," Joey said in warning, but Carpenter spoke over him.

"—and on the off chance it's not you, will most likely be at the bachelor party. Although the bachelorette party could be interesting."

"Focus," Shane said.

"There's a shower in the barn in the rear," Carpenter said. "I could grab some clothes for us from my van. We could get cleaned up." He sniffed. "You might not be aware of it, but we smell of—"

"Get the clothes." Shane turned on his heel and headed down the path for the barn. Carpenter disappeared into the dark, and Joey fell in beside Shane. They trudged up the path, their shoes making squeaking noises as water squished out of them.

Shane reached the barn. The music was overwhelming, and he could see a crowd of men inside split into two distinct groups: a bunch of a-couple-years-out-of-college former frat boys on one side with mugs of beer in their hands acting stupid with several kegs surrounding them and Palmer looking miserable in the middle with a flamingo hat on his head; and a smaller bunch of goombahs from New Jersey seated on the other side, shot glasses in hand, a neat row of bottles stacked on one of their tables. Shane noticed Hammond standing off to one side, looking equally miserable, with neither group.

"This looks like fun," Joey muttered.

"Downer invited the Don's men?" Shane shook his head. First the flamingos, now this. He recognized a tall figure seated at the rear of the mobsters. "That's the consigliere. You know him?"

Joey shook his head. "Nah. It's been twenty-five years since I seen any of those mutts."

"Let's go around and take the back stairs."

They skirted around the building and climbed up the stairs to the loft apartment. "You use the shower first," he told Joey. "Carpenter should be here in a minute."

Joey went into the bathroom while Shane went to the balcony door and cracked it open so he could look down on the barn floor. The frat boys were now chanting something Shane couldn't make out, all looking in one direction at something underneath the balcony. Shane opened the door further to see, when the lights in the barn went out for a moment, then a spotlight, controlled by Downer—*who else?*—was trained in the direction everyone had been staring. Shane edged forward and looked down.

Two of the groomsmen appeared below, pushing a large round bed toward the light. They stopped it and then ran to join their buddies. Shane noted that even the goombahs were perking up in anticipation.

The music suddenly changed, going from the loud thumping techno-whatever that had been playing, to what sounded like monks chanting in Latin.

Shane stepped back as Downer drunkenly turned the spotlight, which flickered over a slight figure dressed in black robes at the top of the stairs from the balcony. Downer corrected, bringing it back and fixing the figure in the glare: a woman dressed in a nun's habit and dress.

"This is going to be interesting," Carpenter said, coming up behind Shane.

The woman moved down the stairs, head bowed in apparent prayer—*I'd be praying, too, with that crowd,* Shane thought. She reached the bed, and the music abruptly shifted to Madonna's "Like a Virgin," and the nun began to dance, dropping pieces of her habit, which came as a surprise to no one, although the frat boys roared anyway. She took off her wimple to reveal her long blonde hair, and then she dropped her robe to reveal a lace bustier, a black leather miniskirt, and fishnet stockings. Downer yelled, "I always wondered what they wore under there!" and his buddies roared again while Palmer continued to drink and look miserable.

"And that's the future of America," Shane said.

"Downer?" Carpenter said. "Surely not."

The blonde jumped on the bed and unhooked her bustier to reveal perfect breasts, covered with pasties of pink-sequined flamingos. When she bumped, her breasts bumped, and the flamingos' sparkly heads bobbed. The flamingos were a terrible thing to do to a great pair of breasts, Shane thought, but you really couldn't help but watch the shiny pink sequins, and after a minute, there was something almost Zen about it. Then she shimmied the miniskirt off her washboard abs and the hoot grew louder: she was wearing garters and a

G-string, also decorated with sequined flamingos so that with every bump and grind, spangled flamingos bounced on her beautiful body. *Jesus,* Shane thought. *That is truly tasteless.*

Agnes would look great in those flamingos.

And she'd laugh her ass off, too, if he showed up and handed them to her.

"That's for you, buddy!" Downer said as the stripper began to de-flamingo herself toward her big finish. He slapped Palmer on the back, making him spill his drink.

The goombahs watched, the consigliere in the back row with his arms folded. Evidently the flamingos weren't impressing them.

"Flamingos," Carpenter said. "Tasteful."

"Downer," Shane said. "Most likely to be shot by accident on purpose on Halloween."

Carpenter's phone rang and he answered it, his face growing serious. "I'll be right there," he said finally, and when Shane looked curious, he said, "Lisa Livia. She had a really bad day. If we're done, I'll go see her."

"What's going on?" Joey asked, coming out of the bathroom, rubbing his head with a towel. He looked out. "Flamingos?"

Shane shook his head. "We're done. I'm going to shower and then go find Agnes."

Carpenter nodded. "The flamingos got the blood going, didn't they?"

"Yeah," Shane said. "Flamingos. They do it for me every time. If Casey Dean's target is down there, he can have him."

By the time the rehearsal dinner ended, Agnes had been ready to go out and stand in the water with Cerise and Hot Pink and scream. Jefferson Keyes had pinched the bridesmaids, Evie had ignored him by drinking steadily, and Lisa Livia had stared like a basilisk at her mother throughout. That, Agnes thought, was entirely understandable, given that LL had gone out to the yacht and confronted Brenda about her theft, and Brenda had flat-out denied it and then accused Lisa Livia of breaking her heart with her suspicion. Because LL hadn't been quiet about it, the rest of the party had found out and had pretty much cut a wide swath around Brenda instead of making her the belle of the party as usual, so that by the end of the evening she was thin-lipped, her eyes narrow and sharp and often as not fixed on Agnes, who was getting all the compliments. Only Taylor had come through, serving a perfect dinner on the beautiful china he'd bought for his catering, and even he had kept up a running commentary that was practically a prospectus for Taylor's Two Rivers Catering Service. "The best thing you can say about this dinner," Agnes told Lisa Livia, tying on her Cranky Agnes apron to help with the cleanup, "is that it's over."

"The food was really good, and Garth was terrific," Lisa Livia said as they watched the teenager clear the tables with what was almost a practiced hand, looking like a fine upstanding citizen in the clothes Palmer had bought him and the haircut Palmer had made him get in exchange for the clothes. "And you got a lot of payback tonight. Taylor was all but wearing a hair T-shirt that said, *I Married the Wrong Woman.*"

"Yes, and Brenda's going to make him pay for that," Agnes said.

"My heart bleeds for him," Lisa Livia said, and went back to the house.

Taylor had caught her arm. "Thank you," he said, and his sincerity was clear.

"Dinner was great," Agnes said, because that was true.

"The wedding luncheon will be, too," he said eagerly. "I'm going to make it up to you—"

"Did you sign the house over to me?" Agnes said flatly.

"Barry's bringing the papers tomorrow," Taylor said. "When he comes to the wedding. He's got them drawn up. We'll do it tomorrow morning. You can call him and ask."

"Until those papers are signed, you haven't even begun to make it up to me," Agnes said. "But the food was terrific."

When the barn had been cleared for the bachelor party, and Garth had been given money to go into town to the movies so he wouldn't be corrupted by the sight of the stripper, Agnes had gone down to talk to the flamingos as usual—"Butch is coming for you in the morning, swear to God, but at least you have each other, how's the shrimp?"—and then gone back to the house where the bachelorette party was in full swing upstairs and finally worked on her column.

Two hours later, she was still staring at her laptop screen. The recipe was done. She had the points she wanted to make: sturdy enough to hold the fondant, tastes great, reflects the personality of the bride and groom, and oh, those Romans, what a bunch of cutups, breaking the cake on the bride's head. But the column was . . . blah.

She looked up at Palmer's groom's cake, the flamingo cake with the lurid green icing and the equally lurid pink flamingos on the sides and the golf balls on white springs popping out from the layers, topped with the two pink flamingo pens, one with a paper top hat and the other with a paper doily veil. Not blah. And right beside it, Maria's white wedding cake—with the concentric circles—easy—and the fondant butterflies on springs—a little harder—pearl trim— much harder—and the antique bride and groom—expensive—that was a work of art. *I did good,* she thought, and relaxed a little before she went to back to the column.

It's worse than blah, she thought. *Anybody could have written this—it's ordinary. I'm not saying anything new, there's nothing here that would make people think, "Gee, she's a great writer, better rush out and get ten copies of Mob Food." Damn it, what do I know about wedding cake that's important? C'mon, Cranky Agnes, be brilliant: Your future's on the line.*

Inside her skull, the emptiness echoed for eternity.

Nothing, I got nothing. God, I'm a fraud. The two hundred columns I've done up to now have all been flukes. I got lucky. Now the truth is here. I can't write, it's all been a fake, I'm going to have to eat worms and die.

Maybe she could do a column on eating worms.

She saved the file and got up and saw the Venus. She looked awful.

Okay, she thought, *accomplish something.* She got the cleanser out and began to scrub the statue down, getting more vigorous as it became apparent that the thing was made out of some kind of eternal compound that wasn't going to collapse under her enthusiasm. And once the scrubbing became automatic and the pearly plastic began to shine, she began to think about the week she'd just survived.

Things were good, if you looked at them just right. For example, she'd survived. And she was going to pull off the wedding, with a lot of help from her friends: The lawn was manicured to golf course perfection, the house gleamed in its new white paint, the shutters were up, the stolen landscaping was beautiful, and the gazebo was magnificent. Even the pink sand had a certain kitsch glow to it. And Taylor was going to cater and Maisie was going to do the white daisies with a few pink accents, and Maria was going to wear her white gown down the aisle, and Evie would be relieved and wouldn't ask questions, and Butch was coming for Cerise and Hot Pink early in the morning so they'd be gone before the wedding, and everything would be beautiful. And at the end of all of it would be Shane—she slowed her scrubbing—he was worth the whole week right there, getting shot at was a small price to pay for a guy like that. She thought about him and scrubbed harder, cleaning the last of the mildew off because he'd be back soon, and she wanted—

"AGNES!" Maria screamed.

"Mother of God," Agnes said, almost dropping her sponge as Maria came running into the kitchen. *"What?"*

Maria grabbed her arms. "Palmer is in the barn having sex with the stripper!"

"Oh, he is not," Agnes said, shaking her off and going back to scrubbing the Venus. "This is Palmer we're talking about. He adores you. And he has much too much good taste to have sex with a stripper. He doesn't know where she's been. Or who her people are. He wouldn't dream of it." She put the sponge down on the counter and said, "Listen, could you read this column and tell me what's missing? Because I—"

"Don't make jokes," Maria said, her face sheet white with stress and too many champagne cocktails. "He's just like his father."

"He is not." Agnes went over and got her a cup of coffee. "Drink this and stop hyperventilating or I'll make you breathe into a paper bag. He's just like his mother. Evie would never have sex with a stripper. Who told you this garbage?"

Maria got a wary look on her face and sipped her coffee. "Somebody who knows about men," she said finally.

"Oh," Agnes said. "Brenda called, did she?"

Maria put the cup down on the counter. "She and Taylor had finished up in the barn kitchen and were coming back and they looked through the double doors and saw him. He had that dumb flamingo hat on his head that Downer got him for the party. She knew it was him."

"Because nobody else could be wearing that hat since Palmer sure as hell wouldn't have taken it off the first chance he got," Agnes said.

"She saw his face," Maria said. "She told me to go down and look."

"She's a lying bitch from hell," Agnes said. "But let's be adults about this and do what she said. Let's go find out."

"What?" Maria pulled back.

"Let's go find out." Agnes came out from around the counter. "Let's go down to the barn and see what old Palmer and the boys are doing."

"We can't go down there," Maria said, aghast.

"Why?" Agnes looked her straight in the eye. "Afraid you'll find out he's innocent?"

"Hey," Maria said, getting some of her old temper back.

"That's more like it." Agnes sighed. "Look, if you don't want to marry him, don't marry him. But he's a good guy. Be up front about it. Don't let your bitch of a grandmother frame him for something he didn't do. Go down there and tell him you don't want him."

Maria swallowed. "I do want him. If he's really the man I thought he was—"

"Why do you listen to Brenda?" Agnes asked tiredly.

"Because she sounds right," Maria said.

"Well, she isn't. She preys on your fears to destroy your happiness so she can get this house back." Agnes opened the drawer in the counter by the basement door and got out her flashlight. "Did your mother tell you what she did to her?"

Maria shook her head.

"She will. Come on. Let's see who's getting up close and personal with the stripper. I'll bet you six M&M'S it's not Palmer."

"I don't want that bet," Maria said.

"Good girl," Agnes said, and opened the screen door, looking back at the Venus as she went.

She was looking pretty good. *Well, there's one thing I finally got right,* Agnes thought, and then followed Maria down the path to the barn.

When Shane came out of the shower, Joey and Carpenter were gone. He went downstairs and saw that the large round bed was still there below the balcony, but the party appeared to have moved outside toward the lawn and dock, where he heard male voices chanting "Drink, drink, drink." *Yeah, there's a good time,* he thought, and went down the balcony stairs and started for the big house, but paused when he heard a woman's voice raised in anger coming from the one of the rooms under the balcony.

Great. Some stupid frat boy and an angry stripper. Just what Agnes needed, a scandal the night before the wedding.

The woman's voice was definitely coming from the door marked OFFICE. "You fucking tried to rip us off," she was yelling. "You think you can short us?"

Downer was probably trying to stiff her, Shane thought. In more ways than one.

"Twenty-five large," the woman said, and Shane frowned. No stripper got paid twenty-five large. "I want the damn money. Tonight."

Shane opened the door and paused. In the moonlight coming in the window he could see the stripper, in her miniskirt and bustier, standing at the side of a desk. She had a gun against the forehead of the man seated in the desk chair. The Don's consigliere, Shane realized.

She turned at the sound of the door, and Shane lunged forward, grabbing her gun hand with both hands as she brought it to bear on him. She smacked him on the side of the head with her free hand, the open palm against his ear, stunning him on top of the damage from the RPG explosion earlier in the day.

Shane squeezed her hand and she dropped the gun just as she brought her knee up hard, missing his groin by scant inches to slam into his right hip as the consigliere scrambled across the room. Shane jerked her arm up and then twisted it, spinning her about as he kicked the gun under the desk.

He put his other arm around her neck in a half nelson and applied pressure, bending the stripper forward, and saw the compass tattoo in the gap between the skirt and bustier.

"Casey Dean's girl," Shane said.

She was bent over the desk, her ass in his crotch, just as it had been in Savannah.

"Fuck you," she said, but she was grinding against him again.

"Didn't work last time, won't work this time," Shane said. "I've finally—"

He didn't finish as she turned her body counterclockwise under him, locking his arm under her body, and smashed her free elbow into his face, the perfect reversal move to a half nelson.

Stunned, Shane let go for a moment, and she slithered out of his grip. She dived for the floor, searching for the gun. He leapt for her just as she decided to make a break for it and grabbed her ankle, and she kicked her foot into his face, breaking free. Shane scrambled to his feet, saw her silhouetted against the door to the room, and jumped, and his momentum shoved both of them through the door and onto the big round bed where she'd stripped, the girl squirming in his arms, trying to get away from under him where he had her pinned facedown.

That's when he heard Maria's voice from the open sliding glass door: *"Oh, God, Agnes, now Shane's doing her, too!"*

Oh, fuck, Shane thought as the girl elbowed him low.

Maria turned and tried to run and Agnes caught her and said, "Don't be ridiculous," and then looked past her to where Shane had a half-naked squirming woman under him on a bed. "Okay, that looks bad," Agnes said, clamping down on her automatic urge to kill him, "but that's not what it looks like."

Maria looked at her, outraged. "How can you be so *blind! Look at them!*"

Agnes looked at them. Shane was pinning the woman to the bed, bearing down on her, and it was hard to tell, sex and violence being so closely related but . . . "No," she said. "I'm pretty sure he's trying to kill her."

Maria looked at the bed and then at Agnes. "You're *insane,*" she said, and then took off down the path.

"I didn't mean it the way it sounded," Agnes said, and went after her. "Maria!" She caught up with her halfway down the path. "I'm sorry, that wasn't right, I didn't mean *kill* kill. I mean, you know, subdue, arrest, Shane's kind of a cop, and . . ." Her voice trailed off as Maria shook her head. "Look, the bottom line is Shane wouldn't do that to me, and Palmer wouldn't do that to you. Things aren't always what they look like; sometimes you just have to trust the guy you love."

"All guys do that," Maria said. "Brenda said—"

"Brenda is a hag from hell who is trying to destroy your wedding so she can take my house," Agnes snapped.

"And you're trying to push me into this wedding so you can keep your house," Maria said.

Agnes threw up her hands. "You really think that? You fell in love with Palmer, who is a great guy, and you came down here completely in love with him, positive you wanted to marry him, and then that peroxided bitch poured poison in your ear and now I'm the one with the ulterior motive. Thanks a lot."

Off in the woods, they heard voices and then someone gag, and Maria made a disgusted sound. "Probably Palmer barfing." She raised her voice toward the sounds. "Sex and booze don't mix, you dummy, and neither does cheating and marriage."

"Well, it's clear to see you love him and care about his well-being," Agnes said, fed up with her. "Don't put yourself out any. I'll go see if he's all right."

"*Hey,*" Maria said as a male voice up on the path said, "Maria? Is that you?"

"No, really, stay here," Agnes said, turning her back on her. "You've never looked more like your grandmother than you do right now."

She left the path and went into the woods, shining the flash on the ground so she didn't trip on any tree roots, and she saw his shoe first. "Palmer," she said, and played the light up his leg onto this shirt and then his face, seeing his eyes staring terrified at the same time she saw the meat fork sticking out of his throat, not Palmer but Taylor, and then she screamed as he reached for her, she screamed and screamed and screamed.

Shane cursed to himself as the stripper tried to worm free. Then she pulled a stiletto from some hidden sheath on the miniskirt and jabbed with it and he felt it pierce into his shoulder.

Fuck this, Shane thought. He pulled back his left fist and hit her in the base of her skull as hard as he could. Her head bounced off the bed, but she was still conscious, albeit stunned. She slashed at him, narrowly missing his eyes.

Shane punched again, this time aiming for her temple, but she moved just enough so the blow didn't strike dead on, but rather bounced off her skull. He ducked as the knife came for his eyes once more, and then forgot all but total combat, blocked the knife hand, grabbed her head, left hand on the back, right hand on her jaw, and twisted violently. The sound of her neck snapping echoed through the barn even as he felt the point of the knife pierce the skin in his shoulder.

Shane felt the body spasm beneath him, then become still.

He rolled over onto his back, breathing hard and staring up at the ceiling of the barn.

Agnes, he thought, but he couldn't summon the energy to get up and go after her.

He checked his shoulder. Not deep. He'd killed her before she could do real damage. He reached over and pulled off the blonde wig, revealing the short red hair.

Finally, he reached into his pocket and pulled out his replacement satellite phone. He hit speed-dial.

"Yes?" Carpenter whispered.

"I've got a package," Shane said, still trying to catch his breath.

"Another amateur? Can it wait? I'm with Lisa Livia at the movies. She's had a rough day. And I thought—"

"Casey Dean's girl. The one with the RPG on the boat."

"Oh." Carpenter was silent for a few seconds. "Where?"

"The barn."

"I'll be there in twenty minutes."

"Thanks."

Shane hung up and looked down at the body. The eyes had the blank look of the dead. Seeing nothing. Ever again. Soon they would cloud up, as if what remained of the soul was turning into mist. Not that he imagined Casey Dean's girl had much of a soul.

His dark thoughts were interrupted by the sound of sirens in the distance, coming closer. *Now what?* Shane got to his feet and turned toward the door, then paused, looking down at the body. Carpenter had said twenty minutes. The sirens would be here before that. But they were coming for something, and he knew it wasn't what had just happened in here. Which meant there was a very good chance Agnes was in trouble. If she'd gotten angry about seeing him with a naked stripper after everything he'd promised the night before, God knew what havoc she'd wreaked.

Shane took a quick look around the barn and found the stripper's bag. A pink cell phone was in it and he pocketed that. Then he picked up the body and slung it on his shoulder. He carried it and the bag out the back of the barn and hid them behind some palmetto bushes, laying some fronds over them. Enough to escape a quick look from the cops.

He headed up the path and came to a halt as a dark figure came toward him, but he relaxed when he recognized the outline of the straw hat.

"Detective Xavier," Shane called out.

"Mister Shane *Smith*."

Shane walked up to the detective. "What brings you out here this late?"

"I might ask the same of you," Xavier said, looking past Shane toward the barn. "Something going on in there?"

"Nope. Just checking on the damage from the bachelor party."

Xavier nodded. "You all must have had a hell of time out here tonight. All sorts of mayhem."

"Like?" Shane asked.

"Maybe I should check out the barn," Xavier said.

"Nobody in there anymore. Party moved out to the shore."

Xavier nodded. "Most likely you're right. What's important is what happened over yonder." He gestured behind Shane, down the path.

"What happened yonder?" Shane asked.

"Your Miss Agnes," Xavier said.

Shane sighed. "What did she do?"

"She appears to have murdered her former fiancé, Taylor Beaufort. Which is why my associate Robbie Hammond arrested her and why he is currently on his way with her to the county jail."

That's my girl, Shane thought.

"I'm real sorry about this, Miss Agnes," Hammond said as he locked the cell door behind her.

"That makes me feel so much better," Agnes said, hugging herself against the cold. It wasn't that cool in the jail, she knew that, but she'd been cold ever since she'd seen the fork in Taylor's neck and felt his hand grab the edge of her apron in one desperate clutch before he died. "You can't possibly think I killed Taylor. I was with Maria right there on the path—"

"No, ma'am," Hammond said. "I had just joined Maria when you screamed. You were in the woods with the victim."

"You *moron*," Agnes said, shivering with rage and something else.

"Hammond, can you get her a jacket or something?" Maria said.

"Yeah, Hammond, get her a jacket," a voice said from the bottom bunk said, and the woman there rolled over—a blowsy blonde who looked like she rotated in and out of the place on a regular basis— peered out at Agnes, and then sat up to get a better look. "Well, look what we got here. Betty Crocker. Nice apron, Betty. *Mob Food?* That how you got in here, cookin' for the mob?"

"Humor," Agnes said to her, shivering. "Har." She turned back to the cell door. "Hammond, if I'd done it, why would I have screamed?"

"To make me think you hadn't done it," Hammond said, sticking his considerable chin out.

Agnes gazed at him for a moment, thinking of all the things she'd like to do to his stupid, determined face. "Hammond, you're dumb as a rock, but Xavier isn't. When he finds out you've arrested me on the thought process of an addled two-year-old—"

Hammond frowned at her. "He knows. I called him."

Oh, just hell, Agnes thought. *They're all nuts.*

"He said you were better off in here than out there. Probably wanted to keep you from killin' anybody else."

"She didn't kill anybody, Robbie," Maria said, steel in her voice.

Hammond stepped back. "Okay, honey."

"*Honey?*" Agnes said, and thought about reaching through the bars and strangling him.

"Hey," the blonde said. "What are you in for, Betty? Beatin' your egg whites?" She laughed uproariously.

"Murder." Agnes took off her Cranky Agnes apron and tossed it on the bunk above the blonde and then climbed up, looking for a blanket.

"We'll get you right out of here, Agnes," Maria said, looking daggers at the blonde.

"No, you won't," the blonde said. "You ain't gonna find a judge tonight or tomorrow or the next or Monday. Not on a holiday weekend, you ain't. Now what are you really in for, Betty?"

"Murder." Agnes pulled a tissue-thin blanket off the bunk and wrapped it around her, and then stretched out on the mattress and looked at the ceiling. It was peeling. Naturally.

The blonde poked at the thin mattress from underneath. "I ain't askin' you again."

"For the love of God, Hammond, tell her," Agnes snarled.

"She killed her ex-fiancé with a meat fork," Hammond told the blonde.

"*She did not,*" Maria said, turning on him.

"*Allegedly,*" Hammond said hastily. "She *allegedly* was found standing over her ex-fiancé with an alleged meat fork."

"I didn't have the meat fork," Agnes said tiredly. "He did."

"Right," Hammond said. "The fork was in him. She wasn't touching it. Still, you know, he was holding on to you. That's pretty bad."

"Just like the rest of my day," Agnes said to the ceiling.

"A meat fork," the blonde said with newfound respect in her voice. "Nice touch, Betty."

"And right after you found Shane with a stripper, too," Maria said, her face crumpling again.

"A girl's gotta earn a living," the blonde said, sounding defensive.

"And she'd just been doing Palmer ten minutes earlier," Maria wailed.

"I don't think so," Agnes said tiredly, still staring at the ceiling. "That just does not sound like Palmer."

"He was wearing the flamingo hat!" Maria said.

"That also does not sound like Palmer." Agnes took a deep breath, mostly to keep from screaming. "Nothing's been what it seems so far. Why should tonight be any different?"

"Those rich guys," Hammond said.

"*You stay out of this,*" Agnes said, rolling so she could look down to see him. "You just stay *out* of this. Somebody just died horribly out there, *do not* use this as an opportunity to make time, damn it."

Hammond put his arm around Maria. "It'll be different with me," he told her.

Maria nodded with a sniffle.

"Listen to me, young lady," Agnes said, sitting up. "What are you trying to do? Ruin your life? Fine, go ahead. Throw your life away in a big dramatic gesture even though you love Palmer and he's the one you should be with. What the hell."

"You want me to forgive him for cheating on me?" Maria said, grabbing on to the bars so she could glare through them. "That's why you stabbed Taylor!"

"I didn't kill Taylor," Agnes said, glaring back. "Although it worries me that you think I did."

"Of course I don't," Maria said, outraged. "I meant the first time."

"There was a first time?" Hammond said.

"No," Agnes and Maria said together.

"And anyway, I don't see you forgiving Shane," Maria said, changing the subject. "I don't see you saying, 'Hey, you boinking the stripper, not a problem, I still love you.'"

"I don't love him," Agnes said. "I just met him. And I don't have to forgive him. He didn't boink her."

"You are so *naïve,*" Maria said.

Hammond tugged on her arm. "We have to go. You shouldn't even be back here."

"*Maria,*" Agnes said.

"We'll get you a lawyer," Maria said as Hammond pulled her through the door.

"Won't do you no good," the blonde said, and then it was quiet, which gave Agnes plenty of time to think.

Not that there was much to think about.

Like, who killed Taylor? Well, he'd been willing to leave Brenda to come back to her and Brenda had almost certainly overheard that, and he'd flouted her to cater the rehearsal dinner, so Brenda was one suspect. And then there was . . .

Brenda. That was it. Nobody else would want to kill poor old Taylor. And nobody else would know that Agnes had stabbed him in the throat with a meat fork. And nobody else would be so viciously cruel as to tell Maria a story that would drive her out to the barn knowing Agnes would go with her, and then arrange for Taylor to be there at the same time, and stab him when Agnes was there, and leave him to die slowly in the woods for Agnes to find him. . . .

Brenda. Hell, she'd already killed Frankie and Four Wheels; Taylor was just filling out her dance card. Of course it was Brenda. She'd stolen her own daughter's life savings.

Well, that filled up a minute. Now what was she going to think about?

Well, there was Shane, having sex with a stripper. Of course he was a guy, and guys did tend to like strippers, but he also knew she was waiting for him back at the house, and Shane just did not strike her as the kind of guy who'd do that. Which was odd because ordinarily she was paranoid about that kind of thing and could work up a really good outrage, but Shane boinking a stripper a hundred yards from where she was waiting after he'd promised to come home to her?

Nah. Whatever he was doing, it wasn't sex. Something energetic and violent, and she really didn't want to think about where the stripper was now and what she'd done to deserve it. Maybe Taylor was hooking up with her in the afterlife. That was some comfort.

That killed another minute.

Which left her with the rest of her life.

Two Rivers was gone unless she could convince Maria that Palmer was not likely to put on a flamingo hat and screw a stripper. That was so self-evident that she was still having trouble understanding why Maria couldn't see it—

"Why a meat fork?" the blonde said.

"Huh?" Agnes said.

"Why'd you do it with a meat fork?"

"I didn't," Agnes said. "As God is my witness, I did not kill him."

"Okay, okay. What did you stab him with the first time?"

Agnes sighed. "A meat fork."

"Why a meat fork?"

"It was the first thing I grabbed. We'd had tenderloin and I'd just washed it and it was on the counter."

"So it was just a coincidence that it was a meat fork this time, too?"

"No, somebody's trying to frame me."

"A lot of people knew about the first time, huh?"

"No," Agnes said, and then stopped. "No, we kept that quiet. She must be planning on making that connection clear to the police herself, unless she already did. Huh. Wonder if she knows that's going to backfire on her?" It wasn't like Brenda to leave a loose end like that. Maybe she really was losing it. Beyond the craziness of murdering Taylor, maybe she was losing it completely.

"She who?"

"The woman who really did it."

"Well, at least she killed him and not you."

"She's trying to kill me," Agnes said. "It's just not working out for her." Which might be what was pushing her over the edge. If she was furious at Agnes for taking LL from her, if she was rabidly determined to get Two Rivers back, if she was so insane that she'd killed Taylor because he was leaving her for Agnes . . .

Oh, hell, Agnes thought. *She's completely psycho and she thinks all her problems are my fault. Just in time for the wedding.*

"Well, you're safe in here for the weekend," the blonde said.

Agnes sighed again. "No, I'm not. My guy will be coming to get me pretty soon."

"The one who fucked the stripper? Nah. I'm telling you, he can't get bail."

"He didn't fuck the stripper." Agnes rolled over on her side. "And he won't bother with bail."

"What's he going to do? Break you out?"

Agnes shrugged. "Whatever it takes. I have to put on a wedding tomorrow, or I lose my house, and he won't let that happen."

"The wedding for Barbie there? I don't think she's gonna get married, I think she's leaving with Deputy Dawg."

"My guy'll bring her back if she does."

The blonde craned her neck up to see Agnes. "So this guy who fucked the stripper, he's going to break you out of jail and help with the runaway bride so you won't lose your house. What is he, Robin Hood?"

"No, he's a hitman."

"Uh-huh. You're crazy."

"No," Agnes said. "But I did have a court-appointed psychiatrist once."

Then she rolled over and made a mental To Do List for when Shane came to get her.

"Agnes didn't kill Taylor," Shane said as he and Xavier headed up the path back to the house. He saw the crime scene tape off to the side of the trail and the deputies tripping over each other trying to investigate it.

"I wouldn't think so," Xavier said, "except Hammond found her standing over Taylor with her meat fork through his throat and him holding on to her apron as he departed this mortal coil. I'm not looking at suicide here, by the way. And she does have that anger problem. Which is why I feel it's best that she stay in custody for tonight."

You want to see anger, Shane thought, *check out Casey Dean's girl's neck.* "You can't keep her locked up. She's got to make this wedding happen tomorrow."

Xavier stared at him. "Let a potential murderer out of jail to put on a wedding? I might be a small-town cop and not so smart as everyone keeps reminding me, but . . ."

He paused because someone was coming this way. Shane turned to see who it was.

Palmer. He came staggering out of the woods, one hand on his forehead, the other extended to keep himself balanced.

"You need to go find Maria," Shane told him when came up to them.

Palmer blinked and his unfocused eyes peered at Shane. "Maria?"

"Your bride," Shane said. "The woman you're marrying tomorrow." Shane held out a hand. "About this tall. Thick, dark hair. Pretty. Loves you."

Palmer was nodding. "Maria. Yeah. Right." He looked about. "Where is she?"

"Probably in the house—" Shane began but Xavier cut him off.

"She's at the jail."

"You arrested her, too?" Shane demanded. "What for? Accessory to forking?"

"She's not under arrest," Xavier said. "She wanted to go with Agnes and Hammond. He'll bring her back once Agnes is settled in." He looked at Shane. "And I do mean settled in. Permanently. No wedding furloughs."

"Hammond?" Palmer said, trying to frown without pain. "She's with Hammond?"

"So if anybody was to have any ideas about early-release programs," Xavier went on, "like, say, waking up a judge—"

Another person came down the path, this one in heels. "Palmer Anderson Keyes." The voice was sharp, and Palmer winced, and Shane recognized Evie as she joined them. Only a mother could make a man's full name go back to childhood. "What are you doing?"

"He's pretty much working on standing up," Shane said.

Evie gave Palmer a look that said she'd be dealing with him later and it wouldn't be pretty, and then she turned to Xavier. "Maria called and said you arrested Agnes."

"Yes."

"Well, let her go," Evie said. "We have a wedding in the morning."

Xavier shook his head. "You people need to get something through your heads. This is a *murder* investigation. Taylor Beaufort is dead. Agnes's meat fork was in his neck. She was standing over the body."

"Agnes *did not* kill Taylor," Evie said with finality. "You know that, Simon."

"I don't know—"

"*Simon,*" Evie said in a very low and husky voice. She stood very still, as did Xavier, her voice apparently taking him back a few years. "Shane, would you take care of Palmer while I talk to Detective Xavier?"

"Yes, ma'am." Shane took Palmer's arm as Evie reached out and took Xavier's.

Xavier looked at her sternly. "Evie, I am sorry if this upsets you, but Agnes Crandall is staying in jail." He put his hat back on his head firmly and with intent.

"Now, Xavier," Evie said.

Shane guided Palmer to the house, listening with one ear to Evie alternately browbeating and cajoling Xavier into freeing Agnes, and by the time they reached the porch, he had a great deal of respect for Evie's powers of persuasion and Xavier's powers of resistance, not to mention a real curiosity about why Evie was married to a blowhard like Jefferson Keyes. The last thing Xavier said was, "Evie, I am sorry, but no, I will not," and then Shane opened the porch door and saw Lisa Livia, white-faced and hollow-eyed, pacing while Carpenter made soothing noises, which he seemed to be good at. Beyond them, through the open kitchen door, he could see Joey and Doyle in the kitchen looking worried.

"Where's Maria?" Lisa Livia demanded.

"She went with Agnes to jail," Shane said, immediately realizing he'd phrased that badly when Lisa Livia turned on Xavier.

"She wasn't arrested," Xavier said hastily. "She was just accompanying Miss Agnes."

"Who *was* arrested," Shane added, feeling that Xavier deserved all the grief he could get.

"For *what?*" Lisa Livia said to Xavier.

"She is helping us with our inqui—"

"Killing Taylor," Shane said, and while Lisa Livia zeroed in on the hapless Xavier, Shane took Carpenter aside. "The package is past the barn, behind some palmettos."

Carpenter frowned. "Perhaps it would be prudent to move the package at a later time."

Shane nodded. "It's secure for now, assuming Downer doesn't trip over it and get creative." He looked over at Xavier now speaking sternly to Lisa Livia, who was snapping right back. "I don't think Xavier is going to go looking for any more trouble tonight."

Lisa Livia turned on Palmer. "And where the hell were you when all this was going on?"

"I was—" Palmer's perfectly smooth forehead furrowed as he tried to think through the alcohol.

"He was under the weather," Shane said.

"Under a keg more likely," Lisa Livia said. "One of the bridesmaids said Maria said he had sex with a stripper."

"Of course not," Palmer said, but he swayed as he said it.

"Absolutely not," Evie said, but she gave her son the fish eye.

Shane shook his head. "Palmer didn't do anything with the stripper."

"How do you know?" Lisa Livia demanded.

"Because this was a special kind of stripper," Shane said, and Lisa Livia opened her mouth to argue and then shut up.

Xavier looked at him oddly.

"Have you questioned the widow yet?" Shane asked him. "Brenda Dupres, uh, Beaufort?"

"She's distraught," Xavier said, his voice dry. "I do, however, have some queries for you—"

"She killed him just like she killed my daddy," Lisa Livia snapped at him. "Go out on that damn boat and beat it out of her, and then bring Agnes home."

"And Maria," Palmer said, his swaying much more pronounced. "Maria should be home. . . ."

"Go on, Xavier," Evie said. "We're waiting. Bring Agnes back." She folded her arms and lifted her chin, and Xavier looked at her, exasperated. "Don't look at me like that. You picked the wrong side on this one. Agnes is innocent. You're always picking the wrong side. You did it twenty-five years ago and you're doing it now."

"Evie," Xavier said.

Palmer's swaying became downright dangerous, and Shane grabbed the front of his shirt and sat him down on the swing, which brought Shane close to Evie's ear. "Walk Xavier to his car," he whispered.

Evie stepped forward. "Come on, Xavier," she said, smooth as glass. "It's dark out there. Walk me to my car."

Xavier started to speak, and she took his arm. "You can harass Shane tomorrow," she said, and tugged him toward the screen door, and he shot Shane a glare full of suspicion and then he looked down at Evie, sighed, and went.

Shane straightened Palmer on the swing. "You stay here and get to know your mother-in-law."

"Where are you going?" Lisa Livia said, almost in tears. "What about Maria? What about *Agnes?*"

"I'm on it," Shane told her.

"It'll be all right," Carpenter said, his voice low. "We'll be right back. And tomorrow, I'll take care of the other thing for you. Rest."

Lisa Livia took a deep breath, nodded, and then turned to Palmer. "You're an idiot. But I like you. I'll make coffee."

Shane looked in the back door to the kitchen at Joey. "You take care of things here."

Joey nodded and patted the gun-shaped bulge under his T-shirt.

Great, Shane thought. *Just what we need. More people with firepower.*

"What's the plan?" Carpenter said.

"We break Agnes out of jail," Shane said. "Then I convince her that I wasn't having sex with the stripper so she doesn't kill me. Then we come back here and take care of the package and hit Casey Dean. Then we find proof that Brenda killed Taylor and give it to Xavier so he doesn't prosecute Agnes for going AWOL. Then we make sure Maria marries Palmer. Then we meet Wilson and I get his job and you get a promotion and a big raise."

"Why does that sound like a To Do List?" Carpenter said.

"Get in the van," Shane said.

Maria had come back with Agnes's lawyer, Barry, who said the same thing about judges and holiday weekends as the blonde—"Told you so," the blonde said—but who added that the prosecution was going to have a damn hard time explaining why Agnes's fingerprints were on a meat fork that she'd committed premeditated murder with on the spur of the moment in the middle of her woods while she asked her alibi to wait on the footpath. "I don't understand why they arrested you at all," Barry said, his face cheerful through the bars. "Xavier's usually smarter than this. We may even get a wrongful arrest out of this. I doubt it, but I can certainly try."

"Detective Hammond is hoping to seduce my goddaughter and break up her wedding and was trying to get me out of the way so he could do it," Agnes said, throwing Hammond to the wolves, and Barry turned to Hammond, even happier to add sexual misconduct and alienation of affection to the list, and shortly after that, Hammond's night got worse when Maria went back to Two Rivers to stay in the second bedroom upstairs because her mother had called her and read her the riot act about behaving like a slut the night before her wedding. Hammond had come back to the cell to complain bitterly when Maria was gone, so when Agnes heard footsteps at the cell door again, she ignored them until she heard a key scrape in the lock. Then she rolled over to see Shane pushing the door open.

"You didn't kill anybody to get in here, did you?" she said as she sat up.

"Here? No." He walked over to her and looked up. "About the stripper. That was not sex."

"I know. You wouldn't do that to me." He looked surprised, and she took a deep breath. "Is she dead?"

"Yeah," he said, clearly regrouping. "She was Casey Dean's girl. She tried to kill us on the boat. She tried to kill me tonight."

"Then you had to do it." Agnes began to climb down from the bunk, and he put his hand on her waist to help her down, sliding his arm around her as her feet hit the floor, and she leaned against him and let him take her weight because he wouldn't let her down.

"I heard about Taylor," he said.

She clung to him. "It was bad. He was still alive when I found him, it was a terrible way to die."

He nodded.

"You know that cool, unemotional killer thing I was going to master? It ain't happening. I'm just not the cool type."

He nodded.

"But I'm not Crazy Rage Person anymore, either. I think I finally got what Dr. Garvin was trying to tell me."

He nodded.

She tilted her head so she could see his face. "You okay there, silent guy?"

"You really do believe me?" He held on to her tighter. "I really wasn't having sex with her, I swear, but you really do believe me?"

She nodded. "Yeah. You're the guy I believe in."

He bent and kissed her, and she held on to him, so grateful he was there, she could have cried. The blonde got up and began to sidle toward the door, and he reached out and grabbed the back of her shirt and put her back on the bunk, but he never let go of Agnes.

"Let's go home," he whispered, and she nodded, the words hitting her hard.

"Yes, please," she said, and they went out the door, his arm still around her.

Shane turned back to the blonde. "Sorry," he said, and closed and locked the cell door behind them.

"Damn," the blonde said and lay back down. "*I* didn't kill any-one. How come you guys get to leave?"

"Clean living," Agnes said, and headed back to Two Rivers with the guy she trusted, thinking fast.

Two Rivers looked calm as they walked up to it, Shane thought. No police cars, no parties going on, just the glow of lights from the windows and the occasional raucous honk from the river. Peaceful enough that you might forget that two people had just died there in the past six hours.

"I'll get the package," Carpenter said as Agnes walked up the back porch steps, and then Agnes said, "Shane?" her voice too high as she looked through the back door.

Shane took the steps two at a time to look over her shoulder.

Joey and Doyle were standing on opposite sides of the table with the Venus between them: Joey had his revolver out pointed at the old handyman, Doyle had a gun in his hand pointed back at Joey, and the Venus looked off into the distance, disavowing all knowledge of their presence.

Shane pushed past Agnes. "What's going on?"

"Ask him," Joey said, nodding at Doyle.

Shane felt Agnes behind him, and now she moved around him, looking at the two old men. "What are you *doing*?"

Joey gave his sharklike smile, but the gun didn't waver. "Agnes Crandall, meet Frankie Fortunato."

"Great," Shane said. "Just great."

saturday

cranky agnes column #116
"Sedate Your Family
with Love and Gravy"

In an attempt to bring health to the holidays, I adapted a recipe for dressing using olive oil and high-fiber whole-wheat bread, and ended up with a pan of something that had a definite this-is-good-for-you vibe that lacked the all-right-I'll-go-to-hell flavor of true celebration food. But it doesn't matter, because while I like dressing a lot, it's really just a delivery system for the gravy. In fact, the Cranky Agnes Theory of Holiday Cooking can be summed up in two words: More Gravy.

You son of a bitch."

Shane turned to look at the door to the hallway and saw Lisa Livia dressed in white pajamas with baby chicks on them, looking ready to kill as she stared at Doyle, two high spots of color on her cheekbones.

"Top of the evening, lass," Doyle called out, but his heart obviously wasn't in it.

Shane looked closer at him, seeing past the beard now, the white hair, the smashed nose, the different-colored eyes, the fake accent, the extra weight, twenty-five years of damage and disguise.

"You *son of a bitch*." Lisa Livia said, her voice close to breaking.

"Now, lass—" Doyle began; then he sighed as Shane took a step toward him, and gave up the pretense and the accent. "All right, all right, jeez, I'm sorry already." Frankie Fortunato looked back at Lisa Livia. "Hi, Livie. Daddy's home."

"Fuck you," Lisa Livia said.

Shane looked at Joey. "How did you figure it out?"

Joey looked at Frankie, murder in his eye. "He told me."

"And you drew down on him?"

"He's got some explaining to do," Joey said.

"You took off and *left me*," Lisa Livia said, still standing in the doorway, as if she were afraid to come in the room. "My daddy. The one who loved me, the one who'd never leave me, you left me with *Brenda*. You *son of a bitch*."

"She tried to *kill* me," Frankie said, as if that explained everything. "She hit me right in the face with that frying pan, broke my nose, look—"

"Now why would she do that?" Agnes said, her hands on her hips, lightning in her eyes, and Shane thought, *Oh, hell, here we go.*

"She thought I was cheating on her," Frankie said, rolling his eyes.

"You were," Joey said, keeping his gun hand steady.

"*Son of a bitch,*" Lisa Livia said, and leaned on the doorframe.

"I'd have hit you with the frying pan, too," Agnes snapped.

"You listening to this?" Frankie said to Shane.

"I'm not planning on cheating," Shane said. *Especially on Agnes.*

"Oh, but if you could have seen Maisie back then," Frankie said, shaking his head.

"Maisie *Shuttle*?" Agnes said, distracted for a second. "Well, that explains why Brenda threatened her with death."

"You *son of a bitch,*" Lisa Livia said weakly, evidently stuck in second gear.

Carpenter appeared in the doorway to the porch, a body bag over one shoulder and—when he saw the firepower at the kitchen table—a gun in his free hand.

Everybody turned to look at him and there was a moment of silence, and then almost by mutual consent everybody turned back to Frankie as the more interesting option.

Frankie sighed. "Brenda saw the necklace and yelled, 'Is that for that bitch Maisie?' and swung that pan and knocked me cold, and when I woke up I was locked in that shelter covered in blood, left for dead—"

"*Totally* understandable," Agnes said, and went around the counter toward the fridge, as if she'd given up on him completely.

Shane sympathized but kept his eyes on the guns.

"—and I almost did die in the river, getting away. I even got a plate here." Frankie pointed to his head. "Shoulda been dead, but us Fortunatos, we got thick skulls."

"Jesus," Joey said, shaking his head but still keeping his gun steady. "You sure fooled me. You musta put on fifty, sixty pounds, you tub o' lard."

"Used to have black hair, too," Frankie said, scowling at him. "Look at this." He popped a blue contact out of one eye with his free hand, then out of the other, revealing the Fortunato trademark: shark black eyes. "You were a lot lighter twenty-five years ago, too, Joey. We all changed."

"Son of a bitch," Lisa Livia said again, but she sounded tired now, and when Shane pulled a chair up to the table for her, between the newly scrubbed Venus and Joey, she came in and sank down into it and just stared at her father, sad and lost.

"I'm sorry, Livie," he said, but he sounded more uncomfortable than sorry.

"Between you and my mother—" Lisa Livia just shook her head.

Shane cleared his throat. "I suggest we put the guns away. There are a lot of secrets here. And I'm tired of them."

Frankie nodded at him, keeping his gun out. "So, you know about your parents?"

"What about my parents?" Shane frowned as Frankie looked at Joey. He caught Joey glaring, raising the gun a little, and he stiffened, but Frankie spoke again.

"You know. That I'm your uncle Frankie. Your good uncle, not your lying snake of a shit-head rat-fuck uncle, the Don."

"*Jesus,* you're a bad liar," Shane said, and Frankie started to swing the gun his way, and Joey raised his even more, and Carpenter said, "Guns away, gentlemen," from the doorway, in that deep voice that brooked no argument, and then Agnes came around the counter, her arms full of food, looking like she had every dish in the refrigerator, and dumped it all on the table between them.

"This is *my kitchen,*" she said, an edge of hysteria in her voice, "and enough goddamn people have been shot in it. You are my family, you're the only family I've got, so you're going to put those guns away and eat something *right now*. Or *there's gonna be hell to pay.*"

She slapped a loaf of bread down on the table and looked at them both, blood in her eyes, and Joey and Frankie both hesitated. "You do not want me *angry*," Agnes said, and they both nodded once and, like the unhappy, dysfunctional family they were, they put the guns away together.

Rhett sighed and went to sleep.

"And now you're gonna *eat*," Agnes said.

"What'd you come back for, Frankie?" Shane said as Joey began to help Agnes take the covers off the dishes.

"My granddaughter's wedding, of course," Frankie said, craning his neck to look into the bowls. "I read about it in the paper and I thought it would be nice. Hey, are those ribs—?"

"Cut the crap," Shane said. "Where's the five million? And what score are you settling with the Don?"

"I was wondering about the five mil myself," Agnes said as she slung plates around the table like she was dealing cards, clearly still mad as hell. "And the necklace. That was a *lousy* thing to do to me, *Doyle.*"

"Aw, Agnes," Frankie said.

"I mean it. I worried about you, I fussed over you. I *fed* you—" She smacked the container with the ribs down in front of him hard.

"Darlin', I know it—"

"And you put a necklace on my dog and almost got me killed." Agnes finished almost throwing his plate at him. "What the hell was that about?"

Frankie looked shamefaced but relieved, Shane thought. *Doesn't want to talk about the Don.*

"That was just a joke," Frankie told Agnes. "Justice for Brenda. I been knocking around all over the world while she stayed here livin' the good life, never paying for half-killing me, never losing one night's sleep over it, so I thought, 'That bitch needs some payback.' So I put the necklace on Rhett so she'd see it and start to worry—"

"Jesus." Lisa Livia sighed and took the cover off the turkey bowl. "You are a piece of work."

"What?" Frankie said, picking up a rib. "I just—"

"Because of you," Agnes said, her voice like cut glass, "Four Wheels sent his grandson here to die. Because of you, Four Wheels came here and died. Because of you, Brenda thought there was five million dollars here and hired hitmen to kill me."

"What the hell?" Frankie said, jolted. He looked at Joey, who nodded. "That bitch hired those hairballs?"

"Because of you, she got so desperate, she killed Taylor tonight with a meat fork," Agnes went on savagely. "I don't even know what the collateral damage is, what happened when Shane went to Savannah that got blood all over my fondant, or if that body bag over Carpenter's shoulder is part of this—"

"No, no, this is professional," Carpenter said.

"—but your joke killed at least five people—"

"Six," Shane said, thinking of Rocko.

"—so forgive me if I'm not slapping you on the back right now."

"Aw, hell," Frankie said, waving the rib at her. "I didn't kill them, Brenda did."

"You're missing the point, Frankie," Shane said, thinking it probably wasn't the first time. "But I'm a lot more interested in your first lie."

"Hey," Frankie said, and bit into the rib.

"The one about how you came back for Maria's wedding." Shane met the old man's dark shark eyes, hooded now as he bent over to demolish the rib. "You didn't come home for the wedding; you came home to turn state's evidence. You came home to roll on the Don. Which means you're the one he hired Casey Dean to hit."

"Ah, *fuck.*" Frankie dropped the stripped rib bone on his plate, annoyed. "Goddamn Wilson must be getting old, he leaks stuff like that."

Silent Carpenter got more silent as Shane shut down any reaction he might have had, to say, "He is."

Frankie reached for another rib, shaking his head, and Lisa Livia got up and headed for the microwave with the entire bowl of gravy.

"Save some for me," Agnes said, dropping into the chair on the other side of Joey.

"Get two straws," Lisa Livia said, and slung the bowl into microwave.

Shane turned to look at Carpenter. *Fucking Wilson knew.* Carpenter met his eyes for a long moment and then nodded and headed for the basement with the body bag, moving past Frankie without looking at him.

"That means that body bag over Carpenter's shoulder *is* your fault," Shane said. "In fact, we can pretty much trace the entire body count back to you."

"Now wait just a fuckin' minute," Frankie said, trying to look indignant with barbecue sauce on his face.

"So now you make it up to us," Agnes said quietly from her seat beside Joey.

Frankie said, "Huh?" and Shane almost did, too, but Joey just put his hand on the back of her chair, one hundred percent behind her as always.

"We have many problems, Frankie," Agnes said, calmer now. "I need this wedding to happen tomorrow. Shane needs to take out Casey Dean. Lisa Livia lost everything she had and more when Brenda emptied the accounts she managed." Frankie turned to LL as she sat down with her hot plate and heated gravy, but Agnes kept on talking. "And Brenda needs to go down for Taylor's murder. So you're going to help us with all of that."

"How?" Frankie said, mystified but not unwilling.

"You're going to give the bride away tomorrow," Agnes said.

"Yeah?" Frankie brightened. "Yeah. I'd like that."

"That should slow Brenda down long enough that with any luck she won't kill anybody during the ceremony," Agnes went on. "If we get real lucky, she'll have a heart attack."

"Hell, yes." Frankie wiped his fingers on the napkins Lisa Livia had dumped by his plate. "You got a tux for me?"

"You can use the Don's," Joey said with an undercurrent in his voice that Shane knew was important, but not as important as the fact that Wilson was fucking them over for some reason.

The son of a bitch had known all along. What else had he known? What other games was he playing? And why was he playing games at all?

"Plus if you show up in the open as Frankie Fortunato," Agnes went on, "that'll draw Casey Dean out in the open, too, so Shane can care of him, so that'll finally be done."

"Good," Frankie said, nodding as he reached for the turkey. "That's good."

Agnes was on a roll. "Of course you might get shot, but you can't make an omelet without breaking eggs." She handed him a plate of deviled eggs. "Have one."

"Hey," Frankie said, frowning.

"And as for Lisa Livia, what did you do with the five million, Frankie?" Agnes asked, an edge in her voice Shane had never heard before. Maybe something about fathers lying to daughters, he thought now, maybe something about too many lies. "Because Lisa Livia needs some of it and you're going to give it to her."

Lisa Livia sat very still across from Frankie, watching, her fork poised above her plate.

"The five million. Oh, that's a sad story," Frankie said, mixing Irish and Jersey and sounding like a lying bastard.

Rhett lifted his head and barked at the back door.

"Already I know you're lying, Frankie," Xavier said from the doorway.

An hour later, Agnes looked at the group crowded around her kitchen table stuffing their faces on a week's worth of leftovers and thought, *The Gang That Could Shoot Straight.* One cop, two hit men, two mobsters, a mob princess, and a food columnist, plus an ancient bloodhound for a mascot; if Evie showed up, they could do *Eight Is Enough.* Without Evie, lucky seven. Please God.

Shane pushed his plate away and then caught sight of her face. "Agnes?"

My team. My family.

"You okay?"

"I'm thinking."

Frankie had spun them the sad story of how he'd lost the five million trying to swim across the Blood River in his escape from Brenda and her frying pan. He tried to make it an epic story of one man's struggle against the flood, but it was basically one cheating goombah's story of how his wife tried to kill him and he hit the road with five mil, which he lost because he couldn't swim very well. The only thing that kept Agnes from killing him was that he was eating the entire time. You couldn't kill somebody who was eating your food. There were rules about things like that.

When Frankie was done with his tall tale, Agnes looked across the table to Lisa Livia. "So. How are you doing?"

"I liked him better dead."

Agnes nodded. "I'm starting to be grateful to mine for staying dead."

"So, Frankie, the five million is gone," Xavier said, shaking his head as she tried to offer him a deviled egg. "And you've just come home because you were so homesick."

"He's come home to roll on the Don," Agnes said, and Shane winced.

"Could I *talk to you* for a minute?" he said, and she handed him the scalloped potatoes, figuring that would hold him for a while.

"No," she said. "Xavier isn't stupid and he's going to notice I'm missing from his jail and he's not going to buy any 'she has to put on a wedding' garbage. In fact, I'm willing to bet that's why he's here now, to arrest me for breaking out of jail and probably to take you in, too, just from sheer exasperation. So I think we tell him what the hell's going on."

She looked at Xavier. "Shane works for the government. He's trying to keep Frankie alive to testify against the Don. Frankie wants to see

Maria get married and then he's going into the Witness Protection Program. He won't testify until the wedding is over, so the wedding has to go off tomorrow, then he testifies, then the Don goes to jail and Frankie disappears, and Palmer and Maria go off to wedded bliss. Since Frankie is here, we're going to use him to rattle Brenda. Nobody's managed to make a dent in her so far, but Frankie showing up alive should do it. That might help you get a confession out of her that she killed Taylor, which you know she did." She stopped for a minute, pretending to think, and did a quick survey of the assembled team. They were all looking at her with various degrees of admiration and relief. *What,* she thought. *You thought I was going to tell him that Shane was a hitman? Am I nuts?* "I think that's it," she finished. "Any questions?"

Xavier looked at Shane. "And you've known all of this from the beginning."

"National security," Shane said.

"Fucking FBI," Xavier said.

"Not quite," Shane said. "But close enough."

"So why didn't I get a visit from men in black suits telling me that I had to let Agnes go?"

"You did," Shane said. "I just don't own a suit, and I don't talk much."

"I'll need to see some identification," Xavier said, and Agnes thought, *Oh, hell,* but Shane took him aside while Joey and Frankie exchanged one of those glances again.

Agnes poked Joey hard in the side. "What aren't you telling Shane?"

Joey pushed his plate away. "He don't want to know."

"I have news for you," Agnes said. "He wants to know. You explode one more bomb under him, *he's* going to explode. I've never seen him lose it, but I've seen him when he *doesn't* lose it, and he's scary as hell. You tell him everything now, or—"

"Okay," Xavier said, coming back. "I'll hold the arrest warrant." He looked at Agnes. "You will not leave the jurisdiction."

"Hell, Xavier," Agnes said. "I won't leave Two Rivers. Do you have any idea what tomorrow—no, *today*, it's Saturday already—is going to be like around here?"

Xavier looked grim, which meant he had a good idea, and picked up his hat. "Good luck to you." He turned for the door.

"Hold it," Agnes said, and he turned back. "You're not going anywhere. I want Brenda arrested and in an orange jumpsuit by Sunday. We need you on this. Sit down and eat."

"Agnes," Shane said.

"We need a plan," Agnes said. "And we need the law in on it. What do we need to nail Brenda Fortunato for good?"

Xavier hesitated and then said, "Proof." He sat down beside Frankie, next to the Venus, and took the bowl of ribs away from him. Frankie looked like he was going to protest and then shut up and reached for the coleslaw instead.

Agnes passed him a fork as Shane said, "Okay, we need a plan. So part A is, Frankie walks Maria down the aisle tomorrow and scares Brenda so that she confesses all to Xavier. Good luck with that. Part B, Casey Dean sees Frankie, makes his move, and I . . . arrest him."

"Casey Dean is Shane's bad guy," Agnes said to Xavier.

"And Shane's going to arrest him," Xavier said around his rib. "Would that be cardiac arrest?"

Okay, Agnes thought, and reached for the deviled eggs. They were all eating and talking. She could eat now, too.

"And then part C, Frankie and I discuss Lisa Livia's inheritance," Shane said, fixing Frankie with a look that said, *You and me, Uncle Frankie*.

Frankie tried to look old and frail and innocent.

"Ha," Agnes said, and he gave up and passed the coleslaw back to her.

"And if Brenda doesn't freely confess to murder?" Xavier asked.

"She'll fuck up something else," Shane said. "You be ready for it."

They all began to talk at once, arguing out the best plan, overlapping each other's words as they reached over each other to get to the food, arguing and eating, Lisa Livia finally joining in as Carpenter pulled up a chair next to her, making Joey and Agnes scoot over, which brought her close to Shane.

Right where I want to be, she thought, and watched to make sure everybody had enough food. When the table was pretty much cleared she said, "Okay, here's my last word: Nobody shoots anybody tonight. We're a team now, one big *happy* family. We need each other. If everybody shows up here tomorrow breathing and with all working body parts, and I do mean *everybody,* I'll make breakfast. Anything you want. But if anybody hurts anybody else on the team, I'm going to be *upset.* Understand?"

Joey and Frankie looked in different directions.

"And nobody wants Agnes upset," Shane said.

Joey and Frankie nodded.

"Good." Agnes shoved her chair back. "Now let's all get some sleep. And somebody check on Garth, please."

"I'll check on the lad," Frankie said, getting up.

"You're not fucking Irish," Joey said, getting up to go with him.

"*Family,*" Agnes said, steel in her voice.

"I can't wait for the holidays," Xavier said, and left them to their slumbers.

Shane followed Agnes up the stairs to the second floor as she said, "Do you think any of this is going to work?"

"It's a place to start," he said. "We'll play it by ear—what's wrong?"

Agnes had stopped at the top of the stairs. "Maria and the bridesmaids are in three of the bedrooms up here, and Carpenter and LL are in the other one. We'll have to use the housekeeper's room again—"

"Nope," he said, and steered her toward the attic stairs, his hands on her waist.

She hesitated and then went along, saying, "I suppose you're right," sounding exhausted. "That whole saving-the-attic-bedroom-as-commitment thing was dumb."

"Nope," he said, letting his hands slide down to her hips, patting her beautiful round butt as she climbed in front of him. His world was going to hell, but Agnes still had a great ass and right now that was enough.

She opened the door at the top of the stairs and then went into the bedroom on the right, and the moonlight flooded the room from the low windows, making it feel almost underwater, peaceful. The big low bed had looked inviting before, but now Agnes said, *"Oh,"* with an ache in her voice that was almost a moan, and he felt the same way.

Shane looked at her in the dim light, round everywhere. "Long day."

"I need a shower first," she said. "I was in *jail.*"

"Been there," Shane said, and watched her pad across the hardwood floor to the half-finished bath on the other side, telling himself that she was exhausted and they were both mind-fried from thinking about the next day until he heard the shower go on, and then he gave up being the Sensitive Guy and stripped and went in to join her.

She hadn't turned the lights on in the bathroom, either, so he found her by the moonlight coming through the skylight, making the soap blue on her wet skin. "Hey," she said, but it was a soft welcome, not a protest, and his hands slid on her soapy lush curves, and he forgot the next day and lost himself in Agnes and in the feel of her hands as she stroked the soap over him, and the soft sound of her giggle and sigh under the water, and the taste of her as she tangled her tongue with his, the way her body yielded to the shove of his, the way she shivered against the scrape of his beard, drew breath at the slide of fingers, and urged him on, hungry for him as he invaded her, but mostly the way she *wanted* him, wrapped herself around him and demanded him, and by the time they fell onto the bed, she was so hot, so desperate for him, and he was so insane for her, that he drove into her, into the shock and the need, into everything she was, obliterating himself in her, nothing but him in her, rolling in those satin sheets, until they both exploded, and when he came back to the cool blue room and the moonlight and the quiet with Agnes shuddering in his arms, holding on to him as if she'd never let him go, for the first time in his life he thought, *Don't let go,* and held on.

The sunlight woke Agnes up because it came in at such a funny angle, and then when she realized where she was, she sat bolt upright and said, *"Oh, my God!"* and Shane sat up, too, and said, *"What?"* reaching for his gun, which, probably for the first time in his life, wasn't within reach because she'd kicked it last night, flailing around. Even Rhett jerked awake under the windows and looked around.

"I overslept. I think." Agnes looked around for a clock, but there wasn't any. "Do you have a watch? What time is it?"

Rhett gave them both a dirty look and went back to sleep.

Shane reached over her, which felt so good that she didn't fall back against the pillows until he pressed her down there with his body as he grabbed his gun and his watch out of the pile of clothing next to the bed. "Six," he said to her, keeping her pinned down.

"Oh, good," she said, nestling back into the pillows. "I still have to get up, but it's not a complete disaster. How's your gun?" She grinned at him, and he put the gun on the bedside table and rolled her to him so that they lay side by side.

"My gun is fine," he said, and pulled her leg over his hip so she could feel him hard against her.

"I guess it is." She settled in closer as he began to kiss her neck. "This was a good idea, sleeping up here. I should have been up here a long time ago instead of saving this place for some dumb commitment idea."

"Nope," he said, and kissed her, and she settled into the kiss the way she'd settled into his body as his hand slid down her stomach, practically following a path by now. She started to giggle at the thought—Shane blazing a trail—and he said, "What?" but he grinned against her mouth.

"You're going to wear a groove there," she said, and then stopped smiling. "Not that I'm assuming you're staying—"

"I'm staying," he said, and kissed her again.

When she came up for air, she said, "You don't have to say—"

"Can we have this conversation tonight?" he said, and she looked up at him, not sure. "I think a lot of things are going to happen to both of us today. But I know I'm going to be back in this bedroom with you tonight. Can we talk about this then?"

Agnes swallowed. "Sure." *He knows he's going to be back here tonight.* She wriggled a little with happiness, and he grinned and pulled her closer.

"Because if we keep talking, you're going to have to leave to go do wedding stuff," he said, letting his hand drift lower, "and I'm not going to get laid."

"Right," Agnes said, and sighed against him, but she thought, *God, I hope we're both still alive to be back here tonight.*

Then he kissed her, and she stopped thinking at all.

An hour later, the buzz of Shane's sat phone woke him up.

"I hate that thing," Agnes murmured, buried under the blanket, her head resting on his chest.

Rhett lifted his head from his place on the floor and communicated his displeasure with a long look before he collapsed back onto the pillow Agnes had put there for him.

"Yeah, I'm starting to feel that way, too," Shane told them both as he checked the phone.

DOCK—FIFTEEN MINUTES

"I've got to meet Wilson," he told her.

"I hate him, too."

"Yeah," Shane said, his mind reluctantly turning to things he didn't want to face.

Wilson had kept information back, vital information. That could have been part of his fucking No Need To Know, part of the whole responsibility of the guy who's in charge—the reality of taking Wilson's place suddenly swept over him, ensconced in Washington, sending others out into the field to do the dirty work, others like Carpenter—but it could be something else, too, and his gut was telling him it was something else and it wasn't good.

He sat up, hating to move away from her warmth. "I'll tell you about it later."

"Can you?" She raised herself up a little, wide awake now. "Because if you can't, just say you can't. Please."

Shane paused and looked down at her. He'd always seen her as capable, angry—definitely angry—and in charge. But right now she just looked vulnerable. He leaned over and kissed her. "Right. I promise."

Another promise. "I'll be back tonight." Getting to be a habit.

Agnes sighed and nodded and rolled out of bed in all her naked splendor. "Okay, then. Breakfast to make. Maria's wedding day. I'm sure everything will go well." She crossed her eyes at him and went into the bathroom, and he sat looking at the space where she'd been for a second, just in case she came back.

"Yeah," he said, and got dressed and went outside into the early morning quiet. The sun was behind him, shooting over the trees and lighting up the far shoreline of the Blood River. The only sound was the quiet lap of water against the pink sand and the honking of Cerise and Hot Pink as they greeted the new day. For a few minutes, he could pretend it was peaceful. Until he heard the boat engine.

Shane looked toward the dock and saw Wilson's boat pull up to it. The old man stepped onto the floating dock and the boat pulled away to a holding position. As Shane went to the long walkway, Wilson made his way slowly up the metal gangplank to the high dock.

Shane heard a car door slam and looked over his shoulder. Frankie Fortunato had just gotten out of his pickup and was stretching, his white hair now dyed black, his beard gone. He was still fifty pounds heavier, but now he looked like Frankie. A second pickup was coming down the drive: Joey. Shane imagined the two had spent an interesting night talking over old times. And threatening to shoot each other. Good thing they were both afraid of Agnes.

Shane stepped onto the wooden dock and began the long walk out.

As he neared Wilson, he could finally see how old his boss was. Older than Joey, older than all the others involved in this. Shane wondered how that felt, how tired Wilson was. How done he was with what he'd been doing for over sixty years. Or was he really done?

Wilson was already seated when Shane arrived at the high dock. Glancing over at the *Brenda Belle,* Shane saw no sign of the boat's owner. Brenda must be biding her time to make her grand entrance. Or sleeping in so she'd have plenty of energy to let loose the dogs of war.

Shane sat down across from his boss. "Good morning."

Wilson nodded. "Today's the day. Casey Dean will—"

"You knew about Frankie Fortunato."

Wilson hesitated for a fraction of a second and then nodded.

"It would have helped if you had informed me," Shane said.

"Doubtful," Wilson said. "You had more than enough intelligence on Casey Dean to do your job. As you might learn, if you achieve my position, less information in the field is preferable most of the time."

"I don't agree."

Wilson shrugged. "It doesn't matter. Given your recent failures, it will be difficult to convince my associates to have you replace me."

"It might be difficult to convince me."

Wilson looked at him, displeased.

Shane stared back at him. "I took out Casey Dean's girlfriend last night."

Wilson stared at him, startled. "Why didn't you or Carpenter report this? And where is she?"

"We were busy."

Wilson's lip curled. "Breaking a suspected murderer out of jail."

"Yes."

"I have allowed you a great deal of latitude here," Wilson began, "and—"

Shane interrupted him. "You've been testing me."

"Very good," Wilson said, practically patting him on the head. "And the girlfriend?"

"We have her. You knew Casey Dean used a woman as his front."

Wilson shrugged. "There were suspicions to that effect."

"That was also part of the test." Shane tried to keep the bitterness from his voice. Carpenter and Joey had almost died so that Wilson could test a job applicant.

"Flexibility of thinking is critical for my job."

Shane sat silent for several moments, staring at the old man. Finally he looked away. He could see Joey on the back porch now, a mug of coffee in his hand, looking out at them. Frankie was moving chairs around in front of the gazebo, getting it ready for the ceremony. Agnes was at the kitchen window, at the kitchen sink, making breakfast for the crowd again. Upstairs, Lisa Livia walked past her bedroom window in her bra, talking a mile a minute, probably to Maria. Even the flamingos were honking as usual.

"The test isn't over, is it?" Shane asked, knowing that Wilson still held all the cards.

"No."

"Yesterday I thought I might be Casey Dean's target."

"Why is that?" Wilson asked.

"Because my real name is Fortunato. My uncle Joey told me my father was the Don's older brother, Roberto."

"You were not Casey Dean's target," Wilson said.

"No."

"But your uncle told you only half the story."

There was something snakelike in the way Wilson said the words, almost as if his tongue were flicking in and out. He *savored* the words, and Shane realized he'd savored a lot of the information he'd been dropping recently.

Behind that desiccated mask, Wilson was enjoying this.

Shane made himself still. "And the other half?"

"Torcelli told you that your parents died in a boating accident, correct?" Wilson's lips twitched, almost imperceptively, too little to notice unless you were watching for it.

Shane was watching for it. He nodded.

"Not true." Wilson lifted his chin, watching Shane from under lizardlike eyelids. "They were murdered by Don Michael Fortunato."

Shane was perfectly still.

"Your father, the eldest brother, stood in Michael's way, so he rigged their boat to explode. They went out on the water, and he blew it up by remote control from a nearby cruiser." Wilson watched Shane.

Shane sat, unmoving.

"They say your father tried to save your mother even though he was horribly wounded."

Shane looked past Wilson to the Blood, beautiful in the early morning.

"They say he screamed her name as he died."

He was aware of the sound of the water lapping against the floating dock and the slight creak of metal on wood as it moved against the steel gangplank.

"They say she cried out yours."

Shane turned back to Wilson. *Look for what he wants.*

Wilson was sitting, looking impassive, but that light was behind his eyes. "I believe she drowned, according to intelligence. There was no coroner's report. The Don let the bodies go down with the boat."

What does he want?

"You don't believe me? Ask your uncle Joey. Or your uncle Frankie. They've known for years."

Frankie and Joey at the table last night. Joey shaking his head. Shane felt heat now—it had been rising the entire time, filling his head, blanking out his brain, but now he could feel it—the old heat from when he'd been a kid, fists flailing. *Don't go there, that's what Wilson wants, do not go there.*

"The real question," Wilson was saying, "is what do you intend to do about it? Because you have a job to do, Mr. Fortunato. One that does not allow for distraction because of personal issues. Can you still do your job and protect the Don?"

He sat back and allowed himself a small complacent smile.

Shane got up and began the long walk down the dock to Joey.

Agnes tipped a pan of pineapple-orange muffins out onto the counter, wiped her hands on her Cranky Agnes apron, and then stepped back beside Carpenter to look out the kitchen window toward the dock, where Shane was meeting with his boss. She felt a little ridiculous baking muffins in a cherry pink halter dress covered with a promo apron, until she saw the man she loved standing like the Grim Reaper, staring down the wizened old goat he worked for. Then she forgot the dress. There was something definitely wrong down on that dock.

"He said something about getting a better job."

Carpenter nodded. "He's in line for a promotion."

Agnes's heart sank. So much for hoping for a new line of work. "So that would be good?"

Carpenter turned his head and looked down at her. "Not for Shane. Shane has been finding his way to the light this week."

"Oh, hell," Agnes said, watching Shane stride back from the dock. He looked tense. As he got closer, she realized that was too tame a description: He looked white with rage, something she'd never seen before.

Carpenter went rigid beside her, as if he, too, knew something was very wrong, beyond the kind of wrong he'd seen before.

Lisa Livia ambled into the kitchen in her pink halter dress and said, "What's new?" She threw an arm around Carpenter's waist and then stopped smiling to look up at him. "What?"

"I don't know," Agnes said, but Carpenter walked away from both of them, as if neither of them were there, out through the porch and down the steps to meet Shane.

"What the hell?" Lisa Livia said, and Agnes went out onto the porch, where Joey was standing, also watching Shane, who was striding toward Frankie in the gazebo.

"This is bad," Joey muttered.

"What?" Agnes asked, but she didn't wait for an answer as she went down the back stairs and across the lawn to meet Shane. She was vaguely aware that Joey was right behind her, but all she cared about was Shane.

Frankie had climbed down and was waiting for him.

"My parents." Shane said it with a fury Agnes had never heard. He was glaring at Frankie, who said nothing, and, as they came up, he burned Joey with the same look.

"That bum Wilson tell you?" Joey asked.

"It's true?" Shane said.

Joey nodded.

"What?" Agnes asked.

Shane met her eyes, the cold, controlled man she'd met five days before obliterated by rage. "We'll be back." He looked at Carpenter. "You take care of things here."

Carpenter nodded once.

"What's going on?" Agnes said, but Shane was already crossing the lawn to the van, Joey and Frankie following him, their shoulders squared with the same determination. *"What the hell—"* she began, but Lisa Livia touched her arm.

"Let it go," she said, and Carpenter nodded, too, and Agnes swallowed and thought, *Well, he didn't lie to me,* and said, "Pineapple-orange muffins for breakfast," and went back to the house, praying that nobody was going to die, especially Shane.

"Do you know where the Don is staying?" Shane asked, working hard to keep a cap on his anger. He was driving Carpenter's van, Frankie and Joey in the captain's chairs behind him, looking like two old extras for some mob movie. Except they were the real deal.

Joey nodded. "Yeah. The Rice Plantation B-and-B. The Don likes quiet, classy joints. The rest of his men are at the Victory Motel with the hookers."

Shane looked back at Joey. "Why didn't you tell me?"

"If I'd of told you, you'd have gone after the Don and gotten yourself killed."

"I'd rather have heard it from you than Wilson," Shane said.

"I was more worried about keeping you alive," Joey said. "Wilson tells you stuff to control you."

"Give me the short version," Shane said as they turned onto the main road out of Agnes's driveway.

Frankie had been talking into his cell phone, and he turned it off before saying, "I just talked to the broad who runs the B-and-B. She says the Don and another guy, most likely his consigliere, are just wrapping up breakfast. So that's good. They gotta come this way for the wedding."

Shane nodded and drove to the B&B, following Joey's terse directions. Half a mile from the place, he pulled the van off the road, then backed into a narrow dirt trail.

"We're gonna stop the Don's car and I talk to him." He climbed between the seats, opened one of the lockers, and grabbed a platter-shaped device and a remote that went with it. Then he opened the side panel and climbed out. "You guys stay here," he told Joey and Frankie.

He went out to the narrow road and lay the platter down in the center, then grabbed a piece of Spanish moss and covered it.

When he was back in the van, he pulled out his Glock and checked the round in the chamber. Then he said, "Tell me what happened."

"We came down here for vacations every year," Frankie said. "Roberto, Michael, me, and Joey. And the families. Your parents went out fishing one day on a small boat, never came back. We got the call from the rental place that the boat hadn't come back; we went out looking, nothing. No one ever found your parents or the boat."

"But we know Michael did it," Joey said with loathing. "He was supposed to be in Savannah when they went missing, but when he showed up again he was different. Confident. Cocky. The son of a bitch."

"You let him get away with it?" Shane said, disbelief in his voice.

"What was we gonna do?" Joey said. "We had no proof. Everyone suspected, but nobody could say for certain, 'cause nobody knew nothin' about it. And I mean, *nothin'*. And where would a guy like Mikey get that kind of bomb on his own? He had to have help, smart help. And not just that snake of a consigliere of his, although he was down here then, too. We couldn't figure it out. And we couldn't whack Michael, or Don Carlo would be all over us. And you were in danger, you were his next hit. So we made a deal."

"To stay in Keyes," Shane said. "And keep me in the dark. Give me a different name. Tell me you didn't know who my father was."

Frankie and Joey nodded once more, two grim, bobblehead old goombahs.

"That's how we ended up staying down here," Frankie said. "Brenda was pissed as hell about that. But I always thought she knew. She offered to babysit you that day, and she never did that before."

Joey jerked his head up.

Frankie nodded. "Yeah. I never said nothin' because she was my wife, but that bothered the hell out of me. We fought about it, and she cried, big hysterics, but you gotta wonder why she wanted to take care of a baby just that one day. She didn't like babies much. But just that one day, she said, 'Give me the baby,' and they handed you over and went off for a big romantic day on the water."

Shane could see them, his dad and his mom on the boat, both of them laughing, probably the first day they'd had alone since he'd been born, a day on the water—

The heat in his head made him dizzy for a minute and then he heard Joey say, "Jesus, she knew. Why—?"

"I think she thought it was gonna move me up in the Family," Frankie said. "She was gonna be Our Lady of the Fortunatos, open the doors to a big house and invite everybody in, sit at the head of the table, queen of New Jersey."

The scene played again, but this time it was him, taking Agnes aboard a boat, her laughing up at him . . . *What if I couldn't get to her? What if she was screaming, in agony, and I couldn't get to her?*

"Maybe we don't leave her to Xavier," Joey said.

"*No,*" Shane said, and Joey shut up. He took a deep breath. "You told me you never saw the consigliere before."

Joey shrugged. "I was just trying to protect you."

Thirty-five years ago, Joey was a thirty-year-old widowed mobster looking at a baby he was going to have take care of. Considering his limitations and what he was up against, he'd done a pretty damn good job. The fact that he couldn't stop now was possibly understandable.

"Okay," Shane asked. "Wilson. How does he play into all this? How does he know?"

Joey frowned. "I don't know. But he's a spook, and spooks and the Organization have worked together before, ever since the big war when the government needed help in Italy. So you're talking over sixty years. Wilson's probably got people wired in."

Literally, Shane thought, remembering the transcript of Don Fortunato's phone call with Casey Dean. Sixty years. About as long as Wilson headed the Organization.

He heard a car coming and slid out of the van into the shade on the side of the road.

A black Lincoln Town Car came rumbling down the road. Shane waited until it was over the platter, then pressed the remote. The platter sent out a massive electromagnetic pulse that fried all the electronics in the car. The engine died and the car rolled by, slowing to a halt about forty feet down the road.

The driver's door opened and the consigliere got out, cursing. Shane's jaw tightened as the passenger door opened and Don Michael stepped out, dapper as all hell. The years had been damn good to him. The consigliere popped the hood and both men disappeared around the front of the car as they tried to figure out what had happened. Shane stepped onto the road, Glock at the ready. He walked to car, then edged around to where he could see the two men.

"Don't move," Shane said.

They both swiveled their heads and stared at him. Then the Don smiled. "Shane," he said. "Am I correct?"

Shane nodded. "Uncle Michael."

The Don and his consigliere exchanged a glance.

"Who told ya?" the Don asked. "Joey?"

"You killed my parents."

The Don laughed, and Shane's hand tightened so much on the gun, he realized the barrel was shaking. *Not good,* he thought.

"You ain't gonna shoot me," the Don said. "Not in cold blood. Your father wouldn't, and you can't."

"I want the truth," Shane said. "About how they died."

"Wasn't me," the Don said. "I was in Savannah. Got witnesses to that."

"Then who was it?" Shane asked. "Him?" He nodded at the consigliere.

The consigliere's eyes slid left, almost a twitch.

"Better yet," Shane said. "Where did you get the bomb? Remote detonated, right? Who gave it to you?"

"I don't know what you're talking about," the Don said, his face smooth.

"And why did *he* give it to you?" Shane said. "Did *he* think you were such a dumb fuck, you'd be easier to manipulate than my father?"

"What?" the Don said, looking rattled for the first time.

"Did *he* figure that since you are the dumbest fucking Fortunato to ever draw breath, *he* wanted you in charge of the Family so *he* could use you like a two-dollar whore, something *he* knew my father would never allow?"

"Hey," the Don said, his face darkening, "nobody uses me, I use *him*—"

"And did he know my mother was on that boat when he blew it up? Did you tell him that, you murdering bastard? Or did you tell him it was just another mob hit?" Shane heard his own breathing, saw the landscape in a red mist, and some small part of him said, *Walk away now.* "He still thinks you're a dumb fuck, you know. That's why he just told me. He thinks I'm going to kill you, which is good with him because he's finished with you. He wants me to take your place. Consolidation. Government hitman and mob boss in one person. Easier. And then he thinks he can control me. All I have to do is kill you and I get it all."

The Don's eyes widened.

Shane shook his head. "But I'm not going to."

The Don let out his breath and nodded. "You're a good boy, Shane. You're a good Fortunato. My heir. Next in line. You can put the gun down now."

"I'm not going to kill you because I don't have to," Shane said, and turned and walked away as Frankie and Joey walked past him, their faces like stone.

The last thing he heard was the Don saying, *"Frankie?"* and then a fusillade of shots ripping apart the Saturday morning as he began the long walk back to Two Rivers.

He never looked back.

Agnes had fed Carpenter and Lisa Livia and Maria and the brides-maids and a dazzled Garth—all that beauty in bathrobes and curlers stunned him—and then sent Garth off to help that floozy Maisie double-check the flowers, and to make sure everything for the wedding was in place, including the flamingo pen place cards, and to keep an eye out for Butch, who was late to pick up Cerise and Hot Pink. She also cleaned raspberry sauce off the pantry door, which had been locked the night before to prevent anybody getting at the cakes, Downer and his damn practical jokes, in particular. The raspberry sauce there made no sense, but then it was hardly the only incomprehensible thing in her life, so she let it go to step over Rhett, clean up the rest of the kitchen with Lisa Livia and Carpenter, and try not to wonder if Shane was lying in a pool of blood somewhere with two old mobsters dying beside him.

It was about nine when they heard Maria scream. Again.

"If she thinks Palmer is having sex with another stripper somewhere, I'm going to be annoyed," Agnes said, but Lisa Livia shook her head and headed for the hallway calling, "What's wrong, baby?" as Carpenter took the dish towel from her hands and said, "Go upstairs and do the bride stuff. I'll hold the fort down here."

"He's okay, right?" Agnes said, not able to stand it anymore.

"He's fine," Carpenter said. "Somebody else isn't, but he's fine."

Agnes nodded. "Okay, then. Do you think there's any chance he's going into a new line of work soon?"

"I think he could be persuaded," Carpenter said.

"Yes, but would it be fair if I did that?" Agnes said. "I mean, it's his work—" and then Lisa Livia yelled, *"Agnes, get up here!"* and she said, "Oh, just hell, Carpenter, what should I do?" and he said, "Get up there," and she went.

When she followed the sounds of outraged female babbling, she found them all—Lisa Livia, Maria, and three bridesmaids all in slips and curlers—staring at Maria's white wedding dress, now covered with purply red stains, the worst of which were two purply red handprints over the breast cups on the bodice. Small, Brenda-sized hands. *She's completely out of control,* Agnes thought. *She's just destroying things now, anything to screw up the wedding.*

"It's *ruined!*" Maria wept, and her bridesmaids clustered round her and wept with her.

"Yep." Agnes looked at it as she listened for the van. A car door slammed outside and she jerked her head to see out the window, praying it was Shane, but it was just the first wedding guests, complete with a little girl who was probably going to cry through the whole ceremony. *Damned early birds, stay home and give your kid a nap.*

"What is that horrible stuff?" Maria wept.

"Huh?" Agnes said. "Oh, that's the raspberry sauce from dessert last night."

Maria looked at her, horror-struck. "That's all you can say? It's dessert? My God, Agnes, *it's my wedding dress!*"

Another car door slammed, and Agnes looked again. Still not Shane. What was it with all these people coming early? It wasn't like you got extra cake.

"Look, honey," Lisa Livia said to Maria. "You—"

"And you stay out of this," Maria said, turning on her, with her acolytes around her. "You and your mouth, butting in all the time, that's what got me that damn flamingo dress and that's what I'm going to have to wear now and it's all because of *you*—"

"*Hey!*" Agnes said, seeing Lisa Livia flinch.

"I know," Lisa Livia said to Maria, miserable. "Really, I know I screwed up—"

"That's not good enough," Maria snapped. "You swear to me that you won't say anything today, not one word at my wedding besides polite conversation, you will not interfere in any way, you swear it to me now."

Lisa Livia swallowed and nodded. "I swear I won't say a word all day that isn't 'Hello, how are you, beautiful day for a wedding.' I will not screw up anything else, I promise."

Another car door. Agnes looked out the window. Not Shane. *Damn it.* He wasn't dead. Other people died, not Shane—

"I don't believe it," Maria was saying, the bridesmaids nodding. "Like you could *stop* talking or interfering. This is like the worst thing that could happen—"

"*Okay, that's it,*" Agnes said.

Everybody turned at looked at her.

"I know this is wedding nerves," Agnes said to Maria. "I know you're a good sweet girl and you've had a terrible week, I know you love your mother, I know this isn't you, but you just crossed the line."

"Oh, please," Maria said, looking put upon.

Agnes looked at the bridesmaids. "You should go get dressed.

Now." When they hesitated, she added, "Go!" and Maria nodded, and they went. Agnes took a step closer to Maria. "Now listen, you. Taylor died last night with a fork through his throat. I know in the excitement of getting married you probably forgot that—"

Maria flushed. "No, but—"

"—but he died in pain and terror choking on his own blood, so the fact that you're going to have to wear a pink dress sewn in one night by a woman who makes a fraction of what you're going to be spending on lunch once you marry this very nice boy who loves you—a woman, I might add, who stayed up all night to fix a dress that you dyed pink to play a joke on the mother of that boy—well, I just can't get too worked up over your tragedy, Maria. You're nineteen, you're marrying a man who adores you, you're going to be filthy rich, and, oh yeah, you're going to have everything your mother never had because she worked her ass off to make sure you got it, and now your fucking grandmother just took all of it and her future from her, which is something you don't seem to have much sympathy for. So while you're screaming and moaning, you might want to look around and notice that you're the luckiest person in this damn place and the rest of us have zero sympathy for you. Now go get those dumb curlers out of your hair and put on your pink dress and don't give me any more tragedy about how you're not sure Palmer loves you. If he's been putting up with this drama princess act and he still wants to spend the rest of his life with you, he loves you."

Maria looked at her, outraged, and then looked at her mother for support.

Lisa Livia shrugged. "Hello, how are you, beautiful day for a wedding."

"Oh, well that's just fine," Maria said, and flounced off, but there was a wavering edge to her voice that gave Agnes hope.

Lisa Livia looked back at the dress. "Brenda did that."

Agnes said, "Yep, and if she was nuts enough to do that, then she's going to do some more stupid things today and get herself caught."

She heard a door slam below and this time it sounded like a van, but when she looked out, she saw only Joey and Frankie getting out of Carpenter's van.

"No," she said, her blood going cold, and ran for the stairs.

Shane was surveying the backyard when he felt somebody sack him from behind, her arms going around him so tightly, his air went out with an *oomph*. He turned around, not easy as tightly as Agnes was clinging to him, and said, "Hey," as his arms went around her. She said into his chest, "I thought you were dead, I didn't see you come back with Joey and Frankie," and he said, "Nah, I told you, I'll always come back." Then she lifted her face, and he saw how terrified she'd been and he kissed her hard, and she held him a little longer than he'd intended, and the longer she held on and kissed him, the more the ugliness of the past receded, and all the good that was Agnes and Two Rivers washed over him.

When she broke the kiss, she said, "I want you to quit that damn job," and he nodded. "Okay, then," she said, and kissed him again, and then he let her go and realized she was wearing something very un-Agnes, a low-cut, tight pink dress that made her look like Jessica Rabbit.

"Nice dress," he said, trying not to laugh, and more of the ugliness went away. It was never all going to go away—there was too much of it, and some of it still had to be dealt with—but Agnes was a pretty good antidote for right now.

"Lisa Livia picked it out," Agnes said, starting to grin, too, which was good; he hated it when she was worried. Another reason to stop killing people for a living.

"Well, it looks great," he said, because it did. Kind of.

"She bought one for Evie, too," Agnes said. "I don't believe Evie's going to wear it, but it was kind of a mother-of-the-bride thing. Or something. Sometimes I don't follow Lisa Livia's thought processes."

"I don't follow Carpenter's either sometimes, but it's always good,"

Shane said, holding her away from him to look at the dress again. "It's not the kind of dress you could run in."

"That's very practical of you, dear," Agnes said, and turned to go back to the house, which was when Shane saw that it was really tight through the rear and had no back at all.

"I really like that dress," he said, and her laugher floated back to him.

Shane grinned, thinking, *That's my girl,* and she turned and smiled back at him, and just for that second before she went on he imagined that she looked like his mother might have, smiling back at his father, and the need for vengeance rose up again like a knife. But vengeance had been Frankie and Joey's to take, not his. And his father and mother had found each other in the beginning, had had each other for a while, had had a life together for a while.

It would have been so much worse never having found each other.

Agnes stopped at the porch door and looked back at him again in her Jessica Rabbit dress, so much love in her smile, so grateful he was back, and he grinned at her and she went inside and he walked down to see what was going wrong at the wedding.

Because everything was just fine at the house.

Agnes walked into the kitchen, trying not to beam, but it was hard. He was going to quit. Maria was mad but she was going to marry Palmer. If Butch would just show up with his van and pick up Cerise and Hot Pink, and Frankie would cough up the money, and she could get her column done—

"Uncle Michael isn't here," Maria said, her hands on hips, splendid in her pink wedding dress.

Agnes blinked at her. "What?"

"Uncle Michael. The Don." Maria folded her arms. "The guy who was giving me away. He's not here."

"He ain't gonna be here," a brand-new Frankie said from the

doorway as Rhett padded past him, oblivious to the drama going on around him. "And you ain't gonna miss him." He straightened the jacket of his tux and lifted his newly shaven chin, and he looked every inch a Fortunato.

"Oh, God," Agnes said. "What happened to the Don?"

"I'm giving you away, Maria," Frankie said, offering Maria his arm.

Maria blinked at him. "Doyle?"

"I'm your grandpa Frankie, honey," Frankie said.

Maria looked at Lisa Livia.

"This is my daddy," Lisa Livia said. "Frankie Fortunato. Your grandmother tried to kill him twenty-five years ago, so he swam the Blood River and got away from her, but now he's come back and he's going to walk you down the aisle."

Maria sat down on of the kitchen chairs.

"Want a drink?" Agnes said. " 'Cause I'm thinking I'm going to need one after the next question." She looked at Frankie. "Where's the Don, Frankie?"

"He's sleeping with those he did wrong to," Frankie said.

"Oh." Agnes got out the bourbon. "Did Shane kill him?"

"Nope," Frankie said while Agnes poured herself a shot. "Don't ask no more questions, Agnes," he added with affection.

"Wouldn't dream of it, Frankie," Agnes said, and knocked back her drink. "Maria?" she said, offering her the bottle.

"No, I'm good," Maria said. "So. Grandpa. You're going to walk me down the aisle. Okay." She looked at Agnes. "You find out who ruined my dress yet?"

"Oh, that was Brenda," Agnes said.

Maria's nodded. "So when she sees me coming down the aisle in her dress with Grandpa Frankie . . ."

"Could be a coronary," Agnes said.

Maria stood up. "Hello, Grandpa."

"Wonderful," Agnes said. "And you really do look beautiful, Maria." When Maria didn't look at her again, she thought, *Well, I have to earn that,* and started for the door, almost toppling over as her knees met the hem of her pencil skirt, a problem she'd been having all morning. *Small steps,* she told herself, and tried again.

To Do List, she thought as she minced her way down the porch steps. *Take back Maria's wedding from the clowns. Get Brenda to incriminate herself. Get Lisa Livia her money back. Get Shane a better job. Write column.*

Burn this damn dress.

Shane surveyed the wedding party. There were about a hundred people gathered. The Don's goombahs were clustered together on Maria's side, and they were going to be surprised when Frankie walked down the aisle instead of the Don. Brenda was not there yet. Probably waiting to make an entrance. That should be good, too.

He checked off the players on the groom's side: the groom, best man, ushers, preacher, musicians, and photographer were in place, and yes, there in the front row was Evie wearing something in that same pink that Agnes had been slinking around in. Evie had a jacket over hers, though. *Good plan,* Shane thought. Then he frowned as he looked out past the lawn: Wilson's boat was back, anchored just off the dock and to the left of Brenda's yacht. Coming to watch the hit?

Had he watched a hit before? Shane wondered. Had the consigliere reported to him so that he knew the details of the deaths—the words *they say* echoing in his mind—or had Wilson known firsthand? What the fuck was the real deal?

Shane walked across the lawn to the photographer, an attractive woman with several cameras dangling on straps around her neck. "Could I borrow your camera with the best zoom for a second?"

The woman turned to him and smiled. "Sure." She pulled one off and held it out for him.

Shane took it. "Thanks." He took the camera and zoomed in on the yacht. Wilson was on the bridge with another old man Shane recognized from intelligence briefings: the head of the mob in New York City. Another of Wilson's puppets, Shane thought. Come to see the coronation of the successor in New Jersey. He handed the camera back to her.

"Appreciate it," he said.

"No sweat." She went back to the guests, and Shane walked over to Carpenter at the edge of the gazebo.

"You do what you had to?" Carpenter asked.

"Joey and Frankie handled it," Shane said. "There've been some changes in the plan. Let's find Casey Dean first." He pulled out the pink cell phone he'd taken from Abigail's bag the night before and hit number 1 on the speed-dial.

Shane stiffened as a woman's voice answered: "Where are you, sis?"

He was still processing that when Carpenter nudged him and pointed. "Over there."

Shane looked across the cluster of guests. The photographer had a cell phone in her hand, and she tossed her hair away from it as she listened in a way Shane remembered.

"Princess," Shane said into the phone. "What's your sign?"

He saw the photographer turn her head and stare right back at him.

"Where's Abigail?" she said into the phone

"I've got her," Shane said. "Casey Dean, I presume? We met before. In a bar in Savannah."

"What do you want?" Casey Dean asked, glaring at Shane.

"The Don's dead, so your contract is, how should I say, defunct." Shane could see her go rigid. "Bullshit."

"You see Don Fortunato or his consigliere anywhere around?"

There was silence. Shane continued. "When the grandfather of the bride escorts her down the aisle, you'll know I'm telling the truth. You do anything, I'll have your ass."

There were several seconds of silence; then Casey Dean spoke. "Where's my sister?"

"We have her, along with the five million."

"What do you want?"

"For now, the wedding to go off without a hitch. Are you clear on that?"

"Yes." The word was a hiss. "But you're fucking up, big-time."

"Make sure to take some good pictures." Shane hit the OFF button, but paused, thinking about what Casey Dean had just said. He looked at the pink phone, then hit 2 on the speed-dial and listened as the phone was answered.

"Yes?" Wilson said.

Shane turned the phone off, cold all over, and looked at Carpenter. "That thing we've been missing?"

"Yes?"

"I just found it."

Fifteen minutes earlier, Agnes had met Lisa Livia in the kitchen and found her wearing not only the Bon Ton pink-hearts dress, but also the pink-heart necklace that had started the whole mess as Rhett's collar.

"You're kidding," she said, and started to laugh.

"My *daddy* gave it to me," Lisa Livia said, holding it out with one finger. "He said he'd had it appraised and it was worth about ten grand and he wanted me to have it."

"Ten grand?" Agnes said doubtfully.

"He's wrong," Lisa Livia said. "It's worth at least thirty. The big hearts are pink quartz, but the spacers are pink diamonds. Good ones, too. He probably went to some fence in Savannah who lowballed him."

"Oh, my God," Agnes said. "And he put it on Rhett."

"Here," Lisa Livia said, and held out her hand, and when Agnes put out her palm, Lisa Livia dropped a pink ribbon onto it. "It's one of the hearts and a couple of the diamonds. It's not much, probably only five grand, but it's a thank-you and a souvenir. In case you ever forget Maria's wedding. Or need some quick cash."

Agnes held up the ribbon to see the heart sparkle in the sunlight, the diamonds sparkling brighter. It was godawful ugly. "I'll never give it up," she said truthfully.

"We gotta wear them," Lisa Livia said, and helped her tie it on. Then she stood back and smiled happily. "Brenda's going to have a heart attack."

They made their way down to the gazebo with Rhett, the flamingos honking in the background because that idiot Butch had not shown up, and they both stopped, stunned, when they saw Evie, dressed in the same cherry dress and wearing a pink jacket and a pink straw hat with a giant pink daisy on it, looking cute as all hell, sitting beside her husband, Jefferson, in all his grayed *Dynasty* dignity.

"I don't believe it," Agnes said as they sat down in the front row, Rhett collapsing at their feet. "Evie wore the dress."

"She cheated," Lisa Livia said. "She's wearing a jacket."

"Yes, but it matches," Agnes said, impressed. "I bet she had that made. I bet it cost ten times what the dress did. And the hat is killer."

"She's gonna outshine Brenda," Lisa Livia said. "I just love Evie Keyes."

Garth was sitting right behind them with a pretty girl in her Sunday best named Tara, who was looking around wide-eyed at everybody. He looked serious, sitting straight in a very nice suit jacket that Palmer had helped him pick out and then paid for, and Agnes thought, *Good for Palmer.* She turned around and whispered, "You've done a great job here, Garth. I don't know what we would have done without you."

The girl looked at Garth with awe. Garth blushed brighter than Cerise.

Agnes turned around and grinned.

Palmer and Downer took their places next to Reverend Miller, a big man who looked extremely unhappy to be there. Downer, on the other hand, looked ecstatic, which meant he probably had something horrible up his sleeve. And Palmer looked like death, or at least hungover to the point of death, staring off into the distance with that If I Don't Move, My Head Won't Fall Off look in his eyes.

The reverend nodded to the band, which immediately struck up very fast Latin dance music that spooked Cerise and Hot Pink into wild honking.

"What the hell?" Palmer said, turning on Downer, who was laughing his ass off.

"Don't you get it?" Downer said, holding on to Palmer now, he was laughing so hard. "It's flamingo music."

"What?" Palmer said, completely confused.

"Flamenco music," Agnes said grimly, but at that point the entire assembly was looking the other direction, and even the band slowed and then stopped playing as the musicians gaped.

Brenda had arrived.

She'd probably been expecting the wedding march and intended to slide in front of Maria, so the flamenco music took her by surprise, but she carried on anyway, walking down the aisle in a black lace dress, holding a black lace handkerchief to her lips at intervals and nodding to anyone who murmured their sympathy to the widow as she glided to the front. By responding only to those who said something, she stayed just this side of good taste, but Brenda in black lace was always going to be hot, and the black lace mantilla she had added had an unfortunate Bride of Dracula effect that threatened to topple the whole thing over into comedy, except that Taylor was really dead.

"Morticia Addams does Seville?" Lisa Livia whispered.

"She's a widow," Agnes whispered back. "Show some respect."

"She ain't as much of a widow as she thinks she is," Lisa Livia said.

Brenda reached the gazebo and gave a sad smile to the groom's family in the front row and then turned to her side of the aisle to take her seat.

Lisa Livia waved to her.

Brenda saw the necklace and went rigid. Then she saw Agnes and went berserk. "We can't have this wedding," she said loudly, and pointed to Agnes. "That woman is a murderer. Detective Xavier, I saw you back there, why isn't this woman in jail?"

Xavier took a couple of steps out from underneath the old oak. "I believe Miss Agnes is on a recreational furlough. Don't you worry, Mrs. Beaufort. I got my eye on her." He nodded to Reverend Miller. "You can go on, Reverend."

"Well, I'm making a citizen's arrest," Brenda said, rigid and righteous in black lace.

"You can't, ma'am," Xavier said. "She's already under arrest. Now let's just all sit down and get started on this nice wedding." He came strolling over to the chairs on the bride's side, looking more relaxed than Agnes had ever seen him. On his way, he tipped his hat at Evie Keyes and gave her a roguish grin, and she smiled back at him, dimpling under her pink daisy.

Jefferson Keyes looked startled.

"I demand an arrest!" Brenda said, her voice growing sharper.

"If you don't sit down," Xavier said, his voice growing softer, "that arrest is gonna be you for disturbing the peace."

Brenda drew a deep breath, which did amazing things for her cleavage, and sat down next to Lisa Livia. "Where'd you get that necklace?" she spat.

"It was a gift," Lisa Livia snapped back.

Xavier sat down behind Brenda, next to Garth, who clearly wished he hadn't.

Up at the front, Reverend Miller was now conferring with Jefferson Keyes. Jefferson finally shook his head and sat back down.

Reverend Miller drew himself up to his full rotund height. "I'm sorry," he said, clearly not. "But I feel the irregularities present at this ceremony make it impossible for me to continue."

Lisa Livia tensed, but Brenda smiled, showing her teeth.

The reverend flared his nostrils. "I don't know what's going on, but there are undercurrents here that make this wedding less than the holy occasion it should be."

Agnes drew a deep calming breath, the way Dr. Garvin had taught her. *I'm going to kick your pompous ass into the Blood River and let the flamingos and the gators fight over it, you dickless wonder.*

Reverend Miller bowed his head. "Let's all close with a prayer—"

"Let's not."

Agnes looked at Lisa Livia, thinking for the moment that she'd broken her promise to Maria, but then she realized that Evie Keyes was standing up, pink daisy quivering with repressed emotion.

"If you don't feel you can perform the wedding ceremony of my son, who will someday inherit a significant portion of the Keyes land and fortune," Evie said, very distinctly, "then I understand. I'm just not sure *he* will." She fixed the reverend with the iciest blue eyes since the Snow Queen, and the reverend froze. Understandably.

Go, Evie, Agnes thought.

"What the hell?" Brenda murmured under her breath, leaning forward.

The reverend turned and smiled weakly at Palmer, who did not smile back, which wasn't surprising since Palmer hadn't smiled since Thursday, but Agnes wasn't about to tell Reverend Miller that.

The reverend turned back to Evie. "Can you assure me that nothing untoward is happening in occasion with this wedding?" he said, trying to work some sternness back into his voice.

"No," Evie said, having no trouble at all lacing her voice with a lot of *fuck you* and earning Agnes's undying respect in the process.

"Perhaps I was hasty," the reverend was saying, going down in ignominious defeat.

No doubt about it, Agnes thought as Evie took her seat again.

Brenda made a little shrieking sound beside her, full of rage and frustration.

"Very well." Reverend Miller nodded to the band, which struck up that goddamned flamenco music again, setting off Cerise and Hot Pink all over again.

"Stop that," Agnes said, standing up, and the whole wedding now looked at her as she scowled at the band. "You, classical music from now on. If you can't play that, you don't get paid. You know the wedding march?"

"Of course we know the wedding march," the bandleader said. "We had to learn the damn flamenco for this gig."

Downer burst out laughing again.

"*Grow up,*" Agnes said, and he stopped. Then she nodded to the band, and it began the wedding march.

"Jesus," Lisa Livia said.

"If we'd had this at the country club—" Brenda began.

"Shut your thieving, murdering mouth," Lisa Livia said, and Agnes thought, *That's fair,* and turned to watch Maria come down the aisle.

Maria appeared at the top of the porch steps, unsmiling but lovely in flamingo pink, and Frankie paused beside her, too, beaming and majestic in tuxedo black, and they walked across the lawn together until they reached the edge of the chairs. Then somebody said, "Who the hell is that?" and Brenda turned, and gasped, "*Frankie?*" rising to her feet on the word as her face went paper white, and Frankie waved to Lisa Livia, and then made a gun out of his thumb and forefinger and shot Brenda.

She fainted dead away and the wedding march trailed off.

Agnes looked at the bandleader. "Don't make me hurt you."

He nodded to the band, which struck up the wedding march again, and Maria began her walk down the white cotton runner, her chin up, her long dark hair ruffling in the breeze, and Frankie on her arm, still beaming.

Lisa Livia uncapped a bottle of water and poured it over her mother's head, ruining her hair and makeup and making Maria smile, and Brenda came to sputtering. Lisa Livia grabbed one arm and hauled her into her seat. Maria and Frankie reached the end of the aisle as a lot of the guests on the bride's side of the aisle suddenly developed a pressing need to be elsewhere.

Maria gave her maid of honor her flowers, Frankie patted her hand and gave it to Palmer, and then they both turned to Reverend Miller, Maria's smile fading as she saw him.

Frankie sat down beside Agnes and said, "Damn fine wedding, Agnes." Then he leaned forward so he could look past her and Lisa Livia to the dripping Brenda and said, "Hello, Brenda. I'm back. Miss me?"

She gazed back at him with such loathing that both Lisa Livia and Agnes pulled back a little.

"Hello, Frankie," she snarled. "Maisie's in the back row if you want a quickie."

"A marriage is a lifetime bond," Reverend Miller intoned loudly, gazing sternly at Maria, who stepped back a little. "One that should not be entered into lightly."

"I saw her," Frankie said. "She hasn't held up like you have, baby. What'd you do, kill a virgin and drink her blood, you murderous bitch?"

"They were a hell of a lot easier to find once you left town, you cheating bastard," Brenda said.

"Shut up," Lisa Livia hissed. "This is my kid's *wedding.*"

"Much soul searching should be done to ascertain that the two souls seeking to be joined *forever* are indeed soul mates," Reverend Miller said to Maria, whose shoulders slumped, "coming from the same kind of communities, speaking the same language—"

"Hey, I was just trying to find a little fuckin' *warmth,*" Frankie said. "Which I sure as hell wasn't gettin' at home."

"You weren't gettin' it at home because you were gettin' it every-place else," Brenda said. "*Fuckin'* everyplace else."

"*Shut up,*" Lisa Livia whispered savagely, and Agnes smacked Frankie on the arm and nodded toward Maria and Palmer.

"—because those who come from different backgrounds, from different *cultures,* may never truly find a common ground to bond upon." Reverend Miller looked sternly at Maria while Palmer continued to look off into the distance for a hangover remedy, having missed the entire speech.

"What the fuck is that minister saying to my little Maria?" Frankie said, startled.

"You let the goddamned minister alone," Brenda said.

"Did he just say my kid wasn't good enough for Palmer?" Lisa Livia said.

"Oh, for the love of God." Agnes stood up to face Reverend Miller.

"I don't know what 'celebrate' means in your vocabulary, but in mine, it doesn't mean making the bride feel like an outsider and everybody else want to kill themselves. You're done here. Go away."

"I tried to leave before," Reverend Miller snapped.

"I know," Agnes said. "But you were a real putz about it, so I'm not giving you any points for that." She looked around for Carpenter but saw only Shane, who was standing next to a large black trunk on a dolly. *That's new,* Agnes thought. "Carpenter?" she called.

"Right behind you," he said, and when she turned around, he was there, straightening his tie.

"Saw this coming, did you?"

"Didn't everybody?"

She leaned closer and whispered, "You swear to me this will be legal?"

"Yes," he whispered back. "I'm legal everywhere except Utah, North Carolina, and Las Vegas."

Agnes closed her eyes. "Okay," she whispered. "The bride and the groom are a little depressed. That hag from hell Brenda has convinced Palmer that Maria is marrying him for his money and convinced Maria that Palmer only wants her because she's beautiful and that he'll cheat on her. One of them might even say, 'I don't.'"

"Got it covered," he said, and moved to the front, majestic in his black suit.

"Welcome friends of Maria and Palmer," he said as he took his place in the gazebo, moving Reverend Miller out of the way at the same time by the sheer force of his bulk, and his voice rolled over them, rich and warm. "Many of you have made long trips to come here, some of them fraught with difficulties, and we are grateful to you for that. Maria and Palmer's trip to this moment has also been fraught with difficulties, and their willingness to surmount those challenges will speak to their hope for the future."

Palmer still looked as though he wasn't listening, but Maria turned to Agnes, giving her a *What the hell?* look.

"Six M&M'S," Agnes whispered. "Swear to God, Maria."

Maria took in a deep breath, nodded, and turned back to Carpenter.

Carpenter cleared his throat.

"Dearly beloved," he said. "We are gathered here today to honor a couple who have shown that they truly know the meaning of love through adversity, of staying the course no matter what life brings. Maria, a lovely girl who could marry any man she chose, is giving her hand to Palmer, a young man of great promise, in spite of his recent losses due to the disastrous lawsuits at the Flamingo Golf Course—"

"What?" Maria said, startled.

"—that have left him penniless—"

"*Dude,*" Downer said, taking a step away from Palmer.

"—and virtually unable to support her—"

"What?" Palmer said, finally waking up to frown at Carpenter. "What are you talking about?"

"*Palmer,*" Maria said, leaning closer to him.

"Really, Maria," Palmer said stiffly. "You don't need to worry about the money."

"I'm *not,*" Maria snapped. "I work, you know. I've worked since I was fifteen. I was *raised* to work. Have you *met* my mother? You think she'd raise a daughter to rely on a man for money?"

Palmer blinked. "I didn't mean . . ."

"I love you, you moron," Maria said, looking like she wanted to kill him. "And now that you're broke, I can prove it to you. In fact . . ." Her face cleared. "Palmer, this is good. We can make a fortune together."

"I'm *not broke,*" Palmer said, scowling at her.

"You're *not listening,*" Maria said. "You're a genius at golf courses, but you're not so smart at practical things. *I* am. I have my mother's brains, and I'm here to tell you, my mother is something else. With your creative brain and my street smarts, we're going to be millionaires in no time. And we'll do it together, Palmer. It'll be *better this way.*" She reached out and grabbed his arm. "We'll be broke for a while, but not for long. You have no idea how smart I am."

Palmer looked exasperated. "Of course I know how smart you are. Why do you think I'm marrying you? You're the smartest woman I've ever met. I knew that on our first date when the car broke down and you fixed it and then we got lost and you figured out the GPS system. I knew damn well that you were the perfect match for me."

Maria's mouth dropped open. "Palmer?"

"Well, it's great that you're hot, too, of course, but it's not important. And I love you. I don't know what the hell's been going on this week." Palmer squared his shoulders. "But I'm telling you now, if you're marrying me for my money, I don't like it much, but I'm marrying you anyway."

"I'm *not*," Maria said. "I never was, that's what I'm trying to tell you, I don't care if you're rich. I want money, but we can make it together. We'll make lots of it. I'm good at it, you'll see. You design the golf courses, and I'll make sure we get lots of money for it and that it gets invested and we have retirement and our kids have college savings, I'll take care of all of it. We'll be rich again. We'll do it together. It'll be *better this way*, Palmer, we'll do it *together*."

"No, we won't," Palmer said. "I don't know what he's talking about. I didn't lose my money. The Flamingo is fine. I'm still rich."

Maria looked at Carpenter.

Carpenter nodded. "I was just checking."

"We're rich?" Maria said.

"Sorry," Palmer said.

"Oh, *thank God*," Maria said, and fell into his arms

"So what I need to know right now is that the two of you really do want to get married," Carpenter said.

"Yes," Palmer said.

"*Absolutely*," Maria said, clinging to him.

"And do you each really believe that the other loves you and wants to marry you?" Carpenter said.

"Yes," Palmer said.

"Yes, *I do*," Maria said.

"And do you promise to live together in contentment with the past, happiness in the present, and hope for the future?"

They both looked taken aback, but Palmer said, "Yes, I do," his voice strong, and Maria said, "Yes, I do, too."

"Then I now pronounce you man and wife," Carpenter said, his voice ringing out.

"You can do that?" Maria said. "Just like that?"

"Yes, I can," Carpenter said. "Do you want to kiss the bride, Palmer?"

"Yes, *I do*," Palmer said, and kissed Maria.

Agnes looked at Lisa Livia, who was crying.

"Did you hear what my daughter said about me?" Lisa Livia said.

"Yes, I did," Agnes said, putting her arm around her. "Damn fine wedding."

"Damn fine minister, too," Lisa Livia said, sobbing.

"Tip him well for the ceremony," Agnes said, "as only you can," and turned to see how Brenda was taking it.

Brenda was gone.

Shane had been so busy watching Casey Dean that he missed what happened in the gazebo, although it was evidently good because people applauded and Maria and Palmer came down the aisle looking like they were in love again, and Agnes was up in the gazebo kissing Carpenter, which meant Carpenter had probably saved the day. *You can count on Carpenter,* he thought, but his focus was already back on Casey Dean.

He pulled out Abigail's cell phone with one hand as he began to roll the trunk down the dock.

"Hey, Princess," Shane said when Casey Dean answered. "Come join me. I've got the money."

"Where's my sister?"

"One thing at a time," Shane said.

"Fuck you."

"Funny, that's what Abigail tried to do." Shane turned the phone off. He saw she was coming toward the dock, despite her outrage. He could see Agnes now talking to Xavier as they headed with the wedding guests for the reception in the barn.

Shane rolled the trunk down the gangplank and onto the floating dock. He looked out at the boat and saw the shadowy figures on the bridge. He punched in speed-dial 2 on his phone.

Wilson answered on the first ring. "Yes?"

"I've got Casey Dean."

There was a slight pause. "Terminated?"

"No, she's coming this way right now. I can deliver her to you for questioning."

"All right."

"And I have the five million."

There was a short silence. "All right. I'll be there in a minute."

The phone went dead.

No *"Atta-boy, good job."*

No *"You mean Frankie had the five mil?"*

No, *"Wow, you mean Casey Dean's female?"*

No shit, Shane thought.

Casey Dean arrived, leading with a large-caliber automatic pistol that was aimed right between his eyes. "Shane. Nice to meet you again. Come here often?" She sounded tough, but Shane could tell she was off-balance in more ways than one as she came down the metal ramp, keeping the gun pointed at him.

"I plan on it." Shane watched as she reached the bottom, easily recognizing the blond princess from the bar, now that she'd lost the dark wig. "So you're Casey Dean."

She smiled. "What's that mean to you, Shane?"

"I heard you were for hire to the lowest bidder."

"You've heard wrong."

Shane shook his head. "You're supposed to say, 'Prove it.' "

"Not all of us live in movie-land, Shane."

"Want a dose of reality? Your client is dead, and your contract is void, so I'm thinking I'm better."

"You're not thinking at all," Casey Dean said with a smile. "I've got the drop on you, dumbass."

"Yeah, but you'd rather have Abigail than shoot me." Shane smiled. "Plus, my team is still intact. Look behind you."

"Nice try—" Casey Dean began, but Carpenter's deep voice cut her off.

"I'd lower the gun, miss." He was at the top of the ramp, gun pointed at the back of her head.

Casey Dean sighed. "Fuck." She lowered the gun.

Shane nodded toward the Wilson's boat, which was approaching. "You're leaving with my boss—"

Casey Dean laughed. "You really are stupid."

Shane smiled. "Not anymore."

Agnes had followed the wedding party to the barn, which wasn't easy in her mother-of-the-bride dress, and made sure that everything had started well there. Garth had everything hopping, dazzling his date, Tara, with his expertise and general command, and Agnes stopped long enough to say, "Garth, you're amazing, what would we do without you?" which probably set him up for the next school year. Frankie dominated the room like a father of the bride, charming the hell out of everybody, and Maria and Palmer were so dazzled with each other that it would have been almost embarrassing if they weren't the bride and groom. Jefferson Keyes *was* embarrassing, no almost about it, but after Xavier told Agnes that a morose Hammond had taken Brenda into custody for questioning, he'd picked up two flutes of champagne and gone over to Evie, and Evie's sad face had blushed and brightened as she'd taken her glass from him, so Agnes was fairly sure that Jefferson's payback was coming at him shortly. Lisa Livia was beaming happily at her baby girl, forgetting for right now that she was broke, even forgetting for the evening that Frankie had deserted her for twenty-five years, patting his shoulder when he stopped to kiss her cheek, so it looked like for the space of the afternoon, everybody in her family would get their happily ever after. Only Carpenter and Shane were missing.

Shane, she thought, and felt the chill again. She looked around the reception hall one more time and then left and went down the path to the house. He was standing on the dock talking to Wilson on the boat, and if she stayed by the porch steps, it was too obvious that she was watching, but if she went into the kitchen, she could see from the window, even from the open door. And maybe finally finish her damn column. That would be a real sign that things were back to normal: meeting her deadline tomorrow.

She opened the porch door and went in, trying not to think about everything that could be wrong down on the boat, and at the last minute, as she went into the kitchen, she turned back to look at him, only to jerk back as she felt a cast-iron skillet miss crushing her skull by inches.

Shane saw Joey walking down the dock from the reception as Wilson's boat bounced against the bumpers. He grabbed the rope Wilson threw and secured the boat as Carpenter held his gun on Casey Dean.

Wilson stepped onto the dock and nodded. "Good job." He glanced at the locker. "The money?"

"Yes," Shane said as Joey came down the metal walkway.

Wilson motioned to Casey Dean. "Take care of her and let's go."

Shane heard her suck in her breath. *Yeah, he's not much for loyalty,* he thought. *Sorry about that, babe.*

"Shane, you can't go with this guy, he's got no soul," Joey called out. "You're not like him, you're like me."

"That's touching," Wilson said to Joey. "But you're his past. I'm his future. And it's a very lucrative and rewarding future. What can you give him? A diner? He's not your heir, he's mine."

"The hell he is." Joey pulled his gun from his waistband and held it on Wilson.

Shane thought, *Another gun. I'm sick of guns.*

"I had to take family away from him once to save him," Joey said. "If I have to kill you to give family back to him, I will."

"No," Wilson said. "I've got you covered from the boat. You'll never make it off this dock alive."

"You can't just shoot him down," Shane said to Wilson, his voice tired.

"Of course I can," Wilson said. "In the interests of national security, I can do anything. You have to understand this if you're going to take my position. You must weigh the benefits of the many against the needs of the few. I've been doing it for decades. When you are National Security, you are the ultimate power. You are above the law. You must grow comfortable with that, making the difficult decisions easily and quickly. People are expendable; security is not."

"This might be that aspect we've been uneasy about all week," Carpenter said mildly from beside him.

"Difficult decisions," Shane said to Wilson. "Like murdering my mother and father in order to make my uncle the power in the family."

"Ah," Wilson said, staring at him. "You're letting personal feelings cloud your judgment again."

Joey growled and raised his gun, and Shane reached out and took it away from him.

"Enough." He looked between the two old men. "I'm not either one of you. If I ever have a kid, no, *when* I have a kid, nobody will ever take him away from me. I'll kill any son of a bitch who tries." He stopped. "Not that I'll have to. Anybody who wants him will have to come through his mother first, and God help that poor bastard."

Wilson's eyes grew even more wintry. "I gather you're refusing the promotion."

Shane prodded Casey Dean forward, her slender body rigid with fury now as she stared at Wilson. "Yes, but I'm giving you your Princess back."

Wilson blinked at her. "You're leaving her alive? Knowing that she'll come after you again? That makes no sense. You'll be looking over your shoulder for the rest of your life, which for one of you will be short. Is that what you want?"

Shane looked into his uncomprehending eyes. "What I want, when I'm done here, is to go back to the house and tell Agnes about my day, find out what happened during hers. That's always interesting. After that, I don't know. We'll think of something."

He slung Joey's gun out into the river, and Joey said, "Hey!" and Carpenter deposited the trunk onto Wilson's boat and escorted Casey Dean on, too, where she glared at Shane and said, "This isn't over."

"I know," Shane said.

Wilson got back on his boat, ignoring Dean, quivering with rage beside him. "You could have had it all. You're throwing away immense power."

"I know," Shane said. "But nobody is above the law."

"I am." Wilson cast off, and the mobster on the bridge backed the boat away.

"Wait a minute, *where's my sister?*" Dean snarled.

"In the trunk," Shane said, and she ran to it and began to flip the latches open.

Shane gave the boat time to make some separation, then hit 2 again on his phone even as he heard Dean scream, *"Abigail!"*

"What?" Wilson sounded distracted as he answered.

Shane could see his former boss on the bridge of the boat, staring at him. "One question," he said as the boat drew even with the *Brenda Belle*.

"What?" Wilson said as Dean came running to the prow of the boat, her gun drawn even though she was out of range.

"How far away was my father's boat when you pushed the button?" Shane said, and held up the detonator from the bomb Dean had put on his truck, the bomb now under Abigail's body in the trunk.

Wilson's jaw went slack, Casey Dean screamed again, and Shane pushed the button.

"*Stop it!*" Agnes yelled, trying to duck under Brenda's skillet, and getting a glancing blow for her pains that made her head ring. She shoved her away and put the kitchen table between them, saying, "Ouch. *Damn it,* Brenda, *stop it.* You're *finished!*"

"No." Brenda started around the table. "*You took my life and you're gonna die!*"

Agnes kept moving, trying to buy some time for her head to clear, the damn skirt making it hard to move sideways around the table. "*Jesus,* that hurt. What *the hell* are you doing? There are people everywhere, you're not going to get away with this—"

"You killed *my clock,*" Brenda said.

"You killed your own clock," Agnes said, trying to gauge how far it was to the back door. "I told you, one of those whack jobs you hired to kill me shot it up."

"You *ruined my wedding dress!*" Brenda circled the table, cutting her off from the back door.

Agnes tried to edge toward the hall door, and Brenda switched directions and cut her off there, too. "Look, the dress was Evie's idea—"

"You *stole my husband!*"

Agnes stopped. "Hey, I was *engaged to him first.*"

"You stole *my family,*" Brenda said, breathing hard, her eyes narrowing as she came closer.

"You ran your family off," Agnes said. Maybe if she shoved the table at Brenda and—

"You took *my house—*"

"I *bought* your house, Brenda," Agnes said as calmly as she could.

"You took *everything: Lisa Livia was mine, Taylor was mine, this house was mine—*"

"Uh, Brenda . . ."

"*—those were my goddamn black shutters!*"

"You have excellent taste," Agnes said, trying a different route.

"It's *my damn house*," Brenda shrieked, and swung the pan again, missing by a mile because the table was between them.

"Brenda, *it's over*. The wedding is *over. I keep the house.*"

"Not if you're *dead*," Brenda snarled, and started around the table, frying pan raised.

Agnes gave up on talking her way out and screamed, *"Hammond!"* as she backed around the table.

"Forget him," Brenda said, circling the table as Agnes circled, too. "Cops go down when you hit them with a frying pan just like any other man. You know that, Agnes."

"No," Agnes said, keeping the table between them. "Oh, God, is he still alive?"

"How should I know?" Brenda snapped. "Is it my day to watch him? No. Stand *still*, damn it."

"Brenda," Agnes said, kicking off her heels to make moving easier. "This is not a good plan. If you kill me, you don't get the house. You're not married to Taylor, you're married to Frankie. You won't inherit anything."

"Fucking *Frankie*," Brenda said, still circling, and Agnes decided her only chance was the back door. If she threw a chair in Brenda's way and then sprinted for it, she might be able to attract enough attention from the dock that somebody down there would shoot Brenda before she got brained with the frying pan.

Except Brenda wouldn't let her on the side of the table toward the door.

Damn it, Brenda, Agnes thought. *Be nuts or cunning, not both, you bitch.* She edged closer to the door, and Brenda moved to cut her off.

"You killed my clock and you stole my daughter," Brenda said, literally spitting as she said it. "She thinks you're family and I'm not. You helped that bitch Evie ruin my wedding dress. She wouldn't invite me to a pigsticking, but she's friends with you, she's *wearing the same dress you are*. You've got my house. My husband was leaving me for you. You stole my *life*, you damn *Yankee*."

"Brenda, you're from fucking New Jersey!" Agnes yelled, and then

Brenda swung the pan again, and Agnes said, "Oh, my God, look!" and pointed to the housekeeper's room.

Brenda looked and Agnes shoved a chair at her and lunged for the back door, only to scream as Brenda threw the frying pan, and caught her in the small of her back and knocked her to her knees. She rolled and grabbed for the pan as Brenda flung herself at her to get it back and then they were both rolling on the floor for it, claws and knees flying to the sound of ripping cloth. Agnes wrenched it away, and Brenda leapt to grab for another pan hanging too high above her head as Agnes scrambled painfully to her feet, trying to get out the back door, only to see Brenda fling herself across the counter for a knife instead.

Oh, fuck, Agnes thought and then screamed as Brenda came at her with the knife, deflecting it with the pan at the last minute.

Brenda slashed again and Agnes realized that she was going to have to kill her, that there was no way to run without getting the knife in the back, no way to defend herself without losing. Even as she had the thought, Brenda slashed again and the knife laid Agnes's arm open, blood spurting all over the black-and-white tile, and she lost her breath and staggered back and slipped to one knee, and Brenda's eyes lit up as she came at her.

Then a boom shook the house, and Brenda looked past her out the screen door, and yelled, "My yacht!" and Agnes gritted her teeth and swung the frying pan into Brenda's knees as hard as she could.

Brenda went down in the blood on the floor, and Agnes got to her feet, ignoring whatever hell was breaking loose outside, and said, "*Stop it,* Brenda, we're both hurt, just *stop,*" but Brenda got up, her eyes insane, and said, "*You killed my yacht! My money was on that yacht, my passwords, you ruined my life!*" and came for her, knife over her head, and Agnes swung the frying pan with everything she had right into Brenda's crazy-eyed head, connecting and making her stagger back. She swung the pan again before Brenda could lunge again, driving her back toward the wall, and then Brenda slipped in Agnes's blood and fell back hard into the basement door, grabbing for the

Venus, her hands slipping off the shiny surface of the unforgiving plastic, and then she disappeared without even a scream into the basement.

Agnes stood there holding the frying pan, waiting for the scream. There should have been a scream. *How fucking crazy do you have to be to die without a scream?* she thought, and then she realized that she was light-headed, which could be from catching the edge of a cast-iron frying pan on the temple or it could be from all the blood that was on her floor that used to be in her veins.

She dropped the pan and tried to stagger out the back door, but she slipped again and fell, the world looping around her, and she thought, *Oh, God, I'm going to die alone in my kitchen,* and then as the light narrowed down and she gave up, she heard the screen door slap and saw Shane bending over her, looking like he was shouting except Shane never got upset, so she was hallucinating, maybe it was her future flashing before her eyes, and then he picked her up and Carpenter was there and she thought, *I'll be okay now,* and passed out cold.

sunday

cranky agnes column #100

"Wedding Cake Is Not a Piece of Cake"

The ancient Romans used to break the wedding cake over the bride's head for "fruitfulness and good fortune." I say there's a time and a place for everything, and a wedding is not the place to smack people with cake, or shove it in their faces, or do anything except admire it, cut it, and eat it. Civilization depends on us being kind to each other, and so does long-term commitment, so a wedding is as good a place as any to give up violence against people and pastry and start playing well with others.

the sun was coming up when Agnes got out of the Defender and saw Joey on the front porch waiting for them, Rhett snoozing at his feet. Joey came down the steps like lightning to help her, although Shane was right there, more than capable of carrying her up the steps all by himself, and in fact she was feeling pretty good, she could make it up on her own.

So she leaned on both of them.

"I love you guys," she said, and they grinned at each other over her head as she went up on the porch to pat her dog, who looked up at her with the same adoration he always gave her. "Hello, baby," she said. "I'm home," and almost wept because she really was: Two Rivers was hers, and it was going to stay hers now.

They were almost to the door when Lisa Livia came out with two pieces of her pink luggage and Carpenter behind her with the other three and a large canvas bag.

"Hey," Agnes said, and Lisa Livia slowed enough to say, "The wedding was *amazing,* Ag, especially the part where you blew up my mother's boat and knocked her ass into the basement. If you'd killed her, it would have been perfect."

"Yeah, I'm sorry about that, I tried," Agnes said. "Where are you going?"

"The Caymans," LL said, and then leaned in and whispered, "Carpenter tossed Brenda's boat before it blew up and found the numbers to her account. I'm going to go find my money, but I'll be back. Save Venus for me."

She kissed Agnes's cheek and then went down the path toward Maria's pink Mustang.

Agnes watched Carpenter load the pink luggage and the canvas bag in the trunk. "Where did she get the money for a ticket to the Caymans?" She looked at Joey, who kept his arm around her, as if she'd fall down if he wasn't there.

"You want to go upstairs and rest," he said, concern in his voice. "You got the place to yourself now, it'll be quiet, you can sleep. Maria and Palmer left on their honeymoon, but they said they'd be back in two weeks. Frankie sent his love but he had someplace he had to be."

"Testifying," Agnes said, watching Carpenter kiss LL good-bye.

"No," Joey said, and Agnes looked at Shane.

"Nobody to testify against," Shane said. "Nobody to testify for."

"So, he just *left*?" Agnes said.

"Yeah," Joey said, looking at her with worry in his eyes. "Shane said you were okay when he called, but . . . you okay?"

Agnes nodded. "Concussion and loss of blood. I'll be fine. Brenda's in traction, but they have nice hospitals in the prison psych wards, which she's going to hate. I hear you stay there a long time when you murder somebody and then hit a cop who stays alive to testify."

Joey snorted. "Hammond. That'll teach him."

Lisa Livia honked, and Agnes waved as she drove away, feeling bereft but not too much. She'd be back. *They'll all come back,* she thought.

Joey waved and then looked past Agnes to Shane, tightening his arm around her. "You take care of my little Agnes."

"That's what I came for," Shane said, and Joey let go of her.

"I'll be back out tomorrow for dinner," he said, and went down the steps, nodding to Carpenter as he passed him on his way up.

"How are you?" Carpenter said to Agnes, meaning every word.

"Good," Agnes said. "I am good. Well, I have to write my column this afternoon but . . ."

"Everything is fine here," Carpenter said. "Garth has everything under control."

"Amazing," Agnes said.

Carpenter nodded. "I have to go to Washington for a few days. They need a cleaner. Different kind of cleaning than I'm used to, but nothing I can't handle."

"You're taking Wilson's place," Shane said.

"We'll see." Carpenter smiled. "Stay centered."

"Hard not to here," Shane said. "You'll be back?"

"Yes," Carpenter said.

"I'm feeling much better, then," Agnes said, but she was actually starting to feel worse, her head beginning to throb again.

"Upstairs," Shane said, and steered her inside and up two flights of stairs to the cool blue bedroom, Rhett padding patiently behind them.

In the middle of the big bed was a large canvas bag.

"I think that's yours," Agnes said, and lay down on the bed because her head really hurt.

Shane picked the bag up and opened it. It was, not surprisingly, full of money. "Why me?"

"I'm guessing that's half of Joey's half of the take from the five mil Frankie came back to get from the basement," Agnes said, and Shane sat down.

"Five million," he said. "Frankie got twenty percent, Joey got twenty, and Four Wheels got ten. And the Don got fifty. Except the Don isn't getting fifty."

"So Frankie and Joey get two million each." Agnes rubbed her forehead carefully. "Frankie split his with Lisa Livia, and she's taking her mil and going down to the Caymans to see what her mother did with her money. And Joey took his two million and split it with you."

Shane took a handful of bills out of the bag. "We can finish the bathroom. And I'd like a boat."

"The IRS is watching you. Spend it slow." Agnes closed her eyes. Then she started to laugh.

"What?" He crawled onto the bed beside her, and Rhett collapsed in a patch of sunshine under the low windows and sighed himself into sleep.

"Frankie and Joey are honorable guys, right?" she said, snuggling against him.

"Right," he said, his voice exhausted.

"Garth's a millionaire."

He laughed, too, warm beside her, and then he stopped, and she looked up at him.

"What?"

"Carpenter said this thing to me." He settled closer to her. "Happiness in the world?"

"Oh, yeah." Agnes smiled against his shoulder. "Contentment with the past, happiness in the present, and hope for the future. It was in the wedding vows."

"He said when I had that, I'd be able to talk to you."

"Oh. Well, all things in good time."

"I'm close." Shane yawned. "I'm close to the middle one, I think. And the last one, I've got that." He closed his eyes as his hand rested on her waist. "Nah," he said, and yawned again. "I'm good with all of them."

She watched him as his breathing slowed and he slept, and then she curled close to him thinking, *I'm good with them, too.*

Outside the windows, the sun came up over the Blood River, and Cerise and Hot Pink honked their fury as Butch loaded them onto the truck. Beyond the truck, Garth showed Tara around the kitchen in the barn and stole a kiss and kept his mouth shut about a million dollars. Farther up the road, the rest of the Thibaults went about their lives in total ignorance of the indoor plumbing that was about to come their way. And farther still up the road, Joey opened the diner and began to make breakfast for the shrimpers and for Xavier and Evie on their way out of town.

It was a damn fine morning.

ML